the devil wears prada

the devil wears prada

LAUREN WEISBERGER

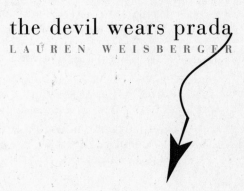

Doubleday

New York London Toronto Sydney Auckland

"Material Girl" by Peter Brown and Robert Rans © 1984 Candy Castle Music. All Rights administered by Warner-Tamerlane Publishing Corp. All Rights Reserved. Used by Permission. WARNER BROS. PUBLICATIONS U.S. INC., Miami, FL 33014

"Wannabe" Words and Music by Matt Rowebottom, Richard Stannard, Geri Halliwell, Emma Bunton, Melanie Brown, Melanie Chisholm, and Victoria Adams. © 1996 EMI MUSIC PUBLISHING LTD. and UNIVERSAL-POLYGRAM INTERNATIONAL PUBLISHING, INC. All Rights for EMI MUSIC PUBLISHING LTD. in the U.S. and Canada Controlled and Administered by EMI FULL KEEL MUSIC. All Rights Reserved. International Copyright Secured. Used by Permission.

"I Think We're Alone Now" Words and Music by Ritchie Cordell. © 1967 (Renewed 1995) EMI LONGITUDE MUSIC. All Rights Reserved. International Copyright Secured. Used by Permission.

"American Pie" Words and Music by Don McLean. © Copyright 1971 Songs of Universal, Inc. on behalf of itself and Benny Bird Co., Inc. All rights reserved. Used by permission.

PUBLISHED BY DOUBLEDAY
a division of Random House, Inc.

DOUBLEDAY and the portrayal of an anchor with a dolphin are registered trademarks of Random House, Inc.

Library of Congress Cataloging-in-Publication Data
Weisberger, Lauren, 1977–
The Devil wears Prada / Lauren Weisberger.—1st ed.
        p.   cm.
1. Periodicals—Publishing—Fiction.   2. New York (N.Y.)—Fiction.
3. Fashion editors—Fiction.   4. Women editors—Fiction.
5. Supervisors—Fiction.   I. Title.
PS3623.E453D485 2003
813'.6—dc21   2003040937

ISBN 0-385-50926-X
Copyright © 2003 by Lauren Weisberger

All Rights Reserved

PRINTED IN THE UNITED STATES OF AMERICA

April 2003
First Edition
1   3   5   7   9   10   8   6   4   2

dedicated to the only three
people alive who genuinely believe it rivals
War and Peace:

my mother, Cheryl, *the mom*
"a million girls would die for";

my father, Steve, *who is handsome, witty,*
brilliant, and talented, and who
insisted on writing his own dedication;

my phenomenal sister, Dana, *their favorite*
(until I wrote a book).

acknowledgments

Thanks to the four people who helped make it happen:

Stacy Creamer—my editor. If you don't enjoy the book, blame her . . . she edited out all the really funny stuff.

Charles Salzberg—writer and teacher. He pushed me hard to keep this project going, so if you don't enjoy it, blame him, too.

Deborah Schneider—agent extraordinaire. She keeps assuring me she loves at least fifteen percent of everything I do, say, or, especially, write.

Richard David Story—my former boss. Easy to love him now that I no longer have to see him before nine A.M. each day.

And of course a huge thanks to all those who offered no assistance whatsoever but who promised to buy multiple copies for a name mention:

Dave Baiada, Dan Barasch, Heather Bergida, Lynn Bernstein, Dan Braun, Beth Buschman-Kelly, Helen Coster, Audrey Diamond, Lydia Fakundiny, Wendy Finerman, Chris Fonzone, Kelly Gillespie, Simone Girner, Cathy Gleason, Jon Goldstein, Eliza Harris, Peter Hedges, Julie Hootkin, Bernie Kelberg, Alli Kirshner, John Knecht, Anna Weber

ACKNOWLEDGMENTS

Kneitel, Jaime Lewisohn, Bill McCarthy, Dana McMakin, Ricki Miller, Daryl Nierenberg, Wittney Rachlin, Drew Reed, Edgar Rosenberg, Brian Seitchik, Jonathan Seitchik, Marni Senofonte, Shalom Shoer, Josh Ufberg, Kyle White, and Richard Willis.

And especially to Leah Jacobs, Jon Roth, Joan and Abe Lichtenstein, and Weisbergers: Shirley and Ed, Judy, David and Pam, Mike and Michele.

Beware of all enterprises that require new clothes.

—HENRY DAVID THOREAU, *WALDEN*, 1854

1

The light hadn't even officially turned green at the intersection of 17th and Broadway before an army of overconfident yellow cabs roared past the tiny deathtrap I was attempting to navigate around the city streets. *Clutch, gas, shift* (neutral to first? Or first to second?), *release clutch*, I repeated over and over in my head, the mantra offering little comfort and even less direction amid the screeching midday traffic. The little car bucked wildly twice before it lurched forward through the intersection. My heart flip-flopped in my chest. Without warning, the lurching evened out and I began to pick up speed. Lots of speed. I glanced down to confirm visually that I was only in second gear, but the rear end of a cab loomed so large in the windshield that I could do nothing but jam my foot on the brake pedal so hard that my heel snapped off. Shit! Another pair of seven-hundred-dollar shoes sacrificed to my complete and utter lack of grace under pressure: this clocked in as my third such breakage this month. It was almost a relief when the car stalled (I'd obviously forgotten to press the clutch when attempting to brake for my life). I had a few seconds—peaceful seconds if one could overlook the angry honking and varied forms of the word "fuck" being hurled at me from all directions—to pull off my Manolos and toss them into the passenger seat. There was nowhere to wipe my sweaty hands except for the suede Gucci pants that hugged my thighs and hips so tightly they'd both begun to tingle within minutes of my securing the final button. My fingers left wet streaks across the supple suede that swathed the tops of my now numb thighs. Attempting to drive this $84,000 stick-shift convertible through the obstacle-fraught streets of midtown at lunchtime pretty much demanded that I smoke a cigarette.

"Fuckin' move, lady!" hollered a swarthy driver whose chest hair threatened to overtake the wife-beater he wore. "What do you think this is? Fuckin' drivin' school? Get outta the way!"

I raised a shaking hand to give him the finger and then turned my attention to the business at hand: getting nicotine coursing through my veins as quickly as possible. My hands were moist again with sweat, evidenced by the matches that kept slipping to the floor. The light turned green just as I managed to touch the fire to the end of the cigarette, and I was forced to leave it hanging between my lips as I negotiated the intricacies of *clutch, gas, shift* (neutral to first? Or first to second?), *release clutch*, the smoke wafting in and out of my mouth with each and every breath. It was another three blocks before the car moved smoothly enough for me to remove the cigarette, but it was already too late: the precariously long line of spent ash had found its way directly to the sweat stain on the pants. Awesome. But before I could consider that, counting the Manolos, I'd wrecked $3,100 worth of merchandise in under three minutes, my cell phone bleated loudly. And as if the very essence of life itself didn't suck enough at that particular moment, the caller ID confirmed my worst fear: it was Her. Miranda Priestly. My boss.

"Ahn-dre-ah! Ahn-dre-ah! Can you hear me, Ahn-dre-ah?" she

trilled the moment I snapped my Motorola open—no small feat considering both of my (bare) feet and hands were already contending with various obligations. I propped the phone between my ear and shoulder and tossed the cigarette out the window, where it narrowly missed hitting a bike messenger. He screamed out a few highly unoriginal "fuck yous" before weaving forward.

"Yes, Miranda. Hi, I can hear you perfectly."

"Ahn-dre-ah, where's my car? Did you drop it off at the garage yet?"

The light ahead of me blessedly turned red and looked as though it might be a long one. The car jerked to a stop without hitting anyone or anything, and I breathed a sigh of relief. "I'm in the car right now, Miranda, and I should be at the garage in just a few minutes." I figured she was probably concerned that everything was going well, so I reassured her that there were no problems whatsoever and we should both arrive shortly in perfect condition.

"Whatever," she said brusquely, cutting me off midsentence. "I need you to pick up Madelaine and drop her off at the apartment before you come back to the office." Click. The phone went dead. I stared at it for a few seconds before I realized that she'd deliberately hung up because she had provided all of the details I could hope to receive. Madelaine. Who the hell was Madelaine? Where was she at the moment? Did she know I was to pick her up? Why was she going back to Miranda's apartment? And why on earth—considering Miranda had a full-time driver, housekeeper, and nanny—was I the one who had to do it?

Remembering that it was illegal to talk on a cell phone while driving in New York and figuring the last thing I needed at that moment was a run-in with the NYPD, I pulled into the bus lane and switched my flashers on. *Breathe in, breathe out,* I coached myself, even remembering to apply the parking brake before taking my foot off the regular one. It had been years since I'd driven a stick-shift car—five years, actually, since a high school boyfriend had volunteered his car up for a few lessons that I'd decidedly flunked—but Miranda hadn't seemed to consider that when she'd called me into her office an hour and a half earlier.

"Ahn-dre-ah, my car needs to be picked up from the place and dropped off at the garage. Attend to it immediately, as we'll be needing it tonight to drive to the Hamptons. That's all." I stood, rooted to the carpet in front of her behemoth desk, but she'd already blocked out my presence entirely. Or so I thought. "That's *all*, Ahn-dre-ah. See to it right now," she added, still not glancing up.

Ah, sure, Miranda, I thought to myself as I walked away, trying to figure out the first step in the assignment that was sure to have a million pitfalls along the way. First was definitely to find out at which "place" the car was located. Most likely it was being repaired at the dealership, but it could obviously be at any one of a million auto shops in any one of the five boroughs. Or perhaps she'd lent it to a friend and it was currently occupying an expensive spot in a full-service garage somewhere on Park Avenue? Of course, there was always the chance that she was referring to a new car—brand unknown—that she'd just recently purchased that hadn't yet been brought home from the (unknown) dealership. I had a lot of work to do.

I started by calling Miranda's nanny, but her cell phone went straight to voice mail. The housekeeper was next on the list and, for once, a big help. She was able to tell me that the car wasn't brand-new and it was in fact a "convertible sports car in British racing green," and that it was usually parked in a garage on Miranda's block, but she had no idea what the make was or where it might currently be residing. Next on the list was Miranda's husband's assistant, who informed me that, as far as she knew, the couple owned a top-of-the-line black Lincoln Navigator and some sort of small green Porsche. Yes! I had my first lead. One quick phone call to the Porsche dealership on Eleventh Avenue revealed that yes, they had just finished touching up the paint and installing a new disc-changer in a green Carrera 4 Cabriolet for a Ms. Miranda Priestly. Jackpot!

I ordered a Town Car to take me to the dealership, where I turned over a note I'd forged with Miranda's signature that instructed them to release the car to me. No one seemed to care whatsoever that I was in no way related to this woman, that some stranger had cruised into the place and requested someone else's Porsche. They tossed me the keys and only laughed when I'd asked them to back it out of the garage because I wasn't sure I could handle a stick shift in reverse. It'd taken me a half hour to get ten blocks, and I still hadn't figured out where or how to turn around so I'd actually be heading uptown, toward the parking place on

Miranda's block that her housekeeper had described. The chances of my making it to 76th and Fifth without seriously injuring myself, the car, a biker, a pedestrian, or another vehicle were nonexistent, and this new call did nothing to calm my nerves.

Once again, I made the round of calls, but this time Miranda's nanny picked up on the second ring.

"Cara, hey, it's me."

"Hey, what's up? Are you on the street? It sounds so loud."

"Yeah, you could say that. I had to pick up Miranda's Porsche from the dealership. Only, I can't really drive stick. But now she called and wants me to pick up someone named Madelaine and drop her off at the apartment. Who the hell is Madelaine and where might she be?"

Cara laughed for what felt like ten minutes before she said, "Madelaine's their French bulldog puppy and she's at the vet. Just got spayed. I was supposed to pick her up, but Miranda just called and told me to pick the twins up early from school so they can all head out to the Hamptons."

"You're joking. I have to pick up a fucking *dog* with this Porsche? Without crashing? It's *never going to happen.*"

"She's at the East Side Animal Hospital, on Fifty-second between First and Second. Sorry, Andy, I have to get the girls now, but call if there's anything I can do, OK?"

Maneuvering the green beast to head uptown sapped my last reserves of concentration, and by the time I reached Second Avenue, the stress sent my body into meltdown. *It couldn't possibly get worse than this*, I thought as yet another cab came within a quarter-inch of the back bumper. A nick anywhere on the car would guarantee I lose my job— that much was obvious—but it just might cost me my life as well. Since there was obviously not a parking spot, legal or otherwise, in the middle of the day, I called the vet's office from outside and asked them to bring Madelaine to me. A kindly woman emerged a few minutes later (just enough time for me to field another call from Miranda, this one asking why I wasn't back at the office yet) with a whimpering, sniffling puppy. The woman showed me Madelaine's stitched-up belly and told me to drive very, very carefully because the dog was "experiencing some discomfort." Right, lady. I'm driving very, very carefully solely to save my job and possibly my life—if the dog benefits from this, it's just a bonus.

With Madelaine curled up on the passenger seat, I lit another cigarette and rubbed my freezing bare feet so my toes could resume gripping
the clutch and brake pedal. *Clutch, gas, shift, release clutch,* I chanted,
trying to ignore the dog's pitiful howls every time I accelerated. She al-
ternated between crying, whining, and snorting. By the time we reached
Miranda's building, the pup was nearly hysterical. I tried to soothe her,
but she could sense my insincerity—and besides, I had no free hands
with which to offer a reassuring pat or nuzzle. So this was what four
years of diagramming and deconstructing books, plays, short stories, and
poems were for: a chance to comfort a small, white, batlike bulldog while
trying not to demolish someone else's really, really expensive car. Sweet
life. Just as I had always dreamed.

I managed to dump the car at the garage and the dog with Miranda's
doorman without further incident, but my hands were still shaking when
I climbed into the chauffeured Town Car that had been following me all
over town. The driver looked at me sympathetically and made some sup-
portive comment about the difficulty of stick shifts, but I didn't feel
much like chatting.

"Just heading back to the Elias-Clark building," I said with a long
sigh as the driver pulled around the block and headed south on Park Avenue. Since I rode the route every day—sometimes twice—I knew I had
exactly eight minutes to breathe and collect myself and possibly even figure out a way to disguise the ash and sweat stains that had become permanent features on the Gucci suede. The shoes—well, those were beyond
hope, at least until they could be fixed by the fleet of shoemakers *Runway* kept for such emergencies. The ride was actually over in six and a
half minutes, and I had no choice but to hobble like an off-balance gi-
raffe on my one flat, one four-inch heel arrangement. A quick stop in the
Closet turned up a brand-new pair of knee-high maroon-colored Jimmy
Choos that looked great with the leather skirt I grabbed, tossing the
suede pants in the "Couture Cleaning" pile (where the basic prices for
dry cleaning started at seventy-five dollars per item). The only stop left
was a quick visit to the Beauty Closet, where one of the editors there took
one look at my sweat-streaked makeup and whipped out a trunk full of
fixers.

Not bad, I thought, looking in one of the omnipresent full-length mirrors. You might not even know that mere minutes before I was hovering precariously close to murdering myself and everyone around me. I strolled confidently into the assistants' suite outside Miranda's office and quietly took my seat, looking forward to a few free minutes before she returned from lunch.

"And-re-ah," she called from her starkly furnished, deliberately cold office. "Where are the car and the puppy?"

I leaped out of my seat and ran as fast as was possible on plush carpeting while wearing five-inch heels and stood before her desk. "I left the car with the garage attendant and Madelaine with your doorman, Miranda," I said, proud to have completed both tasks without killing the car, the dog, or myself.

"And why would you do something like that?" she snarled, looking up from her copy of *Women's Wear Daily* for the first time since I'd walked in. "I specifically requested that you bring both of them to the office, since the girls will be here momentarily and we need to leave."

"Oh, well, actually, I thought you said that you wanted them to—"

"Enough. The details of your incompetence interest me very little. Go get the car and the puppy and bring them here. I'm expecting we'll be all ready to leave in fifteen minutes. Understood?"

Fifteen minutes? Was this woman hallucinating? It would take a minute or two to get downstairs and into a Town Car, another six or eight to get to her apartment, and then somewhere in the vicinity of three hours for me to find the puppy in her eighteen-room apartment, extract the bucking stick shift from its parking spot, and make my way the twenty blocks to the office.

"Of course, Miranda. Fifteen minutes."

I started shaking again the moment I ran out of her office, wondering if my heart could just up and give out at the ripe old age of twenty-three. The first cigarette I lit landed directly on the top of my new Jimmys, where instead of falling to the cement it smoldered for just long enough to burn a small, neat hole. *Great*, I muttered. *That's just fucking great.* Chalk up my total as an even four grand for today's ruined merchandise—a new personal best. Maybe she'd die before I got back, I thought, deciding that now was the time to look on the bright side. Maybe, just maybe, she'd keel over from something rare and exotic and we'd all be released from her wellspring of misery. I relished a last drag before stamping out the cigarette and told myself to be rational. *You don't want her to die*, I thought, stretching out in the backseat. *Because if she does, you lose all hope of killing her yourself. And* that *would be a shame.*

2

I knew nothing when I went for my first interview and stepped onto the infamous Elias-Clark elevators, those transporters of all things *en vogue*. I had no idea that the city's most well-connected gossip columnists and socialites and media executives obsessed over the flawlessly made-up, turned-out, turned-in riders of those sleek and quiet lifts. I had never seen women with such radiant blond hair, didn't know that those brand-name highlights cost six grand a year to maintain or that others in the know could identify the colorists after a quick glance at the finished product. I had never laid eyes on such beautiful men. They were perfectly toned—not too muscular because *"that's* not sexy"—and they showed off their lifelong dedication to gymwork in finely ribbed turtlenecks and tight leather pants. Bags and shoes I'd never seen on real people shouted *Prada! Armani! Versace!* from every surface. I had heard from a friend of a friend—an editorial assistant at *Chic* magazine—that every now and then the accessories get to meet their makers in those very elevators, a touching reunion where Miuccia, Giorgio, or Donatella can once again admire their summer '02 stilettos or their spring couture teardrop bag in person. I knew things were changing for me—I just wasn't sure it was for the better.

I had, until this point, spent the past twenty-three years embodying small-town America. My entire existence was a perfect cliché. Growing up in Avon, Connecticut, had meant high school sports, youth group meetings, "drinking parties" at nice suburban ranch homes when the parents were away. We wore sweatpants to school, jeans for Saturday night, ruffled puffiness for semiformal dances. And college! Well, that was a world of sophistication after high school. Brown had provided endless activities and classes and groups for every imaginable type of artist, misfit, and computer geek. Whatever intellectual or creative interest I wanted to pursue, regardless of how esoteric or unpopular it may have been, had some sort of outlet at Brown. High fashion was perhaps the single exception to this widely bragged-about fact. Four years spent muddling around Providence in fleeces and hiking boots, learning about the French impressionists, and writing obnoxiously long-winded English papers did not—in any conceivable way—prepare me for my very first postcollege job.

I managed to put it off as long as possible. For the three months following graduation, I'd scrounged together what little cash I could find and took off on a solo trip. I did Europe by train for a month, spending much more time on beaches than in museums, and didn't do a very good job of keeping in touch with anyone back home except Alex, my boyfriend of three years. He knew that after the five weeks or so I was starting to get lonely, and since his Teach for America training had just ended and he had the rest of the summer to kill before starting in September, he surprised me in Amsterdam. I'd covered most of Europe by then and he'd traveled the summer before, so after a not-so-sober afternoon at one of the coffee shops, we pooled our traveler's checks and bought two one-way tickets to Bangkok.

Together we worked our way through much of Southeast Asia, rarely spending more than $10 a day, and talked obsessively about our futures. He was so excited to start teaching English at one of the city's underprivileged schools, totally taken with the idea of shaping young minds and mentoring the poorest and the most neglected, in the way that only Alex could be. My goals were not so lofty: I was intent on finding a job in magazine publishing. Although I knew it was highly unlikely I'd get hired at *The New Yorker* directly out of school, I was determined to be writing for them before my fifth reunion. It was all I'd ever wanted to do, the only place I'd ever really wanted to work. I'd picked up a copy for the first time after I'd heard my parents discussing an article they'd just read and my mom had said, "It was so well written—you just don't read things like that anymore," and my father had agreed, "No doubt, it's the only smart thing being written today." I'd loved it. Loved the snappy reviews and the witty cartoons and the feeling of being admitted to a special, members-only club for readers. I'd read every issue for the past seven years and knew every section, every editor, and every writer by heart.

Alex and I talked about how we were both embarking on a new stage in our lives, how we were lucky to be doing it together. We weren't in any rush to get back, though, somehow sensing that this would be the last period of calm before the craziness, and we stupidly extended our visas in Delhi so we could have a few extra weeks touring in the exotic countryside of India.

Well, nothing ends the romance more swiftly than amoebic dysentery. I lasted a week in a filthy Indian hostel, begging Alex not to leave me for dead in that hellish place. Four days later we landed in Newark and my worried mother tucked me into the backseat of her car and clucked the entire way home. In a way it was a Jewish mother's dream, a real reason to visit doctor after doctor after doctor, making absolutely sure that every miserable parasite had abandoned her little girl. It took four weeks for me to feel human again and another two until I began to feel that living at home was unbearable. Mom and Dad were great, but being asked where I was going every time I left the house—or where I'd been every time I returned—got old quickly. I called Lily and asked if I could crash on the couch of her tiny Harlem studio. Out of the kindness of her heart, she agreed.

← →

I woke up in that tiny Harlem studio, sweat-soaked. My forehead pounded, my stomach churned, every nerve shimmied—shimmied in a *very* unsexy way. *Ah! It's back*, I thought, horrified. The parasites had found their way back into my body and I was bound to suffer eternally! Or what if it was worse? Perhaps I'd contracted a rare form of late-developing dengue fever? Malaria? Possibly even Ebola? I lay in silence, trying to come to grips with my imminent death, when snippets from the night before came back to me. A smoky bar somewhere in the East Village. Something called jazz fusion music. A hot-pink drink in a martini glass—oh, nausea, oh, make it stop. Friends stopping by to welcome me home. A toast, a gulp, another toast. Oh, thank god—it wasn't a rare strain of hemorrhagic fever, it was just a hangover. It never occurred to me that I couldn't exactly hold my liquor anymore after losing twenty pounds to dysentery. Five feet ten inches and 115 pounds did not bode well for a hard night out (although, in retrospect, it boded very well for employment at a fashion magazine).

I bravely extracted myself from the crippling couch I'd been crashing on for the past week and concentrated all my energy on not getting sick. Adjustment to America—the food, the manners, the glorious showers—hadn't been too grueling, but the houseguest thing was quickly becoming stale. I figured I had about a week and a half left of exchanging leftover baht and rupees before I completely ran out of cash, and the only way to get money from my parents was to return to the never-ending circuit of second opinions. That sobering thought was the single thing propelling me from bed, on what would be a fateful November day, to where I was expected in one hour for my very first job interview. I'd spent the last week parked on Lily's couch, still weak and exhausted, until she finally yelled at me to leave—if only for a few hours each day. Not sure what else to do with myself, I bought a MetroCard and rode the subways, listlessly dropping off résumés as I went. I left them with security guards at all the big magazine publishers, with a halfhearted cover letter explaining that I wanted to be an editorial assistant and gain some magazine writing experience. I was too weak and tired to care if anyone actually read them, and the last thing I was expecting was an interview. But Lily's phone had rung just the day before and, amazingly, someone from human resources at Elias-Clark wanted me to come in for a "chat." I wasn't sure if it would be considered an official interview or not, but a "chat" sounded more palatable either way.

I washed down Advil with Pepto and managed to assemble a jacket and pants that did not match and in no way created a suit, but at least they stayed put on my emaciated frame. A blue button-down, a not-too-perky ponytail, and a pair of slightly scuffed flats completed my look. It wasn't great—in fact, it bordered on supremely ugly—but it would have to suffice. *They're not going to hire me or reject me on the outfit alone,* I remember thinking. Clearly, I was barely lucid.

I showed up on time for my eleven A.M. interview and didn't panic until I encountered the line of leggy, Twiggy types waiting to be permitted to board the elevators. Their lips never stopped moving, and their gossip was punctuated only by the sound of their stilettos clacking on the floor. *Clackers,* I thought. *That's perfect.* (The elevators!) *Breathe in, breathe out,* I reminded myself. *You will not throw up. You will not throw up. You're just here to talk about being an editorial assistant, and then it's straight back to the couch. You will not throw up. "Why yes, I'd love to work at* Reaction! *Well, sure, I suppose* The Buzz *would be suitable. Oh, what? I may have my pick? Well, I'll need the night to decide between there and* Maison Vous. *Delightful!"*

Moments later I was sporting a rather unflattering "guest" sticker on my rather unflattering pseudosuit (not soon enough, I discovered that guests in the know simply stuck these passes on their bags, or, even better, discarded them immediately—only the most uncouth losers actually *wore* them) and heading toward the elevators. And then . . . I boarded. Up, up, up and away, hurtling through space and time and infinite sexiness en route to . . . human resources.

I allowed myself to relax for a moment or two during that swift, quiet ride. Deep, pouty perfumes mixed with the smell of fresh leather to turn those elevators from the merely functional to the almost erotic. We whisked between floors, stopping to let out the beauties at *Chic, Mantra, The Buzz,* and *Coquette.* The doors opened silently, reverently, to stark white reception areas. Chic furniture with clean, simple lines dared people to sit, ready to scream out in agony if anyone—horror!—spilled. The magazines' names rested in bold black and identifiable, individual typeface along the walls that flanked the lobby. Thick, opaque glass doors protected the titles. They're names the average American recognizes but never imagines to be turning and churning and spinning under one very high city roof.

While I'd admittedly never held a job more impressive than frozen yogurt scooper, I'd heard enough stories from my newly minted professional friends to know that corporate life just didn't look like this. Not even close. Absent were the nauseating fluorescent lights, the never-shows-dirt carpeting. Where dowdy secretaries should have been ensconced, polished young girls with prominent cheekbones and power suits presided. Office supplies didn't exist! Those basic necessities like organizers, garbage cans, and books were simply not present. I watched as six floors disappeared in swirls of white perfection before I felt the venom and heard the voice.

"She. Is. Such. A. Bitch! I *cannot* deal with her anymore. Who does that? I mean, really—WHO DOES THAT?" hissed a twenty-something girl in a snakeskin skirt and a very mini tank top, looking more suited for a late night at Bungalow 8 than a day at the office.

"I know. I *knooooooow*. Like, what do you think I've had to put up with for the past six months? Total bitch. And terrible taste, too," agreed her friend, with an emphatic shake of her adorable bob.

Mercifully, I arrived at my floor and the elevator slid open. *Interesting*, I thought. If you're comparing this potential work environment to an average day in the life of a cliquey junior high girl, it might even be better. Stimulating? Well, maybe not. Kind, sweet, nurturing? No, not exactly. The kind of place that just makes you want to smile and do a great job? No, OK? No! But if you're looking for fast, thin, sophisticated, impossibly hip, and heart-wrenchingly stylish, Elias-Clark is mecca.

The gorgeous jewelry and impeccable makeup of the human resources receptionist did nothing to allay my overwhelming feelings of inadequacy. She told me to sit and "feel free to look over some of our titles." Instead, I tried frantically to memorize the names of all the editors in chief of the company's titles—as if they were going to actually quiz me on them. Ha! I already knew Stephen Alexander, of course, for *Reaction* magazine, and it wasn't too hard to remember *The Buzz*'s Tanner Michel. Those were really the only interesting things they published anyway, I figured. I'd do fine.

A short, svelte woman introduced herself as Sharon. "So, dear, you're looking to break into magazines, are you?" she asked as she led me past a string of long-legged model look-alikes to her stark, cold office. "It's a tough thing to do right out of college, you know. Lots and lots of competition out there for very few jobs. And the few jobs that are available, well! They're not exactly high-paying, if you know what I mean."

I looked down at my cheap, mismatched suit and very wrong shoes and wondered why I'd even bothered. Already deep in thought over how I was going to crawl back to that sofa bed with enough Cheez-Its and cigarettes to last a fortnight, I barely noticed when she almost whispered, "But I have to say, there's an amazing opportunity open right now, and it's going to go fast!"

Hmm. My antennae perked up as I tried to force her to make eye contact with me. Opportunity? Go fast? My mind was racing. She wanted to help me? She liked me? Why, I hadn't even opened my mouth yet—how could she *like* me? And why exactly was she starting to sound like a car salesman?

"Dear, can you tell me the name of the editor in chief of *Runway*?" she asked, looking pointedly at me for the first time since I'd sat down.

Blank. Completely and totally blank, I couldn't remember a thing. I couldn't believe she was *quizzing* me! I'd never read an issue of *Runway* in my life—she wasn't allowed to ask me about *that* one. No one cared about *Runway*. It was a *fashion* magazine, for chrissake, one I wasn't even sure contained any writing, just lots of hungry-looking models and glossy ads. I stammered for a moment or two, while the different names of editors I'd just before forced my brain to remember all swirled inside my head, dancing together in mismatched pairs. Somewhere in the deep recesses of my mind, I was sure I knew her name—after all, who didn't? But it wouldn't gel in my addled brain.

"Uh, well, it seems I can't recall her name right now. But I know I know it, of course I know it. Everyone knows who she is! I just, well, don't, uh, seem to know it right now."

She peered at me for a moment, her large brown eyes finally fixated on my now perspiring face. "Miranda Priestly," she near-whispered, with a mixture of reverence and fear. "Her name is Miranda Priestly."

Silence ensued. For what felt like a full minute, neither of us said a word, but then Sharon must have made the decision to overlook my crucial misstep. I didn't know then that she was desperate to hire another assistant for Miranda, couldn't know that she was desperate to stop this woman from calling her day and night, grilling her about potential candidates. Desperate to find someone, anyone, whom Miranda wouldn't reject. And if I might—however unlikely—stand even the smallest chance of getting hired and thereby relieve her, well, then attention must be paid.

Sharon smiled tersely and told me I was going to meet with Miranda's two assistants. *Two* assistants?

"Why yes," she confirmed with an exasperated look. "Of course Miranda needs two assistants. Her current senior assistant, Allison, has been promoted to be *Runway*'s beauty editor, and Emily, the junior assistant, will be taking Allison's place. That leaves the junior position open for someone!

"Andrea, I know you've just graduated from college and probably aren't entirely familiar with the inner workings of the magazine world . . ." She paused dramatically, searching for the right words. "But I feel it's my duty, my *obligation*, to tell you what a truly incredible opportunity this is. Miranda Priestly . . ." She paused again just as dramatically, as though she were mentally bowing. "Miranda Priestly is the single most influential woman in the fashion industry, and clearly one of the most prominent magazine editors in the world. The world! The chance to work for her, to watch her edit and meet with famous writers and models, to help her achieve all she does *each and every day*, well, I shouldn't need to tell you that it's a job a million girls would die for."

"Um, yeah, I mean yes, that does sound wonderful," I said, briefly wondering why Sharon was trying to talk me into something that a million other people would die for. But there wasn't time to think about it.

She picked up the phone and sang a few words, and within minutes she'd escorted me to the elevators to begin my interviews with Miranda's two assistants.

I thought Sharon was starting to sound a bit like a robot, but then came my meeting with Emily. I found my way down to the seventeenth floor and waited in *Runway*'s unnervingly white reception area. It took just over a half hour before a tall, thin girl emerged from behind the glass doors. A calf-length leather skirt hung from her hips, and her unruly red hair was piled in one of those messy but still glamorous buns on top of her head. Her skin was flawless and pale, not so much as a single freckle or blemish, and it stretched perfectly over the highest cheekbones I'd ever seen. She didn't smile. She sat next to me and looked me over, earnestly but with little apparent interest. Perfunctory. And then, un-prompted and still having not introduced herself, the girl I presumed to be Emily launched into a description of the job. The monotone of her statements told me more than all of her words: she'd obviously gone through this dozens of times already, had little faith that I was any different from the rest, and as a result wouldn't be wasting much time with me.

"It's hard, no doubt about it. There will be fourteen-hour days, you know—not often, but often enough," she rattled on, still not looking at me. "And it's important to understand that there will be no editorial work. As Miranda's junior assistant, you'd be solely responsible for antic-ipating her needs and accommodating them. Now, that could be anything from ordering her favorite stationery to accompanying her on a shopping trip. Either way, it's always fun. I mean, you get to spend day after day, week after week, with this absolutely amazing woman. And amazing she is," she breathed, looking slightly animated for the first time since we started speaking.

"Sounds great," I said and meant it. My friends who'd begun work-ing immediately after graduation had already clocked in six full months in their entry-level jobs, and they all sounded wretched. Banks, adver-tising firms, book publishing houses—it didn't matter—they were all ut-terly miserable. They whined about the long days, the coworkers, and the office politics, but more than anything else, they complained bitterly about the boredom. Compared with school, the tasks required of them were mindless, unnecessary, fit for a chimp. They spoke of the many, many hours spent plugging numbers in databases and cold-calling people who didn't want to be called. Of listlessly cataloging years' worth of information on a computer screen and researching entirely irrelevant subjects for months on end so their supervisors thought they were productive. Each swore she'd actually gotten dumber in the short amount of time since graduation, and there was no escape in sight. I might not particularly love fashion, but I'd sure rather do something "fun" all day long than get sucked into a more boring job.

"Yes. It is great. Just great. I mean, really, really great. Anyway, nice to meet you. I'm going to go get Allison for you to meet. She's great, too." Almost as quickly as she finished and departed behind the glass in a rustle of leather and curls, a coltish figure appeared.

This striking black girl introduced herself as Allison, Miranda's senior assistant who'd just been promoted, and I knew immediately that she was simply *too* thin. But I couldn't even focus on the way her stomach caved inward and her pelvic bones pushed out because I was captivated by the fact she exposed her stomach at work at all. She wore black leather pants, as soft as they were tight, and a fuzzy (or was it furry?) white tank top strained across her breasts and ended two inches above her belly button. Her long hair was as dark as ink and hung across her back like a thick, shiny blanket. Her fingers and toes were polished with a luminescent white color, appearing to glow from within, and her open-toe sandals gave her already six-foot frame an additional three inches. She managed to look incredibly sexy, seminaked, and classy all at the same time, but to me she looked mostly cold. Literally. It was, after all, November.

"Hi, I'm Allison, as you probably know," she started, picking some of the tank top fur from her barely there leather-clad thigh. "I was just promoted to an editor position, and that's the really great thing about working for Miranda. Yes, the hours are long and the work is tough, but it's incredibly glamorous and a million girls would die to do it. And Miranda is such a wonderful woman, editor, *person*, that she really takes care of her own girls. You'll skip years and years of working your way up the ladder by working just one year for her; if you're talented, she'll send you straight to the top, and . . ." She rambled on, not bothering to look up or feign any level of passion for what she was saying. Although I didn't get the impression she was particularly dumb, her eyes were glazed over in the way seen only in cult members or the brainwashed. I had the distinct impression I could fall asleep, pick my nose, or simply leave and she wouldn't necessarily notice.

When she finally wrapped things up and went to go notify yet another interviewer, I nearly collapsed on the unwelcoming reception-area sofas. It was all happening so fast, spiraling out of control, and yet I was excited. So what if I didn't know who Miranda Priestly was? Everyone else certainly seemed impressed enough. Yeah, so it's a fashion magazine and not something a little more interesting, but it's a hell of a lot better to work at *Runway* than some horrible trade publication somewhere, right? The prestige of having *Runway* on my résumé was sure to give me even more credibility when I eventually applied to work at *The New Yorker* than, say, having *Popular Mechanics* there. Besides, I'm sure a million girls *would* die for this job.

After a half hour of such ruminations, another tall and impossibly thin girl came to the reception area. She told me her name but I couldn't focus on anything except her body. She wore a tight, shredded denim skirt, a see-through white button-down, and strappy silver sandals. She was also perfectly tanned and manicured and exposed in such a way that normal people are not when there's snow on the ground. It wasn't until she actually motioned for me to follow her back through the glass doors and I had to stand up that I became acutely aware of my own horrendously inappropriate suit, limp hair, and utter lack of accessories, jewelry, and grooming. To this day, the thought of what I wore—and that I carried something resembling a *briefcase*—continues to haunt me. I can feel my face flame red as I remember how very, very awkward I was among the most toned and stylish women in New York City. I didn't know until later, until I hovered on the periphery of being one of them, just how much they had laughed at me between the rounds of the interview.

After the requisite look-over, Knockout Girl led me to Cheryl Kerston's office, *Runway*'s executive editor and all-around lovable lunatic. She, too, talked at me for what seemed like hours, but this time I actually listened. I listened because she seemed to love her job, speaking excitedly about the "words" aspect of the magazine, the wonderful copy she reads and writers she manages and editors she oversees.

"I have absolutely nothing to do with the fashion side of this place," she declared proudly, "so it's best to save those questions for someone else."

When I told her that it was really her job that sounded appealing, that I had no particular interest or background in fashion, her smile broadened to a genuine grin. "Well, in that case, Andrea, you might be just what we need around here. I think it's time for you to meet Miranda. And if I may offer a piece of advice? Look her straight in the eye and sell yourself. Sell yourself hard and she'll respect it."

As if on cue, Knockout Girl swept in to escort me to Miranda's office. It was only a thirty-second walk, but I could sense that all eyes were on me. They peered at me from behind the frosted glass of the editor's office and from the open space of the assistants' cubicles. A beauty at the copier turned to check me out, and so did an absolutely magnificent man, although he was obviously gay and intent on examining only my outfit. Just as I was about to walk through the doorway that would lead me to the assistants' suite outside of Miranda's office, Emily grabbed my briefcase and tossed it under her desk. It took only a moment for me to realize that the message was *Carry that, lose all credibility.* And then I was standing in her office, a wide-open space of huge windows and streaming bright light. No other details about the space made an impression that day; I couldn't take my eyes off of her.

Since I'd never seen so much as a picture of Miranda Priestly, I was shocked to see how *skinny* she was. The hand she held out was small-boned, feminine, soft. She had to turn her head upward to look me in the eye, although she did not stand to greet me. Her expertly dyed blond hair was pulled back in a chic knot, deliberately loose enough to look casual but still supremely neat, and while she did not smile, she did not appear particularly intimidating. She seemed rather gentle and somewhat shrunken behind her ominous black desk, and although she did not invite me to sit, I felt comfortable enough to claim one of the uncomfortable black chairs that faced her. And it was then I noticed: she was watching me intently, mentally noting my attempts at grace and propriety with what seemed like amusement. Condescending and awkward, yes, but not, I decided, particularly mean-spirited. She spoke first.

"What brings you to *Runway*, Ahn-dre-ah?" she asked in her upper-crust British accent, never taking her eyes away from mine.

"Well, I interviewed with Sharon, and she told me that you're looking for an assistant," I started, my voice a little shaky. When she nodded, my confidence increased slightly. "And now, after meeting with Emily, Allison, and Cheryl, I feel like I have a clear understanding of the kind of person you're looking for, and I'm confident I'd be perfect for the job," I said, remembering Cheryl's words. She looked amused for a moment but seemed unfazed.

It was at this point that I began to want the job most desperately, in the way people yearn for things they consider unattainable. It might not be akin to getting into law school or having an essay published in a campus journal, but it was, in my starved-for-success mind, a real challenge—a challenge because I was an imposter, and not a very good one at that. I had known the minute I stepped on the *Runway* floor that I didn't belong. My clothes and hair were wrong for sure, but more glaringly out of place was my attitude. I didn't know anything about fashion and I didn't *care*. At all. And therefore, I had to have it. Besides, a million girls would die for this job.

I continued to answer her questions about myself with a forthrightness and confidence that surprised me. There wasn't time to be intimidated. After all, she seemed pleasant enough and I, amazingly, knew nothing to the contrary. We stumbled a bit when she inquired about any foreign languages I spoke. When I told her I knew Hebrew, she paused, pushed her palms flat on her desk and said icily, "Hebrew? I was hoping for French, or at least something more *useful*." I almost apologized, but stopped myself.

"Unfortunately, I don't speak a word of French, but I'm confident it won't be a problem." She clasped her hands back together.

"It says here that you studied at Brown?"

"Yes, I, uh, I was an English major, concentrating on creative writing. Writing has always been a passion." *So cheesy!* I reprimanded myself. *Did I really have to use the word "passion"?*

"So, does your affinity for writing mean that you're not particularly interested in fashion?" She took a sip of sparkling liquid from a glass and set it down quietly. One quick glance at the glass showed that she was the kind of woman who could drink without leaving one of those disgusting lipstick marks. She would always have perfectly lined and filled-in lips regardless of the hour.

"Oh no, of course not. I adore fashion," I lied rather smoothly. "I'm looking forward to learning even more about it, since I think it would be wonderful to write about fashion one day." Where the hell had I come up with that one? This was becoming an out-of-body experience.

Things progressed with the same relative ease until she asked her final question: Which magazines did I read regularly? I leaned forward eagerly and began to speak: "Well, I only subscribe to *The New Yorker* and *Newsweek*, but I regularly read *The Buzz*. Sometimes *Time*, but it's dry, and *U.S. News* is way too conservative. Of course, as a guilty pleasure, I'll skim *Chic*, and since I just returned from traveling, I read all of the travel magazines and . . ."

"And do you read *Runway*, Ahn-dre-ah?" she interrupted, leaning over the desk and peering at me even more intently than before.

It had come so quickly, so unexpectedly, that for the first time that day I was caught off-guard. I didn't lie, and I didn't elaborate or even attempt to explain.

"No."

After perhaps ten seconds of stony silence, she beckoned for Emily to escort me out. I knew I had the job.

3

"It sure doesn't sound like you have the job," Alex, my boyfriend, said softly, playing with my hair as I rested my throbbing head in his lap after the grueling day. I'd gone straight from the interview to his apartment in Brooklyn, not wanting to sleep on Lily's couch for another night and needing to tell him about everything that had just happened. I'd thought about staying there all the time, but I didn't want Alex to feel suffocated. "I don't even know why you'd want it." After a moment or two, he reconsidered. "Actually, it does sound like a pretty phenomenal opportunity. I mean, if this girl Allison started out as Miranda's assistant and is now an editor at the magazine, well, that'd be good enough for me. Just go for it."

He was trying so hard to sound really excited for me. We'd been dating since our junior year at Brown, and I knew every inflection of his voice, every look, every signal. He'd just started a few weeks earlier at PS 277 in the Bronx and was so worn down he could barely speak. Even though his kids were only nine years old, he'd been disappointed to see how jaded and cynical they already were. He was disgusted that they all spoke freely about blow jobs, knew ten different slang words for pot, and loved to brag about the stuff they stole or whose cousin was currently residing in a tougher jail. "Prison connoisseurs," Alex had taken to calling them. "They could write a book on the subtle advantages of Sing Sing over Rikers, but they can't read a word of the English language." He was trying to figure out how he could make a difference.

I slid my hand under his T-shirt and started to scratch his back. Poor thing looked so miserable that I felt guilty bothering him with the details of the interview, but I just had to talk about it with someone. "I know. I understand that there wouldn't be anything editorial about the job whatsoever, but I'm sure I'll be able to do some writing after a few months," I said. "You don't think it's completely selling out to work at a *fashion* magazine, do you?"

He squeezed my arm and lay down next to me. "Baby, you're a brilliant, wonderful writer, and I know you'll be fantastic anywhere. And of course it's not selling out. It's paying your dues. You're saying that if you put in a year at *Runway* you'll save yourself three more years of bullshit assistant work somewhere else?"

I nodded. "That's what Emily and Allison said, that it was an automatic quid pro quo. Work a year for Miranda and don't get fired, and she'll make a call and get you a job anywhere you want."

"Then how could you not? Seriously, Andy, you'll work your year and you'll get a job at *The New Yorker*. It's what you've always wanted! And it sure sounds like you'll get there a whole lot faster doing this than anything else."

"You're right, you're totally right."

"And besides, it would guarantee that you're moving to New York, which, I have to say, is very appealing to me right now." He kissed me, one of those long, lazy kisses it seemed we had personally invented. "But stop worrying so much. Like you said yourself, you're still not sure you have the job. Let's wait and see."

We cooked a simple dinner and fell asleep watching Letterman. I was dreaming about obnoxious little nine-year-olds having sex on the playground while they swigged forties of Olde English and screamed at my sweet, loving boyfriend when the phone rang.

Alex picked it up and pressed it to his ear but didn't bother to open his eyes or say hello. He quickly dropped it next to me. I wasn't sure I could muster the energy to pick it up.

"Hello?" I mumbled, glancing at the clock and seeing that it was 7:15 A.M. Who the hell would call at such an hour?

"It's me," barked a very angry-sounding Lily.

"Hi, is everything OK?"

"Do you think I'd be calling you if everything was OK? I'm so hungover I could die, and I finally stop puking long enough to fall asleep, and I'm awakened by a scarily perky woman who says she works in HR at Elias-Clark. And she's looking for you. At *seven-fifteen* in the freakin' morning. So call her back. And tell her to lose my number."

"Sorry, Lil. I gave them your number because I don't have a cell yet. I can't believe she called so early! I wonder if that's good or bad?" I took the portable and crept out of the bedroom, quietly closing the door as I went.

"Whatev. Good luck. Let me know how it goes. Just not in the next couple hours, OK?"

"Will do. Thanks. And sorry."

I looked at my watch again and couldn't believe I was about to have a business conversation. I put on a pot of coffee and waited until it had finished brewing and brought a cup to the couch. It was time to call. I had no choice.

"Hello, this is Andrea Sachs," I said firmly, although my voice betrayed me with its deep, raspy, just-woke-up-ness.

"Andrea, good morning! Hope I didn't call too early," Sharon sang, her own voice full of sunshine. "I'm sure I didn't, my dear, especially since you'll have to be an early bird soon enough! I have some very good news. Miranda was very impressed with you and said she's very much looking forward to working with you. Isn't that wonderful? Congratulations, dear. How does it feel to be Miranda Priestly's new assistant? I imagine that you're just—"

My head was spinning. I tried to pull myself off the couch to get some more coffee, water, anything that might clear my head and turn her words back into English, but I only sank further into the cushions. Was she asking me if I would like the job? Or was she making an official offer? I couldn't make sense of anything she'd just said, anything other than the fact that Miranda Priestly had liked me.

"—delighted with this news. Who wouldn't be, right? So let's see, you can start on Monday, right? She'll actually be on vacation then, but that's a great time to start. Give you a little time to get acquainted with the other girls—oh, they're all such sweeties!" Acquainted? What? Starting Monday? Sweetie girls? It was refusing to make sense in my addled brain. I picked a single phrase that I'd understood and responded to it.

"Um, well, I don't think I can start Monday," I said quietly, hoping I'd indeed said something coherent. Saying those words had shocked me into semiwakefulness. I'd walked through the Elias-Clark doors for the very first time the day before, and was being awakened from a deep sleep to listen to someone tell me that I was to begin work in three days. It was Friday—*at seven o'clock in the goddamn morning*—and they wanted me to start on Monday? It began to feel like everything was spiraling out of control. Why the ridiculous rush? Was this woman so important that she needed me so badly? And why exactly did Sharon herself sound so scared of Miranda?

Starting Monday would be impossible. I had nowhere to live. Home base was my parents' house in Avon, the place I'd grudgingly moved back to after graduation, and where most of my things remained while I'd traveled during the summer. All of my interview-related clothes were piled on Lily's couch. I'd been trying to do the dishes and empty her ashtrays and buy pints of Häagen-Dazs so she wouldn't hate me, but I thought it only fair to give her a much-needed break from my unending presence, so I camped out on weekends at Alex's. That put all of my weekend going-out clothes and fun makeup at Alex's in Brooklyn, my laptop and mismatched suits at Lily's Harlem studio, and the rest of my life at my parents' house in Avon. I had no apartment in New York and didn't particularly understand how everyone knew that Madison Avenue ran uptown but Broadway ran down. I didn't actually know what uptown was. And she wanted me to start Monday?

"Um, well, I don't think I can do this Monday because I don't currently live in New York," I quickly explained, clutching the phone, "and I'll need a couple days to find an apartment and buy some furniture and move."

"Oh, well, then. I suppose Wednesday would be OK," she sniffed.

After a few more minutes of haggling, we finally settled on November 17, a week from Monday. That left me a little more than eight days to find and furnish a home in one of the craziest real estate markets in the world.

I hung up and flopped back down on the couch. My hands were trembling, and I let the phone drop to the floor. A week. I had a week to start working at the job I'd just accepted as Miranda Priestly's assistant. But, wait! That's what was bothering me . . . I hadn't actually accepted the job because it hadn't even been officially offered. Sharon hadn't even had to utter the words "We'd like to make you an offer," since she took it for granted that anyone with some semblance of intelligence would obviously just accept. No one had so much as mentioned the word "salary." I almost laughed out loud. Was this some sort of war tactic they'd perfected? Wait until the victim was finally deep into REM sleep after an extremely stressful day and then throw some life-altering news at her? Or had she just assumed that it would be wasted time and breath to do something as mundane as make a job offer and wait for acceptance, considering that this was *Runway* magazine? Sharon had just assumed that of course I'd jump all over the chance, that I'd be thrilled with the opportunity. And, as they always were at Elias-Clark, she was right. It had all happened so fast, so frenetically, that I hadn't had time to debate and deliberate as usual. But I had a good feeling that this *was* an opportunity I'd be crazy to turn down, that this could actually be a great first step to getting to *The New Yorker*. I had to try it. I was lucky to have it.

Newly energized, I gulped the rest of my coffee, brewed another cup for Alex, and took a quick, hot shower. When I went back into his room, he was just sitting up.

"You're dressed already?" he asked, fumbling for the tiny wire-rimmed glasses he was blind without. "Did someone call this morning, or did I dream that?"

"Not a dream," I said, crawling back under the covers even though I was wearing jeans and a turtleneck sweater. I was careful not to let my wet hair soak his pillows. "That was Lily. The HR woman from Elias-Clark called her place because that's the number I gave them. And guess what?"

"You got the job?"

"I got the job!"

"Oh, come here!" he said, sitting up and hugging me. "I'm so proud of you! That's great news, it really is."

"So you really think it's a good opportunity? I know we talked about it, but they didn't even give me a chance to decide. She just assumed that I'd want the job."

"It's an amazing opportunity. Fashion isn't the worst thing on earth—maybe it'll even be interesting."

I rolled my eyes.

"OK, so maybe that's going a little far. But with *Runway* on your résumé and a letter from this Miranda woman, and maybe even a few clips by the time you're done, hell, you can do anything. *The New Yorker* will be beating down your door."

"I hope you're right, I really do." I jumped up and starting throwing my things in my backpack. "Is it still OK if I borrow your car? The sooner I get home, the sooner I can get back. Not that it really matters, because I'm *moving to New York*. It's official!"

Since Alex went home to Westchester twice a week to babysit his little brother when his mom had to work late, his mom had given him her old car to keep in the city. But he wouldn't be needing it until Tuesday, and I'd be back before then. I had been planning to go home that weekend anyway, and now I'd have some good news to bring with me.

"Sure. No problem. It's in a spot about a half-block down on Grand Street. The keys are on the kitchen table. Call me when you get there, OK?"

"Will do. Sure you don't want to come? There'll be great food—you know my mom orders in only the best."

"Sounds tempting. You know I would, but I organized some of the younger teachers to get together tomorrow night for happy hour. Thought it might help us all work as a team. I really can't miss it."

"Goddamn do-gooder. Always doing good, spreading good cheer wherever you go. I'd hate you if I didn't love you so much." I leaned over and kissed him good-bye.

I found his little green Jetta on the first try and only spent twenty minutes trying to find the parkway that would take me to 95 North, which was wide open. It was a freezing day for November; the temperature was in the midthirties, and there were slick frozen patches on the back roads. But the sun was out, the kind of winter glare that causes unaccustomed eyes to tear and squint, and the air felt clean and cold in my lungs. I rode the entire way with the window rolled down, listening to the "Almost Famous" soundtrack on repeat. I worked my damp hair into a ponytail with one hand to keep it from flying in my eyes, and blew on my hands to keep them warm, or at least warm enough to grip the steering wheel. Only six months out of college, and my life was on the verge of bursting forward. Miranda Priestly, a stranger until yesterday but a powerful woman indeed, had handpicked me to join her magazine. Now I had a concrete reason to leave Connecticut and move—all on my own, as a real adult would—to Manhattan and make it my home. As I pulled into the driveway of my childhood house, sheer exhilaration took over. My cheeks looked red and windburned in the rearview mirror, and my hair was flying wildly about. There was no makeup on my face, and my jeans were dirty around the bottom from trudging through the city slush. But at that moment, I felt beautiful. Natural and cold and clean and crisp, I threw open the front door and called out for my mother. It was the last time in my life I remember feeling so light.

←→

"A week? Honey, I just don't see how you're going to start work in a week," my mother said, stirring her tea with a spoon. We were sitting at the kitchen table in our usual spots, my mother drinking her usual decaf tea with Sweet'N Low, me with my usual mug of English Breakfast and sugar. Even though I hadn't lived at home in four years, all it took was an oversize mug of microwaved tea and a couple Reese's peanut butter cups to make me feel like I'd never left.

"Well, I don't have a choice, and, honestly, I'm lucky to have that. You should've heard how hard-core this woman was on the phone," I said. She looked at me, expressionless. "But, whatever, I can't worry about it. I did just get a job at a really famous magazine with one of the most powerful women in the industry. A job a million girls would die for."

We smiled at each other, but her smile was tinged with sadness. "I'm so happy for you," she said. "Such a beautiful, grown-up daughter I have. Honey, I just know this is going to be the start of a wonderful, wonderful time in your life. Ah, I remember graduating from college and moving to New York. All alone in that big, crazy city. Scary but so, so exciting. I want you to love every minute of it, all the plays and films and people and shopping and books. It's going to be the best time of your life—I just know it." She rested her hand on mine, something she didn't usually do. "I'm so proud of you."

"Thanks, Mom. Does that mean you're proud enough of me to buy me an apartment, furniture, and a whole new wardrobe?"

"Yeah, right," she said and smacked the top of my head with a magazine on her way to the microwave to heat two more cups. She hadn't said no, but she wasn't exactly grabbing her checkbook, either.

I spent the rest of the evening e-mailing everyone I knew, asking if anyone needed a roommate or knew of someone who did. I posted some messages online and called people I hadn't spoken to in months. No luck. I decided my only choice—without permanently moving onto Lily's couch and inevitably wrecking our friendship, or crashing at Alex's, which neither of us was ready for—was to sublet a room short-term, until I could get my bearings in the city. It would be best to find my own room somewhere, and preferably one that was already furnished so I wouldn't have to deal with that, too.

The phone rang at a little after midnight, and I lunged for it, nearly falling off my twin-size childhood bed in the process. A framed, signed picture of Chris Evert, my childhood hero, smiled down from my wall, just below a bulletin board that still had magazine cutouts of Kirk Cameron plastered across it. I smiled into the phone.

"Hey, champ, it's Alex," he said with that tone of voice that meant something had happened. It was impossible to tell if it was something good or bad. "I just got an e-mail that a girl, Claire McMillan, is looking for a roommate. Princeton girl. I've met her before, I think. Dating Andrew, totally normal. You interested?"

"Sure, why not? Do you have her number?"

"No, I only have her e-mail, but I'll forward you her message and you can get in touch with her. I think she'll be good."

I e-mailed Claire while I finished talking to Alex and then finally got some sleep in my own bed. Maybe, just maybe, this would work out.

Claire McMillan: not so much. Her apartment was dark and depressing and in the middle of Hell's Kitchen, and there was a junkie propped up on the doorstep when I arrived. The others weren't much better. There was a couple looking to rent out an extra room in their apartment who made indirect references to putting up with their constant and loud love-making; an artist in her early thirties with four cats and a fervent desire for more; a bedroom at the end of a long, dark hallway, with no windows or closets; a twenty-year-old gay guy in his self-proclaimed "slutty stage." Each and every miserable room I'd visited was going for well over $1,000 and my salary was cashing in at a whopping $32,500. And although math had never been my strong suit, it didn't take a genius to figure out that rent would eat up more than $12,000 of it and taxes would take the rest. Oh, and my parents were confiscating the emergencies-only credit card, now that I was an "adult." Sweet.

Lily pulled through after three straight days of letdowns. Since she had a vested interest in getting me off her couch for good, she e-mailed everyone she knew. A classmate from her Ph.D. program at Columbia had a friend who had a boss who knew two girls who were looking for a roommate. I called immediately and spoke to a very nice girl named Shanti, who told me she and her friend Kendra were looking for someone to move into their Upper East Side apartment, in a room that was miniscule but had a window, a closet, and even an exposed brick wall. For $800 a month. I asked if the apartment had a bathroom and kitchen. It did (no dishwasher or bathtub or elevator, of course, but one can hardly expect living in luxury their first time out). Bingo. Shanti and Kendra ended up being two very sweet and quiet Indian girls who'd just graduated from Duke, worked hellishly long hours at investment banks, and seemed to me, that first day and every day thereafter, utterly indistinguishable from each other. I had found a home.

I'd slept in my new room for three nights already and still felt like a stranger living in a very strange place. The room was minute. Perhaps slightly larger than the storage shed in the backyard of my house in Avon, but not really. And unlike most empty spaces that actually looked bigger with furniture, my room had shrunk to half its size. I had naively eyed the tiny square and decided that it had to be close to a normal-size room and that I'd just buy the usual bedroom set: a queen-size bed, a dresser, maybe a night-stand or two. Lily and I had taken Alex's car to Ikea, the postcollege apartment mecca, and picked out a beautiful light-colored wood set and a woven rug with shades of light blue, dark blue, royal blue, and indigo.

Again, like fashion, home decorating was not my strong suit: I believe that Ikea was into its "Blue Period." We bought a duvet cover with a blue-flecked pattern and the fluffiest comforter they sold. She persuaded me to get one of those Chinese rice-paper lamps for the nightstand, and I chose some preframed black-and-white pictures to complement the deep red roughness of my much-hyped exposed brick wall. Elegant and casual, and not a little Zen. Perfect for my first adult room in the big city.

Perfect, that is, until it all actually arrived. It seems simply eyeing a room isn't quite the same as measuring it. Nothing fit. Alex put the bed together and by the time he'd pushed it against the exposed-brick wall (Manhattan code for "unfinished wall") it had consumed the entire room. I had to send the delivery men back with the six-drawer dresser, the two adorable nightstands, and even the full-length mirror. The men and Alex did lift up the bed, however, and I was able to slip the tri-blue rug under it, and a few blue inches peeked out from underneath the wooden behemoth. The rice-paper lamp had no nightstand or dresser on which to rest, so I simply placed it on the floor, wedged in the six inches between the bed frame and the sliding closet door. And even though I tried special mounting tape, nails, duct tape, screws, wires, Krazy Glue, double-sided tape, and much cursing, the framed photos refused to adhere to the exposed brick wall. After nearly three hours of effort and knuckles rubbed bleeding and raw from the brick, I finally propped them up on the windowsill. It was for the best, I thought. Blocked a bit of the direct view the woman living across the airshaft had into my room. None of it mattered, though. Not the airshaft instead of a majestic skyline or the lack of drawer space or the closet that was too small to hold a winter coat. The room was mine—the first I could decorate all on my own, with no input from parents or roommates—and I loved it.

It was the Sunday night before my first day of work, and I could do nothing but agonize over what to wear the next day. Kendra, the nicer of my two apartmentmates, kept poking her head in and asking quietly if she could help at all. Considering the two of them wore ultraconservative suits to work each day, I declined any fashion input. I paced the living room as much as I could manage when each length only took four strides, and sat down on the futon in front of the TV. Just what does one wear to the first day working for the most fashionable fashion editor of the most fashionable fashion magazine in existence? I'd heard of Prada (from the few Jappy girls who carried the backpacks at Brown) and Louis Vuitton (because both of my grandmothers sported the signature-print bags without realizing how cool they were) and maybe even Gucci (because who hasn't heard of Gucci?). But I sure didn't own a single stitch of it, and I wouldn't have known what to do with it if the entire contents of all three stores resided in my miniature closet. I walked back to my room—or, rather, the wall-to-wall mattress that I called a room—and collapsed on that big, beautiful bed, banging my ankle on the bulky frame. Shit. What now?

After much agonizing and clothes-flinging, I finally decided on a light blue sweater and a knee-length black skirt, with my knee-high black boots. I already knew that a briefcase wouldn't fly there, so I was left with no choice but to use my black canvas purse. The last thing I remember about that night was trying to navigate around my massive bed in high-heeled boots, a skirt, and no shirt, and sitting down to rest from the exhaustion of the effort.

I must have passed out from sheer anxiety, because it was adrenaline alone that awakened me at 5:30 A.M. I bolted from the bed. My nerves had been in perpetual overdrive all week, and my head felt like it would explode. I had exactly an hour and a half to shower, dress, and make my way from my fraternity-like building at 96th and Third to midtown via public transportation, a still sinister and intimidating concept. That meant I had to allot an hour for travel time and a half hour to make myself beautiful.

The shower was horrific. It made a high-pitched squealing noise like one of those dog-training whistles, remaining steadfastly lukewarm until just before I stepped out into the freezing-cold bathroom, at which point the water turned scalding. It took a mere three days of *that* routine before I began sprinting from my bed, turning on the shower fifteen minutes early, and heading back under the covers. When I snoozed three more times with the alarm clock and went back for round two in the bathroom, the mirrors would be all steamed up from the gloriously hot—although trickling—water.

I got myself into my binding and uncomfortable outfit and out the door in twenty-five minutes—a record. And it took only ten minutes to find the nearest subway, something I should've done the night before but was too busy scoffing at my mother's suggestion to take a "run-through" so I wouldn't get lost. When I'd gone for the interview the week before I'd taken a cab, and I was already convinced that this subway experiment was going to be a nightmare. But, remarkably, there was an English-speaking attendant in the booth who instructed me to take the 6 train to 59th Street. She said I'd exit right on 59th and would have to walk two blocks west to Madison. Easy. I rode the cold train in silence, one of the only people crazy enough to be awake and actually moving at such a miserable hour in the middle of November. So far, so good—no glitches until it was time to make my way up to street level.

I took the nearest stairs and stepped out into a frigid day where the only light I saw was emanating from twenty-four-hour bodegas. Behind me was Bloomingdale's, but nothing else looked familiar. Elias-Clark, Elias-Clark, Elias-Clark. Where was that building? I turned in my place 180 degrees until I saw a street sign: 60th Street and Lexington. Well, 59th can't be that far away from 60th, but which way should I walk to make the streets go west? And where was Madison in comparison to Lexington? Nothing looked familiar from my visit to the building the week before, since I'd been dropped off right in front. I strolled for a bit, happy to have left enough time to get as lost as I was, and finally ducked into a deli for a cup of coffee.

"Hello, sir. I can't seem to find my way to the Elias-Clark building. Could you please point me in the right direction?" I asked the nervous-looking man behind the cash register. I tried not to smile sweetly, remembering what everyone had told me about not being in Avon anymore, and how people here don't exactly respond well to good manners. He scowled at me, and I got nervous it was because he thought me rude. I smiled sweetly.

"One dollah," he said, holding out his hand.

"You're charging me for directions?"

"One dollah, skeem or bleck, you peek."

I stared at him for a moment before I realized he knew only enough English to converse about coffee. "Oh, skim would be perfect. Thank you so much." I handed over a dollar and headed back outside, more lost than ever. I asked people who worked at newsstands, as street sweepers, even a man who was tucked inside one of those movable breakfast carts.

Not a single one understood me well enough to so much as point in the direction of 59th and Madison, and I had brief flashbacks to Delhi, depression, dysentery. *No! I will find it.*

A few more minutes of wandering aimlessly around a waking midtown actually landed me at the front door of the Elias-Clark building. The lobby glowed behind the glass doors in the early-morning darkness, and it looked, for those first few moments, like a warm, welcoming place. But when I pushed the revolving door to enter, it fought me. Harder and harder I pushed, until my body weight was thrust forward and my face was nearly pressed against the glass, and only then did it budge. When it did begin to move, it slid slowly at first, prompting me to push ever harder. But as soon as it picked up some momentum, the glass behemoth whipped around, hitting me from behind and forcing me to trip over my feet and shuffle visibly to remain standing. A man behind the security desk laughed.

"Tricky, eh? Not the first time I seen that happen, and won't be the last," he chortled, fleshy cheeks jiggling. "They getcha good here."

I looked him over quickly and decided to hate him and knew that he would never like me, regardless of what I said or how I acted. I smiled anyway.

"I'm Andrea," I said, pulling a knit mitten from my hand and reaching over the desk. "Today's my first day of work at *Runway*. I'm Miranda Priestly's new assistant."

"And I'm sorry!" he roared, throwing his round head back with glee. "Just call me 'Sorry for You'! Hah! Hah! Hah! Hey, Eduardo, check this out. She's one of Miranda's new *slaves*! Where you from, girl, bein' all friendly and shit? Topeka fuckin' Kansas? She is gonna eat you alive, hah, hah, hah!"

But before I could respond, a portly man wearing the same uniform came over and with no subtlety whatsoever looked me up and down. I braced for more mocking and guffaws, but it didn't come. Instead, he turned a kind face to mine and looked me in the eyes.

"I'm Eduardo, and this idiot here's Mickey," he said, motioning to the first man, who looked annoyed that Eduardo had acted civilly and ruined all the fun. "Don't make no never mind of him, he's just kiddin' with you." He spoke with a mixed Spanish and New York accent, as he picked up a sign-in book. "You just fill out this here information, and I'll

give you a temporary pass to go upstairs. Tell 'em you need a card wit
your pitcher on it from HR."

I must have looked at him gratefully, because he got embarrassed
and shoved the book across the counter. "Well, go on now, fill 'er out.
And good luck today, girl. You gonna need it."

I was too nervous and exhausted at this point to ask him to explain,
and besides, I didn't really have to. About the only thing I'd had time to
do in the week between accepting the job and starting work was to learn
a little bit about my new boss. I had Googled her and was surprised to
find that Miranda Priestly was born Miriam Princhek, in London's East
End. Hers was like all the other orthodox Jewish families in the town,
stunningly poor but devout. Her father occasionally worked odd jobs, but
mostly they relied on the community for support since he spent most of
his days studying Jewish texts. Her mother had died in childbirth with
Miriam, and it was *her* mother who moved in and helped raise the children. And were there children! Eleven in all. Most of her brothers and sis-
ters went on to work blue-collar jobs like their father, with little time to
do anything but pray and work; a couple managed to get themselves into
and through the university, only to marry young and begin having large
families of their own. Miriam was the single exception to the family tradition.

After saving the small bills her older siblings would slip her whenever
they were able, Miriam promptly dropped out of high school upon turning seventeen—a mere three months shy of graduation—to take a job as
an assistant to an up-and-coming British designer, helping him put together his shows each season. After a few years of making a name for herself as one of the darlings of London's burgeoning fashion world and
studying French at night, she scored a job as a junior editor at the French
Chic magazine in Paris. By this time, she had little to do with her family:
they didn't understand her life or ambitions, and she was embarrassed by
their old-fashioned piety and overwhelming lack of sophistication. The
alienation from her family was completed shortly after joining French
Chic when, at twenty-four years old, Miriam Princhek became Miranda
Priestly, shedding her undeniably ethnic name for one with more
panache. Her rough, cockney-girl British accent was soon replaced by a
carefully cultivated, educated one, and by her late twenties, Miriam's

transformation from Jewish peasant to secular socialite was complete. She rose quickly, ruthlessly, through the ranks of the magazine world.

She spent ten years at the helm of French *Runway* before Elias transferred her to the number-one spot at American *Runway*, the ultimate achievement. She moved her two daughters and her rock-star then husband (himself eager to gain more exposure in America) to a penthouse apartment on Fifth Avenue at 76th Street and began a new era at *Runway* magazine: the Priestly years, the sixth of which we were nearing as I began my first day.

By some stroke of dumb luck, I would be working for nearly a month before Miranda was back in the office. She took her vacation every year starting a week before Thanksgiving until right after New Year's. Typically, she'd spend a few weeks at the flat she kept in London, but this year, I was told, she had dragged her husband and daughters to Oscar de la Renta's estate in the Dominican Republic for two weeks before spending Christmas and New Year's at the Ritz in Paris. I'd also been forewarned that even though she was technically "on vacation," she'd still be fully reachable and working at all times, and therefore, so should every single other person on staff. I was to be appropriately prepped and trained without her highness present. That way, Miranda wouldn't have to suffer my inevitable mistakes while I learned the job. Sounded good to me. So at 7:00 A.M. on the dot, I signed my name into Eduardo's book and was buzzed through the turnstiles for the very first time. "Strike a pose!" Eduardo called after me, just before the elevator doors swept shut.

Emily, looking remarkably haggard and sloppy in a fitted but wrinkled sheer white T-shirt and hypertrendy cargo pants was waiting for me in the reception area, clutching a cup of Starbucks and flipping though the new December issue. Her high heels were placed firmly on the glass coffee table, and a black lacy bra showed obviously through the completely transparent cotton of her shirt. Lipstick, smeared a bit around her mouth by the coffee cup, and uncombed, wavy red hair that spilled down over her shoulders made her look as though she'd spent the last seventy-two hours in bed.

"Hey, welcome," she muttered, giving me my first official up-down look-over by someone other than the security guard. "Nice boots."

My heart surged. Was she serious? Or sarcastic? Her tone made it impossible to tell. My arches ached already and my toes were jammed up against the front, but if I'd actually been complimented on an item of my outfit by a *Runway*-er, it might be worth the pain.

Emily looked at me a moment longer and then swung her legs off the table, sighing dramatically. "Well, let's get to it. It's *really* lucky for you that she's not here," she said. "Not that she's not great, of course, because she is," she added in what I would soon recognize—and come to adopt myself—as the classic *Runway* Paranoid Turnaround. Just when something negative about Miranda slips out from a Clacker's lips—however justified—paranoia that Miranda will find out overwhelms the speaker and inspires an about-face. One of my favorite workday pastimes became watching my colleagues scramble to negate whatever blasphemy they'd uttered.

Emily slid her card through the electronic reader, and we walked side by side, in silence, through the winding hallways to the center of the floor, where Miranda's office suite was located. I watched as she opened the suite's French doors and tossed her bag and coat on one of the desks that sat directly outside Miranda's cavernous office. "This is your desk, obviously," she motioned to a smooth, wooden, L-shaped Formica slab that sat directly opposite hers. It had a brand-new turquoise iMac computer, a phone, and some filing trays, and there were already pens and paper clips and some notebooks in the drawers. "I left most of my stuff for you. It's easier if I just order the new stuff for myself."

Emily had just been promoted to the position of senior assistant, leaving the junior assistant position open for me. She explained that she would spend two years as Miranda's senior assistant, after which she'd be skyrocketed to an amazing fashion position at *Runway*. The three-year assistant program she'd be completing was the ultimate guarantee of going places in the fashion world, but I was clinging to the belief that my one-year sentence would suffice for *The New Yorker*. Allison had already left Miranda's office area for her new post in the beauty department, where she'd be responsible for testing new makeup, moisturizers, and hair products and writing them up. I wasn't sure how being Miranda's assistant had prepared her for this task, but I was impressed nonetheless. The promises were true: people who worked for Miranda got places.

The rest of the staff began streaming in around ten, about fifty in all of editorial. The biggest department was fashion, of course, with close to thirty people, including all the accessories assistants. Features, beauty, and art rounded out the mix. Nearly everyone stopped by Miranda's office to schmooze with Emily, overhear any gossip concerning her boss, and check out the new girl. I met dozens of people that first morning, everyone flashing enormous, toothy white smiles and appearing genuinely interested in meeting me.

The men were all flamboyantly gay, adorning themselves in second-skin leather pants and ribbed T's that stretched over bulging biceps and perfect pecs. The art director, an older man sporting champagne blond, thinning hair, who looked like he dedicated his life to emulating Elton John, was turned out in rabbit-fur loafers and eyeliner. No one batted an eye. We'd had gay groups on campus, and I had a few friends who'd come out the past few years, but none of them looked like this. It was like being surrounded by the entire cast and crew of *Rent*—with better costumes, of course.

The women, or rather the girls, were individually beautiful. Collectively, they were mind-blowing. Most appeared to be about twenty-five, and few looked a day older than thirty. While nearly all of them had enormous, glimmering diamonds on their ring fingers, it seemed impossible that any had actually given birth yet—or ever would. In and out, in and out they walked gracefully on four-inch skinny heels, sashaying over to my desk to extend milky-white hands with long, manicured fingers, calling themselves "Jocelyn who works with Hope," "Nicole from fashion," and "Stef who oversees accessories." Only one, Shayna, was shorter than five-nine, but she was so petite it seemed impossible for her to carry another inch of height. All weighed less than 110 pounds.

As I sat in my swivel chair, trying to remember everyone's name, the prettiest girl I'd seen all day swooped in. She wore a rose-colored cashmere sweater that looked like it was spun from pink clouds. The most amazing, white hair swirled down her back. Her six-one frame looked as though it carried only enough weight to keep her upright, but she moved with the surprising grace of a dancer. Her cheeks glowed, and her multi-carat, flawless diamond engagement ring emanated an incredible light-ness. I thought she'd caught me staring at it, since she flung her hand under my nose.

"I created it," she announced, smiling at her hand and looking at me. I looked to Emily for an explanation, a hint as to who this might be, but she was on the phone again. I thought the girl was referring to the ring, meant that she had actually designed it, but then she said, "Isn't it a gor-geous color? It's one coat Marshmallow and one coat Ballet Slipper. Ac-tually, Ballet Slipper came first, and then a topcoat to finish it off. It's perfect—light colored without looking like you painted your nails with White Out. I think I'll use this every time I get a manicure!" And she turned on her heels and walked out. *Ah, yes, a pleasure to meet you, too,* I mentally directed toward her back as she strutted away.

I'd been enjoying meeting all my coworkers; everyone seemed kind and sweet and, except for the beautiful weirdo with the nail polish fetish, they all appeared interested in getting to know me. Emily hadn't left my side yet, seizing every opportunity to teach me something. She provided running commentary on who was really important, whom not to piss off, whom it was beneficial to befriend because they threw the best parties. When I described Manicure Girl, Emily's face lit up.

"Oh!" she breathed, more excited than I'd heard her about anyone else yet. "Isn't she just amazing?"

"Um, yeah, she seemed nice. We didn't really get a chance to talk, she was just, you know, showing me her nail polish."

Emily smiled widely, proudly. "Yes, well, you do know who she is, don't you?"

I wracked my brain, trying to remember if she looked like any movie stars or singers or models, but I couldn't place her. So, she was famous! Maybe that's why she hadn't introduced herself—I was supposed to rec-ognize her. But I didn't. "No, actually, I don't. Is she famous?"

The stare I received in response was part disbelief, part disgust. "Um, *yeah,*" Emily said, emphasizing the "yeah" and squinting her eyes as if to say, *You total fucking idiot.* "That is Jessica Duchamps." She waited. I waited. Nothing. "You do know who that is, right?" Again, I ran lists through my mind, trying to connect something with this new information, but I was quite sure I'd never, ever heard of her. Besides, this game was getting old.

"Emily, I've never seen her before, and her name doesn't sound familiar. Would you please tell me who she is?" I asked, struggling to remain calm. The ironic part was that I didn't even care who she was, but Emily was clearly not going to give this up until she'd made me look like a complete and total loser.

Her smile this time was patronizing. "Of course. You just had to say so. Jessica Duchamps is, well, a Duchamps! You know, as in the most successful French restaurant in the city! Her parents own it—isn't that crazy? They are so unbelievably rich."

"Oh, really?" I said, feigning enthusiasm for the fact that this superpretty girl was worth knowing because her parents were restaurateurs. "That's great."

I answered a few phone calls with the requisite "Miranda Priestly's office," although both Emily and I were worried that Miranda herself would call and I wouldn't know what to do. Panic set in during a call when an unidentified woman barked something incoherent in a strong British accent, and I threw the phone to Emily without thinking to put it on hold first.

"It's her," I whispered urgently. "Take it."

Emily gave me my first viewing of her specialty look. Never one to mince emotions, she could raise her eyebrows and drop her chin in a way that clearly conveyed equal parts disgust and pity.

"Miranda? It's Emily," she said, a bright smile lighting up her face as if Miranda might be able to seep through the phone and see her. Silence. A frown. "Oh, Mimi, so sorry! The new girl thought you were Miranda! I know, how funny. I guess we have to work on *not thinking every British accent is necessarily our boss!*" She looked at me pointedly, her overtweezed eyebrows arching even higher.

She chatted a bit longer while I continued to answer the phone and take messages for Emily, who would then call the people back—with nonstop narration on their order of importance, if any, in Miranda's life. About noon, just as the first hunger pangs were beginning, I picked up a call and heard a British accent on the other end.

"Hello? Allison, is that you?" asked the icy-sounding but regal voice. "I'll be needing a skirt."

I cupped my hand over the receiver and felt my eyes open wide. "Emily, it's her, it's definitely her," I hissed, waving the receiver to get her attention. "She wants a skirt!"

Emily turned to see my panic-stricken face and promptly hung up the phone without so much as "I'll call you later" or even "good-bye." She pressed the button to switch Miranda to her line, and plastered on another wide grin.

"Miranda? It's Emily. What can I do?" She put her pen to her pad and began writing furiously, forehead furrowing intently. "Yes, of course. Naturally." And as fast as it happened, it was over. I looked at her expectantly. She rolled her eyes at me for appearing so eager.

"Well, it looks like you have your first job. Miranda needs a skirt for tomorrow, among other things, so we'll need to get it on a plane by tonight, at the latest."

"OK, well, what kind does she need?" I asked, still reeling from the shock that a skirt would be traveling to the Dominican Republic simply because she'd requested it do so.

"She didn't say exactly," Emily muttered as she picked up the phone.

"Hi, Jocelyn, it's me. She wants a skirt, and I'll need to have it on Mrs. de la Renta's flight tonight, since she'll be meeting Miranda down there. No, I have no idea. No, she didn't say. I really don't know. OK, thanks." She turned to me and said, "It makes it more difficult when she's not specific. She's too busy to worry about details like that, so she didn't say what material or color or style or brand she wants. But that's OK. I know her size, and I definitely know her taste well enough to predict exactly what she'll like. That was Jocelyn from the fashion department. They'll start calling some in." I pictured Jerry Lewis presiding over a skirt telethon with a giant scoreboard, drum role, and voilà! Gucci and spontaneous applause.

Not quite. "Calling in" the skirts was my very first lesson in *Runway* ridiculousness, although I do have to say that the process was as efficient as a military operation. Either Emily or myself would notify the fashion assistants—about eight in all, who each maintained contacts within a specified list of designers and stores. The assistants would immediately begin calling all of their public relations contacts at the various design houses and, if appropriate, at upscale Manhattan stores and tell them that Miranda Priestly—yes, Miranda Priestly, and yes, it was indeed for her *personal* use—was looking for a particular item. Within minutes, every PR account exec and assistant working at Michael Kors, Gucci, Prada, Versace, Fendi, Armani, Chanel, Barney's, Chloé, Calvin Klein, Bergdorf, Roberto Cavalli, and Saks would be messengering over (or, in some cases, hand-delivering) every skirt they had in stock that Miranda Priestly could conceivably find attractive. I watched the process unfold like a highly choreographed ballet, each player knowing exactly where and when and how their next step would occur. While this near-daily activity unfolded, Emily sent me to pick up a few other things that we'd need to send with the skirt that night.

"Your car will be waiting for you on Fifty-eighth Street," she said while working two phone lines and scribbling instructions for me on a piece of *Runway* stationery. She paused briefly to toss me a cell phone and said, "Here, take this in case I need to reach you or you have any questions. Never turn it off. Always answer it." I took the phone and the paper and headed down to the 58th Street side of the building, wondering how I was ever going to find "my car." Or even, really, what that meant. I had barely stepped on the sidewalk and looked meekly around before a squat, gray-haired man gumming a pipe approached.

"You Priestly's new girl?" he croaked through tobacco-stained lips, never removing the mahogany-colored pipe. I nodded. "I'm Rich. The dispatcher. You wanna car, you talka to me. Got it, blondie?" I nodded again and ducked into the backseat of a black Cadillac sedan. He slammed the door shut and waved.

"Where you going, miss?" the driver asked, pulling me back to the present. I realized I had no idea and pulled the piece of paper from my pocket.

First stop: Tommy Hilfiger's studio at 355 West 57th St., 6th Floor.
Ask for Leanne. She'll give you everything we need.

I gave the driver the address and stared out the window. It was one o'clock on a frigid winter afternoon, I was twenty-three years old, and I was riding in the backseat of a chauffeured sedan, on my way to Tommy Hilfiger's studio. And I was positively starving. It took nearly forty-five minutes to go the fifteen blocks during the midtown lunch hour, my first glimpse of real city gridlock. The driver told me he'd circle the block until I came out again, and off I went to Tommy's studio. When I asked for Leanne at the receptionist's desk on the sixth floor, an adorable girl not a day older than eighteen came bounding down the stairs.

"Hi!" she called, stretching out the "I" sound for a few seconds. "You must be Andrea, Miranda's new assistant. We sure do love her around here, so welcome to the team!" She grinned. I grinned. She pulled a massive plastic bag out from underneath a table and immediately spilled its contents on the floor. "Here we have Caroline's favorite jeans in three colors, and we threw in some baby T's, too. And Cassidy just adores Tommy's khaki skirts—we gave them to her in olive and stone." Jean skirts, denim jackets, even a few pair of socks came flying out of the bag, and all I could do was stare: there were enough clothes to constitute four or more total preteen wardrobes. *Who the hell are Cassidy and Caroline?* I wondered, staring at the loot. What self-respecting person wears Tommy Hilfiger jeans—in three different colors, no less?

I must've looked thoroughly confused, because Leanne quite purposely turned her back while repacking the clothes and said, "I just know Miranda's daughters will love this stuff. We've been dressing them for years, and Tommy insists on picking the clothes out for them himself." I shot her a grateful look and threw the bag over my shoulder.

"Good luck!" she called as the elevator doors closed, a genuine smile taking up most of her face. "You're lucky to have such an awesome job!" Before she could say it, I found myself mentally finishing the sentence— *a million girls would die for it.* And for that moment, having just seen a famous designer's studio and in possession of thousands of dollars worth of clothes, I thought she was right.

Once I got the hang of things, the rest of the day flew. I debated for a few minutes whether anyone would be mad if I took a minute to pick up a sandwich, but I had no choice. I hadn't eaten anything since my croissant at seven this morning, and it was nearly two. I asked the driver to pull over at a deli and decided at the last minute to get him one, too.

His jaw dropped when I handed him the turkey and honey mustard, and I wondered if I had made him uncomfortable.

"I just figured you were hungry, too," I said. "You know, driving around all day, you probably don't have much time for lunch."

"Thank you, miss, I appreciate it. It's just that I've been driving around Elias-Clark girls for twelve years, and they are not so nice. You are very nice," he said in a thick but indeterminate accent, looking at me in the rearview mirror. I smiled at him and felt a momentary flash of foreboding. But then the moment passed and we each munched our turkey wraps while sitting in gridlock and listening to his favorite CD, which sounded to me like little more than a woman shrieking the same thing over and over in an unknown language, the whole thing set to sitar music.

Emily's next written instruction was to pick up a pair of white shorts that Miranda desperately needed for tennis. I figured we'd be headed to Polo, but she had written Chanel. Chanel made white tennis shorts? The driver took me to the private salon, where an older saleswoman whose facelift had left her eyes looking like slits handed me a pair of white cotton-Lycra hot pants, size zero, pinned to a silk hanger and draped in a velvet garment bag. I looked at the shorts, which appeared as though they wouldn't fit a six-year-old, and looked back to the woman.

"Um, do you really think Miranda will wear these?" I asked tentatively, convinced the woman could open that pit-bull mouth of hers and consume me whole. She glared at me.

"Well, I should hope so, miss, considering they're custom measured and cut, according to her exact specifications," she snarled as she handed the minishorts over. "Tell her Mr. Kopelman sends his best." *Sure, lady. Whoever that is.*

My next stop was what Emily wrote as "way downtown," J&R Computer World near City Hall. Seemed it was the only store in the entire city that sold Warriors of the West, a computer game that Miranda wanted to purchase for Oscar and Annette de la Renta's son, Moises. By the time I made it downtown an hour later, I'd realized that the cell phone could make long-distance calls, and I was happily dialing my parents and telling them how great the job was.

"Um, Dad? Hi, it's Andy. Guess where I am now? Yes, of course I'm at work, but that happens to be in the backseat of a chauffeured car cruising around Manhattan. I've already been to Tommy Hilfiger and Chanel, and after I buy this computer game, I'm on my way to Oscar de la Renta's apartment on Park Avenue to drop all the stuff off. No, it's not for him! Miranda's in the DR and Annette's flying there to meet them all tonight. On a private plane, yes! Dad! It stands for the Dominican Republic, of course!"

He sounded wary but pleased that I was so happy, and I came to decide that I was hired as college-educated messenger. Which was absolutely fine with me. After leaving the bag of Tommy clothes, the hot pants, and the computer game with a very distinguished-looking doorman in a very plush Park Avenue lobby (so this is what people mean when they talk about Park Avenue!), I headed back to the Elias-Clark building. When I walked into my office area, Emily was sitting Indian-style on the floor, wrapping presents in plain white paper with white ribbons. She was surrounded by mountains of red-and-white boxes, all identical in shape, hundreds, perhaps thousands, scattered between our desks and overflowing into Miranda's office. Emily was unaware that I was watching her, and I saw that it took her only two minutes to wrap each individual box perfectly and an additional fifteen seconds to tie on a white satin ribbon. She moved efficiently, not wasting a single second, piling the wrapped white boxes in new mountains behind her. The wrapped pile grew and grew, but the unwrapped pile didn't shrink. I estimated that she could be at it for the next four days and still not finish.

I called her name over the eighties CD she had playing from her computer. "Um, Emily? Hi, I'm back."

She turned toward me and for a brief moment appeared to have no idea who I was. Completely blank. But then my new-girl status came rushing back. "How'd it go?" she asked quickly. "Did you get everything on the list?"

I nodded.

"Even the video game? When I called, there was only one copy left. It was there?"

I nodded again.

"And you gave it all to the de la Rentas' doorman on Park? The clothes, the shorts, everything?"

"Yep. No problem. It went very smoothly, and I dropped it all off a few minutes ago. I was wondering, will Miranda actually wear those—"

"Listen, I need to run to the bathroom and I've been waiting for you to get back. Just sit by the phone for a minute, OK?"

"You haven't gone to the bathroom since I left?" I asked incredulously. It had been five hours. "Why not?"

Emily finished tying the ribbon on the box she had just wrapped and looked at me coolly. "Miranda doesn't tolerate anyone except her assistants answering her phone, so since you weren't here, I didn't want to go. I suppose I could have run out for a minute, but I know she's having a hectic day, and I want to make sure that I'm always available to her. So no, we do not go to the bathroom—or anywhere else—without clearing it with each other. We need to work together to make sure that we are doing the best job possible for her. OK?"

"Sure," I said. "Go ahead. I'll be right here." She turned and walked away, and I put my hand on the desk to steady myself. No going to the bathroom without a coordinated war plan? Did she really sit in that office for the past five hours willing her bladder to behave because she worried that a woman across the Atlantic may call in the two and a half minutes it would take to run to the ladies' room? Apparently so. It seemed a little dramatic, but I assumed that was just Emily being overly enthusiastic. There was no way that Miranda actually demanded that of her assistants. I was sure of it. Or did she?

I picked up a few sheets of paper from the printer and saw that it was titled "X-Mas Presents Received." One, two, three, four, five, *six* single-spaced pages of gifts, with sender and item on one line each. Two hundred and fifty-six presents in all. It looked like a wedding registry for the Queen of England, and I couldn't take it in fast enough. There was a Bobby Brown makeup set from Bobby Brown herself, a one-of-a-kind leather Kate Spade handbag from Kate and Andy Spade, a Smythson of Bond Street burgundy leather organizer from Graydon Carter, a mink-lined sleeping bag from Miuccia Prada, a multistrand beaded Verdura bracelet from Aerin Lauder, a diamond-encrusted watch from Donatella Versace, a case of champagne from Cynthia Rowley, a matching beaded tank top and evening bag from Mark Badgley and James Mischka, a collection of Cartier pens from Irv Ravitz, a chinchilla muffler from Vera Wang, a zebra-print jacket from Alberto Ferretti, a Burberry cashmere blanket from Rosemarie Bravo. And that was just the start. There were handbags in every shape and size from everyone: Herb Ritts, Bruce Weber, Giselle Bundchen, Hillary Clinton, Tom Ford, Calvin Klein, Annie Leibovitz, Nicole Miller, Adrienne Vittadini, Michael Kors, Helmut Lang, Giorgio Armani, John Sahag, Bruno Magli, Mario Testino, and Narcisco Rodriguez, to name a few. There were dozens of donations made in Miranda's name to various charities, what must have been a hundred bottles of wine and champagne, eight or ten Dior bags, a couple dozen scented candles, a few pieces of Oriental pottery, silk pajamas, leather-bound books, bath products, chocolates, bracelets, caviar, cashmere sweaters, framed photographs, and enough flower arrangements and/or potted plants to decorate one of those five-hundred-couple mass weddings they have in soccer stadiums in China. Ohmigod! Was this reality? Was this actually happening? Was I now working for a woman who received 256 presents at Christmas from some of the world's most famous people? Or not so famous? I wasn't sure. I recognized a few of the really obvious celebrities and designers, but didn't know then that the others comprised some of the most sought-after photographers, makeup artists, models, socialites, and a whole slew of Elias-Clark executives. Just as I was wondering if Emily actually knew who all the people were, she walked back in. I tried to pretend I wasn't reading the list, but she didn't mind at all.

"Crazy, isn't it? She is the coolest woman ever," she gushed, snatching the sheets off her desk and gazing at them with what can only be described as lust. "Have you ever seen more amazing things in your life? This is last year's list. I just pulled it out so we know what to expect since the gifts have begun coming in already. That's definitely one of the best parts of the job—opening all her presents." I was confused. *We* opened her presents? Why wouldn't she open them herself? I asked as much.

"Are you out of your mind? Miranda won't like ninety percent of the stuff people send. Some of it is downright insulting, things I won't even show her. Like this," she said, picking up a small box. It was a Bang and Olufsen portable phone in their signature sleek silver with all rounded edges and the capability to remain clear for something like 2,000 miles. I had been in the store just a couple weeks earlier, watching Alex salivate over their stereo systems, and I knew the phone cost upward of five hundred dollars and could do everything short of holding a conversation *for* you. "A phone? Do you believe someone had the nerve to send Miranda Priestly a *phone*?" She tossed it to me. "Keep it if you want it: I would never even let her see this. She'd be annoyed that someone sent something *electronic*." She pronounced the word "electronic" as though it were synonymous with "covered in bodily fluids."

I tucked the phone box under my desk and tried to keep the smile off my face. It was too perfect! A portable phone was on my list of stuff that I still needed for my new room, and I'd just gotten a five-hundred-dollar one for free.

"Actually," she continued, flopping down again on the floor of Miranda's office, Indian-style, "let's put in a few hours wrapping some more of these wine bottles, and then you can open the presents that came in today. They're over there." She pointed behind her desk to a smaller mountain of boxes and bags and baskets in a multitude of colors.

"So, these are gifts that we're sending out from Miranda, right?" I asked her as I picked up a box and began wrapping it in the thick white paper.

"Yep. Every year, it's the same deal. Top-tier people get bottles of Dom. This would include Elias execs, and the big designers who aren't also personal friends. Her lawyer and accountant. Midlevel people get Veuve, and this is just about everyone—the twins' teachers, the hair stylists, Uri, et cetera. The nobodies get a bottle of the Ruffino Chianti—usually they go to the PR people who send small, general gifts that aren't personalized for her. She'll have us send Chianti to the vet, some of the babysitters who fill in for Cara, the people who wait on her in stores she goes to often, and all the caretakers associated with the summer house in Connecticut. Anyway, I order about twenty-five thousand dollars' worth of this stuff at the beginning of November, Sherry-Lehman delivers it, and it usually takes nearly a month to do all the wrapping. It's good she's out of the office now or we'd be taking this stuff home with us to wrap. Pretty good deal, because Elias picks up the tab."

"I guess it would cost double that to have the Sherry-Lehman place wrap them, huh?" I wondered, still trying to process the hierarchy of the gift-giving.

"What the hell do we care?" she snorted. "Trust me, you'll learn quickly that cost is no issue around here. It's just that Miranda doesn't like the wrapping paper they use. I gave them this white paper last year, but they just didn't look as nice as when we do it." She looked proud.

We wrapped like that until close to six, with Emily telling me how things worked as I tried to wrap my mind around this strange and exciting world. Just as she was describing exactly how Miranda likes her coffee (tall latte with two raw sugars), a breathless blond girl I remembered as one of the many fashion assistants walked in carrying a wicker basket the size of a baby carriage. She hovered just outside Miranda's office, looking as though she thought the soft gray carpeting might turn to quicksand under her Jimmy Choos if she dared to cross the threshold.

"Hi, Em. I've got the skirts right here. Sorry that took so long, but no one's around since it's that weird time right before Thanksgiving. Anyway, hopefully you'll find something she'll like." She looked down at her basket full of folded skirts.

Emily looked up at her with barely disguised scorn. "Just leave them on my desk. I'll return the ones that won't work. *Which I imagine will be most of them, considering your taste.*" The last part was under her breath, just loud enough for me to hear.

The blond girl looked bewildered. Definitely not the brightest star in the sky, but she seemed nice enough. I wondered why Emily so obviously hated her. It'd been a long day already, what with the running commentary and errands all over the city and hundreds of names and faces to try to remember, so I didn't even ask.

Emily placed the large basket on her desk and looked down on it, hands on her hips. From what I could see from Miranda's office floor, there were perhaps twenty-five different skirts in an incredible assortment of fabrics, colors, and sizes. Had she really not specified what she wanted at all? Did she really not bother to inform Emily whether she'd be needing something appropriate for a black-tie dinner or a mixed-doubles match or perhaps to use as a bathing suit cover-up? Did she want denim, or would something chiffon work better? How exactly were we supposed to predict what *might* please her?

I was about to find out. Emily carried the wicker basket to Miranda's office and carefully, reverentially, placed it on the plush carpeting beside me. She sat down and began removing the skirts one by one and laying them in a circle around us. There was a beautiful crocheted skirt in shocking fuchsia by Celine, a pearl gray wraparound by Calvin Klein, and a black suede one with black beads along the bottom by Mr. de la Renta himself. There were skirts in red and ecru and lavender, some with lace and others in cashmere. A few were long enough to sweep gracefully along the ankles, and others were so short they looked more like tube tops. I picked up a midcalf, brown silk beauty and held it up to my waist, but the material covered only one of my legs. The next one in the pile reached to the floor in a swirl of tulle and chiffon and looked as though it would feel most at home at a Charleston garden party. One of the jean skirts was prefaded and came with a gigantic brown leather belt already looped around it, and another had a crinkly, silver-material overlay on top of a slightly more opaque silver liner. Where on earth were we going here?

"Wow, looks like Miranda has a thing for skirts, huh?" I said, simply because I had nothing better to say.

"Actually, no. Miranda has a slight obsession with scarves." Emily refused to make eye contact with me, as though she'd just revealed that she herself had herpes. "It's just one of those cute, quirky things about her you should know."

"Oh, really?" I asked, trying to sound amused and not horrified. An obsession with scarves? I like clothes and bags and shoes as much as the next girl, but I wouldn't exactly declare any of them an "obsession." And something about the way Emily was saying it wasn't so casual.

"Yes, well, she must need a skirt for something specific, but it's scarves that's she's really into. You know, like her signature scarves?" She looked at me. My face must have betrayed my complete lack of a clue. "You do remember meeting her during the interview, do you not?"

"Of course," I said quickly, sensing it'd probably not be the best idea to let this girl know that I couldn't so much as remember Miranda's name during my interview, never mind remember what she was wearing. "But I'm not sure I noticed a scarf."

"She always, always, always wears a single white Hermès scarf somewhere on her outfit. Mostly around her neck, but sometimes she'll have her hairdresser tie one in a chignon, or occasionally she'll use them as a belt. They're like, her signature. Everyone knows that Miranda Priestly wears a white Hermès scarf, no matter what. How cool is that?"

It was at that exact moment that I noticed Emily had a lime green scarf woven through the belt loops on her cargo pants, just peeking out from underneath the white T-shirt.

"She likes to mix it up sometimes, and I'm guessing that this is one of those times. Anyway, those idiots in fashion never know what she'll like. Look at some of these, they're hideous!" She held up an absolutely gorgeous flowy skirt, slightly dressier than the rest with its little flecks of gold shimmering from the deep tan background.

"Yep," I agreed, in what was to become the first of thousands, if not millions, of times I agreed with whatever she said simply to make her stop talking. "It's horrendous-looking." It was so beautiful I thought I'd be happy to wear it to my own wedding.

Emily continued prattling on about patterns and fabrics and Miranda's needs and wants, occasionally interjecting a scathing insult about a coworker. She finally chose three radically different skirts and set them aside to send to Miranda, talking, talking, talking the whole time. I tried to listen, but it was almost seven, and I was trying to decide whether I was ravenously hungry, utterly nauseated, or just plain exhausted. I think it was all three. I didn't even notice when the tallest human being I'd ever seen swooped into the office.

"YOU!" I heard from somewhere behind me. "STAND UP SO I CAN GET A LOOK AT YOU!"

I turned just in time to see the man, who was at least seven feet tall, with tanned skin and black hair, pointing directly at me. He had 250 pounds stretched over his incredibly tall frame and was so muscular, so positively ripped, that it looked as though he might just explode out of his denim . . . catsuit? Ohmigod! He was wearing a catsuit. Yes, yes, a denim, one-piece catsuit with tight pants and a belted waist and rolled-up sleeves. And a cape. There was actually a blanket-size fur cape tied twice around his thick neck, and shiny black combat boots the size of tennis rackets adorned his mammoth feet. He looked around thirty-five years old, although all the muscles and the deep tan and the positively chiseled jawbone could have been hiding ten years or adding five. He was flapping his hands at me and motioning for me to get up off the floor. I stood, unable to take my eyes off him, and he turned to examine me immediately.

"WELL! WHO DO WE HAVE HEEEEERE?" he bellowed, as best as one can in a falsetto voice. "YOU'RE PRETTY, BUT TOO WHOLE-SOME. AND THE OUTFIT DOES NOTHING FOR YOU!"

"My name's Andrea. I'm Miranda's new assistant."

He moved his eyes up and down over my body, inspecting every inch. Emily was watching the spectacle with a sneer on her face. The silence was unbearable.

"KNEE-HIGH BOOTS? WITH A KNEE-LENGTH SKIRT? ARE YOU KIDDING ME? BABY GIRL, IN CASE YOU'RE UNAWARE—IN CASE YOU MISSED THE BIG, BLACK SIGN BY THE DOOR—THIS IS *RUNWAY* MAGAZINE, THE FUCKING *HIIPPEST* MAGAZINE ON EARTH. ON EARTH! BUT NO WORRIES, HONEY, NIGEL WILL GET RID OF THAT JERSEY MALL-RAT LOOK YOU'VE GOT GOING SOON ENOUGH."

He put both his massive hands on my hips and twirled me around. I could feel his eyes looking at my legs and tush.

"SOON ENOUGH, SWEETIE, I PROMISE YOU, BECAUSE YOU'RE GOOD RAW MATERIAL. NICE LEGS, GREAT HAIR, AND NOT FAT. I CAN WORK WITH NOT FAT. SOON ENOUGH, SWEETIE."

I wanted to be offended, to pull myself away from the grip he had on my lower body, to take a few minutes and mull over the fact that a complete stranger—and a coworker, no less—had just provided an unsolicited and unflinchingly honest account of my outfit and my figure, but I wasn't. I liked his kind green eyes that seemed to laugh instead of taunt, but more than that, I liked that I had passed. This was Nigel—single name, like Madonna or Prince—the fashion authority whom even I recognized from TV, magazines, the society pages, everywhere, and he had called me pretty. And said I had nice legs! I let the mall-rat comment slide. I *liked* this guy.

I heard Emily tell him to leave me alone from somewhere in the background, but I didn't want him to go. Too late, he was already heading for the door, his fur cape flapping behind him. I wanted to call out, tell him it had been nice to meet him, that I wasn't offended by what he said and was excited that he wanted to redo me. But before I could say a thing, Nigel whipped around and covered the space between us in two strides, each the length of a long jump. He planted himself directly in front of me, wrapped my entire body with his massive, rippling arms, and pressed me to him. My head rested just below his chest, and I smelled the unmistakable scent of Johnson's Baby Lotion. And just as I had the presence of mind to hug him back, he flung me backward, engulfed both of my hands in his, and screeched:

"WELCOME TO THE DOLLHOUSE, BABY!"

5

"He said what?" Lily asked as she licked a spoonful of green tea ice cream. She and I had met at Sushi Samba at nine so I could update her on my first day. My parents had grudgingly forked over the emergencies-only credit card again until I got my first paycheck. Spicy tuna rolls and seaweed salads certainly felt like an emergency, and so I silently thanked Mom and Dad for treating Lily and me so well.

"He said, 'Welcome to the dollhouse, baby.' I swear. How cool is that?"

She looked at me, mouth hung open, spoon suspended in midair.

"You have the coolest job I've ever heard of," said Lily, who always talked about how she should've worked for a year before going back to school.

"It does seem pretty cool, doesn't it? Definitely weird, but cool, too. Whatever," I said, digging in to my oozing chocolate brownie. "It's not like I wouldn't rather be a student again than doing any of this."

"Yeah, I'm sure you'd just love to work part-time to finance your obscenely expensive and utterly useless Ph.D. You would, wouldn't you? You're jealous that I get to bartend in an undergrad pub, get hit on by freshmen until four A.M. every night, and then head to class all day, aren't you? All of it knowing that if—and that's a big, fat if—you manage to finish at some point in the next seventeen years, you'll never get a job. Anywhere." She plastered on a big, fake smile and took a swig of her Sapporo. Lily was studying for her Ph.D. in Russian Literature at Columbia and working odd jobs every free second she wasn't studying. Her grandmother barely had enough money to support herself, and Lily wouldn't qualify for grants until she'd finished her master's, so it was remarkable she'd even come out that night.

I took the bait, as I always did when she bitched about her life. "So why do you do it, Lil?" I asked, even though I'd heard the answer a million times.

Lily snorted and rolled her eyes again. "Because I love it!" she sang sarcastically. And even though she'd never admit it because it was so much more fun to complain, she did love it. She'd developed a thing for Russian culture ever since her eighth-grade teacher told her that Lily looked how he had always pictured Lolita, with her round face and curly black hair. She went directly home and read Nabokov's masterpiece of lechery, never allowing the whole teacher-Lolita reference to bother her, and then read everything else Nabokov wrote. And Tolstoy. And Gogol. And Chekhov. By the time college rolled around, she was applying to Brown to work with a specific Russian lit professor who, upon interviewing seventeen-year-old Lily, had declared her one of the most well read and passionate students of Russian literature he'd ever met—undergrad, graduate, or otherwise. She still loved it, still studied Russian grammar and could read anything in its original, but she enjoyed whining about it more.

"Yeah, well, I definitely agree that I have the best gig around. I mean,

Tommy Hilfiger? Chanel? Oscar de la Renta's apartment? Quite a first day. I have to say, I'm not quite sure how all of this is going to get me any closer to *The New Yorker*, but maybe it's just too early to tell. It's just not seeming like reality, you know?"

"Well, anytime you feel like getting back in touch with reality, you know where to find me," Lily said, taking her MetroCard out of her purse. "If you get a craving for a little ghetto, if you're just dying to keep it real in Harlem, well, my luxurious two-hundred-and-fifty-square-foot studio is all yours."

I paid the check and we hugged good-bye, and she tried to give me specific instructions on how to get from Seventh Avenue and Christopher Street to my own sublet all the way uptown. I swore up and down that I understood exactly where to find the L-train and then the 6, and how to walk from the 96th Street stop to my apartment, but as soon as she left, I jumped in a cab.

Just this once, I thought to myself, sinking into the warm backseat and trying not to breathe in the driver's body odor. *I'm a* Runway *girl now*.

I was pleased to discover that the rest of that first week wasn't much different than the first day. On Friday, Emily and I met in the stark white lobby again at seven A.M., and this time she handed me my own ID card, complete with a picture that I didn't remember taking.

"From the security camera," she said when I stared at it. "They're everywhere around here, just so you know. They've had some major problems with people stealing stuff, the clothes and jewelry called in for shoots; it seems the messengers and sometimes even the editors just help themselves. So now they track everyone." She slid her card down the slot and the thick glass door clicked open.

"Track? What exactly do you mean by 'track'?"

She moved quickly down the hallway toward our offices, her hips swishing back and forth, back and forth in the skintight tan Seven cords she was wearing. She'd told me the day before that I should seriously consider getting a pair or ten, as these were among the only jeans or corduroys that Miranda would permit people to wear in the office. Those and the MJ's were OK, but only on Friday, and only if worn with high heels. MJ's? "Marc Jacobs," she had said, exasperated.

"Well, between the cameras and the cards, they kind of know what everyone's doing," she said as she dropped her Gucci logo tote on her desk. She began unbuttoning her very fitted leather blazer, a coat that looked supremely inadequate for the late-November weather. "I don't think they actually look at the cameras unless something's missing, but the cards tell everything. Like, every time you swipe it downstairs to get past the security counter or on the floor to get in the door, they know where you are. That's how they tell if people are at work, so if you have to be out—and you never will, but just in case something really awful happens—you'll just give me your card and I'll swipe it. That way you'll still get paid for all the days you miss, even if you go over. You'll do the same for me—everyone does it."

I was still reeling from the "and you never will" part, but she continued her briefing.

"And that's how you'll get food in the dining room also. It's a debit card: just put on some money and it gets deducted at the register. Of course, that's how they can tell what you're eating," she said, unlocking Miranda's office door and plopping herself on the floor. She immediately reached for a boxed bottle of wine and began wrapping.

"Do they care what you eat?" I asked, feeling as though I'd just stepped directly into a scene from *Sliver*.

"Um, I'm not sure. Maybe? I just know they can tell. And the gym, too. You have to use it there, and at the newsstand to buy books or magazines. I think it just helps them stay organized."

Stay organized? I was working for a company who defined good "organization" as knowing which floor each employee visited, whether they preferred onion soup or Caesar salad for lunch, and just how many minutes they could tolerate the elliptical machine? I was a lucky, lucky girl.

Exhausted from my fourth morning of waking up at five-thirty, it took me another five full minutes to work up the energy to climb out of my coat and settle down at my desk. I thought about putting my head down to rest for just a moment, but Emily cleared her throat. Loudly.

"Um, you want to get in here and help me?" she asked, although it was clearly no question. "Here, wrap something." She thrust a pile of white paper my way and resumed her task. Jewel blasted from the extra speakers attached to her iMac.

Cut, place, fold, tape: Emily and I worked steadily through the morning, stopping only to call the downstairs messenger center each time we'd finished with twenty-five boxes. They'd hold them until we gave the green light for them to be fanned out all over Manhattan in mid-December. We'd already completed all of the out-of-town bottles during my first two days, and those were piled in the Closet waiting for DHL to pick them up. Considering each and every one was set to be sent first-day priority, arriving at their locations at the earliest possible time the very next morning, I wasn't sure what the rush was—considering it was only the end of November—but I'd already learned it was better not to ask questions. We would be FedExing about 150 bottles all over the world. The Priestly bottles would make it to Paris, Cannes, Bordeaux, Milan, Rome, Florence, Barcelona, Geneva, Brugges, Stockholm, Amsterdam, and London. Dozens to London! FedEx would jet them to Beijing and Hong Kong and Capetown and Tel Aviv and Dubai (Dubai!). They would be toasting Miranda Priestly in Los Angeles, Honolulu, New Orleans, Charleston, Houston, Bridgehampton, and Nantucket. And those all before any went out in New York—the city that contained all of Miranda's friends, doctors, maids, hair stylists, nannies, makeup artists, shrinks, yoga instructors, personal trainers, drivers, and personal shoppers. Of course, this was where most of the fashion-industry people were, too: the designers, models, actors, editors, advertisers, PR folks, and all-around style mavens would each receive a level-appropriate bottle lovingly delivered by an Elias-Clark messenger.

"How much do you think all of this costs?" I asked Emily, while snipping what felt like the millionth piece of thick white paper.

"I told you, I ordered twenty-five thousand dollars' worth of booze."

"No, no—how much do you think it costs altogether? I mean, to overnight all these packages all over the world, well, I bet that in some cases the shipping costs more than the bottle itself, especially if they're getting a nobody bottle."

She looked intrigued. It was the first time I'd seen her look at me with anything other than disgust, exasperation, or indifference. "Well, let's see. If you figure that all the domestic FedExes are somewhere in the twenty-dollar range, and all the international are about $60, then that equals $9,000 for FedEx. I think I heard somewhere that the messengers charge eleven bucks a package, so sending out 250 of those would be $2,750. And our time, well, if it takes us a full week to wrap everything, then added together, that's two full weeks of both our salaries, which is another four grand—"

It was here I flinched inwardly, realizing that both of our salaries together for an entire week's work was by far the most insignificant expense.

"Yeah, it comes to around $16,000 in total. Crazy, huh? But what choice is there? She is Miranda Priestly, you know."

At about one Emily announced she was hungry and was heading downstairs to get some lunch with a few of the girls in accessories. I assumed she meant she would pick up her lunch, since that's what we'd been doing all week, so I waited for ten minutes, fifteen minutes, twenty, but she never reappeared with her food. Neither of us had actually eaten in the dining room since I'd started in case Miranda called, but this was ridiculous. Two o'clock came and then two-thirty and then three, and all I could think about was how hungry I was. I tried calling Emily's cell phone, but it went directly to voice mail. Could she have died in the dining room? I wondered. Choked on some plain lettuce, or simply slumped over after downing a smoothie? I thought about asking someone to pick something up for me, but it seemed too prima donna–ish to ask a perfect stranger to fetch me lunch. After all, *I* was supposed to be the lunch-fetcher: *Oh, yes, darling, I'm simply too important to abandon my post here wrapping presents, so I was wondering if you might pick me up a turkey and brie croissant? Lovely*. I just couldn't do it. So when four o'clock rolled around and there was still no sign of Emily and no call from Miranda, I did the unthinkable: I left the office unattended.

After peeking down the hall and confirming that Emily was nowhere in sight, I literally ran to the reception area and pushed the down button twenty times. Sophy, the gorgeous Asian receptionist, raised her eyebrows and looked away, and I wasn't sure if it was my impatience or her knowledge that Miranda's office was abandoned that made her look at me that way. No time to figure it out. The elevator finally arrived, and I was able to throw myself onboard even as a sneering, heroin-thin guy with spiky hair and lime green Pumas was pushing "Door Close." No one moved aside to give me room even though there was plenty of space. And while this would've normally driven me crazy, all I could concentrate on was getting food and getting back, ASAP.

The entrance to the all-glass-and-granite dining room was blocked by a group of Clackers-in-training, all leaning in and whispering, examining each group of people who got off the elevator. Friends of Elias employees, I immediately recalled from Emily's description of such groups, obvious from their unmasked excitement to be standing at the center of it all. Lily had already begged me to take her to the dining room since it'd been written up in nearly every Manhattan newspaper and magazine for its incredible food quality and selection—not to mention its gaggle of gorgeous people—but I wasn't ready for that yet. Besides, due to the complex office-sitting schedule Emily and I negotiated each day so far, I'd yet to spend more time there than the two and a half minutes it took to choose and pay for my food, and I wasn't sure I ever would.

I pushed my way past the girls and felt them turn to see if I was anyone important. Negative. Weaving quickly, intently, I bypassed gorgeous racks of lamb and veal marsala in the entrees section and, with a push of willpower, cruised right past the sundried tomato and goat cheese pizza special (which resided on a small table banished to the sidelines that everyone referred to as "Carb Corner"). It wasn't as easy to navigate around the *pièce de résistance* of the room, the salad bar (also known just as "Greens," as in "I'll meet you at Greens"), which was as long as an airport landing strip and accessible from four different directions, but the hordes let me pass when I loudly assured them that I wasn't going after the last of the tofu cubes. All the way in the back, directly behind the panini stand that actually resembled a makeup counter, was the single, lone soup station. Lone because the soup chef was the only one in the entire dining room who refused to make a single one of his offerings low fat, reduced fat, fat-free, low sodium, or low carb. He simply refused. As a result, his was the single table in the entire room without a line, and I sprinted directly toward him every day. Since it appeared that I was the only one in the entire company who actually bought soup—and I'd only been there a week—the higher-ups had slashed his menu to a solitary soup per day. I prayed for tomato cheddar. Instead, he ladled out a giant cup of New England clam chowder, proudly declaring it was made with heavy cream. Three people at Greens turned to stare. The only obstacle left was dodging the crowds around the chef's table, where a visiting chef in full whites was arranging large chunks of sashimi for what appeared to be adoring fans. I read the nametag on his starched white collar: Nobu Matsuhisa. I made a mental note to look him up when I got upstairs, since I seemed to be the only employee in the place who wasn't fawning all over him. Was it worse to have never heard of Mr. Matsuhisa or Miranda Priestly?

The petite cashier looked first at the soup and then at my hips when she rang me up. Or had she? I'd already grown accustomed to being looked up and down every time I went anywhere, and I could've sworn she was looking at me with the same expression I would've given a five-hundred-pound person with eight Big Macs arrayed in from of him: the eyes raised just enough as if to ask, "Do you *really* need that?" But I brushed my paranoia aside and reminded myself that the woman was simply a cashier in a cafeteria, not a Weight Watchers counselor. Or a fashion editor.

"So. Not many people buying the soup these days," she said quietly, punching numbers on the register.

"Yeah, I guess not that many people like New England clam chowder," I mumbled, swiping my card and willing her hands to move faster, faster.

She stopped and turned her narrowed brown eyes directly toward mine. "No, I think it's because the soup chef insists on making these really fattening things—do you have any idea how many calories are in that? Do you have any idea how fattening that little cup of soup is? I'm just saying is, someone could put on ten pounds from just looking at it—" *And you're not one who could afford to gain ten pounds*, she implied.

Ouch. As if it hadn't been hard enough convincing myself that I was a normal weight for a normal height as all the tall, willowy *Runway* blondes had openly examined me, now the *cashier* was—for all intents and purposes—telling me I was fat? I snatched my takeout bag and pushed past the people, and walked into the bathroom that was conveniently located directly outside the dining room, where one could purge any earlier bingeing problems. And even though I knew that the mirror would reveal nothing more or less than it had that morning, I turned to face it head on. A twisted, angry face stared back at me.

"What the hell are you doing here?" Emily all but shouted at my reflection. I whipped around in time to see her hanging her leather blazer through the handle of the Gucci logo tote, as she pushed her sunglasses on top of her head. It occurred to me that Emily had meant what she'd said three and a half hours before quite literally: she'd gone out for lunch. As in, outside. As in, left me all alone for three straight hours with no warning, practically tethered to a phone line with no hopes of food or bathroom breaks. As in, none of that mattered because I still knew I was wrong to leave and I was about to get screamed at for it by someone my own age. Blessedly, the door swung open and the editor in chief of *Coquette* strode in. She looked us both up and down as Emily grabbed my arm and steered me out of the bathroom and toward the elevator. We stood like that together, her clutching my arm and me feeling as though I'd just wet the bed. We were living one of those scenes where the kidnapper puts a gun to a woman's back in broad daylight and quietly threatens her as he leads her to his basement of torture.

"How could you do this to me?" she hissed as she pushed me through *Runway*'s reception-area doors and we hurtled together back to our desks. "As the senior assistant, I am responsible for what goes on in our office. I know you're new, but I've told you from the very first day: we do not leave Miranda unattended."

"But Miranda's not here." It came out as a squeak.

"But she could've called while you were gone and no one would've been here to answer the goddamn phone!" she screamed as she slammed the door to our suite. "Our first priority—our only priority—is Miranda Priestly. Period. And if you can't deal with that, just remember that there are millions of girls who would die for your job. Now check your voice mail. If she called, we're dead. *You're* dead."

I wanted to crawl inside my iMac and die. How could I have screwed up so badly during my very first week? Miranda wasn't even in the office and I'd already let her down. So what if I was hungry? It could wait. There were genuinely important people trying to get things done around here, people who depended on me, and I'd let them down. I dialed my mailbox.

"Hi, Andy, it's me." Alex. "Where are you? I've never heard you not answer. Can't wait for dinner tonight—we're still on, right? Anywhere you want, your pick. Call me when you get this, I'll be in the faculty lounge anytime after four. Love you." I immediately felt guilty, because I'd already decided after the whole lunch debacle that I'd rather reschedule. My first week had been so crazy that we'd barely seen each other, and we'd made a special plan to have dinner that night, just the two of us. But I knew I wouldn't be any fun if I fell asleep in my wine, and I kind of wanted a night to unwind and be alone. I'd have to remember to call and see if we could do it the next night.

Emily was standing over me, having already checked her own voice mail. From her relatively calm face, I guessed that Miranda had not left her any death threats. I shook my head to indicate that I hadn't gotten one from her yet.

"Hi, Andrea, it's Cara." Miranda's nanny. "So, Miranda called here a little while ago"—heart stoppage—"and said she's tried the office and no one was picking up. I figured something was going on down there, so I told her that I'd spoken to both you and Emily just a minute before, but don't worry about it. She wanted a *Women's Wear Daily* faxed to her, and I had a copy right here. Already confirmed that she got it, too, so don't stress. Just wanted to let you know. Anyway, have a good weekend. I'll talk to you later. 'Bye."

Lifesaver. The girl was an absolute saint. It was hard to believe I'd only known her a week—and not even in person, only over the phone—because I thought I was in love with her. She was the opposite of Emily in every regard: calm, grounded, and entirely fashion-oblivious. She recognized Miranda's absurdity but didn't begrudge her it; she had that rare, charming quality of being able to laugh at herself and everyone else.

"Nope, not her," I told Emily, lying sort of but not really, smiling triumphantly. "We're in the clear."

"*You're* in the clear, this time," she said flatly. "Just remember that we're in this together, but I am in charge. You'll cover for me if I want to go out to lunch once in a while—I'm entitled. This will never happen again, right?"

I bit back the urge to say something nasty. "Right," I said. "Right."

We'd managed to finish wrapping the rest of the bottles and get them all to the messengers by seven that night, and Emily didn't mention the office-abandonment issue again. I finally fell into a taxi (just this one time) at eight, and was spread-eagle, still fully dressed, on top of my covers at ten. And I still hadn't eaten because I couldn't bear the thought of going out in search of food and getting lost again, as I had the past four nights, in my own neighborhood. I called Lily to complain on my brand-new Bang and Olufsen phone.

"Hi! I thought you and Alex had a date tonight," she said.

"Yeah, we did, but I'm dead. He's fine with doing it tomorrow night, and I think I'll just order. Whatever. How was your day?"

"I have one word: screwed up. OK, so that was two. You'll never imagine what happened. Well, of course you will, it happens all the—"

"Cut to it, Lil. I'm going to pass out any minute."

"OK. Cutest guy ever came to my reading today. Sat through the whole thing looking absolutely fascinated, and waited for me afterward. Asked if he could take me for a drink and hear all about the thesis I had published at Brown, which he'd already read."

"Sounds great. What was he?" Lily went out with different guys almost every night after getting off work, but had yet to complete her fraction. She had founded the Scale of Fractional Love one night after listening to a few of our guy friends rate the girls they were dating on their own invention, the Ten-Ten Scale. "She's a six, eight, B-plus," Jake would declare of the advertising assistant he'd been set up with the night before. It was assumed everyone knew that it was a ten-point scale, with face always being the first numerical ranking, body the second, and personality coming in last with a slightly more generalized letter grade. Since there were clearly more factors at work in judging guys, Lily devised the Fractional Scale, which had a total of ten pieces that each earned a point. The Perfect Guy would obviously have all five of the primary pieces: intelligence, sense of humor, decent body, cute face, and any sort of job that fell under the generous umbrella of "normal." Since it was next to impossible to find The Perfect Guy, someone could up their fraction by earning points on the secondary five, which included a definitive lack of psycho ex-girlfriends, psycho parents, or date-rapist roommates, and any sort of extracurricular interests or hobbies that weren't sports- or porn-related. So far, the highest anyone had received was a nine-tenths, but he had broken up with her.

"Well, at first he was going strong at seven-tenths. He was a theater major at Yale *and* he's straight, and he could discuss Israeli politics so intelligently that he never once suggested that we 'just nuke 'em,' so that was good."

"Sure sounds good. I can't wait for the clincher. What was it? Did he talk about his favorite Nintendo game?"

"Worse." She sighed.

"Is he thinner than you?"

"Worse." She sounded defeated.

"What on earth could be worse than that?"

"He lives on Long Island—"

"Lily! So he's geographically undesirable. That doesn't make him undateable! You know better than to—"

"With his parents," she interrupted.

Oh.

"For the past four years."

Oh, my.

"And he absolutely loves it. Says he can't imagine wanting to live alone in such a big city when his mom and dad are such great company."

"Whoa! Say no more. I don't think we've ever had a seven-tenths fall all the way to a zero after the first date. Your guy set a new record. Congratulations. Your day was officially worse than mine." I leaned over to kick my bedroom door closed when I heard Shanti and Kendra come home from work. I heard a guy's voice with them and wondered if either of my roommates had boyfriends. I'd seen them a combined total of only ten minutes in the last week and a half, because they seemed to work longer hours than I did.

"That bad? How could your day be bad? You work in *fashion*," she said.

There was a quiet knocking on the door.

"Hold on a sec, someone's here. Come in!" I called to the door, much too loud for the tiny space. I waited for one of my quiet roommates to timidly ask if I'd remembered to call the landlord to put my name on the lease (no) or bought more paper plates (no) or had taken down any phone messages (no), but Alex appeared.

"Hey, can I call you back? Alex just showed up." I was thrilled to see him, so excited that he'd surprised me, but a small part of me had been looking forward to just taking a shower and crawling into bed.

"Sure. Tell him I say hi. And remember what a lucky girl you are for having completed the fraction with him, Andy. He's great. Hold on to that one."

"Don't I know it. The kid's a goddamn saint." I smiled in his direction.

" 'Bye."

"Hi!" I willed myself to first sit up, then stand up and walk over to him. "What a great surprise!" I went to hug him but he backed away, keeping his arms behind his back. "What's wrong?"

"Nothing at all. I know you've had such a long week, and, knowing you, I figured you hadn't bothered to eat yet, so I brought the food to you." He pulled a huge brown paper bag from behind his back, one of the old-school grocery style ones, and it already had some delicious-smelling grease stains on it. All of a sudden, I was starving.

"You did not! How'd you know that I was sitting here this very second, wondering how I was going to motivate to find food? I was just about to give up."

"So come here and eat!" He looked pleased and pulled open the bag, but we both couldn't fit on the floor of my bedroom together. I thought about eating in the living room since there was no kitchen, but Kendra and Shanti had both collapsed in front of the TV together, their untouched takeout salads open in front of them. I thought they were waiting until the *Real World* episode they were watching was over, but then I noticed that they'd both already fallen asleep. Sweet lives we all had.

"Hold on, I have an idea," he said and tiptoed to the kitchen. He came back with two oversize garbage bags and spread them out over my blue comforter. He dug into the greasy bag and brought out two giant burgers with everything and one extra-large order of fries. He'd remembered ketchup packets and tons of salt for me, and even the napkins. I clapped I was so excited, although a quick visual of the imagined disappointment on Miranda's face appeared, one that said, *You? You're eating a burger?*

"I'm not done yet. Here, check it out." And out of his backpack came a fistful of tiny vanilla tea lights, a bottle of screw-top red wine, and two waxy paper cups.

"You're kidding," I said softly, still not believing that he'd put all this together after I'd canceled our date.

He handed me a cup of wine and tapped it with his. "No, I'm not. You think I was going to miss hearing about the first week of the rest of your life? To my best girl."

"Thank you." I said, slowly taking a sip. "Thank you, thank you, thank you."

6 "Ohmigod, is it the fash-
ion editor herself?" Jill mock-shrieked when she opened the front door.
"Come on over here and let your big sister genuflect a li'l."

"Fashion editor?" I snorted. "Hardly. Try fashion mishap. Welcome
back to civilization." I hugged her for what felt like ten minutes and
didn't want to let go. It was hard when she'd started at Stanford and left
me all alone with our parents when I was a mere nine years old, but it
was even harder when she'd followed her boyfriend—now husband—to
Houston. Houston! The whole placed seemed drenched in humidity and
infested with mosquitoes to the point of unbearability, and if that wasn't
bad enough, my sister—my sophisticated, beautiful big sister who loved

neoclassical art and made your heart melt when she recited poetry—had developed a southern accent. And not just a slight accent with a subtle, charming southern lilt, but an all-out, unmistakable, like-a-drill-through-the-eardrum redneck drawl. I'd yet to forgive Kyle for dragging her to that wretched place, even if he was a pretty decent brother-in-law, and it didn't help when he opened his mouth.

"Hey there, Andy darlin', you're looking more beautiful every time I see you." *Yer lookin' more beeyootiful avery time I see ya.* "What are they feeding y'all at *Runway*, huh?"

I wanted to stick a tennis ball in his mouth to keep him from talking anymore, but he smiled at me and I walked over and hugged him. He might sound like a hick and grin a little too openly and often, but he tried really hard and he clearly adored my sister. I vowed to make a sincere effort not to visibly cringe when he spoke. "It's not really what I'd call a feeding-friendly kind of place, if you know what I mean. Whatever it is, it's definitely in the water and not the food. But never mind. Kyle, you look great yourself. Keeping my sister busy in the city of misery, I hope?"

"Andy, just come and visit, sweetie. Bring Alex along and y'all can make it a li'l vacation. It's not that bad, you'll see." He smiled first at me and then at Jill, who smiled back and brushed the back of her hand across his cheek. They were disgustingly in love.

"Really, Andy, it's a culture-rich place with a whole lot to do. We both wish you'd come visit us more often. It's just not right that the only time we see each other is in this house," she said, waving expansively around our parents' living room. "I mean, if you can stand Avon, you can certainly stand Houston."

"Andy, you're here! Jay, the big New York City career girl is here, come say hi," my mom called as she rounded the corner coming from the kitchen. "I thought you were going to call when you got to the train station."

"Mrs. Myers was picking Erika up from the same train, so she just dropped me off. When are we eating? I'm starving."

"Now. Do you want to clean up? We can wait. You look a little ragged from the train. You know, it's fine if—"

"Mother!" I shot her a warning look.

"Andy! You look dynamite. Come here and give your old man a hug." My dad, tall and still very handsome in his midfifties, smiled from the hallway. He was holding a Scrabble box behind his back that he only let me see by flashing it quickly by the side of his leg. He waited until everyone looked away from him and pointed to the box and mouthed, "I'll kick your ass. Consider yourself warned."

I smiled and nodded my head. Contrary to all common sense, I found myself looking forward to the next forty-eight hours with my family more than I had in the four years since I'd left home. Thanksgiving was my favorite holiday, and this year I was set to enjoy it more than ever.

We gathered in the dining room and dug into the massive meal that my mother had expertly ordered, her traditional Jewish version of a night-before-Thanksgiving feast. Bagels and lox and cream cheese and whitefish and latkes all professionally arranged on rigid disposable serving platters, waiting to be transferred to paper plates and consumed with plastic forks and knives. My mother smiled lovingly as her brood dug in, with a look of pride on her face as if she'd been cooking for a week to sustain and nurture her babies.

I told them all about the new job, tried as best as I could to describe a job that I didn't yet fully understand myself. Briefly I wondered if it sounded ridiculous to tell them how the skirts were called in and all the hours I'd logged wrapping and sending presents, and how there was a little electronic ID card that tracked everything you did. It was hard to fit into words the sense of urgency each of these had taken on at the time, how when I was at work it seemed that my job was supremely relevant, even important. I talked and talked, but I didn't know how to explain this world that may have been only two hours away geographically but was really in a different solar system. They all nodded and smiled and asked questions, pretending to be interested, but I knew it was all too foreign, too absolutely strange sounding and different to make any sense to people who—like me until a few weeks earlier—had never even heard the name Miranda Priestly. It didn't make much sense to me yet, either: it seemed overly dramatic at times and more than a little Big Brother–esque, but it was exciting. And cool. It was definitely, undeniably a supercool place to call work. Right?

"Well, Andy, you think you'll be happy there for your year? Maybe you'll even want to stay longer, huh?" My mom asked while smearing cream cheese on her salt bagel.

In signing my contract at Elias-Clark, I'd agreed to stay with Miranda for a year—if I didn't get fired, which at this point seemed like a big if. And if I fulfilled my obligation with class and enthusiasm and some level of competence—and this part was not in writing but implied by a half-dozen people in HR, and Emily, and Allison—then I would be in a position to name the job I'd like next. It was expected, of course, that whichever job that may be would be at *Runway* or, at the very least, at Elias-Clark, but I was free to request anything from working on book reviews in the features department to acting as a liaison between Hollywood celebrities and *Runway*. Out of the last ten assistants who had made it through their year in Miranda's office, a full hundred percent had chosen to move to the fashion department at *Runway*, but I didn't let that concern me. A stint in Miranda's office was considered to be the ultimate way to skip three to five years of indignity as an assistant and move directly into meaningful jobs in prestigious places.

"Definitely. So far everyone seems really nice. Emily's a little, um, well, *committed*, but otherwise, it's been great. I don't know, to listen to Lily talk about her exams or Alex talk about all the shitty things he has to deal with at work, I think I got pretty lucky. Who else gets to drive around in a chauffeured car on their first day? I mean, really. So yeah, I think it'll be a great year, and I'm excited for Miranda to come back. I think I'm ready."

Jill rolled her eyes and shot me a look as if to say, *Cut the bullshit, Andy. We all know you're probably working for a psycho bitch surrounded by anorexic fashionistas and are trying to paint this really rosy picture because you're worried you're in over your head*, but instead she said, "It sounds great, Andy, it really does. Amazing opportunity."

She was the only one at the table who could possibly understand, since, before moving to the Third World, she'd worked for a year at a small private museum in Paris and had developed an interest in haute couture. Hers was more of an artistic and aesthetic hobby than a consumer one, but she still had some exposure, at least, to the fashion world. "We have some great news, too," she continued, reaching across the table for Kyle's hand. He had set down his coffee and extended both his hands.

"Oh, thank god," my mother instantly exclaimed, slumping over as if someone had finally lifted the two-hundred-pound dumbbell that had rested on her shoulders for the last two decades. "It's about time."

"Congratulations, you two! I have to say you've had your mother really worried. You're certainly not newlyweds anymore, you know. We were beginning to wonder . . ." From the head of the table my dad raised his eyebrows.

"Hey guys, that's great. It's about time I get to be an aunt. When's the little one due?"

They both looked dumbfounded, and for a moment I worried that we'd gotten it all wrong, that their "good" news was that they were building a newer, bigger home in that swamp they lived in, or that Kyle had finally decided to leave his father's law firm and was going to join my sister in opening the gallery she'd always dreamed of. Maybe we'd jumped the gun on this one, been just a little too eager to hear that a future niece or grandson was on the way. It was all my parents could talk about lately, incessantly hashing and rehashing the reasons why my sister and Kyle—already in their thirties and with four years of marriage behind them—had yet to reproduce. In the past six months, the subject had progressed from time-consuming family obsession to perceived crisis.

My sister looked worried. Kyle frowned. My parents looked as though they might both pass out from the silence. The tension was palpable.

Jill got out of her chair and walked over to Kyle, where she plopped herself in his lap. She wrapped her arm behind the back of his neck and leaned her face next to his, whispering in his ear. I glanced at my mother, who looked about ten seconds away from unconsciousness, the worry causing the small lines near her eyes to grow as deep as trenches.

Finally, finally, they giggled, and turned toward the table, and announced unanimously, "We're going to have a baby." And then there was light. And shrieking. And hugging. My mother flew out of her seat so fast that she knocked it over and, in turn, tipped over a potted cactus that rested by the sliding-glass door. My dad grabbed Jill and kissed her on both cheeks and the top of her head, and for the first time I could remember since their wedding day, he kissed Kyle, too.

I rapped my Dr. Brown's black cherry can with a plastic fork and announced that we needed a toast. "Please raise your glasses, everyone, raise your glasses to the brand-new Sachs baby that will be joining our family." Kyle and Jill looked at me pointedly. "OK, I guess technically it's a Harrison baby, but it will be a Sachs at heart. To Kyle and Jill, future perfect parents to the world's most perfect child." We all clinked soda cans and coffee mugs and toasted the grinning couple and my sister's twenty-four-inch waist. I cleaned up by throwing the entire contents of the table directly into a garbage bag while my mom tried to pressure Jill to name the baby after various dead relatives. Kyle sipped coffee and looked pleased with himself, and just before midnight my dad and I sneaked off to his study for a game.

He turned up the white-noise machine he used when he had patients during the day, both to block out the sounds of the household from them and to keep anyone else in the house from hearing what was discussed in his office. Like any good shrink, my dad had placed a gray leather couch in the far corner, so soft I liked to rest my head on the armrest, and three chairs that angled forward and held a person in a kind of fabric sling. Womblike, he assured me. His desk was sleek and black and topped with a flat-screen monitor, and the matching black leather chair was high-backed and very plush. A wall of psychology books encased in glass, a collection of bamboo stalks in a very tall crystal vase on the floor, and some framed colorblock prints—the only real color in the room— completed the futuristic look. I flopped on the floor between the couch and his desk, and he did the same.

"So, tell me what's really going on, Andy," he said as he handed me a little wooden tile holder. "I'm sure you're feeling really overwhelmed right now."

I picked my seven tiles and carefully arranged them in front of me. "Yeah, it's been a pretty crazy couple weeks. First moving, then starting. It's a weird place, hard to explain. It's like, everyone's beautiful and thin and wearing gorgeous clothes. And they really do seem nice enough—

everybody's been really friendly. Almost like they're all on serious pre-scription drugs. I don't know . . ."

"What? What were you going to say?"

"I can't put my finger on it. There's just this feeling that it's all a house of cards that's going to come crashing down around me. I can't shake the feeling that it's ridiculous to be working for a *fashion* maga-zine, you know? The work's been a little mindless so far, but I don't even care. It's challenging enough because it's all new, you know?"

He nodded.

"I know it's a 'cool' job, but I keep wondering how it's preparing me for *The New Yorker*. I must just be looking for something to go wrong, because so far it seems too good to be true. Hopefully, I'm just crazy."

"I don't think you're crazy, sweetie. I think you're sensitive. But I have to agree, I think you lucked out with this one. People go their entire lives and don't see the things you'll see this year. Just think! Your first job out of college, and you're working for the most important woman at the most profitable magazine at the biggest magazine publishing company in the entire world. You'll get to watch it all happen, from the top down. If you just keep your eyes open and your priorities in order, you'll learn more in one year than most people in the industry will see in their entire careers." He placed his first word in the middle of the board, JOLT.

"Not bad for an opening move," I said and counted its worth, dou-bled it because the first word always went on a pink star, and started a scorecard. Dad: 22 points, Andy: 0. My letters weren't showing much promise. I added an A, M, and E to the L and accepted my paltry six points.

"I just want to make sure you give it a fair shake," he said, switch-ing his tiles around on his holder. "The more I think about it, the more I'm convinced this is going to mean big things for you."

"Well, I sure hope you're right, because I have enough paper cuts from wrapping to last a long, long time. There better be more to the whole thing than that."

"There will be, sweetie, there will be. You'll see. It might feel like you're doing silly stuff, but trust me, you're not. This is the start of some-thing fantastic, I can feel it. And I've studied up on your boss. This Miranda sounds like a tough woman, no doubt about it, but I think you're going to like her. And I think she's going to like you, too."

He placed the word TOWEL down using my E and looked satisfied.

"I hope you're right, Dad. I really hope you're right."

←→

"She's the editor in chief of *Runway*—you know, the fashion magazine?" I whispered urgently into the phone, trying valiantly not to get frustrated.

"Oh, I know which one you mean!" said Julia, a publicity assistant for Scholastic Books. "Great magazine. I love all those letters where girls write in their embarrassing period stories. Are those for real? Do you remember reading the one where—"

"No, no, not the one for teenagers. It's most definitely for grown women." In theory, at least. "Have you really never seen *Runway*?" *Is it humanly possible that she hasn't?* I wondered. "Anyway, it's spelled P-R-I-E-S-T-L-Y. Miranda, yes," I said with infinite patience. I wondered how she'd react if she knew I actually had someone on the line who'd never heard of her. Probably not well.

"Well, if you could get back to me as soon as possible, I'd *really* appreciate it," I told Julia. "And if a senior publicist gets in anytime soon, *please* have her call me."

It was a Friday morning in the middle of December and the sweet, sweet freedom of the weekend was only ten hours away. I had been trying to convince a fashion-oblivious Julia at Scholastic that Miranda Priestly really was someone important, someone worth bending rules and suspending logic for. This proved significantly more difficult than I had anticipated. How could I have known that I'd have to explain the weight of Miranda's position to influence someone who'd never even heard of the most prestigious fashion magazine on earth—or its famous editor? In my four short weeks as Miranda's assistant, I'd already figured out that such weight-throwing and favor-currying was merely part of my job, but usually the person I was attempting to persuade, intimidate, or otherwise pressure yielded completely at the mere mention of my infamous boss's name.

Unfortunately for me, Julia worked for an educational publishing house where someone like Nora Ephron or Wendy Wasserstein was much likelier to get VIP treatment than someone known for her impeccable taste in fur. I inherently understood this. I tried to remember all the way back to a time before I had ever heard of Miranda Priestly—five weeks earlier—and couldn't. But I knew that such a magical time had existed. I envied Julia's indifference, but I had a job to do, and she wasn't helping.

The fourth book in that wretched Harry Potter series was due to be released the next day, a Saturday, and Miranda's ten-year-old twin daughters each wanted one. The first copies wouldn't arrive in stores until Monday, but I had to have them in my hands on Saturday morning—mere minutes after they were released from the warehouse. After all, Harry and the crew had to catch a private flight to Paris.

My thoughts were interrupted by the phone. I picked it up as I always did now that Emily trusted me enough to speak to Miranda. And boy, did we speak—probably in the vicinity of two dozen times a day. Even from afar, Miranda had managed to creep into my life and completely take over, barking orders and requests and demands at a rapid-fire pace from seven A.M. until I was finally allowed to leave at nine P.M.

"Ahn-dre-ah? Hello? Is anyone there? Ahn-dre-ah!" I jumped out of my seat the moment I heard her pronounce my name. It took a moment to remember and accept that she was not, in fact, in the office—or even in the country, and for the time being, at least, I was safe. Emily had assured me that Miranda was completely unaware that Allison had been promoted or I had been hired, that these were insignificant details lost on her. As long as someone answered the phone and got her what she needed, that person's actual identity was irrelevent.

"I simply do not understand what takes you so long to speak after you pick up the phone," she stated. From any other person on earth that would have sounded whiny, but from Miranda it sounded appropriately cold and firm. Just like her. "In case you haven't been here long enough to notice, when I call, you respond. It's actually simple. See? I call. You respond. Do you think you can handle that, Ahn-dre-ah?"

I nodded like a six-year-old who'd just been reprimanded for throwing spaghetti on the ceiling, even though she couldn't see me. I concentrated on not calling her "ma'am," a mistake I'd made a week earlier that had almost gotten me fired. "Yes, Miranda. I'm sorry," I said softly, head bowed. And for that moment I *was* sorry, sorry that her words hadn't registered in my brain three-tenths of a second faster than they had, sorry that my tardiness in saying "Miranda Priestly's office" had taken a fraction of a second longer than absolutely necessary. Her time was, as I was constantly reminded, much more important than my own.

"All right then. Now, after wasting all that time, may we begin? Did you confirm Mr. Tomlinson's reservation?" she asked.

"Yes, Miranda, I made a reservation for Mr. Tomlinson at the Four Seasons at one o'clock."

I could see it coming a mile away. A mere ten minutes earlier she'd called and ordered me to make a reservation at the Four Seasons and call Mr. Tomlinson and her driver and the nanny to inform them of the plans, and now she'd want to rearrange them.

"Well, I've changed my mind. The Four Seasons is not the appropriate venue for his lunch with Irv. Reserve a table for two at Le Cirque, and remember to remind the maître d' that they will want to sit in the *back* of the restaurant. Not on display in the front. *The back.* That's all."

I had convinced myself when I first spoke with Miranda on the phone, that by uttering "that's all," she really intended those words to mean "thank you." By the second week I'd rethought that.

"Of course, Miranda. *Thank you*," I said with a smile. I could sense her pausing on the other end of the line, wondering how to respond. Did she know I was calling attention to her refusal to say thank you? Did it seem odd to her that I was thanking her for ordering me around? I had recently begun thanking her after every one of her sarcastic comments or nasty phone-in commands, and the tactic was oddly comforting. She knew I was mocking her somehow, but what could she say? *Ahn-dre-ah, I never want to hear you thank me again. I forbid you to express your gratitude in such a manner!* Come to think of it, that might not be that much of a stretch.

Le Cirque, Le Cirque, Le Cirque, I said over and over in my head, determined to make that reservation ASAP so I could get back to the significantly more difficult Harry Potter challenge. The Le Cirque reservationist immediately agreed to have a table ready for Mr. Tomlinson and Irv whenever they arrived.

Emily walked in a from a stroll around the office and asked me if Miranda had called at all.

"Only three times, and she didn't threaten to fire me during any of them," I said proudly. "Of course, she did intimate it, but she didn't all-out threaten. Progress, no?"

She laughed in the way she did only when I made fun of myself, and she asked what Miranda, her guru, had wanted.

"Just wanted me to switch around B-DAD's lunch reservation. Not sure why I'm doing that when he has his own assistant, but hey, I don't ask questions around here." Mr. Blind, Deaf, and Dumb was our nickname for Miranda's third husband. Although to the general public he appeared to be none of those, those of us in the know were quite confident he was all three. There was, quite simply, no other explanation for how a nice guy like him could tolerate living with *her*.

Next, it was time to call B-DAD himself. If I didn't call soon, he may not be able to get to the restaurant in time. He'd flown back from their vacation for a couple days of business meetings, and this lunch with Irv Ravitz—Elias-Clark's CEO—was among the most important. Miranda wanted every detail perfect—as though that were something new. B-DAD's real name was Hunter Tomlinson. He and Miranda had gotten married the summer before I started working, after what I'd heard was a rather unique courtship: she pursued, he demurred. According to Emily, she'd chased him relentlessly until he'd yielded from the mere exhaustion of ducking her. She'd left her second husband (the lead singer of one of the most famous bands from the late sixties and the twins' father) with absolutely no warning before her lawyer delivered the papers, and was married again precisely twelve days after the divorce was finalized. Mr. Tomlinson followed orders and moved into her penthouse apartment on Fifth Avenue. I'd only met Miranda once and I'd never met her new husband, but I'd logged enough phone hours with each that I felt, unfortunately, like they were family.

Three rings, four rings, five rings . . . *hmm, I wonder where his assistant is?* I prayed for an answering machine, since I wasn't in the mood for the mindless, friendly chitchat of which B-DAD seemed so fond. Instead, I got his secretary.

"Mr. Tomlinson's office," she trilled in her deep southern drawl. "How may I help you today?" *How mah I hep ya tuhday?*

"Hi, Martha, it's Andrea. Listen, I don't need to talk to Mr. Tomlinson, can you just give him a message for me? I made a reservation for—"

"Darlin', you know Mr. T. always wants to talk to you. Hold just a sec." And before I could protest, I was listening to the elevator version of "Don't Worry, Be Happy" by Bobby McFerrin. Perfect. It was fitting that B-DAD had picked the most annoyingly optimistic song ever written to entertain callers when they were put on hold.

"Andy, is that you, sweetheart?" He asked quietly in his deep, distinguished voice. "Mr. Tomlinson is going to think you're avoiding him. It's been ages since I've had the pleasure of speaking with you." A week and a half, to be precise. In addition to his blindness, deafness, and dumbness, Mr. Tomlinson had the added irritating habit of constantly referring to himself in the third person.

I took a deep breath. "Hello, Mr. Tomlinson. Miranda asked me to let you know that lunch is at one today at Le Cirque. She said that you'd—"

"Sweetheart," he said slowly, calmly. "Enough with all that plan-making for just a second. Give an old man a moment of pleasure and tell Mr. Tomlinson all about your life. Will you do that for him? So tell me, dear, are you happy working for my wife?" Was I happy working for his wife? Hmm, let's see here. Are little baby mammals squealing with glee when a predator swallows them whole? *Why of course, you putz, I'm deliriously happy working for your wife. When neither of us is busy, we give each other mud masks and gossip about our love lives. It's a lot like a slumber party among friends, if you must know. The whole thing is just one big laugh riot.*

"Mr. Tomlinson, I love my job and I adore working for Miranda." I held my breath and prayed that he'd give it up.

"Well, Mr. T. is just thrilled that things are working out." *Great, asshole, but are you thrilled?*

"Sounds great, Mr. Tomlinson. Have a great lunch," I cut him off before he inevitably asked about my weekend plans, and hung up.

I sat back in my chair and gazed across the office suite. Emily was engrossed in trying to reconcile another one of Miranda's $20,000 American Express bills, her highly waxed brow furrowed in concentration. The Harry Potter project loomed ahead of me, and I had to get moving on it immediately if I ever wanted to get away this weekend.

Lily and I had planned a movie marathon weekend. I was exhausted from work and she was stressed out from her classes, so we'd promised to spend the whole weekend parked on her couch and subsist solely on beer and Doritos. No Snackwells. No Diet Coke. And absolutely no black pants. Even though we talked all the time, we hadn't spent any real time together since I'd moved to the city.

We'd been best friends since eighth grade, when I first saw Lily crying alone at a cafeteria table. She'd just moved in with her grandmother and started at our school, after it became clear that her parents weren't coming home any time soon. They'd taken off a few months before to follow the Dead (they'd had her when they were both nineteen and were more into bong hits than babies), leaving her behind to be watched over by their whacked-out friends at the commune in New Mexico (or as Lily preferred, the "collective"). When they hadn't returned almost a year later, Lily's grandmother took her from the commune (or as Lily's grandmother preferred, the "cult") to live with her in Avon. The day I found her crying alone in the cafeteria was the day her grandmother had forced her to chop off her dirty dreadlocks and wear a dress, and Lily was not happy about it. Something about the way she talked, the way she said, "That's so Zen of you," and "Let's just decompress," charmed me, and we immediately became friends. We'd been inseparable through the rest of high school, had roomed together for all four years at Brown. Lily hadn't yet decided whether she preferred MAC lipstick or hemp necklaces and was still a little too "quirky" to do anything totally mainstream, but we complemented each other well. And I missed her. Because with her first year as a graduate student and my being a virtual slave, we hadn't seen a whole lot of each other lately.

I couldn't wait for the weekend. My fourteen-hour workdays were registering in my feet, my upper arms, my lower back. Glasses had replaced the contacts I'd worn for a decade because my eyes were too dry and tired to accept them anymore. I smoked a pack a day and subsisted solely on Starbucks (expensed, of course) and takeout sushi (further expensed). I'd begun losing weight already. The weight I'd lost from the dysentery had returned briefly, but after my stint at *Runway* it had begun to disappear again. Something in the air there, I suppose, or perhaps it was the intensity with which food was eschewed in the office. I'd already weathered a sinus infection and had paled significantly, and it had been only four weeks. I was only twenty-three years old. And Miranda hadn't even been in the office yet. Fuck it. I deserved a *weekend*.

Into this mix leaped Harry Potter, and I was *not* pleased. Miranda had called this morning. It took only a few moments for her to outline what she wanted, although it took me forever to interpret it. I learned quickly that in the Miranda Priestly world, it was better to do something wrong and spend a great deal of time and money to fix it than to admit you didn't understand her convoluted and heavily accented instructions and ask for clarification. So when she mumbled something about getting the Harry Potter books for the twins and having them flown to Paris, intuition alone told me this was going to interfere with my weekend. When she hung up abruptly a few minutes later, I looked to Emily with panic.

"What, oh, what, did she say?" I moaned, hating myself for being too scared to ask Miranda to repeat herself. "Why can I not understand a single word that woman utters? It's not me, Em. I speak English, always have. I know she does it to personally drive me crazy."

Emily looked at me with her usual mix of disgust and pity. "Since the book comes out tomorrow and they're not here to buy it, she wants you to pick up two copies and bring them to Teterboro. The jet will take them to Paris," she summed up coldly, daring me to comment on the ludicrousness of the instructions. I was reminded once again that Emily would do anything—really, anything—if it meant making Miranda a bit more comfortable. I rolled my eyes and kept quiet.

Since I was NOT going to sacrifice a nanosecond of weekend to do her bidding, and because I had an unlimited amount of money and power (hers) at my personal disposal, I spent the rest of the day arranging for Harry Potter to jet his way to Paris. First, a few words for Julia at Scholastic.

> *Dearest Julia,*
>
> *My assistant, Andrea, tells me that you're the sweetheart to whom I should address my most heartfelt appreciation. She has informed me that you are the single person capable of locating a couple copies of this darling book for me tomorrow. I want you to know how much I appreciate your hard work and cleverness. Please know how happy you'll make my sweet daughters. And don't ever hesitate to let me know if you need anything, anything at all, for a fabulous girl like yourself.*
>
> *XOXO,*
> *Miranda Priestly*

I forged her name with a perfect flourish (hour upon hour of practicing with Emily standing over me, instructing me to make the final "a" a little loopier, had finally paid off), attached the note to the latest issue of *Runway*—one not yet on the newsstand—and called for a rush messenger to deliver the entire package to Scholastic's downtown office. If this didn't work, nothing would. Miranda didn't care that we forged her signature—it saved her from bothering with details—but she'd probably be livid to see that I'd penned something so polite, so *adorable*, using her name.

Three short weeks earlier I would have quickly canceled my plans if Miranda called and wanted me to do something for her on the weekends, but I was now experienced—and jaded—enough to bend the rules a little. Since Miranda and the girls would not themselves be at the airport in New Jersey when *Harry* arrived the following day, I saw no reason why I had to be the one to deliver him. Acting under the assumption and prayer that Julia would pull through for me with a couple copies, I worked out some details. Dial, dial, and within an hour a plan had emerged.

Brian, a cooperative editorial assistant at Scholastic—whom I was assured would have permission from Julia within a couple hours—would

take home two office copies of *Harry* that evening, so he wouldn't have
to go back to the office on Saturday. Brian would leave the books with
the doorman of his Upper West Side apartment building, and I would
have a car pick them up the following morning at eleven. Miranda's
driver, Uri, would then call me on my cell phone to confirm that he'd received the package and was on his way to drop it at Teterboro airport,
where the two books would be transferred to Mr. Tomlinson's private jet
and flown to Paris. I briefly considered conducting the entire operation
in code to make it resemble a KGB operation even more, but dropped
that when I remembered that Uri didn't really speak regular English that
well. I had checked to see how fast the fastest DHL option would have
them there, but delivery couldn't be guaranteed until Monday, which was
obviously unacceptable. Hence the private plane. If all went as planned,
little Cassidy and Caroline could wake up in their private Parisian suite
on Sunday and enjoy their morning milk while reading about Harry's ad-
ventures—*a full day earlier than all of their friends*. It warmed my heart,
it really did.

Minutes after the cars had been reserved and all the appropriate
people put on alert, Julia called back. Although it'd be a grueling task
and she was likely to get in trouble, she'd be happy to give Brian two
copies for Ms. Priestly. Amen.

"Do you believe he got *engaged*?" Lily asked as she rewound the copy of
Ferris Bueller we'd just finished. "I mean, we're twenty-three years old
for goodness sake—what's the rush?"

"I know, it does seem weird." I called from the kitchen. "Maybe Mom
and Dad won't let him have access to the massive trust fund until he's
settled down? That'd be enough motivation to put a ring on her finger.
Or maybe he's just lonely?"

Lily looked at me and laughed. "Naturally, he can't just be in love
with her and ready to spend the rest of his life with her, right? I mean,
we've established that that's totally out of the question, right?"

"Correct. That's not an option. Try again."

"Well, then, I'm forced to pick curtain number three. He's gay. He finally came to the realization himself—even though I've known forever—and realizes that Mom and Dad won't be able to handle it, so he'll cover by marrying the first girl he can find. What do you think?"

Casablanca was next on the list, and Lily fast-forwarded past the opening credits while I microwaved cups of hot chocolate in the tiny kitchen of her nonalcove studio in Morningside Heights. We lazed around straight through Friday night—breaking only to smoke and make another Blockbuster run. Saturday afternoon found us particularly motivated, and we managed to saunter down to SoHo for a few hours. We each bought new tank tops for Lily's upcoming New Year's party and shared an oversize mug of eggnog from a sidewalk café. By the time we made it back to her apartment on Saturday, we were exhausted and happy and spent the rest of the night alternating between *When Harry Met Sally* on TNT and *Saturday Night Live*. It was so thoroughly relaxing, such a departure from the misery that had become my daily routine, I'd forgotten all about the Harry Potter mission until I heard a phone ring on Sunday. Ohmigod, it was Her! I overheard Lily speaking in Russian to someone, probably a classmate, on her cell phone. Thank you, thank you, thank you, dear lord: it wasn't Her. But that still didn't let me off the hook. It was already Sunday morning, and I had no idea if those stupid books had found their way to Paris. I had enjoyed my weekend so much—had actually managed to relax enough—that I had forgotten to check. Of course, my phone was on and set to the highest ring level, but I never should've waited for someone to call me with a problem, when of course it'd be too late to do anything. I should've taken preemptive action and confirmed with everyone involved yesterday that all the steps of our highly choreographed plan had worked.

I dug frantically through my overnight bag, searching for the cell phone given to me by *Runway* that would ensure I was always only seven digits away from Miranda. I finally freed it from a tangle of underwear at the bottom of the bag and flopped backward on the bed. The little screen announced immediately that I had no service at that point, and I knew immediately, instinctively, that she had called and it had gone directly to voice mail. I hated that cell phone with my entire soul. I even hated my new Bang and Olufsen home phone by this point. I hated Lily's phone, commercials for phones, pictures of phones in magazines, and I even hated Alexander Graham Bell. Working for Miranda Priestly caused a number of unfortunate side effects in my day-to-day life, but the most unnatural one was my severe and all-consuming hatred of phones.

For most people, the ringing of a phone was a welcome sign. Someone was trying to reach them, to say hello, ask about their well-being, or make plans. For me, it triggered fear, intense anxiety, and heart-stopping panic. Some people considered the many available phone features to be a novelty, even fun. For me, they were nothing short of imperative. Although I'd never had so much as call waiting before Miranda, a few days into my tenure at *Runway* I was signed up for call waiting (so she'd never get a busy signal), caller ID (so I could avoid her calls), call waiting with caller ID (so I could avoid her calls while talking on the other line), and voice mail (so she wouldn't know I was avoiding her calls because she'd still hear an answering machine message). Fifty bucks a month for phone service—before long distance—seemed a small price to pay for my peace of mind. Well, not peace of mind exactly; more like early warning.

The cell phone afforded me no such barriers. Sure, it had all the same features as the home phone, but from Miranda's point of view there was simply no reason *whatsoever* for the cell to ever be turned off. It could never go unanswered. The few reasons for such a situation that I'd thrown out to Emily when she'd first handed me the phone—a standard *Runway* office supply—and told me to always answer it were quickly eliminated.

"What if you were sleeping?" I had stupidly asked.

"So get up and answer it," she'd answered while filing down a scraggly nail.

"Sitting down to a really fancy meal?"

"Be like every other New Yorker and talk at the dinner table."

"Getting a pelvic exam?"

"They're not looking in your ears, are they?" All right then. I got it.

I loathed that fucking cell but could not ignore it. It kept me tied to Miranda like an umbilical cord, refusing to let me grow up or out or away from my source of suffocation. She called *constantly*, and like some sick Pavlovian experiment gone awry, my body had begun responding viscerally to its ring. *Brring-brring.* Increased heart rate. *Brüüing.* Automatic finger clenching and shoulder tensing. *Brrüüüüüüing. Oh, why won't she leave me alone, please, oh, please, just forget I'm alive*—sweat breaks out on my forehead. This whole glorious weekend I'd never even considered the phone might not have service and had just assumed it would've rung if there was a problem. Mistake number one. I roamed the couple hundred square feet until AT&T decided to work again, held my breath, and dialed into my voice mail.

Mom left a cute message wishing me lots of fun with Lily. A friend from San Francisco found himself on business in New York that week and wanted to get together. My sister called to remind me to send a birthday card to her husband. And there it was, almost unexpected but not quite, that dreaded British accent ringing in my ears. "Ahn-dre-ah. It's Mir-ahnda. It's nine in the morning on Sunday in Pah-ris and the girls have not yet received their books. Call me at the Ritz to assure me that they will arrive shortly. That's all." Click.

The bile began to rise in my throat. As usual, the message lacked all niceties. No hello, good-bye, or thank you. Obviously. But more than that, it had been left nearly half a day ago, and I had still not called her back. Grounds for dismissal, I knew, and there was nothing I could do about it. Like an amateur, I'd assumed my plan would work perfectly and hadn't even realized that Uri had never called to confirm the pickup and drop-off. I scanned through the address book on my phone and quickly dialed Uri's cell phone number, another Miranda purchase so that he'd be on call 24/7 as well.

"Hi, Uri, it's Andrea. Sorry to bother you on Sunday, but I was wondering if you picked up those books yesterday from Eighty-seventh and Amsterdam?"

"Hi, Andy, eet's so nice to hear your woice," he crooned in the thick Russian accent I always found so comforting. He'd been calling me Andy like a favorite old uncle would since the first time we met, and coming from him—as opposed to B-DAD—I didn't mind it. "Of course I pick up the bouks, just like you say. You tink I don't vant to help you?"

"No, no, of course not, Uri. It's just that I got a message from Miranda saying that they hadn't received them yet, and I'm wondering what went wrong."

He was quiet for a moment, and then offered me the name and number of the pilot who was flying the private jet yesterday afternoon.

"Oh, thank you, thank you, thank you," I said, scribbling the number down frantically and praying that the pilot would be helpful. "I've got to run. Sorry I can't talk, but have a great weekend."

"Yes, yes, good veekend to you, Andy. I tink the pilot man will help you trace the bouks. Nice luck to you," he said merrily and hung up.

Lily was making waffles and I desperately wanted to join her, but I had to deal with this now or I was out of a job. Or maybe I'd already been fired, I thought, and no one had even bothered to tell me. Not outside the realm of *Runway* possibility, remembering the fashion editor who'd been fired while on her honeymoon. She herself stumbled across her change in job status by reading about it in a copy of *Women's Wear Daily* in Bali. I quickly called the number that Uri had given me for the pilot and thought I'd pass out from frustration when an answering machine picked up.

"Hi, Jonathan? This is Andrea Sachs from *Runway* magazine. I'm Miranda Priestly's assistant, and I needed to ask you a question about the flight yesterday. Oh, come to think of it, you're probably still in Paris, or maybe on your way back. Well, I just wanted to see if the books, and uh, well, you of course, made it to Paris in one piece. Can you call my cell? 917-555-8702. Please, as soon as possible. Thanks. 'Bye."

I thought about phoning the concierge at the Ritz to see if he'd remember receiving the car that would have brought the books from the private airport on the outskirts of Paris but quickly realized that my cell didn't dial internationally. It was quite possibly the only task it was not programmed to handle, and it was, of course, the only one that mattered. At that moment, Lily announced that she had a plate of waffles and a cup of coffee for me. I walked into the kitchen and took the food. She was sipping a Bloody Mary. Ugh. It was a Sunday morning. How could she be drinking?

"Having a Miranda moment?" she asked with a look of sympathy.

I nodded. "Think I screwed up pretty badly this time," I said, gratefully accepting the plate. "This one just might get me fired."

"Oh, sweetie, you always say that. She won't fire you. She hasn't even seen you hard at work yet. At least, she better not fire you—you have the greatest job in the world!"

I looked at her warily and willed myself to remain calm.

"Well, you do," she said. "So she sounds difficult to please and a little crazy. Who isn't? You still get free shoes and makeovers and haircuts and clothes. The clothes! Who on earth gets free designer clothes just for showing up at work each day? Andy, you work at *Runway*, don't you understand? A million girls would kill for your job."

I understood. I understood right then that Lily, for the first time since I met her nine years before, *didn't* understand. She, like all my other friends, loved hearing the crazy work stories I'd accumulated in the past weeks—the gossip and the glamour—but she didn't really understand just how hard each day was. She didn't understand that the reason I continued to show up, day after day, was not for the free clothes, didn't understand that all the free clothes in the world wouldn't make this job bearable. It was time to bring one of my best friends into my world, where, I was quite certain, she *would* understand. She just needed to be told. Yes! It was time to share with someone exactly what was going on. I opened my mouth to start, excited at the prospect of having an ally, but my phone rang.

Dammit! I wanted to throw it against the wall, tell whoever was on the other end to go to hell. But a small part of me hoped it was Jonathan with some information. Lily smiled and told me to take my time. I nodded sadly and answered.

"Is this Andrea?" asked a man's voice.

"Yes, is this Jonathan?"

"It is indeed. I just called home and got your message. I'm flying back from Paris right now, somewhere over the Atlantic as we speak, but you sounded so worried I wanted to call you back right away."

"Thank you! Thank you! I really appreciate it. Yes, I am a bit worried, because I got a call from Miranda earlier today and it seems strange that she hadn't yet received the package. You did give it to the driver in Paris, right?"

"Sure did. You know, miss, in my business I don't ask any questions. Just fly where I'm told and when and try to get everyone there in one piece. But it's sure not often I end up flying overseas with nothing on board but a package. Must've been something real important, I imagine, like an organ for a transplant or maybe some classified documents. So yes, I took real good care of that package and I gave it to the driver, just like I was told. Nice fella from the Ritz. No problems."

I thanked him and hung up. The concierge at the Ritz had arranged for a driver to meet Mr. Tomlinson's private plane at de Gaulle and transfer Harry back to the hotel. If everything went as planned, Miranda should've had those books by seven in the morning local time, and considering it was already late afternoon there, I couldn't imagine what had gone wrong. There was no choice: I had to call the concierge, and since my cell wouldn't dial internationally, I had to find a phone that did.

I took the plate of now cold waffles back to the kitchen and dumped them in the garbage. Lily was lying on the couch again, half-asleep. I hugged her good-bye and told her I'd call her later and headed out to hail a cab back to the office.

"What about today?" she whined. "I have *The American President* all lined up and ready to go. You can't leave yet—our weekend's not over!"

"I know, I'm sorry, Lil. I have to deal with this now. There's nothing I'd rather do than stay here, but she's got me on a pretty short leash right now. I'll call you later?"

The office was, of course, deserted, as everyone was surely brunching at Pastis with their investment banker boyfriends. I sat in my darkened area, took a deep breath, and dialed. Blissfully, Monsieur Renaud, my favorite of the Ritz concierges, was available.

"Andrea, dear, how are you? We're simply delighted to have Miranda and the twins back with us again so soon," he lied. Emily told me that Miranda stayed at the Ritz so frequently that the entire hotel staff knew her and the girls by name.

"Yes, Monsieur Renaud, and I know she's just thrilled to be there," I lied back. No matter how accommodating the poor concierge was, Miranda found fault with his every move. To his credit, he never stopped trying, and he never stopped lying about how much he loved her, either. "Listen, I'm wondering if that car you sent to meet Miranda's plane made it back to the hotel already?"

"Well of course, dear. That was hours ago. He must've returned here before eight o'clock this morning. I sent the best driver we have on staff," he said proudly. If only he knew what his best driver had been sent to shuttle around town.

"Well, that's so strange, because I got a message from Miranda saying that she never received the package, but I've checked with the driver here who swears he dropped it at the airport, the pilot who swears he flew it to Paris and gave it to your driver, and now you who remember it arriving at the hotel. How could she not have received it?"

"It seems the only way to solve this is to ask the lady herself," he trilled in a fake-happy voice. "Why don't I connect you?"

I had hoped against all hope that it wouldn't come to this, that I'd be able to identify and fix the problem without having to speak to her. What would I tell her if she still insisted that she'd never received the package? Was I supposed to suggest that she look on the table in her suite, where it was inevitably left hours earlier? Or was I supposed to go through the whole thing, private jet and all, and get her two more copies by the end of the day? Or perhaps I should hire a secret service agent next time to accompany the books on their journey overseas and ensure that nothing compromises their safe arrival? Something to think about.

"Sure, Monsieur Renaud. Thanks for your help."

A few clicks and the phone was ringing. I was sweating slightly from the tension, so I wiped my palm on my sweatpants and tried not to think what would happen if Miranda saw me wearing sweatpants in her office. *Be calm, be confident*, I coached myself. *She can't disembowel me over the phone.*

"Yes?" I heard from a faraway place, jolting myself out of my self-help thoughts. It was Caroline who, at a mere ten years, had perfected her mother's brusque phone manner perfectly. Cassidy at least had the courtesy to answer the phone with a "hello."

"Hi, sweetie," I crooned, hating myself for sucking up to a child. "It's Andrea, from the office. Is your mom there?"

"You mean my *mum*?" she corrected as she always did when I used the American pronunciation. "Sure, I'll get her."

A moment or two later, Miranda was on the line.

"Yes, Ahn-dre-ah? This had better be important. You know how I feel about being interrupted when I'm spending time with the girls," she stated in her cold, clipped way. *You know how I feel about being inter-rupted when I'm spending time with the girls?* I wanted to scream. *Are you fucking kidding me, lady? You think I'm calling for my goddamn health? Because I couldn't bear to go a single weekend without hearing your miserable voice? And what about me spending time with* my *girls?* I thought I'd pass out from anger, but I took a deep breath and dove right in.

"Miranda, I'm sorry if this is a bad time, but I'm calling to ensure that you received the Harry Potter books. I heard your message saying that you hadn't yet received them, but I've spoken to everyone and—"

She interrupted me midsentence and spoke slowly and surely. "Ahn-dre-ah. You should really listen more closely. I said no such thing. We received the package early this morning. Incidentally, it came so early that they woke us all up for the silly thing."

I couldn't believe what I was hearing. I didn't dream that she'd left the message, did I? I was still too young even for early-onset Alzheimer's, right?

"What I said was that we didn't receive *both* copies of the book, as I had requested. The package included only one, and I'm sure you can imagine just how disappointed the girls are. They were really looking forward to each having their *own* copy, as I had requested. I need you to explain why my orders weren't followed."

This wasn't happening. This couldn't be happening. I was definitely dreaming now, living some sort of alternate-universe existence where anything resembling rationality and logic were suspended indefinitely. I wouldn't even let myself consider the absurdity of what was unfolding.

"Miranda, I do recall that you requested two copies, and I ordered two," I stammered, hating myself yet again for pandering. "I spoke to the girl at Scholastic and am quite sure that she understood that you needed two copies of the book, so I can't imagine—"

"Ahn-dre-ah, you know how I feel about excuses. I'm not particu-larly interested in hearing yours now. I expect something like this will never happen again, correct? That's all." She hung up.

I stood there for what must have been five full minutes, listening to the squawking off-the-hook sound with the receiver pressed against my ear. My mind raced, full of questions. Could I kill her? I wondered, considering the probability of getting caught. Would they automatically assume it was me? Of course not, I concluded—everybody, at least at *Runway*, had a motive. Do I really have the emotional wherewithal to watch her die a long, slow, agonizingly painful death? Well, yes, that much was for sure—what would be the most enjoyable way to snuff out her wretched existence?

I slowly replaced the receiver. Could I really have misunderstood her message when I listened to it earlier? I grabbed my cell phone and replayed the messages. *"Ahn-dre-ah. It's Mir-ahnda. It's nine in the morning on Sunday in Pah-ris and the girls have not yet received their books. Call me at the Ritz to assure me that they will arrive shortly. That's all."* Nothing was really wrong. She may have received one copy instead of two, but she deliberately gave me the impression that I'd made a tremendous, career-ending mistake. She'd called with no concern that her nine A.M. call would have reached me at three A.M., on my most perfect weekend in months. She'd called to drive me a little crazier, push me a little bit harder. She'd called to dare me to defy her. She'd called to make me hate her that much more.

7

Lily's New Year's party was good and low-key, just a lot of paper cups of champagne at Lily's place with a bunch of people from college and some others they managed to drag along. I was never a big fan of the holiday. I don't remember who first called it "Amateur Night" (I think it was Hugh Hefner), saying that he went out the other 364 days a year, but I tend to agree. All that forced drinking and merry-making did not a good time guarantee. So Lily had stepped up and thrown a little party to save us all the $150 tickets to some club or, even worse, any sort of ridiculous thoughts of actually freezing in Times Square. We'd each brought a bottle of something not too poisonous, and she had passed out noisemakers and glittery tiaras, and we got quite drunk and happy and toasted in the New Year on her rooftop overlooking Harlem. Although we'd all had way too much to drink, Lily was pretty much nonfunctional by the time everyone else had left. She had already thrown up twice, and I was scared to leave her alone in the apartment, so Alex and I had packed her a bag and dragged her in the cab with us. We all stayed at my place, Lily on the futon in the living room, and went out for a big brunch the next day.

I was glad the whole holiday thing was over. It was time to get on with my life and get started—really started—on my new job. Even though it felt like I'd been working for a decade, I was technically just beginning. I had a lot of hope that things would improve once Miranda and I started working together day to day. Anyone could be a cold-hearted monster over the phone, especially someone who was uncomfortable with vacations and being so far away from work. But I was convinced that the misery of that first month would give way to a whole new situation, and I was excited to see how it would all unfold.

It was a little after ten on a cold and gray January 3, and I was actually happy to be at work. Happy! Emily was gushing about some guy she met at a New Year's party in LA, some "superhot, up-and-coming songwriter" who had promised to come visit her in New York in the next couple weeks. I was chatting with the associate beauty editor who sat down the hall, a really sweet guy who'd graduated from Vassar and whose parents didn't yet know—even despite the college choice and the fact that he was a *beauty* editor at a *fashion* magazine—that he did, in fact, sleep with guys.

"Oh, come with me, please? It'll be so fun, I promise. I'll introduce you to some real hotties, Andy, you'll see. I have some gorgeous straight friends. Besides, it's *Marshall*'s party—it's got to be great," James crooned, leaning against my desk as I checked my e-mail. Emily was chattering away happily on her side of the suite, detailing her rendezvous with the long-haired singer.

"I would, you know I would, but I've had these plans with my boyfriend tonight since before Christmas," I said. "We've been planning on going out to a really nice dinner together for weeks, and I canceled on him last time."

"So see him after! Come on, it's not every day you get a chance to meet the single most talented colorist in the civilized world, is it? And there will be loads of celebrities and everyone will look gorgeous, and, well, I just know it'll be the most glamorous party of the week! Harrison and Shrift-man is putting it on, for chrissake—you can't beat that. Say yes." He squinted his face into exaggerated puppy eyes, and I had to laugh.

"James, I'd really, really like to—I've never even been to the Plaza! But I really can't change these plans. Alex made reservations at this little Italian place right by his apartment and there's no way I can reschedule." I knew I couldn't cancel, and I didn't want to—I wanted to spend the night alone with Alex and hear how his new after-school pro-gram was shaping up, but I was sorry it had to be the same night as this party. I'd been reading about it in the papers for the past week: it seemed that all of Manhattan was ecstatically waiting for Marshall Madden, hair colorist extraordinaire, to host his annual post–New Year's blowout. They were saying that this year was going to be even bigger than usual because Marshall had just published a new book, *Color Me Marshall*. But I wasn't going to cancel on my boyfriend to go to some star party.

"Well, OK, but don't say I never asked you to go anywhere. And don't come crying to me when you read in *Page Six* tomorrow that I was spot-ted with Mariah or J-Lo. Just don't." And he huffed away, half joking that he was angry, half not, since he seemed to be in a perpetual snit anyway.

So far, the week after New Year's had been easy. We were still un-wrapping and cataloging presents—I had gotten to unveil the most stunning pair of Swarovski-encrusted stilettos this morning—but there were none left to send and the phones were quiet since many people were still away. Miranda would be returning from Paris at the end of the week but wouldn't be in the office until Monday. Emily felt confident that I was ready to handle her, and so was I. We'd run through everything, and I'd taken nearly an entire legal pad full of notes. I glanced down at it, hoping I'd remember everything. Coffee: Starbucks only, tall latte, two raw sugars, two napkins, one stirrer. Breakfast: Mangia delivery, 555–3948, one soft cheese Danish, four slices bacon, two sausage links. Newspapers: newsstand in lobby, *New York Times*, *Daily News*, *New York Post*, the *Financial Times*, the *Washington Post*, *USA Today*, the *Wall Street Journal*, *Women's Wear Daily*, and the *New York Observer* on

Wednesdays. Weekly magazines, available Mondays: *Time, Newsweek, U.S. News, The New Yorker*(!), *Time Out New York, New York,* the *Economist.* And on and on it went, listing her favorite flowers and her most-hated flowers, her doctors' names and addresses and home phone numbers, her household help, her snack preferences, her preferred bottled water, every size she wore in every article of clothing from lingerie to ski boots. I made lists of people she wanted to talk to (*Always*), and separate lists for people she never wanted to talk to (*Never*). I wrote and wrote and wrote as Emily revealed these things throughout our weeks together, and when we were finished, I felt there was nothing I did not know about Miranda Priestly. Except, of course, what exactly made her so important that I'd filled a legal pad with likes and dislikes. Why, exactly, was I supposed to care?

"Yeah, he's amazing," Emily was sighing, twisting the phone cord round and round her forefinger. "It was the most romantic weekend I think I've ever had."

Ping! You have a new e-mail from Alexander Fineman. Click here to open. Oooh, fun. Elias-Clark had firewalled instant messenger, but for some reason I could still receive instant notifications that I'd received a new e-mail. I'd take it.

Hey baby, how's your day?? Things are crazy here, as usual. Remember I told you that Jeremiah had threatened all the little girls with a box cutter he'd brought from home? Well, it seems he was serious—he brought another one to school today and sliced one of the girls' arms at recess and called her a bitch. Not a deep cut at all, but when the teacher on duty asked him where he'd gotten such an idea, he said he saw his mom's boyfriend do it to his mom. He's six years old, Andy, can you believe it? Anyway, the principal called an emergency faculty meeting tonight, so I'm afraid I can't make dinner. I'm so sorry! But I have to say, I'm happy that they're responding to this at all—it's more than I had hoped for. You understand, don't you? Please don't be mad. I'll call you later, and I promise to make it up to you. Love, A

Please don't be mad? I hope you understand? One of his fourth-graders had *slashed* another student and he was hoping I'd be OK with him canceling dinner? I'd canceled on him my first week because I'd thought my week of riding around in a limo and wrapping presents had been too demanding. I wanted to cry, to call him and tell him it was more than OK, that I was proud of him for caring about these kids, for taking the job in the first place. I hit "reply" and was just about to write as much when I heard my name.

"Andrea! She's on her way in. She'll be here in ten minutes," Emily announced loudly, obviously struggling to remain calm.

"Hmm? I'm sorry, I didn't hear what—"

"Miranda is on her way into the office this moment. We need to get ready."

"On her way into the office? But I thought she wasn't even coming back to the country until Saturday . . ."

"Well, clearly she changed her mind. Now, move! Go downstairs and get her papers and lay them out just the way I told you. When you're done, wipe down her desk and leave a glass of Pellegrino on the left-hand side, with ice and a lime. And make sure that her bathroom is stocked, OK? Go! She's already in the car, so she should be here in less than ten minutes, depending on traffic."

As I raced out of the office, I could hear Emily rapid-fire dialing four-digit extensions and all but screaming, "She's on her way—tell every-one." It took me only three seconds to wind through the hallways and pass through the fashion department, but I already heard panicked cries of "Emily said she's on her way in" and "Miranda's coming!" and a particularly blood-curdling cry of "She's *baaaaaaaaaaaaaaaaaaaaaack*!" Assistants were frantically straightening clothes on the racks that lined the halls, and editors were racing into their offices, where I could see one changing from her kitten-heeled shoes to four-inch stilettos while another lined her lips, curled her lashes, and adjusted her bra strap without so much as slowing down. As the publisher walked out of the men's room, I glanced past him and saw James, looking frenzied, checking his black cashmere sweater for lint while spastically popping Altoids in his mouth. Unless the men's room was wired with loudspeakers for these very occasions, I wasn't even sure how he'd heard yet.

I was dying to stop and watch the scene unfold, but I had less than ten minutes to prepare for my first meeting with Miranda as her actual assistant, and I wasn't going to blow it. Until then I'd been trying not to appear as if I'd been actually running, but upon witnessing the utter lack of dignity everyone else had demonstrated, I broke into a sprint.

"Andrea! You know Miranda's on her way here, don't you?" Sophy called from the reception desk as I flew by.

"Yeah, I know, but how do you know?"

"Sweetie pie, I know everything. Now I suggest you get your butt in gear. One thing's for sure: Miranda Priestly does *not* like to be kept waiting."

I leapt onto the elevator and called out a thank you. "I'll be back in three minutes with the papers!"

The two women on the elevator stared at me in disgust, and I realized that I had been screaming.

"Sorry," I said, trying to catch my breath. "We just found out that our editor in chief is on her way to the office and we weren't prepared, so everyone's a little edgy now." *Why am I explaining myself to these people?*

"Ohmigod, you must work for Miranda! Wait, let me guess. You're Miranda's new assistant? Andrea, right?" The leggy brunette flashed what must've been four dozen teeth and moved forward like a piranha. Her friend instantly brightened.

"Um, yeah. Andrea," I said, repeating my own name as though I wasn't entirely sure it was mine. "And yes, I'm Miranda's new assistant."

At that moment the elevator hit the lobby and the doors opened to the stark white marble. I moved ahead of the women and bolted through before the doors had opened entirely and heard one of them call, "You're a lucky girl, Andrea. Miranda's an amazing woman, and a million girls would die for your job!"

I tried not to slam into a group of very unhappy-looking lawyers, and nearly flew into the newsstand in the corner of the lobby, where a little Kuwaiti man named Ahmed presided over a sleek display of glossy titles and a noticeably sparser array of mostly sugar-free candy and diet sodas. Emily had introduced Ahmed and me to each other before Christmas as part of my training, and I was hoping he could be enlisted to help me now.

"Stop right there!" he cried as I began pulling newspapers out of their wire racks by the register. "You are Miranda's new girl, right? Come here."

I swiveled to see Ahmed lean down and ferret under the register, his face turning a bit too red under the strain. "Ah-ha!" he cried again, springing to his feet with all the agility of an old man with two broken legs. "For you. So you don't make a mess of my display, I keep them aside for you each day. And maybe to make sure I don't run out, too." He winked.

"Ahmed, thank you. I can't even tell you how much this helps me. Do you think I should get the magazines now, too?"

"I sure do. Look, it's already Wednesday and they all came out on Monday. Your boss probably don't like that so much," he said knowingly. And again he reached under the register and again he rose with an armful of magazines, which, after a quick glance, I confirmed were all the ones on my list—no more, no less.

ID card, ID card, where the hell was that goddamn ID card? I reached inside my starched white button-down and found the silk lanyard that Emily had fashioned for me out of one of Miranda's white Hermès scarves. "Never actually wear the card when she's around, of course," she had said, "but just in case you forget to take it off, at least you won't be wearing it on a plastic chain." She had practically spit out the last two words.

"Here you go, Ahmed. Thank you so much for your help, but I'm in a big, big rush. She's on her way in."

He swiped my card down the reader on the side of the machine and placed the scarf lanyard around my neck like a lei. "Run, now. Run!"

I grabbed the overflowing plastic bag and ran, pulling my ID card out again to swipe against the security turnstiles that would allow me to enter the Elias-Clark elevator bank. I swiped and pushed. Nothing. I swiped and pushed again, this time harder. Nothing.

"*Some boys kiss me, some boys hug me, I think they're okay-ay,*" Eduardo, the round and slightly sweaty security guard, began singing in a high-pitched voice from behind the security desk. Shit. I already knew without looking that his smile, conspiratorial and enormous, demanded again—as it had every single day for the past few weeks—that I play along. It seems he had a never-ending supply of annoying tunes that he loved to sing, and he wouldn't let me through the turnstiles until I acted them out. The day before was "I'm Too Sexy." As he sang, *"I'm too sexy for Milan, too sexy for Milan, New York and Japan,"* I had to walk down the lobby's imaginary runway. It could be fun when I was in a decent mood. Sometimes it even made me smile. But it was my very first day with Miranda, and I couldn't be late getting her things set up, I just couldn't. I wanted to *hurt* him for holding me up as everyone else breezed past the security desk in the turnstiles on each side of me.

"If they don't give me proper credit, I just walk away-ay," I muttered, allowing the words to stretch and fade, just like Madonna.

He raised his eyebrows. "Where's the enthusiasm, girlfriend?"

I thought I'd do something violent if I heard his voice again, so I dropped my bag of papers on the counter, threw both arms up in the air and thrust my hips to the left, while pursing my lips into a dramatic pout. *"A material! A material! A material! A material . . . WORLD!"* I all but screamed, and he cackled and clapped and *whoosh!* He buzzed me through.

Mental note: Discuss with Eduardo when and where it is appropriate to make a complete ass of me. Once again, I dove onto the elevators and raced past Sophy, who kindly opened the doors to the floor without my even asking. I even remembered to stop in one of the minikitchens and put some ice in one of the Baccarat goblets we kept in a special cabinet over the microwave just for Miranda. Glass in one hand, newspapers in another, I peeled around the corner and smashed directly into Jessica, a.k.a. Manicure Girl. She looked both annoyed and panic-stricken.

"Andrea, are you aware that Miranda is on her way to the office?" she asked, looking me up and down.

"Sure am. I've got her newspapers right here and her water right here, and now I just need to get them back to her office. If you'll excuse me . . ."

"Andrea!" she called as I ran past her, an ice cube flying out of the glass and landing outside the art department. "Remember to change your shoes!"

I stopped dead in my tracks and looked down. I was wearing a pair of funky street sneakers, the kind that weren't designed to do anything but look cool. The rules of dress—unspoken and otherwise—were obviously relaxed when Miranda was away, and even though every single person in the office looked fantastic, each was wearing something they would swear up and down that they'd never, ever wear in front of Miranda. My bright red, mesh sneakers were a prime example.

I had broken a sweat by the time I made it back to our suite. "I've got all the papers and I bought the magazines, too, just in case. The only thing is, I don't think I can wear these shoes, can I?"

Emily tore the headset from her ear and flung it down on her desk. "No, of course you can't wear those." She picked up the phone, dialed four digits, and announced, "Jeffy, bring me a pair of Jimmy's in a size . . ." She looked at me.

"Nine and a half." I pulled a small bottle of Pellegrino out of the closet and filled the glass.

"Nine and a half. No, now. No, Jeff, I'm serious. Right now. Andrea is wearing *sneakers* for chrissake, *red* sneakers, and She's going to be here any minute. OK, thanks."

It was then I noticed that in the four minutes I'd been downstairs, Emily had managed to switch her faded jeans to leather pants and her own funky sneakers to open-toe stilettos. She'd also cleaned up the entire office suite, sweeping the contents of both our desks into drawers and stashing all of the incoming gifts that hadn't yet been transferred to Miranda's apartment in the closet. She had slicked on a fresh coat of lip gloss and added some color to her cheeks and was presently motioning for me to get moving.

I grabbed the bag of newspapers and shook them out in a pile on the lightbox in her office, a sort of underlit table where Emily said Miranda would stand for hours on end and examine film that had come in from photo shoots. But it was also where she liked her papers arranged, and once again, I consulted my legal pad for the correct order. First, the *New York Times*, followed by the *Wall Street Journal*, and then the *Washington Post*. And on and on the order went in a pattern I couldn't distinguish, each placed slightly on top of the one before it until they fanned out across the table in formation. *Women's Wear Daily* was the single exception: this was to be placed in the middle of her desk.

"She's here! Andrea, come out here! She's on her way up," I heard Emily hiss from the outer area. "Uri just called to tell me he just dropped her off."

I put *WWD* on her desk, placed the Pellegrino on a corner of her desk on a linen napkin (which side? I couldn't remember which side it was supposed to go on), and darted from the office, taking one last look around to ensure that everything was in order. Jeffy, one of the fashion assistants who helped organize the fashion closet, tossed me a shoe box with a rubber band around it and bolted. I pulled it open immediately. Inside were a pair of Jimmy Choo heels with straps made of camel hair going every which way and buckles nestled in the middle of it all, probably worth around eight hundred dollars. Shit! I had to get these on. I yanked off my sneakers and my now sweaty socks and tossed them under my desk. The right one went on rather easily, but I couldn't work my stubby fingernail to free the buckle on the left one until—there! I pried it open and thrust my left foot into it, watching the straps bite into the already swollen flesh. In another few seconds I had it buckled and was returning to an upright sitting position just as Miranda walked in.

Frozen. I was absolutely frozen in midmotion, my mind working fast enough to understand how ridiculous I must look, but not quite fast enough to move. She noticed me immediately, probably because she was expecting Emily to still be sitting at her old desk, and walked over. She leaned on the counter that ran over my desk, leaned over it and even closer to me, until she was able to see my entire body as I sat, immobilized, in the chair. Her bright blue eyes moved up and down, side to side, all over my white button-down, my red corduroy Gap miniskirt, my now buckled camel-hair Jimmy Choo sandals. I felt her examine every inch of me, skin and hair and clothes, her eyes moving so quickly but her face remaining frozen. She leaned closer still, until her face was only a foot from mine and I could smell the fantastic aroma of salon shampoo and expensive perfume, so close that I could see the very fine lines around her mouth and eyes that were invisible from a more comfortable distance. But I couldn't look too long at her face, because she was intently examining mine. There wasn't the slightest indication that she recognized that a) we had, in fact, met before; b) I was her new employee; or c) I was not Emily.

"Hello, Ms. Priestly," I squeaked impulsively, even though some-where in the back of my head I knew that she hadn't uttered a word yet. But the tension was unbearable, and I couldn't help but barrel forward. "I'm so excited to be working for you. Thank you so much for the op-portunity to . . ." *Shut up! Just shut your stupid mouth!* Talk about no dignity.

She walked away. Finished looking me up and down, pushed back-ward off the counter, and just walked away while I was stuttering mid-sentence. I could feel heat coming off my face, a flush of confusion and pain and humiliation all wrapped into one, and it didn't help that I could feel Emily glaring at me. I pulled my hot face upward and confirmed that Emily was indeed glaring at me.

"Is the Bulletin updated?" Miranda asked to no one in particular as she walked into her office and, I noticed happily, directly to the light table where I'd arranged her papers.

"Yes, Miranda. Here it is," Emily said obsequiously, racing in behind her and handing her the clipboard where we kept all of Miranda's mes-sages typed as they come in.

I sat quietly, watching Miranda move deliberately around her office in the picture frames that hung on her wall: if I looked at the glass in-stead of at the photos themselves, I could see her reflection. Emily im-mediately busied herself at her desk, and silence prevailed. *Do we never get to talk to each other or anyone else if she's in the office?* I wondered. I wrote a quick e-mail to Emily, asking her as much, which I saw her re-ceive and read. Her answer came back right away: *You got it,* she wrote. *If you and I have to talk, we whisper. Otherwise, no talking. And don't EVER speak to her unless she speaks to you. And do not EVER call her Ms. Priestly—it's Miranda. Got it?* I felt again as if I had been slapped, but I looked up and nodded. And it was then I noticed the coat. It was right there, a great big pile of fabulous-looking fur, all bunched up on the end of my desk, with one arm dangling off the edge. I looked at Emily. She rolled her eyes, waved her hand toward the closet, and mouthed, "Hang it up!" It was as heavy as a wet down comforter com-ing out of the washing machine, and I needed both hands to keep it from dragging on the floor, but I gingerly hung it on one of the silk hangers and gently, quietly, closed the doors.

I hadn't even sat back down when Miranda appeared next to me, and this time her eyes were free to roam over my entire body. Impossible as it seemed, I could feel each body part ignite as she eyed it, but I was frozen, unable to dive back to my chair. Just as my hair was about to catch fire, those relentless blue eyes finally stopped on mine.

"I'd like my coat," she said quietly, looking directly at me, and I wondered if she wondered who I was, or if she didn't notice or care that there was a relative stranger posing as her assistant. There wasn't so much as a glimmer of recognition, even though my interview with her had taken place a few weeks earlier.

"Surely," I managed, and moved toward the closet again, which was an awkward maneuver because she was currently standing between it and me. I turned my body sideways to keep from bumping into her and tried to slide myself past her, reaching to pull open the door I had just shut. She didn't move a single inch to let me pass, and I could feel that the eyes had continued their roving. Finally, blessedly, my hands closed around the fur, and I pulled it carefully to freedom. I wanted to throw it at her and see if she'd catch it, but I restrained myself at the last second and held it open as a gentleman would for a lady. She shrugged into it with one graceful motion and picked up her cell phone, the only item she had brought with her to the office.

"I'd like the Book tonight, Emily," she said as she walked confidently out of the office, probably not even noticing that a cluster of three women standing in the hall outside the suite scattered immediately upon seeing her, chins to their chests.

"Yes, Miranda. I'll have Andrea bring it up."

That was that. She left. And the visit that had inspired office-wide panic, frenzied preparations, even makeup and wardrobe adjustments, had lasted just under four minutes, and had taken place—as far as my inexperienced eyes could see—for absolutely no reason whatsoever.

8

"Don't look now," James said, his mouth as immobile as a ventriloquist's, "but I spy Reese Witherspoon at three o'clock."

I swiveled immediately as he cringed in embarrassment, and, sure enough, there she was, sipping a glass of champagne and throwing her head back in laughter. I didn't want to be impressed, but I couldn't help it: she was one of my favorite actresses.

"James, darling, I'm so glad you could make it to my little party," quipped a thin, beautiful man who came up behind us. "And who do we have here?" They kissed.

"Marshall Madden, color guru, this is Andrea Sachs. Andrea is actually—"

"Miranda's new assistant," Marshall finished, smiling at me. "I've heard all about you, little one. Welcome to the family. I do hope you'll come visit me. I promise that together we can, um, smooth over your look." He ran his hand lovingly over my scalp and picked up the ends of my hair, which he immediately held up against the roots. "Yes, just a touch of something honey-colored and you'll be the next supermodel. Get my number from James, OK, sweetie, and come see me anytime you get a minute. Probably easier said than done!" he sang as he floated toward Reese.

James sighed and looked on wistfully. "He's a master," he breathed, "simply the best. The ultimate. A man among boys, to say the least. And gorgeous." A man among boys? Funny. Whenever anyone had used that phrase before, I'd always pictured Shaquille O'Neal making a move toward the hoop against a small power forward—not a colorist.

"He's definitely gorgeous, I'll agree with you there. Have you ever dated him?" It seemed like the perfect match: the associate beauty editor of *Runway* dating the most sought-after colorist in the free world.

"I wish. He's been with the same guy for four years now. Do you believe it? Four years. Since when are hot gay men allowed to be monogamous? It's just not fair!"

"Hey, I hear you. Since when are hot straight men allowed to be monogamous? Well, unless they're being monogamous with me, that is." I took a long drag from my cigarette and blew out a near-perfect smoke ring.

"So admit it, Andy. Tell me you're glad you came tonight. Tell me this isn't the greatest party ever," he said, smiling.

I'd grudgingly decided to go with James after Alex had canceled, mostly because he wouldn't leave me alone. It seemed utterly impossible that a single interesting thing would transpire at a party for a book about highlights, but I had to admit that I'd been surprised. When Johnny Depp had come over to say hi to James, I was shocked that he not only seemed to have a full command of the English language, but had even managed a few funny jokes. And it was intensely gratifying to see that Gisele, the Ittest It girl of all current It girls, was downright short. Of course it would've been even nicer to discover that she was secretly squat, too, or had a major acne problem that had all been airbrushed out in her gorgeous cover shoots, but I'd settle for short. All in all, it hadn't been a bad hour and a half so far.

"I'm not sure I'd go that far," I said, leaning toward him to catch a glimpse of a great looking guy who appeared to be sulking in the corner near the book table. "But it hasn't been quite as disgusting as I'd imagined. And besides, I'm up for anything after the day I've had."

After Miranda had made her rather abrupt departure after her rather abrupt arrival, Emily informed me that that night would be the first time I would have to bring "the Book" to Miranda's apartment. The Book was a large wire-bound collection of pages as big as a phonebook, in which each current issue of *Runway* was mocked up and laid out. She explained that no substantial work could get done each day until after Miranda left, because all of the art people and editorial people spent all day long consulting with her, and she changed her mind every hour. Therefore, when Miranda left around five each day to spend some time with the twins, the real day's work would begin. The art department would craft their new layout and input any new photos that had come in, and editorial would tweak and print any copy that had finally, finally, gotten Miranda's approval—a giant, looping "MP" scrawled across the entire first page. Every editor would send all the day's new changes to the art assistant, who, hours after nearly everyone else had left, would run the images and layouts and words through a small machine that waxed the backs of the pages and pressed them onto their appropriate page in the Book. It was then my job to take the Book up to Miranda's apartment whenever it was finished—anywhere in the eight to eleven P.M. range, depending on where in the production process we were—at which point she'd mark it all up. She'd bring it back the next day, and the entire staff would go through the whole thing again.

When Emily overheard me tell James that I'd go to the party with him after all, she jumped right in. "Um, you know you can't go anywhere until the Book's finished, right?"

I stared. James looked as though he might tackle her.

"Yeah, I have to say, this is the part of your job I'm most happy to be done with. It can get really, really late sometimes, but Miranda needs to see it every single night, you know. She works from home. Anyway, I'll wait with you tonight and show you how to do it, but then you're on your own."

"OK, thanks. Any idea when it'll be finished tonight?"

"Nope. Changes every night. You'd really have to ask the art department."

The Book was finally ready on the earlier side, at eight-thirty, and after I'd retrieved it from an exhausted-looking art assistant, Emily and I walked down to 59th Street together. Emily was holding an armful of freshly dry-cleaned clothes on hangers, encased in plastic, and she explained to me that dry cleaning always accompanied the Book. Miranda would bring her dirty clothes to the office, where, as my luck would have it, it was my job to call the cleaners and let them know we had a pickup. They would send someone to the Elias-Clark building immediately, pick up the clothes, and return them in perfect condition a day later. We stored them in our office closet until we could either hand them off to Uri or take them to her apartment ourselves. My job was getting more intellectually stimulating by the minute!

"Hey, Rich!" Emily called brightly, fakely, to the pipe-chomping dispatcher I'd met my first day. "This is Andrea. She'll be taking the Book every night, so make sure she gets a good car, OK?"

"Will do, Red." He pulled the pipe out of his mouth and motioned toward me. "I'll take good care of Blondie over here."

"Great. Oh, and can you have another car follow us to Miranda's? Andrea and I are going separate places after we drop off the Book."

Two massive Town Cars pulled up just at that moment, and the mammoth driver in the first car barreled out of the front seat and opened the back door for us. Emily climbed in first, immediately whipped out her cell phone, and called out, "Miranda Priestly's apartment, please." He nodded and threw the car in gear and we were off.

"Is it always the same driver?" I asked, wondering how he knew where to go.

She motioned me to be quiet as she left a message for her roommate. She then said, "No, but there are only so many drivers who work for the company. I've had them all at least twenty times, so they know their way by now." She went back to her dialing. I looked behind us and saw the second empty Town Car carefully mimicking our turns and stops.

We pulled up in front of a typical Fifth Avenue doorman building: immaculate sidewalk, well-kept balconies, and what looked like a gorgeous, warmly lit lobby. A man in a tuxedo and hat immediately came to the car and opened the door for us, and Emily got out. I wondered why we weren't just going to leave the Book and the clothes with him. As far as I understood—and it wasn't a lot, especially when it came to this strange city—that's what doormen were for. As in, that's their job. But Emily pulled a leather Louis Vuitton key chain from her Gucci logo tote and handed it to me.

"I'll wait here. You take the stuff up to her apartment, Penthouse A. Just open her door and leave the book on the table in the foyer and hang the clothes on the hooks by the closet. Not *in* the closet, *by* the closet. And then just leave. Whatever you do, don't knock or ring the doorbell. She doesn't like to be disturbed. Just let yourself in and out and be quiet!" She handed me the tangle of wire hangers and plastic and opened her cell phone again. *All right, I can handle this. Why so much drama for a book and some pants?*

The elevator man smiled kindly at me and silently pressed the PH button after turning a key. He looked like a battered wife, dejected and sad, as though he couldn't fight any longer and had just made peace with his unhappiness.

"I'll wait here," he said softly, staring at the floor. "You shouldn't be more than a minute."

The carpet in the hallways was a deep burgundy color, and I almost toppled over when one of my heels got stuck in the loops. The walls were papered in a thick, cream-colored fabric that had tiny cream pinstripes running the length, and there was a suede cream bench pushed against the wall. The French doors directly in front of me said PH B, but I swiveled and saw identical doors with PH A. It took every ounce of restraint not to ring the bell, but I remembered Emily's warning and slid the key in the lock. It clicked right away, and before I could fix my hair or wonder what was on the other side, I was standing in a large, airy foyer and smelling the most amazing scent of lamb chops. And there she was, delicately bringing a fork to her mouth while two identical, black-haired little girls yelled at each other across the table and a tall, rugged-looking man with silver hair and a broad, face-encompassing nose read a newspaper.

"Mum, tell her that she can't just walk in my room and take my jeans! She won't listen to me," one of them pleaded of Miranda, who'd set down her fork and was taking a sip of what I knew to be Pellegrino with a lime, from the *left* side of the table.

"Caroline, Cassidy, enough. I simply don't want to hear it anymore. Tomas, bring out some more mint jelly," she called. A man I presumed to be the chef hurried into the room holding a silver bowl on a silver serving platter.

And then I realized that I'd been standing there for nearly thirty seconds, observing them all having dinner. They hadn't seen me yet, but would as soon as I moved toward the hall table. I did so gingerly but felt them all turn to look. Just as I was about to offer some sort of greeting, I remembered making a gigantic ass out of myself at our first meeting earlier today, stammering and stumbling like an idiot, and I kept my mouth shut. *Table, table, table.* There it was. *Deposit book on table.* And now for the clothes. I looked around frantically for the place I was supposed to hang the dry cleaning, but I couldn't focus. The dinner table had grown silent, and I could feel them all watching me. No one said hello. It didn't seem to bother the girls that there was a perfect stranger standing in their apartment. Finally, I saw a small coat closet tucked away behind the door, and I managed to get every twisted, slippery hanger on the rod.

"Not in the closet, Emily," I heard Miranda call out, slowly, deliberately. "On the hooks that are provided for this exact occasion."

"Oh, um, hi there." *Idiot! Shut up! She's not looking for a response, just do what she says!* But I couldn't help it. It was just too weird that no one had said hello or wondered who I might be, or in any way acknowledged that someone had just let herself into their apartment and was prowling around. And *Emily?* Was she kidding? Blind? Could she really not tell that I was not the girl who'd worked for her for over a year already? "I'm Andrea, Miranda. I'm your new assistant."

Silence. All-pervasive, unbearable, never-ending, deafening, debilitating silence.

I knew I shouldn't keep talking, knew that I was digging my own grave, but I just couldn't help myself. "Um, well, sorry about the confusion. I'll just put these on the hooks, like you said, and let myself out." *Stop narrating! She doesn't give a shit what you're doing. Just do it and get out.* "OK, then, have a nice dinner. Nice meeting all of you." I turned to leave and realized that not only was the mere act of talking ridiculous, but I was also saying stupid things. *Nice to meet you?* I hadn't been introduced to a single one of them.

"Emily!" I heard just as my hand reached the doorknob. "Emily, let this not happen tomorrow night. We're not interested in the interruption." And the doorknob turned itself in my hand and I was finally in the hallway. The entire thing had taken less than a minute, but I felt like I'd just swum the entire length of an Olympic-size pool without coming up for air.

I slumped onto the bench and took long, controlled breaths. That bitch! The first time she called me Emily could've been a mistake, but the second was undoubtedly deliberate. What better way to belittle and marginalize someone than to insist on calling them the wrong name, after you've refused to so much as acknowledge their presence in your own home? I knew I was the lowest-ranking life-form at the magazine already—as Emily hadn't yet lost an opportunity to impress upon me—but was it really so necessary for Miranda to make sure I was aware of it, too?

It wouldn't have been outside the realm of reality to sit there all night and shoot mental bullets at the PH A doors, but I heard a throat clearing and looked up to find the sad little elevator man watching the floor and patiently waiting for me to join him.

"Sorry," I said as I shuffled aboard.

"No problem," he near-whispered, intently studying the wood-paneled floor. "It'll get easier."

"What? I'm sorry, I didn't hear what you—"

"Nothing, nothing. Here you are, miss. Have a nice evening." The door opened to the lobby, where Emily was loudly chattering on her cell phone. She clicked it closed when she saw me.

"How'd it go? No problem, right?"

I thought about telling her what had transpired, wished fervently that she could be a sympathetic coworker, that we could be a team, but I knew I'd just be setting myself up for another verbal lashing. *So not interested right now.*

"It was totally fine. No problems at all. They were eating dinner and I just left everything exactly where you said."

"Good. Well, that's what you'll do every night. Then just take the car home and you're done. Anyway, have fun at Marshall's party tonight. I'd definitely go, but I have a bikini wax appointment I just can't cancel—do you believe they're booked for the next two months? And it's the middle of winter, too. It must be all the people who are going on winter vacations. Right? I just can't understand why every woman in New York needs a bikini wax right now. It's just so strange, but hey, what can you do?"

My head pounded to the tempo of her voice, and it seemed that no matter what I did or how I responded, I was sentenced to forever listen to her talk about bikini waxes. It may have been better to have her scream at me about interrupting Miranda's dinner.

"Yeah, what can you do? Well, I'd better get going, I told James I'd meet him at nine and it's already ten after. See you tomorrow?"

"Yep. Will do. Oh, just so you know, now that you're pretty much trained, you'll still get in at seven, but I don't come in until eight. Miranda knows—it's understood that the senior assistant comes in later since she works so much harder." I almost lunged at her throat. "So just go through the morning routine like I taught you. Call me if you have to, but you should know the drill by now. 'Bye!" She hopped into the backseat of the second car that was waiting in front of the building.

" 'Bye!" I trilled, a giant fake smile plastered on my face. The driver made a move to get out of the car and open the door for me, but I told him I was fine to let myself into the backseat. "The Plaza, please."

James had been waiting for me on the stairs outside even though it couldn't have been more than twenty degrees. He'd gone home to change and looked very, very skinny in black suede pants and a white ribbed tank top, which showed off his expertly applied midwinter bottle tan. I still looked appropriately amateurish in my Gap miniskirt.

"Hey, Andy, how'd the Book dropping-off go?" We waited in line to check our coats and I had immediately spotted Brad Pitt.

"Ohmigod, you're joking. Brad Pitt's here?"

"Yeah, well, Marshall does Jennifer's hair, natch. So she must be here also. Really, Andy, maybe next time you'll believe me when I tell you to stick with me. Let's get a drink."

The Reese and Johnny spottings had come back to back, and by the time one A.M. rolled around, I'd had four drinks and was happily gabbing away with a fashion assistant from *Vogue*. We were discussing bikini waxes. Passionately. And it didn't even bother me. *Christ*, I thought, as I weaved through the crowd looking for James, flashing a giant kiss-ass smile in the general direction of Jennifer Aniston when I passed by—*this isn't a half-bad party*. But I was tipsy, I had to be at work again in less than six hours, and I hadn't been home in nearly twenty-four, so when I spotted James making out with one of the colorists from Marshall's salon, I was just about to duck out when I felt a hand in the small of my back.

"Hey," said the gorgeous guy I'd spotted earlier lurking in the corner. I waited for him to realize that he'd approached the wrong girl, that I must've looked the same as his girlfriend from behind, but he just smiled even wider. "Not so talkative, are you?"

"Oh, and saying 'hey' makes you articulate, I guess?" *Andy! Shut your mouth!* I berated silently. *Some absolutely beautiful man approaches you out of the blue at a party full of celebrities and you tell him off right away?* But he didn't seem offended, and even though it didn't seem possible, his smile increased in size to an all-out grin.

"Sorry," I muttered while examining my nearly empty drink. "My name's Andrea. There. I think that's a much better way of beginning." I stuck out my hand and wondered what he wanted.

"Actually, I liked your way just fine. Name's Christian. A pleasure to meet you, Andy." He pushed a brown curl out of his left eye and took a swig from a bottle of Budweiser. He looked vaguely familiar, I decided, but I couldn't place him.

"Bud, huh?" I asked, pointing to his hand. "I didn't think they served something so lowbrow at a party like this."

He laughed, a deep, hearty laugh instead of the chuckle I'd expected. "You sure do say what you think, don't you?" I must've looked mortified, because he smiled again and said, "No, no, that's a good thing. And a rare thing, especially in this industry. I couldn't bring myself to drink champagne from a straw out of a minibottle, you know? Something fairly emasculating about that. So the bartender dug one of these out of the kitchen somewhere." Another curl push, but it fell back in his eye the moment he took his hand away. He pulled a pack of cigarettes from the pocket of his black sport coat and offered it to me. I took one and proceeded to drop it immediately, seizing the opportunity to examine him while I reached down to retrieve it.

It landed a few inches from his shiny, square-toed loafers that sported the irrefutable Gucci tassel, and on the way up I noticed that his Diesel jeans were the perfect parts faded, long, and wide enough at the bottom that they dragged a little behind the shiny loafers, the ends frayed from repeated interaction with the soles. A black belt, probably Gucci but thankfully not recognizable, kept the jeans riding in the perfect low spot below his waist, where he had tucked in a plain white cotton T-shirt—one that even though it easily could have been a Hanes was definitely an Armani or a Hugo Boss and was put in place only to offset his beautiful complexion. His black blazer looked just as expensive and well cut, perhaps even custom-made to fit his average-size but inexplicably sexy frame, and it was his green eyes that commanded the most attention. Seafoam, I thought, remembering the old J.Crew colors we'd loved so much in high school, or perhaps just a straightforward teal. The height, the build, the whole package looked vaguely like Alex, just with a whole lot more Euro style and a whole lot less Abercrombie. Slightly cooler, slightly better looking. Definitely older, right around thirty. And probably much too slick.

He immediately produced a flame and leaned in close to make sure my cigarette had caught. "So what brings you to a party like this, Andrea? Are you one of the lucky few who can call Marshall Madden her own?"

"No, I'm afraid not. At least not yet, although he wasn't all that subtle in telling me that I probably should be." I laughed, noticing for a brief moment that I was *desperate* to impress this stranger. "I work at *Runway*. One of the beauty guys dragged me here."

"Ah, *Runway* magazine, huh? Cool place to work, if you're into S&M and that sort of thing. How do you like it?"

I wasn't sure if he meant S&M or the job itself, but I considered the possibility that he got it, that he was enough of an insider to know that it wasn't exactly how it appeared to those on the outside. Perhaps I should charm him with the nightmare involved in dropping off the Book earlier that night? No, no, I had no idea who this guy was . . . for all I knew he also worked at *Runway* in some far-flung department I hadn't even seen yet, or maybe for another Elias-Clark magazine. Or maybe, just maybe, he was one of those sneaky *Page Six* reporters that Emily had so carefully warned me against. "They just appear," she'd said ominously. "They just appear and try to trick you into saying something juicy about Miranda or *Runway*. Just be aware." Between that and the tracking ID cards, I was quite sure that *Runway*'s surveillance put the mob to shame. The *Runway* Paranoid Turnaround was back.

"Yeah," I said, trying to sound casual and noncommittal. "It's a strange place. I'm not so into fashion—I'd actually rather be writing, but I guess it's not a bad start. What do you do?"

"I'm a writer."

"Oh, you are? That must be nice." I hoped I didn't sound quite as condescending as I felt, but it got to be really annoying when anyone and everyone in New York anointed himself or herself a writer or actor or poet or artist. *I used to write for the paper in college,* I thought to myself, *and hell, I even had an essay published in a monthly magazine once in high school.* Did that make me a writer? "What do you write?"

"Mostly literary fiction so far, but I'm actually working on my first historical novel." He took another swig and swatted yet again at that pesky but adorable curl.

"First historical" implied that there other were nonhistorical novels. Interesting. "What's it about?"

He thought for a moment and then said, "It's a story told from the perspective of a young woman, about what it was like to live in this country during World War Two. I'm still finishing my research, transcribing interviews and things like that, but the little writing I've done so far has come along. I think . . ."

He continued talking, but I'd already tuned him out. Holy shit. I recognized the book description immediately from a *New Yorker* article I'd just read. It seemed the entire book world was eagerly anticipating his next contribution and couldn't shut up about the realism with which he depicts his female heroine. I was standing at a party, casually chatting with Christian Collinsworth, the boy genius who'd first been published at the ripe old age of twenty from a Yale library cubicle. The critics had gone crazy over his first book, hailing it as one of the most significant literary achievements of the twentieth century, and he'd followed it up with two more since then, each spending more time on the bestseller list than the one before it. *The New Yorker* piece had included an interview in which the author had called Christian "not only a force for years to come" in the book industry, but one with "a hell of a look, a killer style, and enough natural charm that would ensure—in the unlikely event that his literary success did not—a lifetime of success with the ladies."

"Wow, that's really great," I said, all of a sudden feeling too tired to be witty or funny or cute. This guy was some big-time author—what the hell did he want with me, anyway? Probably just killing time before his girlfriend finished up her $10,000 per day modeling assignment and made her way over. *And what does it matter either way, Andrea?* I asked myself harshly. *In case you conveniently forgot, you do happen to have an incredibly kind and supportive and adorable boyfriend. Enough of this already!* I hastily made up a story about needing to get home right away, and Christian looked amused.

"You're scared of me," he stated factually, flashing me a teasing smile.

"Scared of you? Why on earth would *I* be scared of *you*? Unless there's some reason I should be . . ." I couldn't help but flirt back; he made it so easy.

He reached for my elbow and deftly turned me around. "Come on, I'll put you in a cab." And before I could say no, that I was perfectly fine to find my own way home, that it was nice to meet him but he'd better think again if he thought he was coming home with me, I was standing on the red-carpeted steps of the Plaza with him.

"Need a cab, folks?" the doorman asked us as we walked outside.

"Yes, please, one for the lady," Christian answered.

"No, I have a car, um, right over there," I said, pointing to the strip of 58th Street in front of the Paris Theatre where all the Town Cars had lined up.

I wasn't looking at him, but I could feel Christian smiling again. One of *those* smiles. He walked me over to the car and opened the door, swinging his arm gallantly toward the backseat.

"Thank you," I said formally, not a little awkwardly, while extending my hand. "It was really nice to meet you, Christian."

"And you, Andrea." He took the hand I'd intended him to shake and instead pressed it to his lips, leaving it there just a fraction of a second longer than he should have. "I do hope we see each other again soon." And by then I'd somehow made it into the backseat without tripping or otherwise humiliating myself and was concentrating on not blushing even though I could already feel that it was too late. He slammed the door and watched as the car pulled away.

It didn't seem strange this time that even though I hadn't so much as seen the interior of a Town Car two months earlier, I had personally had one chauffeuring me around for the past six hours, and that even though I'd never really met anyone even remotely famous before, I'd just rubbed elbows with Hollywood celebrities and had my hand nuzzled—yes, that was it, he'd nuzzled it—by one of the undisputed most eligible bachelors in New York City. *No, none of that really matters*, I reminded myself over and over again. *It's all a part of that world, and that world is no place you want to be. It might look like fun from here*, I thought, *but you'd be in way over your head.* But I stared at my hand anyway, trying to remember every last detail about the way he'd kissed it, and then thrust the offending hand into my bag and pulled out my phone. As I dialed Alex's number, I wondered what exactly, if anything, I would tell him.

9

It took me twelve weeks before I gorged myself on the seemingly limitless supply of designer clothes that *Runway* was just begging to provide for me. Twelve impossibly long weeks of fourteen-hour work days and never more than five hours of sleep at a time. Twelve miserable long weeks of being looked up and down from hair to shoes each and every day, and never receiving a single compliment or even merely the impression that I had passed. Twelve horrifically long weeks of feeling stupid, incompetent, and all-around moronic. And so I decided at the beginning of my fourth month (only nine more to go!) at *Runway* to be a new woman and start dressing the part.

Getting myself awake, dressed, and out the door prior to my twelve-week epiphany had sapped me completely—even I had to concede that it'd be easier to own a closetful of "appropriate" clothes. Until that point, putting on clothes had been the most stressful part of an already really lousy morning routine. The alarm went off so early that I couldn't bear to tell anyone what time I actually woke up, as though the mere mention of the words inflicted physical pain. Getting to work at seven A.M. was so difficult it bordered on funny. Sure, I'd been up and out a few times in my life by seven—perhaps sitting in an airport when I had to catch an early flight or having to finish studying for an exam that day. But mostly when I'd seen that hour of daylight from the outside it was because I hadn't yet found my way to bed from the night before, and the time didn't seem so bad when a full day of sleep stretched out ahead. This was different. This was constant, unrelenting, inhumane sleep deprivation, and no matter how many times I tried to go to bed before midnight, I never could. The past two weeks had been particularly rough since they were closing one of the spring issues, so I had to sit at work, waiting for the Book, until close to eleven some nights. By the time I would drop it off and get home, it was already midnight, and I still had to eat something and crawl out of my clothes before passing out.

Blaring static—the only thing I couldn't ignore—began at exactly 5:30 A.M. I would force a bare foot out from under the comforter and stretch my leg in the general direction of the alarm clock (which itself was placed strategically at the foot of my bed to force some movement), kicking aimlessly until I had made contact and the shrieking ceased. This continued, steadily and predictably, every seven minutes until 6:04 A.M., at which point I would inevitably panic and spring from bed to shower.

A tangle with my closet came next, usually between 6:31 and 6:37 A.M. Lily, herself not exactly fashion-conscious in her graduate student uniform of jeans, ratty L.L.Bean sweaters, and hemp necklaces, said every time I saw her, "I still don't understand what you wear to work. It's *Runway* magazine, for god's sake. Your clothes are as cute as the next girl's, Andy, but nothing you own is *Runway* material."

I didn't tell her that for the first few months I had risen extra early with an intense determination to coax *Runway* looks from my very Banana Republic–heavy wardrobe. I'd stood with my microwaved coffee for nearly

a half hour each morning, agonizing over boots and belts, wool, and mi-
crofiber. I'd change stockings five times until I finally had the right color,
only to berate myself that stockings of any style or color were *so not OK*.
The heels on my shoes were always too short, too stacked, too thick. I
didn't own a single thing in cashmere. I had not yet heard of thongs (!) and
therefore obsessed maniacally over how to banish panty lines, themselves
the focus of many a coffee-break critique. No matter how many times I
tried them on, I couldn't bring myself to wear a tube top to work.

And so after three months, I surrendered. I just got too tired. Emo-
tionally, physically, mentally, the daily wardrobe ordeal had sapped me
of all energy. Until, that is, I relented on the three-month anniversary of
my first day. It was a day like any other as I stood with my yellow "I ❤
Providence" mug in one hand, the other hand rifling through my Abercrombie favorites. *Why fight it?* I asked myself. Simply wearing their
clothes wouldn't necessarily mean I was a total sellout, would it? And besides, the comments on my current wardrobe were becoming more fre-
quent and vicious, and I had begun to wonder if my job was at risk. I
looked in the full-length mirror and had to laugh: the girl in the Maid-
enform bra (ich!) and cotton Jockey bikinis (double ich!) was trying to
look the part of *Runway*? Hah. Not with this shit. I was working at *Runway* magazine for chrissake—simply putting on anything that wasn't
torn, frayed, stained, or outgrown really wasn't going to cut it anymore.
I pushed aside my generic button-downs and ferreted out the tweedy
Prada skirt, black Prada turtleneck, and midcalf length Prada boots that
Jeffy had handed me one night while I waited for the Book.

"What's this?" I'd asked, unzipping the garment bag.

"This, Andy, is what you should be wearing if you don't want to get
fired." He smiled, but he wouldn't look me in the eye.

"I'm sorry?"

"Look, I just think you should know that your, uh, your look isn't
really going over well with everyone around here. Now, I know this stuff
gets expensive, but there's ways around that. I've got so much stuff in the
Closet that no one will notice if you need to, uh, borrow some of it sometimes." He made quote marks with his fingers around the word "borrow." "And, of course, you should be calling all the PR people and
getting your discount card for their designers. I only get thirty percent

off, but since you work for Miranda, I'll be surprised if they charge you for anything. There's no reason for this, uh, *Gap thing* you've got going on to continue."

I didn't explain that wearing Nine West instead of Manolos or jeans they sold in Macy's junior department but not anywhere on Barney's eighth floor of couture denim heaven had been my own attempt to show everyone that I wasn't seduced by all things *Runway*. Instead, I just nodded, noticing that he looked supremely uncomfortable having to tell me that I was humiliating myself every day. I wondered who had put him up to it. Emily? Or Miranda herself? Didn't really matter either way. Hell, I'd already survived three full months—if wearing a Prada turtleneck instead of one from Urban Outfitters was going to help me survive the next nine, then so be it. I decided I'd start putting together a new and improved wardrobe immediately.

I finally made it outside by 6:50 A.M., actually feeling pretty damn good about the way I looked. The guy in the breakfast cart closest to my apartment even whistled, and a woman stopped me before I'd taken ten steps and told me she had been eyeing those boots for three months now. *I could get used to this*, I thought. Everyone's got to put something on every day, and this sure felt a hell of a lot better than any of my stuff. As was now habit, I walked to the corner of Third Avenue and promptly hailed a cab and collapsed into the warm backseat, too tired to be thankful that I didn't have to join the commoners on the subway, and croaked, "Six-forty Madison. Quickly, please." The cabbie looked at me through the rearview—with a touch of sympathy, I swear—and said, "Ah, yes. Elias-Clark building," and we squealed left onto 97th Street and made another left onto Lex, flying through the lights until 59th Street, where we headed west to Madison. After exactly six minutes, since there was no traffic, we came to a screeching halt in front of the tall, thin, sleek monolith that set such a fine physical example for so many of its inhabitants. The fare came to $6.40 like it did every single morning, and I handed the cabbie a ten-dollar bill, like I did every single morning. "Keep the change," I sang, feeling the same joy I did every day when I saw their shock and happiness. "It's on *Runway*."

No problem there, that's for sure. It took all of a week on the job to see that accounting wasn't exactly a strong suit at Elias, not even a real priority. It was never a problem to write off ten-dollar cab rides each and every day. Another company might wonder what gave you the right to take a cab to work in the first place; Elias-Clark wondered why you had deigned to take a cab when there was a car service available. Something about gypping the company out of that extra ten bucks each day—even though I don't imagine anyone was directly suffering from my over-spending—made me feel a whole lot better. Some might have called it passive-aggressive rebellion. I called it getting even.

I bolted from the cab, still happy to make someone else's day, and walked toward 640 Madison. Although it was named the Elias-Clark building, JS Bergman, one of the most prestigious banks in the city (obviously), rented half of it. We didn't share anything with them, not even an elevator bank, but it didn't stop their rich bankers and our fashion beauties from checking each other out in the lobby.

"Hey, Andy. What's up? Long time, no see." The voice behind me sounded sheepish and unwilling, and I wondered why whoever it was didn't just leave me alone.

I'd been mentally preparing myself to start the morning routine with Eduardo when I'd heard my name, and I turned to see Benjamin, one of Lily's many ex-boyfriends from college, slumped against the building just outside the entrance, not even seeming to notice that he was sitting on the sidewalk. He was only one of many of Lily's guys, but he'd been the first one she'd really, genuinely liked. I hadn't spoken to good old Benji (he loathed being called that) since Lily had walked in on him having sex with two girls from her a capella singing group. Walked right into his off-campus apartment and found him sprawled out in his living room with one soprano and a contralto, mousy girls who never did manage to look at Lily again. I'd tried to convince her it was just a college prank, but she didn't buy it. Cried for days, and made me promise not to tell anyone what she'd discovered. I didn't have to tell anyone, though, be-cause he did—bragged to anyone who would listen about how he'd "nailed two singing geeks," as he'd put it, while "a third one watched." He'd made it sound as though Lily had been there the entire time, agree-ably perched on the couch and watching her big, bad man go about be-ing manly. Lily had sworn to never let herself really fall for another guy, and so far seemed to be keeping her promise. She slept with plenty of them, but she sure didn't let them stick around long enough to actually run the risk of discovering something likable about them.

I looked at him again and tried to find the old Benji in this guy's face. He had been athletic and cute. Just a normal guy. But Bergman had turned him into a shell of a human. He was wearing an oversize, wrinkled suit and looked as though he was hoping to suck crack cocaine out of his Marlboro. He seemed already overworked even though it was only seven o'clock, and this made me feel better. Because it was payback for being an asshole to Lily, and because I wasn't the only one dragging myself to work at such an obscene hour. He was probably getting paid $150,000 a year to be so miserable, but whatever, at least I wasn't alone.

Benji saluted me with his lit cigarette, glowing eerily in the still dark winter morning, and motioned for me to come over. I was nervous I'd be late, but Eduardo gave me his "Don't worry, she's not here yet—you're fine" look and I walked over to Benji. He looked bleary-eyed and hopeless. He probably thought *he* had a tyrannical boss. Hah! If only he knew. I wanted to laugh out loud.

"Hey, I noticed you're the only one here this early every day," he muttered at me while I dug around in my bag for lipstick before hitting the elevators. "What's the deal?"

He looked so tired, so beaten-down, that I felt a surge of sympathy and kindness. But then I felt my legs nearly give out from exhaustion, and I remembered the way Lily had looked when one of Benji's dumb lacrosse buddies had asked if she'd been happy to watch or really actually wanted to join in, and I lost my cool.

"Well, my deal is that I work for a rather demanding woman, and I need to get here two and a half hours before the rest of the goddamn magazine so that I'm prepared for her," I said, my tone dripping with anger and sarcasm.

"Whoa. Just asking. Sorry, though, it sounds pretty bad. Which one do you work for?"

"I work for Miranda Priestly," I said, and prayed for a nonreaction. Something about having a seemingly well-educated, successful professional have no idea who Miranda was made me very, very happy. Delighted almost. And luckily, this one didn't let me down. He shrugged and inhaled and looked at me expectantly.

"She's the editor in chief of *Runway*," I lowered my voice and began with glee, "and pretty much the biggest bitch I've ever met. I mean, I've honestly never met anyone like her. She's really not even human." I had a litany of complaints I would've liked to have dumped on Benji, but the *Runway* Paranoid Turnaround came on full-force. I became immediately nervous, almost paranoid, convinced that this unknowing, uncaring person was somehow one of Miranda's lackeys, sent to spy on me from the *Observer* or *Page Six*. I knew it was ridiculous, completely absurd. After all, I had personally known Benji for years now and was quite sure he wasn't working for Miranda in any capacity. Just not totally sure. After all, how could you be totally sure? And who knew who could be standing behind me at that very second, overhearing every one of my nasty words? Damage control was required immediately.

"Of course, she IS the most powerful woman in fashion and publishing, and you just can't get to the top of two major industries in New York City handing out candy all day long. Um, it's understandable that she's a little tough to work for, you know? I would be, too. Yeah, so, um, I have to run now. Good seeing you again." And I ducked away, as I often had the past few weeks when I found myself talking to someone other than Lily or Alex or my parents and I couldn't help myself from bashing the witch.

"Hey, don't feel too bad," he called after me as I headed toward the elevator bank. "I've been here since last Thursday morning." And with that, he dropped his smoldering butt and half-heartedly stamped it into the cement.

"Morning, Eduardo," I said, looking at him with my best tired, pathetic eyes. "I fucking hate Mondays."

"Hey, buddy, don't worry. At least you beat her here this morning," he said, smiling. He was referring, of course, to those miserable mornings when Miranda would show up at five A.M. and need to be escorted upstairs since she refused to carry an access card. She'd then pace the office, calling Emily and me over and over until one of us could manage to wake up, get ready, and get to work as if a national security emergency were unfolding.

I pushed against the turnstile, praying that this Monday would be the exception, that he'd let me pass without a performance. Negative.

"Yo, tell me what you want, what you really, really want," he sang with his huge, toothy smile and Spanish accent. And all the pleasure of making the cabbie happy and finding out that I had arrived ahead of Miranda vanished. I was left, as I was every morning, wanting to reach across the security counter and tear the flesh from Eduardo's face. But since I was such a good sport and he was one of my only friends in the place, I weakly acquiesced. *"I'll tell you what I want, what I really, really want, I wanna—I wanna—I wanna—I wanna—I really, really, really wanna zigga zig aaaaaahhhh,"* I sang meekly in a pitiful tribute to the Spice Girls' nineties hit. And once again, Eduardo grinned and buzzed me through.

"Hey, don't forget: July sixteenth!" he called after me.

"I know, July sixteenth . . ." I called back, a reference to our shared birthdays. I don't remember how or why he had discovered my birthdate, but he adored that we had the same one. And for some inexplicable reason, it became a part of our personal morning ritual. Every single goddamn day.

There were eight elevators on the Elias-Clark side, half for floors one to seventeen, half for seventeen and up. Only the first bank really mattered since most of the big names were on the first seventeen floors; they advertised their presence with illuminated panels over the elevator doors. There was a free, state-of-the-art gym on the second floor for employees, complete with a full Nautilus circuit and at least a hundred Stairmasters, treadmills, and elliptical machines. The locker rooms had saunas, hot tubs, steam rooms, and attendants in maids' uniforms, and a salon offered emergency manicures, pedicures, and facials. There was even complimentary towel service, or so I'd heard—not only did I not have the time, the place was always too damn crowded between the hours of six A.M. and ten P.M. to so much as walk around. Writers and editors and sales assistants called three days ahead of time to book themselves into the yoga or kick-boxing classes, and even then they lost their place if they didn't get there fifteen minutes in advance. Like nearly everything at Elias-Clark designed to make employees' lives better, it just stressed me out.

I'd heard a rumor that there was a daycare center in the basement, but I didn't know anyone who actually had children, so I still wasn't entirely positive. The real action began on the third floor with the dining room, where so far Miranda had refused to eat among the peons unless she was lunching with Irv Ravitz, Elias's CEO, who liked to eat there in a show of unity with his employees.

Up, up, up we went, past all the other famous titles. Most of them had to share floors, with one flanking each side of the receptionist's desk, facing off behind separate glass doors. I hopped off at the seventeenth floor, checking my butt in the reflection of the door's glass. In a stroke of empathy and genius, the architect had kindly left mirrors out of the elevators in 640 Madison. As usual, I'd forgotten my electronic ID card— the very same one that tracked all our movements, purchases, and absences in the building—and had to break onto the floor. Sophy didn't come in until nine, so I had to bend down under her desk, find the button that would release the glass doors, and sprint from the middle of the reception area to the doors and yank them open before they snapped locked again. Sometimes I'd have to do this three or four times until I finally caught it, but today I made it on my second attempt.

The floor was always dark when I arrived, and I took the same route to my desk every morning. To my left when I walked in was the advertising department, the girls who most loved adorning themselves in Chloé T-shirts and spike-heeled boots while handing out business cards that screamed "Runway." They were removed, wholly and entirely, from anything and everything that took place on the editorial side of the floor: it was editorial that picked the clothes for the fashion spreads, wooed the good writers, matched the accessories to the outfits, interviewed the models, edited the copy, designed the layouts, and hired the photographers. Editorial traveled to hot spots around the world for shoots, got free gifts and discounts from all the designers, hunted for trends, and went to parties at Pastis and Float because they "had to check out what people were wearing."

Ad sales was left to try and sell ad space. Sometimes they threw promotional parties, but they were celebrity-free and therefore boring to

New York's hipster scene (or so Emily had sneeringly told me). My phone would ring off the hook on a day during a *Runway* ad sales party with people I didn't know really well looking for an invite. "Um, like, I hear *Runway*'s having a party tonight. Why am I not invited?" I always found out from someone on the outside that there was a party that night: editorial was never invited because they wouldn't go anyway. As if it wasn't enough for the *Runway* girls to mock, terrorize, and ostracize any and every person who wasn't one of them, they had to create internal class lines as well.

The ad sales department gave way to a long, narrow hallway. It seemed to stretch forever before arriving at a tiny kitchen on the left side. Here were an assortment of coffees and teas, a fridge for stored lunches— all superfluous, since Starbucks had a monopoly on employees' daily caffeine fixes and all meals were carefully selected in the dining room or ordered in from any one of a thousand midtown takeout places. But it was a nice touch, almost cute; it said, *"Hey, look at us, we have Lipton tea packets and Sweet'N Lows and even a microwave in case you want to warm up some of last night's dinner! We're just like everyone else!"*

I finally made it to Miranda's enclave at 7:05, so tired I could barely move. But as with everything, there was yet another routine that I never thought to question or alter, so I began in earnest. I unlocked her office and turned on all the lights. It was still dark outside, and I loved the drama of standing in the dark in the power monger's office, staring out at a flashing and restless New York City and picturing myself in one of those movies (take your pick—any that have lovers embracing on the expansive terrace of his $6 million apartment with views of the river), feeling on top of the world. And then the lights would blaze forth, and my fantasy was over. The anything-is-possible feel of New York at dawn vanished, and the identical, grinning faces of Caroline and Cassidy were all I could see.

Next I unlocked the closet in our outer office area, the place where I hung her coat (and mine if she wasn't wearing a fur that day—Miranda didn't like Emily's or my pedestrian wools hanging next to her minks) and where we kept a number of supplies: castoff coats and clothes that were worth tens of thousands of dollars, some new dry cleaning that had been delivered to the office but not yet brought up to Miranda's apartment, at least two hundred of the infamous white Hermès scarves. I'd heard that Hermès had decided to discontinue her particular style last year, a simple and elegant white silk square. Someone at the company felt they owed Miranda an explanation and actually called to apologize to her. Unsurprisingly, she'd coldly told them how disappointed she was and promptly purchased their entire remaining stock. About five hundred of the scarves had been delivered to the office a couple years before I'd gotten there, and we were now down to less than half. Miranda left them everywhere: restaurants, movies, fashion shows, weekly meetings, taxis. She left them on airplanes, at her daughters' school, on the tennis court. Of course, she always had one stylishly incorporated into her outfit—I'd yet to see her outside her own home without one. But that didn't explain where they all went. Perhaps she thought they were handkerchiefs? Or maybe she liked jotting notes on silk instead of paper? Whatever it was, she seemed to truly believe they were disposable, and none of us knew how to tell her otherwise. Elias-Clark had paid a couple hundred dollars for each one, but no matter: we handed them out to her as though they were Kleenex. At the rate she was going, in under two years, Miranda was due to run out.

I'd arranged the stiff orange boxes on the ready-to-distribute shelf of the closet, where they never remained for very long. Every third or fourth day, she'd prepare to leave for lunch and sigh, "Ahn-dre-ah, hand me a scarf." I comforted myself with the thought that I'd be long gone by the time she ran out of them completely. Whoever was unlucky enough to be around would have to tell her that there were no more white Hermès scarves, and that none could be made, shipped, created, formed, mailed, ordered, or mandated. The mere thought was terrifying.

Just as I got the closet and office opened, Uri called.

"Andrea? Hello, hello. It is Uri. Could you come downstairs please? I am on Fifty-eighth Street, closer to Park Avenue, right in front of the New York Sports Club. I have things for you."

This call was a good although imperfect way of telling me that Miranda would be arriving somewhat soon. Maybe. Most mornings she sent Uri ahead to the office with her things, an assortment of dirty clothes that needed dry cleaning, any copy she'd taken home to read, magazines, shoes or bags that needed to be fixed, and the Book. This way, she could have me meet the car and carry up all of these rather mundane things ahead of schedule and deal with them before she stepped into the office. She tended to follow her stuff by about a half hour, since Uri would drop off her things and then go pick her up from wherever she might be hiding that morning.

She herself could be anywhere, since, according to Emily, she never slept. I didn't believe it until I started getting to the office ahead of Emily and would be the first to listen to the voice mail. Every night, without exception, Miranda would leave eight to ten ambiguous messages for us between the hours of one and six in the morning. Things like, "Cassidy wants one of those nylon bags all the little girls are carrying. Order her one in the medium size and a color she'd like," and "I'll be needing the address and phone number of that antique store in the seventies, the one where I saw the vintage dresser." As though we knew which nylon bags were all the rage among ten-year-olds or at which one of four hundred antique stores in the seventies—east or west, by the way?—she happened to spot something she liked at some point in the past fifteen years. But each morning I faithfully listened to and transcribed those messages, hitting "replay" over and over and over again, trying to make sense of the accent and interpret the clues in order to avoid asking Miranda directly for more information.

Once, I made the mistake of suggesting that we actually ask Miranda to provide a few more details, only to be met with one of Emily's withering looks. Questioning Miranda was apparently off-limits. Better to muddle through and wait to be told how off the mark our results were. To locate the vintage dresser that had caught Miranda's eye, I had spent two and a half days in a limo, cruising around Manhattan, through the seventies on both sides of the park. I ruled out York Avenue (too residential) and proceeded up First, down Second, up Third, down Lex. I skipped Park (again, too residential) but continued up Madison, and then repeated a similar process on the West Side. Pen poised, eyes peeled, phone book open in my lap, ready to jump out at the first sight of a store that sold antiques. I graced every single antique store—and not a few regular furniture stores—with a personal visit. By store number four, I had it down to an art form.

"Hi, do you sell any vintage dressers?" I'd practically scream the second they buzzed me inside. By the sixth store I wasn't even bothering to move in from the doorway. Some snotty salesperson inevitably looked me up and down—I couldn't escape it!—sizing me up to decide if I was someone to be bothered with. Most would notice the waiting Town Car at this point and grudgingly provide me with a yes or no answer, although some wanted detailed descriptions of the dresser I was looking for.

If they admitted to selling something that fit my two-word requirement, I would immediately follow up with a curt "Has Miranda Priestly been here recently?" If they hadn't thought I was crazy at this point, they now looked ready to call security. A few had never heard her name, which was fantastic both because it was rejuvenating to see firsthand that there were still normally functioning human beings whose lives weren't dominated by her, and also because I could promptly leave without further discussion. The pathetic majority who recognized the name became instantly curious. Some wondered which gossip column I wrote for. But regardless of whatever story I made up, no one had seen her in their shop (with the exception of three stores who hadn't "seen Ms. Priestly in months, and oh, how we miss her! Please do tell her that Franck/Charlotte/Sarabeth sends his/her love!").

When I hadn't located the shop by noon of the third day, Emily finally gave me the green light to come to the office and ask Miranda for clarification. I started sweating when the car pulled in front of the building. I threatened to climb over the turnstile if Eduardo didn't let me pass without a performance. By the time I reached our floor, the sweat had soaked through my shirt. Hands started shaking the moment I entered the office suite, and the perfectly prepared speech (*Hello, Miranda. I'm fine, thanks so much for asking. How are you? Listen, I just wanted to let you know that I've been trying very hard to locate the antique store you described, but I haven't had much luck. Perhaps you could tell me whether it's on the east or west side of Manhattan? Or maybe you even recall the name?*) simply vanished into the fickle regions of my very nervous brain. Against all protocol, I didn't post my question on the Bulletin; I requested permission to approach her at her desk and—probably because she was so shocked I'd had the nerve to speak without being spoken to—she granted it. To make a long story short, Miranda sighed and patronized and condescended and insulted in every delightful way of hers but finally opened her black leather Hermès planner (tied shut inconveniently but chicly with a white Hermès scarf) and produced . . . the business card for the store.

"I left this information on the recording for you, Ahn-dre-ah. I suppose it would have been too much trouble to write it down?" And even though the yearning to make decorative paper-cut designs all over her face with the aforementioned business card filled my entire being, I simply nodded and agreed. It wasn't until I looked down at the card that I noticed the address: 244 East 68th Street. Naturally. East or west or Second Avenue or Amsterdam wouldn't have made a damn bit of difference, because the store I'd just dedicated the past thirty-three working hours to locating wasn't even in the seventies.

I thought of this as I wrote down the last of Miranda's late-night requests before racing downstairs to meet Uri at our designated area. Every morning he described where he parked in great detail so I could theoretically meet him at the car. But every morning, no matter how fast I made it downstairs, he'd bring everything inside himself so I wouldn't have to race up and down the streets searching for him. I was delighted to see that today was no exception: he was leaning against a lobby turnstile, holding bags and clothes and books in his arms like a benevolent, generous grandfather.

"Don't you run to me, you hear?" he said in his thick Russian accent. "All day long, you run, run, run. She makes you work very, very hard. This is why I bring the tings to you," he said, helping me get a grip on the overflowing bags and boxes. "You be a good girl, you hear, and have a nice day."

I shot him a grateful look, glared at Eduardo semijokingly—my way of saying, "I will fucking kill you if you even *think* of asking me to strike a pose right now"—and softened a bit when he buzzed me through the turnstiles, comment-free. I miraculously remembered to stop by the lobby newsstand, where Ahmed piled all of Miranda's requested morning papers into my arms. Although the mailroom delivered each to Miranda's desk by nine each day, I was still to purchase a full second set every morning to help minimize the risk that she would spend a single second in her office without her papers. Same with the weekly magazines. No one seemed to mind that we charged nine newspapers a day and seven magazines a week for someone who read only the gossip and fashion pages.

I dumped all her stuff on the floor under my desk. It was time for the first round of ordering. I dialed the number I'd memorized long ago for Mangia, a gourmet takeout place in midtown, and, as usual, Jorge answered.

"Hi, pumpkin, it's me," I'd say, propping the phone against my shoulder so I could start logging into Hotmail. "Let's get this day started." Jorge and I were friends. Talking three, four, five times a morning had a funny way of bonding two people rather quickly.

"Hey, baby, I'll send one of the boys over right away. Is she there yet?" he asked, understanding that "she" was my lunatic boss and that she worked for *Runway*, but not quite understanding who exactly would be consuming the breakfast I had just ordered. Jorge was one of my morning men, as I liked to call them. Eduardo, Uri, Jorge, and Ahmed gave a decent as possible start to my day. They were deliciously unaffiliated with *Runway*, even though their separate existences in my life were solely meant to make its editor's life more perfect. Not a single one of them truly understood Miranda's power and prestige.

Breakfast number one would be on its way to 640 Madison in seconds, and the chances were good I'd have to throw it out. Miranda ate four slices of greasy, fatty bacon, two sausage links, and a soft cheese Danish every morning, and washed it down with a tall latte from Starbucks (two raw sugars, remember!). As far as I could tell, the office was divided on whether she was permanently on the Atkins diet or just lucky enough to have a superhuman metabolism, the result of some pretty fantastic genes. Either way, she thought nothing of devouring the fattiest, most sickeningly unhealthy foods—even though the rest of us weren't exactly afforded the same luxury. Since nothing stayed hot for more than ten minutes after it arrived, I'd keep reordering and tossing until she showed up. I could get away with microwaving each meal one time, but that bought me only an extra five minutes, and she could usually tell. ("Ahn-dre-ah, this is vile. Get me a fresh breakfast at once.") I would order and reorder every twenty minutes or so until she called from her cell phone and told me to order her breakfast ("Ahn-dre-ah, I'll be at the office shortly. Order my breakfast"). Of course, this was usually only a two- or three-minute warning, so the preordering was necessary both because of the short warning and in the rather common event that she didn't bother to call at all. If I'd done my job, by the time her actual call for breakfast had come, I'd already have two or three on the way.

The phone rang. It had to be her, too early to be anyone else.

"Miranda Priestly's office," I chirped, bracing myself for the iciness.

"Emily, I'll be there in ten minutes and I'd like my breakfast to be ready."

She had taken to calling both Emily and me "Emily," suggesting, quite rightly, that we were indistinguishable from each other and completely interchangeable. Somewhere in the back of my mind I was offended, but I'd grown accustomed to it at this point. And besides, I was too tired to really care about something as incidental as my name.

"Yes, Miranda, right away." But she had already hung up. The real Emily walked into the office.

"Hey, is she here?" she whispered, looking furtively toward Miranda's office as she always did, without a hello or a good morning, just like her mentor.

"Nope, but she just called and she'll be here in ten. I'll be back."

I quickly transferred my cell phone and cigarettes to my coat pocket and ran. I had only a few minutes to get downstairs, cross Madison, and jump the line at Starbucks—and suck down my first precious cigarette of the day while in transit. Stamping out the last embers, I stumbled into the Starbucks at 57th and Lex and surveyed the line. If it was fewer than eight or so people, I preferred to wait like a normal person. Like most days, however, the line today was twenty or more poor professional souls, wearily waiting in line for their expensive caffeine fix, and I had to jump in front of them. It was not something I relished, but Miranda didn't seem to understand that the latte I presented to her each morning could not only *not* be delivered but could easily take a half hour at prime time to purchase. A couple weeks of shrill, angry phone calls on my cell phone ("Ahn-dre-ah, I simply do not understand. I called you a full twenty-five minutes ago to tell you I'd be in, and my breakfast is not ready. This is unacceptable."), and I had spoken to the franchise manager.

"Um, hi. Thanks for taking a minute to talk with me," I said to the petite black woman who was in charge. "I know this sounds absolutely crazy, but I was wondering if we could work something out in terms of me having to wait in line." I went on to explain, as best I could, that I work for a rather important, unreasonable person who doesn't like to wait for her morning coffee, and was there any way I could walk ahead of the line, subtly, of course, and have someone prepare my order immediately? By some stroke of dumb luck, Marion, the manager, was going to FIT at night for a degree in fashion merchandising.

"Ohmigod, are you kidding? You work for Miranda Priestly? And she drinks our lattes? A tall? Every morning? Unbelievable. Oh, yes, yes, of course! I'll tell everyone to help you right away. Don't worry about a thing. She is, like, the most powerful person in fashion," Marion gushed as I forced myself to nod enthusiastically.

And so it came that I could, at will, bypass a long line of tired, aggressive, self-righteous New Yorkers and order before those who had been waiting for many, many minutes. It didn't make me feel good or important or even cool, and I always dreaded the days I had to do it. When the lines were hellishly long like the one today—snaking around the entire counter and pushing its way outside—I felt even worse and knew I'd be walking out with a full load. My head was pounding at this point, and my eyes already felt heavy and dry. I tried to forget that this was my life, the reason I'd spent four long years memorizing poems and examining prose, the result of good grades and lots of kissing up. Instead, I ordered Miranda's tall latte from one of the new baristas and added a few drinks of my own. A grande Amaretto Cappuccino, a Mocha Frappuccino, and a Caramel Macchiato landed in my four-cup carrier, along with a half-dozen muffins and croissants. The grand total came to $28.83, and I made sure to tuck my receipt into the already bulging, specially designated receipt section of my wallet, all of which would be reimbursed by the always reliable Elias-Clark.

I had to hurry now, as it was already twelve minutes since Miranda had called and I knew she'd probably be sitting there, seething, wondering exactly where I disappeared to every morning—the Starbucks logo on the side of the cup didn't ever clue her in. But before I could pick up all the stuff from the counter, my phone rang. And as usual, my heart lurched. I knew it was her, absolutely, positively knew it, but it scared me nonetheless. The caller ID confirmed my suspicion, and I was surprised to hear that it was Emily, calling from Miranda's line.

"She's here and she's pissed," Emily whispered. "You've got to get back here."

"I'm doing everything I can," I growled, trying to balance the carrying tray and the bag of baked goods on one arm and hold the phone with the other.

And thus the basic root of the hatred that existed between Emily and me. Since she was in the "senior" assistant position, I was more of Miranda's personal assistant, there to fetch those coffees and meals, help her kids with their homework, and run all over the city to retrieve the perfect dishes for her dinner parties. Emily did her expenses, made her travel arrangements, and—the biggest job of all—put through her personal clothing order every few months. So when I was out gathering the goodies each morning, Emily was left alone to handle all of the ringing phone lines and an alert, early-morning Miranda and all of her demands. I hated her for being able to wear sleeveless shirts to work, where she wouldn't ever have to leave the warm office six times a day to race around New York fetching, searching, hunting, gathering. She hated me for having excuses to leave the office, where she knew I always took longer than necessary to talk on my cell phone and smoke cigarettes.

The walk back to the building usually took longer than the walk to Starbucks, since I had to distribute my coffees and snacks. I preferred to hand them out to the homeless, a small band of regulars who hung out on stoops and slept in doorways on 57th Street, thumbing the city's attempts to "clean them up." The police always hustled them away before rush hour kicked into high gear, but they were still hanging out when I was doing the day's first coffee run. There was something so fantastic—invigorating, really—in making sure that these overpriced, Elias-sponsored coffee faves made it into the hands of the city's most undesirable people.

The urine-soaked man who slept outside the Chase Bank got a daily Mocha Frappuccino. He never actually woke up to accept it, but I left it (with a straw, of course) next to his left elbow each morning, and it was often gone—along with him—when I returned for my next coffee run a few hours later.

The old lady who propped herself up on her cart and set out a cardboard sign that read NO HOME/CAN CLEAN/NEED FOOD got the Caramel Macchiato. I soon found her name was Theresa, and I used to buy her a tall latte, like Miranda's. She always said thank you, but she never made a move to taste it while it was still hot. When I finally asked her if she wanted me to stop bringing them, she vigorously shook her head and mumbled that she hates to be picky, but she'd actually like something sweeter, that the coffee was too strong. The next day I had her coffee flavored with vanilla and topped with whipped cream. Was this better? Oh yes, it was much, much better, but maybe now it was a touch too sweet. One more day and I finally got it right: it turns out Theresa liked her coffee unflavored, topped with whipped cream and some caramel syrup. She flashed a near-toothless smile and began guzzling it each and every day, the moment I handed it to her.

The third coffee went to Rio, the Nigerian who sold CDs off a blanket. He didn't appear to be homeless, but he walked over to me one morning when I was handing Theresa her daily fix and said, or, rather, sang, "Yo, yo, yo, you like the Starbucks fairy or what? Where's mine?" I handed him a grande Amaretto Cappuccino the next day, and we'd been friends ever since.

I expensed twenty-four dollars more every day on coffee than necessary (Miranda's single latte should've cost a mere four dollars) to take yet another passive-aggressive swipe at the company, my personal reprimand to them for Miranda Priestly's free rein. I handed them out to the filthy, the smelly, and the crazy because that—and not the wasted money—was what would *really* piss them off.

By the time I made it to the lobby, Pedro, the heavily accented Mexican delivery boy from Mangia, was chatting in Spanish with Eduardo near the elevator bank.

"Hey, here's our girlie," said Pedro as a few Clackers peered over at us. "I've got the usual: bacon, sausage, and one nasty-looking cheese thing. You only ordered one today! Don't know how you eat this shit and stay so thin, girl." He grinned. I suppressed the urge to tell him he didn't have a clue what thin looked like. Pedro knew full well that I was not the one eating his breakfasts, but like every one of the dozen or so people I spoke to before eight A.M. each day, he didn't really know the details. I handed him a ten, as usual, for the $3.99 breakfast, and headed upstairs.

She was on the phone when I entered the office, her snakeskin Gucci trench draped across the top of my desk. My blood pressure increased tenfold. Would it kill her to take the extra two steps over to the closet, open it, and hang up her own coat? Why did she have to take it off and fling it over my desk? I put down the latte, looked over at Emily, who was too busy answering three phone lines to notice me, and hung up the snakeskin. I shook off my own coat and bent down to toss it underneath my desk, since mine might infect hers if they mingled in the closet.

I grabbed two raw sugars, a stirrer, and a napkin from a stock I kept in my desk drawer and wrapped them all together. I briefly considered spitting in the drink but was able to restrain myself. Next, I pulled a small china plate from the overhead bin and dumped out the greasy meat and the oozing Danish, wiping my hands on her dirty dry cleaning, which was hidden beneath my desk so she couldn't see it hadn't been picked up yet. I was theoretically supposed to clean her plate each day in the sink in our mock-up kitchen, but I just couldn't bring myself to bother. The humiliation of doing her dishes in front of everyone prompted me to wipe it down with tissues after each meal and scrape off any leftover cheese with my fingernails. If it was really dirty or had been sitting for a long time, I'd open a bottle of the Pellegrino we kept by the case and dump a little bit on. I figured she should be thankful I wasn't using a spritz or two of desk cleaner. I was reasonably sure that I had reached a new moral low—what was worrisome was that I'd sunk to it so naturally.

"Remember, I want my girls smiling," she was saying into the phone. I could tell from her tone she was talking to Lucia, the fashion director who'd be in charge of the upcoming Brazil shoot, about how the models should appear. "Happy, lots of teeth, clean healthy girls. No brooding, no anger, no frowning, no dark makeup. I want them shining. I mean it, Lucia: I will accept nothing less."

I set the plate on the edge of her desk and placed the latte and the napkin with all necessary accessories next to it. She didn't look at me. I paused for a moment to see if she'd hand me a pile of papers off her desk, things to fax or find or file, but she ignored me and I walked out. Eight-thirty A.M. I'd been awake now for three full hours, felt like I'd already worked for twelve, and could finally sit down for the very first time all morning. Just as I was logging on to Hotmail, anticipating some fun e-mails from people on the outside, she walked out. The belted jacket cinched her already tiny waist and complemented the perfectly fitted pencil skirt she wore beneath it. She looked dynamite.

"Ahn-dre-ah. The latte is ice cold. I don't understand why. You were certainly gone long enough! Bring me another."

I inhaled deeply and concentrated on keeping the look of hatred off my face. Miranda set the offending latte on my desk and flipped through the new issue of *Vanity Fair* that a staffer had set on the table for her. I could feel Emily watching me and knew her look would be one of sympathy and anger: she felt bad that I had to repeat the hellish ordeal all over again, but she hated me for daring to be upset about it. After all, wouldn't a million girls die for my job?

And so with an audible sigh—something I'd perfected lately, so it was just enough Miranda could hear but not nearly enough she could ever call me on it—I once again put on my coat and willed my legs to move toward the elevators. It was going to be another long, long day.

The second coffee run in twenty minutes went much more smoothly; the lines at Starbucks had thinned a little and Marion had come on duty. She herself got to work on a tall latte as soon as I walked in the door. I didn't bother overspending on a larger order this time because I was too desperate to just get back and sit down, but I did add *venti* cappuccinos for both Emily and me. Just as I was paying for the coffee, my phone rang. Goddamn it to hell, this woman was impossible. Insatiable, impatient, impossible. I hadn't been gone for more than four minutes; she couldn't possibly be freaking out yet. Again, I balanced my tray in one hand and pulled my phone from my coat pocket. I'd already decided that such behavior on her part warranted my having another cigarette—if just to hold up her coffee a few minutes longer—when I saw that it was Lily calling from her home phone.

"Hey, bad time?" she asked, sounding excited. I looked at my watch and saw that she should've been in class.

"Um, sort of. I'm on my second coffee run, which is really great. I'm really, really enjoying my self, just in case you were wondering. What's up? Don't you have class now?"

"Yeah, but I went out with Pink-Shirt Boy again last night and we each drank a few too many margaritas. Like, eight too many. He's still passed out here, so I can't just leave him. But that's not why I'm calling."

"Yeah?" I was barely listening, since one of the cappuccinos was starting to leak and I had the phone wedged in between my neck and my shoulder as I used my one free hand to pluck a cigarette from the box and light it.

"My landlord had the nerve to knock on my door at eight o'clock this morning to tell me that I'm being evicted," she said with not a little bit of glee in her voice.

"Evicted? Lil, why? What are you going to do?"

"It seems they finally caught on that I'm not Sandra Gers and that she hasn't lived here in six months. Since she's technically not family, she wasn't allowed to pass down the rent-controlled apartment to me. I knew that, of course, so I've just been saying I'm her. I don't really know how they found out. But whatev, it doesn't really matter, because now you and I can live together! Your lease with Shanti and Kendra is just month by month, right? You subletted because you had no place to live, right?"

"Right."

"Well, now you do! We can get a place together, anywhere we like!"

"That's great!" It sounded hollow to my ears even though I was genuinely excited.

"So you're up for it?" she asked, her enthusiasm sounding a bit dampened.

"Lil, definitely. Honestly, it's an awesome idea. I don't mean to sound negative, it's just that it's sleeting and I'm standing outside and I have burning hot coffee running down my left arm . . ." *Beep-beep.* The other line rang, and even though I almost burned my neck with the lit end of the cigarette while trying to pull my phone away from my ear, I was able to see that it was Emily calling.

"Shit, Lil, it's Miranda calling. I've got to run. But congrats on getting evicted! I'm so excited for us. I'll call you later, OK?"

"OK, I'll talk to—"

I had already clicked over and mentally prepared myself for the barrage.

"Me again," Emily said tightly. "What the hell is going on? It's a fucking coffee, for chrissake. You forget that I used to do your job, and I know it doesn't take that long to—"

"What?" I said loudly, holding a few fingers over the microphone on the receiver. "What'd you say? I can't hear you. Well, if you can hear me, I'll be back in just a minute!" And I clicked my phone shut and buried it deep in my pocket. And even though I had at least half a Marlboro left, I dropped it on the sidewalk and ran back to work.

Miranda deigned to accept this slightly warmer latte and even gave us a few moments of peace between ten and eleven, when she sat in her office with the door closed, cooing to B-DAD. I'd officially met him for the first time the week before, when I'd dropped the Book off that Wednesday night around nine. He had been removing his coat from the closet in the foyer and spent the next ten minutes referring to himself in the third person. Since that meeting, he had paid me extra-special attention when I let myself in each night, always taking a few minutes to ask about my day or compliment me on a job well done. Naturally, none of these niceties seemed to rub off on his wife, but at least he was pleasant to be around.

I was just about to begin calling some of the PR people to see about getting a few more decent clothes to wear to work when Miranda's voice shook me from my thoughts. "Emily, I'd like my lunch." She had called from her office to no one in particular, since Emily could mean either of us. The real Emily looked at me and nodded, and I knew it was OK to move. The number for Smith and Wollensky was programmed into my desk phone, and I recognized the voice on the other end as the new girl.

"Hey, Kim, it's Andrea from Miranda Priestly's office. Is Sebastian there?"

"Oh, hi, um, what did you say your name was again?" No matter that I called at the exact same time, twice a week, and had already identified myself—she always acted as though we'd never spoken.

"From Miranda Priestly's office. At *Runway*. Listen, I don't mean to be rude"—*yes, actually, I do*—"but I'm kind of in a hurry. Could you just put Sebastian on?" If anyone else had answered I would've been able to just tell that person to put in an order for Miranda's usual, but since this one was too dumb to be trusted, I had learned to ask for the manager himself.

"Um, OK, let me check and see if he's available." *Trust me, Kim, he's available. Miranda Priestly is his life.*

"Andy, dear, how are you?" Sebastian breathed into the phone. "I hope you're calling because our favorite fashion editor would like some lunch today, yes?"

I wondered what he'd say if I told him, just once, that it wasn't Miranda who was looking for lunch, but me. After all, this wasn't exactly a takeout joint, but they made a special exception for the queen herself.

"Oh, yes, indeed. She was just saying how much she was in the mood for something delicious from your restaurant, and she also said to send her love." If under threat of death or dismemberment Miranda wouldn't have been able to identify the name of the place that made her lunch each day, never even mind the name of its daytime manager, but he always seemed so happy when I said something like this. Today he was so excited he giggled.

"Fab! That's just fabulous! We'll have it ready for you as soon as you get here," he called with fresh excitement in his voice. "Can't wait! And give her my love, too, of course!"

"Of course I will. See you soon." It was exhausting to stroke his ego so enthusiastically, but he made my job so much easier it was well worth it. Every day that Miranda didn't have lunch out, I served her the same meal at her desk, and she leisurely ate it behind closed doors. I kept a supply of china plates in the bins above my desk for this purpose. Most were samples sent by designers whose new "home" lines had just come out, although some I just took directly from the dining room. It would have been too annoying to have to keep stock of things like gravy trays and steak knives and linen napkins, though, so Sebastian was always sure to provide those with the meal.

And once again I shrugged on my black wool coat and jammed my cigarettes and phone in the pocket and headed outside, into a late February day that seemed to get only grayer as it progressed. Although it was just a fifteen-minute walk to the restaurant on 49th and Third, I considered calling for a car but thought better of it when I felt the clean air in my lungs. I lit a cigarette and drew the smoke in; when I exhaled, I wasn't sure if it was smoke or cold air or irritation, but it felt damn good.

Dodging the aimlessly meandering tourists had become easier. I used to stare in disgust at pedestrians on cell phones, but given my hectic days, I'd become a walking talker. I pulled my cell out and called Alex's school where, according to my fuzzy recollection, he could possibly be eating his lunch in the faculty lounge at that moment.

It rang twice before I heard a high-pitched, pinched woman's voice answer.

"Hello. You've reached PS 277 and this is Mrs. Whitmore speaking. How may I help you?"

"Is Alex Fineman there?"

"And who may I ask is calling?"

"This is Andrea Sachs, Alex's girlfriend."

"Ah, yes, Andrea! We've all heard so much about you." Her words were so clipped she sounded as though she might choke any moment.

"Oh, really? That's . . . uh, that's good. I've heard a lot about you too, of course. Alex says wonderful things about everyone at school."

"Well, isn't that nice. But seriously, Andrea, it sounds like you have quite some job there! How interesting it must be, working for such a talented woman. You're a lucky girl, indeed."

Ah, yes. Mrs. Whitmore. I am a lucky girl indeed. I'm so lucky, you have no idea. I can't tell you how lucky I felt when I was sent out just yesterday afternoon to purchase tampons for my boss, only to be told that I'd bought the wrong ones and asked why I do nothing right. And luck is probably the only way to explain why I get to sort another person's sweat- and food-stained clothing each morning before eight and arrange to have it cleaned. Oh, wait! I think what actually makes me luckiest of all is getting to talk to breeders all over the tristate area for three straight weeks in search of the perfect French bulldog puppy so two incredibly spoiled and unfriendly little girls can each have their own pet. Yes, that's it!

"Oh, yes, well, it is a fantastic opportunity," I said by rote. "A job a million girls would die for."

"You can say that again, dear! And guess what? Alex just walked in. I'll put him on."

"Hey, Andy, what's going on? How's your day going?"

"Don't ask. I'm on my way to pick up Her lunch right now. How's your day?"

"Good, so far. My class has music today right after lunch, so I actually have an hour and a half free, which is nice. And then we get to cover more phonics exercises!" he said, sounding just a little defeated. "Even though it seems like they're never going to learn how to actually read something."

"Well, have there been any slashings today?"

"No."

"So, how much can you ask for? You've had a relatively pain-free, bloodless day. Enjoy it. Save the whole reading concept for tomorrow. So, guess what? Lily called this morning. She finally got evicted from her place in Harlem, so we're going to move in together. Fun, right?"

"Hey, congratulations! Couldn't have been better timing for you. You guys will have a great time together. Come to think of it, it's a little scary. Dealing with Lily full-time . . . and Lily's guys . . . Promise we can stay at my place a lot?"

"Of course. But you'll feel right at home—it'll be just like senior year all over again."

"Too bad she's losing that cheap apartment. Other than that, it's great news."

"Yeah, I'm psyched. Shanti and Kendra are fine, but I'm kind of done with the whole living-with-strangers thing." I loved Indian food, but I did not love how the curry smell had seeped into everything I owned. "I'm going to see if Lil wants to meet for a drink tonight to celebrate. You up for it? We'll meet somewhere in the East Village so it's not too far for you."

"Yeah, sure, sounds great. I'm running to Larchmont to watch Joey tonight, but I'll be back in the city by eight. You won't even be out of work by then, so I'll meet Max and we can all meet up afterward. Hey, is Lily seeing anyone? Max could use a, well . . ."

"A what?" I laughed. "Go on, say it. Do you think my friend is a whore? She's just free-spirited, is all. And is she seeing someone? What kind of question is that? Someone named Pink-Shirt Boy stayed over there last night. I don't think I know his real name."

"Whatever. Anyway, the bell just rang. Call me when you're done dropping off the Book."

"Will do. 'Bye."

I was about to stash the phone when it rang again. The number wasn't familiar, though, and I answered it out of sheer relief that it wasn't Miranda or Emily.

"Mir—er, hello?" I'd taken to automatically answering my cell and home phone' "Miranda Priestly's office," which was supremely embarrassing when it was anyone except my parents or Lily. Had to work on that.

"Is this the lovely Andrea Sachs whom I inadvertently terrified at Marshall's party?" asked a somewhat hoarse and very sexy voice on the other end. Christian! I'd been almost relieved when he hadn't resurfaced anywhere after massaging my hand with his lips. But all the feelings of wanting to impress him with my wit and charm that first night came rushing back, and I quickly vowed to play it cool.

"It is. And who may I ask is this? There were a number of men who terrified me that night for dozens of different and varied reasons." *OK, so far, so good. Deep breath, be cool.*

"I didn't realize I had so much competition," he said smoothly. "But I suppose I shouldn't be surprised. How have you been, Andrea?"

"Fine. Great, actually," I lied quickly, remembering a *Cosmo* article I'd read that had exhorted me to "keep it light and airy and happy" when talking to a new guy because most "normal" guys didn't respond so well to hard-bitten cynicism. "Work is going really well. I'm loving my job, actually! It's been really interesting lately—a lot to learn, tons of stuff going on. Yeah, it's great. What about you?" *Don't talk about yourself too much, don't dominate the conversation, get him comfortable enough to chat about his favorite and most familiar topic: him.*

"You're a rather deft liar, Andrea. To an untrained ear that almost sounded believable, but you know what they say, don't you? You can't bullshit a bullshitter. Don't worry, though. I'll let you get away with it this time." I opened my mouth to deny the accusation, but instead I just laughed. A perceptive one indeed. "Let me get right to the point here, because I'm about to get on a plane for D.C. and security doesn't look all too happy that I'm walking through a metal detector while talking on the phone. Do you have plans for Saturday night?"

I hated when people phrased their questions that way, asked if you had plans before they told you what they had in mind. Did his girfriend need someone to run errands for her and he thought I fit the bill? Or maybe he needed someone to walk his dog while he gave yet another eight-hour-long interview to the *New York Times*? I was considering what noncommittal way I could answer that question when he said, "So, I have a reservation at Babbo this Saturday. Nine o'clock. A bunch of friends will be there, too, mostly magazine editors and pretty interesting people. An editor from *The Buzz*, and a couple writers from *The New Yorker*. Good crowd. You up for it?" At that exact moment, an ambulance roared past me with its siren wailing, lights flashing in a fruitless attempt to speed through the hopelessly gridlocked traffic. As usual, the drivers ignored the ambulance and it sat at the red light like all the other vehicles.

Had he just asked me out? Yes, I thought that's exactly what had just happened. He was asking me out! He was asking me out. Christian Collinsworth was asking me on a date—a Saturday-night date, to be specific, and to Babbo, where he just so happened to have a prime-time reservation with a group of smart, interesting people, people just like him. Never even mind the *New Yorker* writers! I racked my brain, trying to remember if I'd mentioned to him at the party that Babbo was the one restaurant I most wanted to try in New York, that I loved Italian and knew how much Miranda loved it and I was dying to go. I'd even thought about blowing a week's pay on a meal and had called to make a reservation for Alex and me, but they'd been booked solid for the next five months. I hadn't been asked on a date by anyone other than Alex in three years.

"Um, Christian, golly, I'd love to," I started, trying to forget immediately that I'd just said "golly." *Golly!* Who said that? The scene where Baby proudly announces to Johnny that she'd carried a watermelon flashed to mind, but I pushed it back and willed myself to forge forward despite the humiliation. "I'd really love to"—*yes, you idiot, you just said that, try to make some progress here*—"but I just can't do it. I, um, I already have plans for Saturday." A good response overall, I thought. I was shouting over the noise of the siren, but I thought I still sounded somewhat dignified. No need to be available for a date that was only two days away, and no real need to reveal existence of boyfriend . . . after all, it really wasn't any of his business. Right?

"Do you really have plans, Andrea, or do you think your boyfriend would disapprove of you going out with another man?" He was fishing, I could tell.

"Either way has nothing to do with you," I said prissily, and I actually rolled my eyes at myself. I crossed Third Avenue without noticing that the light was against me and almost got mowed down by a minivan.

"OK, well, I'll let you off this time. But I'll be asking again. And I think next time you'll say yes."

"Oh, really? What gives you that impression?" The confidence that had seemed so sexy before was now starting to sound a whole lot like arrogance. The only problem was that it made him sound even sexier.

"Just a hunch, Andrea, just a hunch. And no need to worry that pretty little head of yours—or your boyfriend's—I was just extending a friendly invitation for a good meal and good company. Maybe he'd like to join us, Andrea? Your boyfriend. He must be a great guy, I'd really like to meet him."

"No!" I almost shouted, horrified at the thought of the two of them sitting across a table from each other, each so amazing in such radically different ways. I'd be ashamed for Christian to see Alex's wholesomeness, his do-gooder ways. To Christian, Alex would seem like a naïve hick. And I'd be even more ashamed for Alex to see, with his own eyes, all the ugly things I found so incredibly attractive about Christian: the style, the cockiness, a self-assuredness so rock-solid it seemed impossible to insult him.

"No." I laughed or, rather, forced a laugh, as I tried to make it sound casual. "I'm not so sure that's a good idea. Although I'm sure he'd just love to meet you, too."

He laughed with me, but it had turned mocking, patronizing. "I was just kidding, Andrea. I'm sure your boyfriend's a really great guy, but I'm not particularly interested in meeting him."

"Well, of course. Sure. I mean, I knew what you—"

"Listen, I've got to run. Why don't you give me a call if you change your mind . . . or your 'plans,' OK? Offer's still open. Oh, and have a great day." And before I could say another word, he'd hung up.

What the hell had just happened? I ran through it again: Hot Smart Writer had somehow found my cell number, called it, and fully asked me on a date for Saturday night to Hot Trendy Restaurant. I wasn't clear whether he knew ahead of time if I had a boyfriend or not, but he didn't appear particularly daunted by the information. The only thing I knew for sure was that I'd spent way too long chatting on the phone, a fact confirmed by a quick glance at my watch. It had been thirty-two minutes since I'd left the office, longer than the time it usually took me to get lunch and come back.

I stashed the phone and realized I had already made it to the restaurant. I pulled open the lumbering wooden door and stepped into the hushed, darkened dining room. Even though every table was filled with midtown bankers and lawyers gnawing on their favorite steaks, there was barely any noise at all, as if the plush carpeting and manly color scheme just absorbed all the sound.

"Andrea!" I heard Sebastian cry from the hostess stand. He beelined toward me as though I might be holding the last of a life-saving medication. "We're just all so glad you're here!" Two young girls in crisp gray skirt suits nodded seriously behind him.

"Oh, really? Why is that?" I could never help myself toying with Sebastian, just a little. He was such an unbelievable kiss-ass.

He leaned over conspiratorially, his excitement palpable. "Well, you know how the entire staff here at Smith and Wollensky feels about Ms. Priestly, don't you? *Runway* is such a gorgeous magazine, what with all the beautiful shoots and stunning style and, of course, fascinating, literate articles. We all just adore it!"

"Literate articles, huh?" I asked, suppressing the huge smile that was threatening to emerge. He nodded proudly and turned as one of the suited helpers tapped him on the shoulder to hand him a tote bag.

He literally cried out in joy. "Ah-hah! Here we have it, one perfectly prepared lunch for one perfect editor—and one perfect assistant," he added while winking at me.

"Thank you, Sebastian, we both appreciate it." I opened the natural cotton tote, a bag that looked just like those *über*-cool ones from the Strand that all the NYU students slung over their shoulder, but without the logo, and made sure everything was right. One-and-a-quarter-pound ribeye, bleeding all over the container, so raw it just might not have been cooked at all. Check. Two baked potatoes the size of small kittens, each steaming hot. Check. One small side container of smashed potatoes, made soft with lots of heavy cream and extra butter. Check. Precisely eight perfect stalks of asparagus with the tips looking plump and juicy and the ends shaved to a clean, white finish. Check. There was also a metal gravy boat full of softened butter, a pinch-box overflowing with grainy kosher salt, a wooden-handled steak knife, and a crisp white linen napkin, which today was folded into the shape of a pleated skirt. How adorable. Sebastian waited to see if I liked it.

"Very nice, Sebastian," I said as though I were praising a puppy for going number two outside. "You really outdid yourself today."

He beamed and then looked at the ground in practiced humility. "Well, thank you. You know how I feel about Ms. Priestly, and, well, it's really an honor to, well, you know . . ."

"Prepare her lunch?" I supplied, helpfully.

"Well, yes. Exactly. You know what I mean."

"Yes, of course I do, Sebastian. She'll love it, I'm sure." I didn't have the heart to tell him that I immediately unfolded all of his creations because the Ms. Priestly he so adored would throw a hissy fit if faced with a napkin in the shape of anything other than a napkin—never mind a bowling bag or a high-heeled shoe. I tucked the bag under my arm and turned to leave, but just then my phone rang.

Sebastian looked at me expectantly, fervently hoping that the voice on the other line of my cell phone would be his love, his reason for living. He wasn't let down.

"Is this Emily? Emily, is that you, I can barely hear you!" Miranda's voice came over the line in a shrill, angry staccato.

"Hello, Miranda. Yes, this is Andrea." I stated calmly while Sebastian visibly swooned at the sound of her name.

"Are you preparing my lunch yourself, Andrea? Because according to my clock, I asked for it thirty-five minutes ago. I cannot think of a single reason why—if you were doing your job properly—my lunch would not be at my desk yet. Can you?"

She got my name right! A small success, but no time to celebrate.

"Uh, um, well, I'm very sorry it's taken so long, but there was a little mix-up with—"

"You do know just how uninterested I am in such details, do you not?"

"Yes, of course I understand, and it won't be long before—"

"I am calling to tell you that I want my lunch, and I want it *now*. There's really not much room for nuance, Emily. I. Want. My. Lunch. Now!" With that, she hung up the phone, and my hands were shaking so badly I dropped my cell on the floor. It might as well have been covered in burning arsenic.

Sebastian, who looked ready to pass out from the action, swooped down to retrieve the phone and hand it back to me.

"Is she upset with us, Andrea? I hope she doesn't think we let her down! Does she? Does she think that?" His mouth pursed into a tight oval and the already prominent veins in his forehead pulsed, and I wanted to hate him as much as I hated her, but I just felt sorry for him. Why did this man, this man who seemed remarkable only to the extent that he was so unremarkable, why did he care so much about Miranda Priestly? Why was he so invested in pleasing her, impressing her, providing for her? Perhaps he should take over my job, I thought, because I was going to quit. Yes, that was it. I was going to march back to that office and quit. Who needed her shit? What gave her the right to talk to me, to anyone, like that? The position? The power? The prestige? The goddamn Prada? Where, in a just universe, was this acceptable behavior?

The receipt I was supposed to sign every day charging the ninety-five-dollar meal to Elias-Clark was resting on the podium, and I quickly scrawled an illegible signature. Whether it was mine or Miranda's or Emily's or Mahatma Gandhi's at this point I couldn't even be sure, but it wouldn't matter. I grabbed the bag of food that redefined the term "lunch meat" and stomped back outside, leaving a very fragile Sebastian to deal with himself. I threw myself in a cab the moment I hit the street, nearly knocking an elderly man off his feet. No time to be concerned. I had a job to quit. Even with the midday traffic, we covered the few blocks in ten minutes, and I threw the cabbie a twenty. I would've given him fifty if I'd had it and figured out a way to recoup it from Elias, but there were none in my wallet. He immediately began counting out change, but I slammed the door and ran. Let that twenty go to caring for a little girl somewhere or fixing a hot water heater, I decided. Or even for a few postshift beers at the cab park in Queens—whatever the cabbie did with it would somehow be nobler than buying yet another cup of Starbucks.

Full of self-righteous indignation, I stormed inside the building and ignored the disapproving stares from the small group of Clackers in the corner. I saw Benji stepping off the Bergman elevators but quickly turned my
back so I didn't waste any more time, swiped my card, and threw my hip
against the turnstile. Shit! The metal bar smacked against my pelvic bone
and I knew I'd have a splotchy purple bruise within minutes. I looked up to
see two rows of glimmering white teeth and the fat, sweating face that
formed around them. Eduardo. He had to be kidding. He just had to be.

I quickly flashed him my best nasty look, the one that said, quite
simply, *Just die!* but it didn't work today. Maintaining full eye contact, I
swiveled around to the next turnstile in the line, swiped my card
lightning-fast, and lunged against the bar. He'd managed to lock it just
in time, and I stood there as he let the Clackers go through the first turnstile I'd tried, one by one. Six in all, and I still stood there, so frustrated
I thought I might cry. Eduardo was not sympathetic.

"Girlfriend, don't look so down. This ain't torture, it's fun. Now,
please. Pay attention, because . . . *I think we're alone now. There doesn't
seem to be anyone a-rou-ound. I think we're alone now. The beatin' of
our hearts is the only sou-ound.*"

"Eduardo! How on earth am I supposed to act out that one? I don't
have time for this shit right now!"

"OK, OK. No actin' this time, just singin'. I'll start, you finish. *Children behave! That's what they say when we're together. And watch how
you play! They don't understand, and so we're . . .*"

I figured I wouldn't have to quit if I ever actually made it upstairs because I'd be fired by then anyway. Might as well make someone else's
day. *"Running just as fast as we can,"* I continued, not missing a beat.
*"Holdin' on to one another's hand. Tryin' to get away into the night and
then you put your arms around me and we tumble to the ground and
then you say . . ."*

I leaned in closer when I noticed that the jerk from day one, Mickey,
was trying to listen, and Eduardo finished it off: *"I think we're alone
now. There doesn't seem to be anyone a-rou-ound. I think we're alone
now. The beatin' of our hearts is the only sou-ound!"* He guffawed and
threw his hand in the air. I slapped him high five, and I heard the metal
bar click open.

"Have a good lunch, Andy!" he called, still grinning.

"You, too, Eduardo, you, too."

The elevator ride was blissfully uneventful, and it wasn't until I was standing directly outside the doors of our office suite that I decided I couldn't quit. Aside from the obvious—that is, it'd be too terrifying to do it unprepared, she'd probably just look at me and say, "No, I won't allow you to quit" and then what would I say?—I had to remember that it was only a year of my life. A single year to bypass many more of misery. One year, 12 months, 52 weeks, 365 days, of putting up with this garbage to do what I really wanted. It wasn't too great a demand, and besides, I was too tired to even think about looking for another job. Way too tired.

Emily looked up at me when I walked in. "She'll be right back. She just got called up to Mr. Ravitz's office. Seriously, Andrea, what took you so long? You know that she comes down on me when you're late, and what can I tell her? That you're smoking cigarettes instead of buying her coffee, or talking to your boyfriend instead of getting her lunch? It's not fair—it's really not." She turned her attention back to her computer, a resigned expression on her face.

She was right, of course. It wasn't fair. To me, to her, to any semicivilized human being. And I felt bad for making it more difficult for her, which I did every time I took a few extra minutes away from the office to relax and unwind. Because every second I was gone was another second that Miranda focused her relentless attention on Emily. I vowed to try harder.

"You're totally right, Em, and I'm sorry. I'll try harder."

She looked genuinely surprised and a little bit pleased. "I'd really appreciate it, Andrea. I mean, I've done your job. I *know* how much it sucks. Trust me, there were days that I had to go out in the snow and the slush and the rain to get her coffee five, six, seven times in a single day. I was so tired I could barely move—I know what it's like! Sometimes she'd call me to ask where something was—her latte, her lunch, some special, sensitive-teeth toothpaste I'd been sent to find—it was comforting to discover that at least her teeth had a bit of sensitivity—and I hadn't even left the building yet. Hadn't even gotten outside! That's just her, Andy. That's just how it is. You can't fight it anymore, or you'll never survive. She doesn't mean any harm by it, she really doesn't. That's just the way she is."

I nodded and I understood, but I just couldn't accept that. I hadn't worked anywhere else, but I just couldn't believe that all bosses everywhere acted like this. But maybe they did?

I carried the lunch bag over to my desk and began the preparations for serving her. One by one, I used my bare hands to pluck the food from its heat-sealed to-go containers and arrange it (stylishly, I hoped) on one of the china plates from the overhead bin. Slowing only to wipe my now greasy hands on a pair of her dirty Versace pants I hadn't yet sent to the cleaners, I placed the plate on the teak and tile serving tray that resided under my desk. Next to it went the gravy boat full of butter, the salt, and the silverware wrapped in a linen-pleated skirt-no-longer. A quick survey of my artistry revealed a missing Pellegrino. Better hurry—she'd be back any minute! I dashed to one of the minikitchens and palmed a fistful of ice cubes, blowing on them to keep them from freezer-burning my hands. Blowing was only one itsy, bitsy, teensy step from licking them— *do I do it? No! Be above it, rise above it. Do not spit in her food or gum her ice cubes. You're a bigger person than that!*

Her office was still empty by the time I made it back, and the only thing left to do was pour the bottled water and place the whole orchestrated tray on her desk. She'd come back and perch at her mammoth desk and call out for someone to close her doors. And this would be one time I'd jump up happily, enthusiastically, because it meant not only that she'd sit quietly behind those closed doors for a good half hour, on the phone with B-DAD, but also that it was time for us to eat as well. One of us could race down to the dining room and grab the very first thing she saw and race back so the other could go. We would try to hide our food under our desks and behind our computer screens just in case she came out unexpectedly. If there was a single unspoken but still irrefutable rule, it was that members of the *Runway* staff do not eat in front of Miranda Priestly. Period.

My watch said it was quarter after two. My stomach said it was late evening. It had been seven hours since I'd shoved a chocolate scone down my throat on the walk back to the office from Starbucks, and I was so hungry I considered gnawing on her ribeye.

"Em, I might pass out, I'm so hungry. I think I'm going to run down and pick something up. Can I get you something?"

"Are you crazy? You haven't served her lunch yet. She'll be back any minute."

"I'm serious. I really don't feel well. I don't think I can wait." The sleep deprivation and the low blood sugar were combining to make me dizzy. I wasn't sure I'd be able to carry the steak tray into her office even if she did come back sometime soon.

"Andrea, be rational! What if you run into her in the elevator or in reception? She'd know that you left the office. She'd freak! It's not worth the risk. Hold on a sec—I'll get you something." She grabbed her change purse and headed out of the office. Not four seconds later, I saw Miranda making her way down the hall toward me. Any thoughts of dizziness or hunger or exhaustion disappeared the moment I spotted her tight, frowning face, and I flew out of my seat to put the tray on her desk before she reached it herself.

I landed in my seat, head spinning, mouth dry, and totally disoriented, just before her first Jimmy Choo crossed the threshold. She didn't so much as glance in my direction or, thankfully, seem to notice that the real Emily wasn't at her desk. I had a feeling that the meeting she'd just had with Mr. Ravitz hadn't gone so well, although it could have just been her lingering resentment at having to leave her office to go see someone else in theirs. Mr. Ravitz was, so far, the only person in the entire building whom Miranda rushed to accommodate.

"Ahn-dre-ah! What is this? Please tell me, what on earth is this?"

I raced into her office and stood before her desk, where we both looked down at what was, quite obviously, the same lunch she ate whenever she didn't go out. A quick mental checklist revealed that nothing was missing or out of place or on the wrong side or cooked incorrectly. What was her problem?

"Um, it's, uh, well, it's your lunch," I said quietly, making a genuine effort not to sound sarcastic, which was difficult, considering my statement was supremely obvious. "Is something wrong?"

In all fairness, I think she just parted her lips, but to my neardelirious self, it looked like she was baring actual pointed fangs.

"Is something wrong?" she mimicked in a high-pitched voice that sounded nothing like my own, nothing human. She narrowed her eyes to slits and leaned closer, still refusing, as always, to raise her voice. "Yes, there's something wrong. Something very, very wrong. Why do I have to come back to my office to find *this* sitting on my desk?"

It was like trying to solve one of those twisted riddles. Why did she have to come back to her desk to find this sitting on it, I wondered. Clearly, the fact that she had requested it an hour earlier was not the correct answer, but it was the only one I had. Did she not like the tray it was on? No, that wasn't possible: she'd seen it a million times and hadn't ever complained about it. Had they accidentally given her the wrong cut of meat? No, that wasn't it, either. The restaurant had once mistakenly sent me off with a wonderful-looking filet, thinking that she was sure to enjoy it more than the tough ribeye, but she'd almost had a full-fledged heart attack. She'd made me call the chef personally and scream at him over the phone while she stood over me and told me what to say.

"I'm so sorry, miss, really I am," he'd said softly, sounding like the nicest guy in the world. "I really just thought that since Ms. Priestly is such a good customer that she'd prefer to have our best. I didn't charge her extra, but don't worry, it won't happen again, I promise." I felt like crying when she ordered me to tell him that he would never be a real chef anywhere besides some second-rate steak emporium, but I had done it. And he had apologized and agreed, and from that day on she'd always gotten her bloody ribeye. So it wasn't that, either. I had no idea what to say or do.

"Ahn-dre-ah. Did Mr. Ravitz's assistant not tell you that we had lunch together in that wretched dining room just a few moments ago?" she asked slowly, as though she were trying to keep herself from losing control completely.

She *what?* After all of that, after all the running and the Sebastian ridiculousness, and the angry phone calls, and the ninety-five-dollar meal, and the Tiffany song, and the food arranging, and the dizziness, and the waiting to eat until she came back, and *she'd already eaten?*

"Uh, no, we didn't get a call from her at all. So, uh, does that mean you don't want this?" I asked, motioning to the tray.

She looked at me as if I had just suggested she eat one of the twins. "What do you think that means, Emily?" Shit! She'd been doing so well with my name.

"I guess that, uh, well, that you don't want it."

"That's very perceptive of you, Emily. I'm lucky you're such a quick study. Now remove it. And make sure this does not happen again. That's all."

A quick fantasy flashed forward, one in which I would, just like in the movies, sweep my arm across the desk and send the whole tray flying across the room. She would watch and, shocked into contriteness, apologize profusely for speaking to me like that. But the clicking of her nails against the desk brought me back to reality, and I quickly picked up the tray and carefully walked out of her office.

"Ahn-dre-ah, close the door! I need a moment!" she called. I guess that having a gourmet lunch appear on her desk that she didn't feel like eating had been a really stressful part of her day.

Emily had just returned with a can of Diet Coke and a package of raisins for me. This was supposed to be the snack to tide me over to lunch, and of course there wasn't a single calorie or gram of fat or ounce of added sugar in the whole thing. She dropped them on her desk when she heard Miranda calling and ran over to shut her French doors.

"What happened?" she whispered, eyeing the untouched tray of food that I was holding, frozen to the spot near my desk.

"Oh, it seems our charming boss already had her lunch," I hissed through clenched teeth. "And she just reamed me out for not predicting, not divining, not being able to look directly inside her stomach and know that she wasn't hungry anymore."

"You're kidding me," she said. "She yelled at you because you ran to get her lunch—just like she asked—and then couldn't possibly have known that she'd already eaten somewhere else? What a bitch!"

I nodded. It was a phenomenal change of pace to have Emily actually take my side for once, not to lecture me on all the ways I Just Don't Get It. But, wait! It was too good to be true. Like a sun that falls out of the sky, leaving only pink and blue streaks where it had shone seconds before, Emily's face flashed from angry to contrite. The *Runway* Paranoid Turnaround.

"Remember what we talked about before, Andrea." Oh, yes, here it comes. RPT, twelve o'clock. "She doesn't do it to hurt you. She doesn't mean anything by it. She's just way too important to get held up on the little stuff. So don't fight it. Just throw out the food, and let's move on." Emily fixed her features in a determined look and took a seat in front of her computer. I knew she was wondering right then and there if Miranda had had our outer office areas bugged and had heard the whole thing. She was red and flustered and very obviously displeased with her lack of control. I didn't know how she had survived as long as she had.

I thought about eating the steak myself, but the mere thought that it had been on Miranda's desk only moments earlier made me feel nauseated. I took the tray to the kitchen and tilted it so every single item would just slide directly into the garbage—all the expertly cooked and seasoned food, the china plate, the metal butter container, the salt box, the linen napkin, the silver, the steak knife, and the Baccarat glass. Gone. All gone. What did it matter? I'd get it all over again the next day, or whenever it was that she may again be hungry for lunch.

By the time I'd made it to Drinkland, Alex looked annoyed and Lily looked wasted. I immediately wondered if Alex somehow knew that I'd been asked out on a date today, by a guy who was not only famous and older, but also a complete and total dickhead. Could he tell? Did he sense it? Should I tell him? No, no need to get into it with him when it was so insignificant. It wasn't like I was admitting to being interested in some other guy, not like I would actually ever act on it. So there was nothing to gain by mentioning the conversation at all.

"Hey there, fashion girl," Lily slurred, waving her gin and tonic toward me in a salute. Some of it splashed down the front of her cardigan, but she didn't seem to notice. "Or should I say, future roomie? Get a drink. We need to have a toast!" It came out sounding like "toath."

I kissed Alex and sat down next to him.

"Don't you look hot today!" he said, eyeing my Prada outfit appreciatively. "When did this happen?"

"Oh, today. Right around the time it was all but spelled out that if I didn't fix my look I might not have a job anymore. Pretty insulting stuff, but I have to say, if you've got to put something on every day, this stuff isn't half bad.

"Hey, listen, guys. I'm really, really sorry I'm late. The Book took forever tonight, and as soon as I dropped it off at Miranda's she had me run to the corner deli and pick up some basil."

"I thought you said she had a cook," Alex pointed out. "Why couldn't he do it?"

"She does indeed have a cook. She also has a housekeeper, a nanny, and two children. So I have no idea why I was the one sent out for dinner spices. It was especially annoying since Fifth Avenue doesn't have any corner delis, and neither does Madison or Park, so I had to go all the way to Lex to find one. But, of course, they didn't sell basil, so I had to walk up nine blocks until I found an open D'Agostino's. It took me an extra forty-five minutes. I should just expense a fucking spice rack and start traveling with it wherever I go. But let me tell you, those were a really, really worthwhile forty-five minutes! I mean, think of how much I learned shopping for that basil, how better prepared I am for my future in magazines! I'm on the fast track to becoming an editor now!" I flashed a winning smile.

"To your future!" Lily cried, not detecting a single hint of sarcasm in my diatribe.

"She's so far gone," Alex said quietly, watching Lily with the look of someone watching a sick relative sleep in a hospital bed. "I got here on time with Max, who already left, but she must've been here for hours already. Either that, or she drinks really fast."

Lily had always been a big drinker, but it wasn't weird, because Lily was a big everything. She was the first one to smoke pot in junior high and the first one to lose her virginity in high school and the first to go skydiving in college. She loved anyone and anything that didn't love her back, so long as it made her *feel* alive.

"I just don't understand how you can sleep with him when you know he's never going to break up with his girlfriend," I'd said about a guy she'd been secretly seeing our junior year.

"I just don't understand how you can play by so many rules," she'd shot back instantly. "Where's the fun in all your perfectly planned, mapped-out, rule-filled life? Live a little, Andy! Feel something! It's good to be alive!"

Maybe she had been drinking a little more lately, but I knew that her first-year studies were incredibly stressful, even for her, and that her professors at Columbia were more demanding and less understanding than the ones she'd had wrapped around her finger at Brown. *It might not be a bad idea*, I thought, signaling to the waitress. Maybe drinking was the way to handle it. I ordered an Absolut and grapefruit juice and took a long, deep swig. It made me feel more sick than anything, because I still hadn't had time to eat anything except the raisins and the Diet Coke Emily had scraped together for me earlier that day.

"I'm sure she's just had a rough couple of weeks in school," I said to Alex as though Lily weren't sitting with us. She didn't notice we were talking about her because she was preoccupied giving some yuppie guy at the bar heavy-lidded, come-hither looks. Alex put his arm around me and I snuggled closer on the couch. It felt so good to be near him again— it seemed like it had been weeks.

"I hate to be a buzz-kill, but I really have to get home," Alex said, pushing my hair back behind my ear. "Will you be OK with her?"

"You have to leave? Already?"

"Already? Andy, I've been here watching your best friend drink for the past two hours. I came to see you, but you weren't here. And now it's almost midnight, and I still have essays to correct." He said it calmly, but I could see that he was upset.

"I know, I'm sorry about that, I really am. You know that I would've been there if I could've helped it at all. You know that—"

"I do know all that. I'm not saying you did anything wrong or that you could've done anything differently. I understand. But try to understand where I'm coming from, too, OK?"

I nodded and kissed him, but I felt awful. I pledged to make it up to him, to pick a night and plan something really special for just the two of us. He did, after all, put up with a lot from me.

"So, you won't even stay over tonight?" I asked hopefully.

"Not unless you need help with Lily. I really need to get home and work on those papers." He hugged me good-bye, kissed Lily on the cheek, and headed toward the door. "Call me if you need me," he said as he walked out.

"Hey, why'd Alex leave?" Lily asked, even though she'd been sitting there through the entire conversation. "Is he mad at you?"

"Probably," I sighed, hugging my canvas messenger bag to my chest. "I've been a shit to him lately." I went to the bar to ask for an appetizer menu and by the time I came back, the Wall Street guy had curled up on the couch next to Lily. He looked to be in his late twenties, but his receding hairline made it impossible to know for sure.

I grabbed her coat and tossed it at her. "Lily, put that on. We're leaving," I said while looking at him. He was on the shorter side, and his pleated khakis didn't help his pudgy figure. And the fact that his tongue was now two inches from my best friend's ear didn't make me like him any more.

"Hey, what's the rush?" he asked in a whiny, nasal voice. "Your friend and I are just getting to know each other." Lily grinned and nodded, trying to take a gulp from her drink but not realizing her glass was empty.

"Well, that's very sweet, but it's time for us to go. What's your name?"

"Stuart."

"Nice to meet you, Stuart. Why don't you give Lily here your number and she can give you a call when she's feeling a little better—or not. How does that sound?" I flashed him a smile.

"Uh, whatever. No worries. I'll catch you guys later." He was on his feet and headed to the bar so fast that Lily hadn't yet noticed he'd left.

"Stuart and I are getting to know each other, aren't we, Stu?" She turned to the place where he had sat and looked confused.

"Stuart had to run, Lil. Come on, let's get out of here."

I pulled her drab green peacoat on over her sweater and yanked her to her feet, where she swayed precariously until she regained her balance. The air outside was searing and cold and I figured it'd help her sober up.

"I don't feel so good." She was slurring again.

"I know, sweetie, I know. Let's get a cab back to your apartment, OK? Do you think you can make it?"

She nodded and then leaned over very casually and threw up. All over her brown boots, with some of it splashing up the sides of her jeans. *If only the* Runway *girls could see my best friend now.* I couldn't help thinking.

I sat her down on a window ledge that looked reasonably like it wouldn't have an alarm and ordered her not to move. There was a twenty-four-hour bodega right across the street, and this girl clearly needed some water. When I got back, she'd thrown up again—this time all down her front—and her eyes looked droopy. I'd bought two bottles of Poland Spring, one for her to drink and one for cleaning, but she was too gross now. I dumped one all over her feet to wash away the sick, and half of the second one over her coat. Better to be soaking wet than covered in puke. She was so drunk she didn't even notice.

It took a little persuading to get a cabbie to let us in with Lily looking in such bad shape, but I promised a really big tip on top of what was sure to be a really big fare. We were going from the Lower East Side to the far Upper West, and I was already figuring out a way to expense what was sure to be a twenty-dollar ride. I could probably just write it off as a trip I had to make in search of something for Miranda. Yes, that would work.

The trip to her fourth-floor walk-up was even less fun than the cab, but she'd become more cooperative after the twenty-five-minute ride, and she even managed to wash herself in the shower after I'd undressed her. I pointed her in the direction of her bed and watched as she collapsed face-down when her knees hit the box spring. I looked down at her, unconscious, and was momentarily nostalgic for college, for all the things we'd done together then. It was fun now, no question, but it would never again be as carefree as then.

I briefly wondered if Lily might be drinking too much these days. After all, she did seem to be drunk pretty consistently. But when Alex had brought it up the week before, I'd assured him it was because she was still a student, still not living in the real world with real, adult responsibilities (like pouring the perfect Pellegrino!). I mean, it's not like we hadn't together done too many shots at Señor Frog's on spring break or too ambitiously worked our way through three bottles of red wine while celebrating the anniversary of the day we'd first met in eighth grade. Lily had held my hair back as I sat with my face resting on the toilet seat after a postfinals binge, and pulled over four times once while driving me back to my dorm after a night that had included eight rum and Cokes and a particularly horrid karaoke rendition of "Every Rose Has Its

Thorn." I'd dragged her back to my apartment on the night of her twenty-first birthday and tucked her into my bed, checking her breathing every ten minutes, and finally fell asleep on the floor next to her after I'd made sure she'd live through the night. She had awakened twice that night. The first time was to throw up over the side of the bed—making a sincere effort to make it into the garbage can I'd set up beside it but getting confused and vomiting down the side of my wall instead—and once more to apologize sincerely and tell me she loved me and I was the best friend a girl could have. That's what friends did: they got drunk together and did stupid things and looked out for one another, right? Or was that all just college fun, rites of passage that had a time and a place? Alex had insisted that this was different, that *she* was different, but I just didn't see it that way.

I knew I should've stayed with her tonight, but it was nearly two and I had to be at work in five hours. My clothes smelled of vomit and there was no way I could find a single appropriate piece of clothing in Lily's closet to wear to *Runway*—especially with my new upgraded look. I sighed and pulled a blanket over her and set her alarm for 7:00 A.M. so just in case she wasn't too hungover, she'd have a shot at making it to class.

" 'Bye, Lil. I'm heading out. You OK?" I placed the portable phone on the pillow by her head.

She opened her eyes, looked directly at me, and smiled. "Thanks," she muttered, her eyelids dropping again. She wasn't fit to run a marathon, or probably even operate a motorized lawn mower, but she'd be fine to just sleep it off.

"It was my pleasure," I managed, even though this was the first time in twenty-one hours I had stopped physically running, fetching, rearranging, moving, cleaning, or otherwise assisting. "I'll call you tomorrow," I said as I willed my legs not to give out. "If either of us is still alive." And I finally, *finally*, went home.

10

"Hey, I'm glad I caught you," I heard Cara say on the other end of the line. Why was she out of breath at quarter of eight in the morning?

"Uh-oh. You never call this early. What's wrong?" In the split second it took me to say those words, a half-dozen scenarios of what Miranda could need raced through my mind.

"No, no, it's nothing like that. I just wanted to warn you that B-DAD is on his way in to see you, and he's particularly chatty this morning."

"Oh, well, that's sure great news. It's been, what, nearly a week since he's interrogated me about every aspect of my life? I was wondering where my biggest fan had gone." I finished typing my memo and hit "print."

"You're a lucky girl, I have to say. He's lost interest in me entirely," she pined dramatically. "He only has eyes for you. I heard him say that he was coming over to discuss details of the Met party with you."

"Great, that's just great. I can't wait to meet this brother of his. So far I've just spoken to him on the phone, but he sounds like a total schmuck. So, you're sure he's on his way, or is it possible there's a kind spirit up above who just may spare me that particular misery today?"

"Nope, not today. He's definitely on his way. Miranda has a podiatrist appointment at eight-thirty A.M., so I don't think she'll be coming with him."

I checked the appointment book on Emily's desk quickly and confirmed her appointments. A Miranda-free morning was indeed on the schedule. "Fantastic. I couldn't think of anyone dreamier to do a little early-morning bonding with than B-DAD himself. Why does he talk so much?"

"Can't answer that other than to point out the obvious: he married her, so he's clearly not all there. Call if he says anything particularly ridiculous. I have to run. Caroline just smashed one of Miranda's Stila lipsticks into the bathroom mirror for no apparent reason."

"Our lives rock, don't they? We're the coolest girls. Anyway, thanks for the heads up. Talk to you later."

"OK, 'bye."

I glanced over the memo while I waited for B-DAD's arrival. It was a request to the board of trustees of the Metropolitan Museum of Art from Miranda. She was asking permission to throw a dinner party in one of the galleries in March for her brother-in-law, a man I could tell she absolutely despised but who was, unfortunately, family. Jack Tomlinson was B-DAD's younger and wilder brother, and he'd just announced he was leaving his wife and three children and marrying his masseuse. Although he and B-DAD were both quintessential East Coast prep school aristocracy, Jack had shed his Harvard persona in his late twenties and moved to South Carolina, where he'd immediately made a fortune in real estate. Judging from everything Emily had told me, he'd morphed into a first-class Southern boy, a real straw-chewin', tobacco-spittin' hick, which of course appalled Miranda, the epitome of class and sophistication. B-DAD had asked Miranda to organize an engagement party for his baby brother, and Miranda, blinded by love, had no choice but to oblige. And if she had to do something, then she sure as hell was going to do it right. And right was at the Met.

Dear Honored Members, blah, blah, blah, would like to request permission to host a fabulous little soiree, blah, blah, blah, will be hiring only the finest caterers, florists, and band, of course, blah, blah, blah, would welcome your input, blah, blah. Making sure one last time that there were no glaring errors, I quickly forged her name and called for a messenger to come pick it up.

The knock on the office suite door—which I kept closed this early in the morning since no one was in yet anyway—came almost immediately, and I was impressed with their turnaround time, but the door swung open to reveal B-DAD, who was sporting a grin much too enthusiastic for pre-eight A.M.

"Andrea," he sang, immediately walking over to my desk and smiling so genuinely it made me feel guilty for not liking him.

"Good morning, Mr. Tomlinson. What brings you here so early?" I asked. "I'm sorry to tell you that Miranda's not in yet."

He chuckled, his nose twitching like a rodent's. "Yes, yes, she won't be in until after lunch, or so I believe. Andy, it really has been too long since you and I caught up. Tell Mr. T. now: How is everything?"

"Here, let me take those," I said, pulling the monogrammed duffel full of Miranda's dirty clothes that she'd given him to give to me. I also relieved him of the beaded Fendi tote bag that had surfaced again recently. It was a one-of-a-kind tote that had been hand-beaded in an elaborate crystal design just for Miranda from Silvia Venturini Fendi, as a thank-you for all of her support, and one of the fashion assistants had put its value at just under ten grand. But I noticed today that one of the skinny leather handles had broken loose yet again, even though the accessories department had returned it to Fendi for hand-stitching two dozen times already. It was intended to hold a delicate ladies' wallet, perhaps accompanied by a pair of sunglasses or maybe, if absolutely necessary, a small cell phone. Miranda didn't really care about that. She had currently crammed in an extra-large bottle of Bulgari perfume, a sandal with a broken heel that I was probably supposed to get fixed, the blotter-size Hermès daily planner that weighed more than an entire laptop, an oversize spiked dog collar that I thought either belonged to Madelaine or was for an upcoming fashion shoot, and the Book I had delivered to her the night before. I would have hocked a bag worth ten thousand dollars and paid my rent for a year, but Miranda preferred to use it as a trash receptacle.

"Thank you, Andy. You really are a big help to everyone. So Mr. T. would sure like to hear more about your life. What's going on?"

What's going on? What's going on? Hmm, well, let's see here. Really not all that much, I suppose. I spend most of my time trying to survive my term of indentured servitude with your sadistic wife. If there are ever any free minutes during the workday when she's not making some belittling demand, then I'm trying to block out the brainwash drivel that's spoon-fed to me by her assistant in chief. On the increasingly rare occasions that I find myself outside the confines of this magazine, I'm usually trying to convince myself that it really is OK to eat more than eight hundred calories a day and that being a size six does not put me in the plus-size category. So I guess the short answer is, not much.

"Well, Mr. Tomlinson, not too much. I work a lot. And I guess when I'm not working I hang out with my best friend, or my boyfriend. Try to see my family." *I used to read a lot*, I wanted to say, *but I'm too tired now.* And sports have always been a pretty big part of my life, but there wasn't time anymore.

"So, you're twenty-five, right?" He non-sequitured. I couldn't even imagine where he was going with this one.

"Uh, no, I'm twenty-three. I only graduated last May."

"Ah-hah! Twenty-three, huh?" He looked like he was trying to decide whether to say something or not. I braced myself. "So tell Mr. T., what do twenty-three-year-olds do in this city for fun? Restaurants? Clubs? That sort of thing?" He smiled again, and I wondered if he really needed the attention as much as he appeared to: there was nothing sinister behind his interest, just a seemingly driving need to *talk.*

"Um, well, all sorts of things, I guess. I don't really go to clubs, but bars and lounges and places like that. Go out for dinner, see movies."

"Well, that sounds like a lot of fun. Used to do that kind of stuff, too, when I was your age. Now it's just a lot of work events and fund-raisers. Enjoy it while you can, Andy." He winked like a dorky father would.

"Yeah, well, I'm trying," I managed. *Please leave, please leave, please leave*, I willed, staring longingly at the bagel that was just calling my name. I get three minutes of peace and quiet a day, and this man was stealing all of it.

He opened his mouth to say something, but the doors swung open and Emily stomped in. She was wearing her headphones and moving to the music. I watched her mouth drop open when she saw him standing there.

"Mr. Tomlinson!" she exclaimed, yanking off her headphones and tossing her iPod in her Gucci tote. "Is everything OK? Nothing's wrong with Miranda, is it?" She looked and sounded genuinely concerned. An A-plus performance: always the perfectly attentive, unfailingly polite assistant.

"Hello there, Emily. Nothing wrong at all. Miranda will be here shortly. Mr. T. just came by to drop off her things. How are you doing today?"

Emily beamed. I wondered if she actually enjoyed his presence. "Just fine. Thanks so much for asking. And you? Did Andrea help you with everything?"

"Oh, she sure did," he said, throwing smile number 6,000 in my direction. "I wanted to go over a few things about my brother's engagement party, but I realize that it's probably a little early for that, right?"

For a moment I thought he meant too early in the morning and I almost shouted "Yes!" but then I realized that he meant it was too early in the planning to discuss details.

He turned back to Emily and said, "You've got yourself a great junior assistant here, don't you think?"

"Absolutely," Emily managed through clenched teeth. "She's the best." She grinned.

I grinned.

Mr. Tomlinson grinned with extra wattage, and I wondered if he had a chemical imbalance, perhaps hypomania.

"Well, Mr. T. had better be on his way. It's always lovely chatting with you girls. Have a nice morning, both of you. Good-bye now."

"'Bye, Mr. Tomlinson!" Emily called as he rounded the corner in the hallway on his way to reception.

"Why were you so rude to him?" she asked as she pulled the flimsy leather blazer off, only to reveal a flimsier chiffon scoop-neck that was laced all the way up the front like a corset.

"So rude? I helped him unload her stuff and I talked to him before you got here. How is that rude?"

"Well, you didn't say good-bye, for one thing. And you have that look on your face."

"That look?"

"Yes, that look of yours. The one that tells everyone just how far above this you are, just how much you hate it here. That may fly with me, but it won't with Mr. Tomlinson. He's Miranda's *husband*, and you just can't treat him like that."

"Em, don't you think he's a little, I don't know . . . weird? He never stops talking. How can he be so nice when she's such a . . . so not as nice?" I watched as she glanced inside Miranda's office to make sure that I'd set the newspapers correctly.

"Weird? Hardly, Andrea. He's one of the most prominent tax attorneys in Manhattan."

It wasn't worth it. "Never mind, I don't even know what I'm saying. What's going on with you? How was your night?"

"Oh, it was good. I went shopping with Jessica for gifts for her bridesmaids. Everywhere—Scoop, Bergdorf's, Infinity, everywhere. And I tried on a bunch of stuff to get some idea for Paris, but it's still really too early."

"For Paris? You're going to Paris? Does that mean you'll leave me alone with her?" I hadn't meant to say the last part out loud, but it had slipped.

Again, a look like I was crazy. "Yes, I'll be going to Paris with Miranda in October, for the spring ready-to-wear shows. Each year she takes her senior assistant to the spring shows so she can see what it's really like. I mean, I've been to, like, a million at Bryant Park, but the European shows are just different."

I did a quick calculation. "In October, as in seven months from now? You were trying on clothes for a trip seven months from now?" I hadn't meant for it to sound as harsh as it did, and Emily immediately got defensive.

"Well, yes. I mean, obviously I wasn't going to buy anything—so many of the styles will have changed by then. But I just wanted to start thinking about it. It's a really huge deal, you know. Stay in five-star hotels, go to the craziest parties ever. And my god, you get to go to the hottest, most exclusive fashion shows in existence."

Emily had already told me that Miranda went to Europe three or four times a year for the fashion shows. She always skipped London, like everyone did, but she went to Milan and Paris in October for spring ready-to-wear, in July for winter couture, and in March for fall ready-to-wear. Sometimes she'd hit resort, but not always. We'd been working like crazy to get Miranda prepared for the shows coming up at the end of the month. I'd wondered briefly why she wasn't planning on bringing an assistant.

"So why doesn't she take you to all of them?" I decided to just go for it, even though the answer was sure to entail a lengthy explanation. I was excited enough that Miranda would be out of the office for two whole weeks (she spent one in Milan and one in Paris) and was giddy at the thought of getting rid of Emily for a week of that. Visions of bacon cheeseburgers and nonprofessionally ripped jeans and flats—oh hell, maybe even sneakers—filled my head. "Why just in October?"

"Well, it's not like she doesn't have help over there. Italian and French *Runway* always send some of their assistants for Miranda, and most of the time the editors help her themselves. But it's at spring RTW that she throws a huge party, the annual kick-off party that everyone says is the biggest and best at all the shows, all year long. I'll only go for the week while she's in Paris. So obviously she would only trust *me* to help her there." Obviously.

"Mmm, sounds like it'll be a great time. So that means I just hold down the fort here, huh?"

"Yeah, pretty much. But don't think that it'll be a joke. That will probably be the hardest week of all because she needs a lot of assistance when she's away. She'll be calling you a lot."

"Oh, goody," I said. She rolled her eyes.

I slept with my eyes open, staring at a blank computer screen, until the office began to fill up and there were other people to watch. Ten A.M. brought the first of the Clackers, the quiet sipping of no-whip skim lattes to nurse the previous night's champagne hangovers. James stopped by my desk, as he did whenever he saw Miranda wasn't at hers, and proclaimed he'd met his future husband at Balthazar the night before.

"He was just sitting at the bar, wearing the greatest red leather jacket I'd ever seen—and let me tell you, he could pull it off. You should have seen how he slipped those oysters on his tongue . . ." He audibly groaned. "Oh, it was just magnificent."

"So'd you get his number?" I asked.

"Get his number? Try get his pants. He was butt-ass naked on my couch by eleven, and boy, let me tell you—"

"Lovely, James. Lovely. Not one for playing hard to get, are you? Sounds a little slutty of you, to be honest. This is the age of AIDS, you know."

"Sweetie, even you, Miss High and Mighty I-Date-the-World's-Last-Angel, would've been on your knees without a second thought if you saw this guy. He's absolutely amazing. Amazing!"

By eleven everyone had checked everyone else out, making notations of who had scored a pair of the new Theory "Max" pants or the latest, impossible-to-find Sevens. Time for a break at noon, when conversation centered around particular items of clothing and usually took place by the racks lined up against the walls. Each morning Jeffy would pull out all the racks of dresses and bathing suits and pants and shirts and coats and shoes and everything else that had been called in as a potential item to shoot for one of the fashion spreads. He lined up each rack against a wall, weaving them throughout the entire floor so the editors could find what they needed without having to fight their way through the Closet itself.

The Closet wasn't really a closet at all. It was more like a small auditorium. Along the perimeter were walls of shoes in every size and color and style, a virtual Willy Wonka's factory for fashionistas, with dozens of slingbacks, stilettos, ballet flats, high-heeled boots, open-toe sandals, beaded heels. Stacked drawers, some built-in and others just shoved in corners, held every imaginable configuration of stockings, socks, bras, panties, slips, camisoles, and corsets. Need a last-minute leopard-print push-up bra from La Perla? Check the Closet. How about a pair of flesh-colored fishnets or those Dior aviators? In the Closet. The accessories shelves and drawers took up the farthest two walls, and the sheer amount of merchandise—not to mention its value—was staggering. Fountain pens. Jewelry. Bed linens. Mufflers and gloves and ski caps. Pajamas. Capes. Shawls. Stationery. Silk flowers. Hats, so many hats. And bags. The bags! There were totes and bowling bags, backpacks and under-arms, over-shoulders and minis, oversize and clutches, envelopes and messengers, each bearing an exclusive label and a price tag of more than the average American's monthly mortgage payment. And then there were the racks and racks of clothes—pushed so tightly together it was impos-sible to walk among them—that occupied every remaining inch of space.

So during the day Jeffy would attempt to make the Closet a semi-usable space where models (and assistants like myself) could try on clothes and actually reach some of the shoes and bags in the back by pushing all of the racks into the halls. I'd yet to see a single visitor to the floor—whether writer or boyfriend or messenger or stylist—not stop dead in his or her tracks and gape at the couture-lined hallways. Some-times the racks were arranged by shoot (Sydney, Santa Barbara) and other times by item (bikinis, skirt suits), but mostly it just seemed like a haplessly casual mishmash of *really expensive stuff.* And although every-one stopped and stared and fingered the butter-soft cashmeres and the intricately beaded evening gowns, it was the Clackers who hovered pos-sessively over "their" clothes and provided constant, streaming com-mentary on each and every piece.

"Maggie Rizer is the only woman in the *world* who can actually wear these capris," Hope, one of the fashion assistants—weighing a whopping 105 pounds and clocking in at six-one—loudly announced outside our office suite while holding the pants in front of her legs and sighing. "They would make my ass look even more gigantic than it already is."

"Andrea," called her friend, a girl I didn't know very well who worked in accessories, "please tell Hope she's not fat."

"You're not fat," I said, my mouth on autopilot. It would've saved me many, many hours to have a shirt printed up that said as much, or perhaps to just have the phrase tattooed directly on my forehead. I was constantly called on to assure various *Runway* employees that they weren't fat.

"Ohmigod, have you seen my gut lately? I'm like the fucking Firestone store, spare tires everywhere. I'm huge!" Fat was on everyone's minds, if not actually their bodies. Emily swore that her thighs had a "wider circumference than a giant sequoia." Jessica believed that her "jiggly upper arms" looked like Roseanne Barr's. Even James complained that his ass had looked so big that morning when he got out of the shower that he'd "contemplated calling in fat to work."

In the beginning I'd responded to the myriad am-I-fat questions with what I thought to be an exceedingly rational reply. "If you're fat, Hope, what does that make me? I'm two inches shorter than you and I weigh more."

"Oh, Andy, be serious. *I* am fat. *You're* thin and gorgeous!"

Naturally I thought she was lying, but I soon came to realize that Hope—along with every other anorexically skinny girl in the office, and most of the guys—was able to accurately evaluate other people's weight. It was just when it came time to look in the mirror that everyone genuinely saw a wildebeest staring back.

Of course, as much as I tried to keep it at bay, to remind myself over and over that I was normal and they weren't, the constant fat comments had made an impression. It'd only been four months I'd been working, but my mind was now skewed enough—not to mention paranoid—that I sometimes thought these comments were directed intentionally to me. As in: I, the tall, gorgeous, svelte fashion assistant, am pretending to think I'm fat just so you, the lumpy, stumpy personal assistant will realize that you are indeed the fat one. At five-ten and 115 pounds (the same weight as when my body was racked with parasites), I'd always considered myself on the thinner side of girls my age. I'd also spent my life until then feeling taller than ninety percent of the women I met, and at least half the guys. Not until starting work at this delusional place did I know what it was like to feel short and fat, all day, every day. I was easily the troll of the group, the squattest and the widest, and I wore a size six. And just in case I failed to consider this for a moment, the daily chitchat and gossip could surely remind me.

"Dr. Eisenberg said that the Zone only works if you swear off fruit, too, you know," Jessica added, joining the conversation by plucking a skirt from the Narciso Rodriguez rack. Newly engaged to one of the youngest vice presidents at Goldman Sachs, Jessica was feeling the pressures of her upcoming society wedding. "And she's right. I've lost at least another ten pounds since my last fitting." I forgave her for starving herself when she barely had enough body fat to function normally, but I just couldn't forgive her for *talking* about it. I could not, no matter how impressive the doctors' names were or how many success stories she prattled on about, bring myself to *care*.

At around one the office really picked up pace, because everyone began getting ready for lunch. Not that there was any eating associated with the lunch hour, but it was the prime time of day for guests. I watched lazily as the usual array of stylists, contributors, freelancers, friends, and lovers stopped by to revel in and generally soak up the glamour that naturally accompanied hundreds of thousands of dollars' worth of clothes, dozens of gorgeous faces, and what felt like an unlimited amount of really, really, really long legs.

Jeffy made his way over to me as soon as he could confirm that both Miranda and Emily had left for lunch and handed me two enormous shopping bags.

"Here, check this stuff out. This should be a pretty good start."

I dumped the contents of one bag onto the floor beside my desk and began sorting. There were Joseph pants in camel and charcoal gray, both long and lean and low-waisted, made from an incredibly soft wool. A pair of brown suede Gucci pants looked as though they could turn any schlub into a supermodel, while two pairs of perfectly faded Marc Jacobs jeans looked like they were custom cut for my body. There were eight or nine options for tops, ranging from a skintight ribbed turtleneck sweater by Calvin Klein to a teeny, completely sheer peasant blouse by Donna Karan. A dynamite graphic Diane Von Furstenburg wrap-dress was folded neatly over a navy, velvet Tahari pantsuit. I spotted and immediately fell in love with an all-around pleated Habitual denim skirt that would fall just above my knees and look perfect with the decidedly funky floral-printed Katayone Adelie blazer.

"These clothes . . . this is all for me?" I asked, hoping I sounded excited and not offended.

"Yeah, it's nothing. Just some things that have been lying around the Closet forever. We might have used some of it in shoots, but none of it ever got returned to the companies. Every few months or so I clean out the Closet and give this stuff away, and I figured you, uh, might be interested. You're a size six, right?"

I nodded, still dumbfounded.

"Yeah, I could tell. Most everyone else is a two or smaller, so you're welcome to all of it."

Ouch. "Great. This is just great. Jeffy, I can't thank you enough. It's all amazing!"

"Check out the second bag," he said, motioning to where it sat on the floor. "You don't think you can pull off that velvet suit with that shitty messenger bag you're always dragging around, do you?"

The second, even more bulging bag spilled forth a stunning array of shoes, bags, and a couple of coats. There were two pairs of high-heeled Jimmy Choo boots—one ankle- and one knee-length—two pairs of open-toe Manolo stiletto sandals, a pair of classic black Prada pumps, and one pair of Tod loafers, which Jeffy immediately reminded me to never wear to the office. I slung a slouchy red suede bag over my shoulder and immediately saw the two intersecting "C"s carved in the front, but that wasn't nearly as beautiful as the deep chocolate leather from the Celine tote that I threw on my other arm. A long military-style trench with the signature oversize Marc Jacobs buttons topped it all off.

"You're joking," I said softly, fondling a pair of Dior sunglasses he'd apparently thrown in as an afterthought. "You've got to be kidding."

He looked pleased with my reaction and ducked his head. "Just do me a favor and wear it, OK? And don't tell anyone that I gave you first pick on all this stuff, because they live for the Closet clean-outs, you hear?" He bolted from the suite when we heard Emily's voice call out to someone down the hall, and I shoved my new clothes under my desk.

Emily came back from the dining room with her usual lunch: an all-natural fruit smoothie and a small to-go container of iceberg lettuce topped with broccoli and balsamic vinegar. Not vinaigrette. Vinegar. Miranda would be in any minute—Uri had just called to say he was dropping her off—so I didn't have my usually luxurious seven minutes to beeline to the soup table and gulp it down back at my desk. The minutes ticked by and I was starving, but I just didn't have the energy to weave through the Clackers and get examined by the cashier and wonder if I was doing permanent damage by swallowing piping hot (and fattening!) soup so fast that I could feel the heat coursing down my esophagus. *Not worth it*, I thought. *Skipping a single meal won't kill you*, I told myself. *In fact, according to every single one of your sane and stable coworkers, it'll just make you stronger. And besides, $2,000 pants don't look so hot on girls who gorge themselves*, I rationalized. I slumped down in my chair and thought of how well I had just represented *Runway* magazine.

11 The cell phone shrilled from somewhere deep in my dream, but consciousness took over long enough for me to wonder if it was her. After a stunningly fast orientation process—*Where am I? Who is "she"? What day is it?*—I realized that having the phone ring at eight on a Saturday morning was not a good omen. None of my friends would be awake for hours, and after years of getting screened out, my parents had grudgingly accepted that their daughter wasn't answering until noon. In the seven seconds it took to figure all this out, I was also contemplating a reason why I should pick up this phone call. Emily's reasons from the first day came back to me, though, and so I started my arm in a floor sweep from the comfort of my bed. I managed to click it open just before it stopped ringing.

"Hello?" I was proud that my voice sounded strong and clear, as though I'd spent the past few hours working hard at something respectable rather than passed out in a sleep that was so deep, so intense, it couldn't possibly have indicated good things about my health.

"Morning, honey! Glad to hear you're awake. I just wanted to tell you that we're in the sixties on Third, so I'll be there in just ten minutes or so, OK?" My mom's voice came booming over the line. Moving day! It was moving day! I'd forgotten entirely that my parents had agreed to come into the city to help me pack my stuff up and take it to the new apartment Lily and I had rented. We were going to lug the boxes of clothes and CDs and picture albums while the real movers tackled my massive bed frame.

"Oh, hi, Mom," I mumbled, lapsing back into tired-voice mode. "I thought you were her."

"Nope, you've got yourself a break today. Anyway, where should we park? Is there a garage right around there?"

"Yeah, right under my building, just enter right from Third. Give them my apartment number in the building and you'll get a discount. I've got to get dressed. I'll see you soon."

"OK, honey. Hope you're ready to work today!"

I fell back onto my pillow and considered my options for possibly going back to sleep. They were looking really grim, considering they'd driven all the way in from Connecticut to help me move. Just then, the alarm clock blared its signature static. Ah hah! So I *had* remembered that today was moving day. The reminder that I wasn't going completely crazy was a small comfort.

Getting out of bed was, quite possibly, even harder to do than other days even though it was happening a few hours later. My body had been briefly tricked into thinking that it would actually get to catch up, had depended on reducing that infamous "sleep debt" we'd learned about in Psych 101, when I wrenched it from bed. There was a small pile of clothes I'd left folded by the bed, the only things besides my toothbrush that I hadn't yet packed. I pulled on the blue Adidas windpants, the hooded Brown sweatshirt, and the pair of filthy gray New Balance sneak-

ers that had accompanied me around the world. Not a second after I
swooshed the last of my Listerine did the buzzer ring.

"Hi, guys. I'll buzz you up, just a sec."

There was a knock on the door two minutes later, and instead of my
parents there stood a rumpled-looking Alex. He looked great, as usual. His
faded jeans hung low on nonexistent hips, and his long-sleeved navy T-shirt
was just the right amount of tight. The tiny wire-rims he wore only when he
couldn't tolerate his contacts were perched in front of very red eyes, and his
hair was all over the place. I couldn't stop myself from hugging him on the
spot. I hadn't seen him since the Sunday before, when we'd met for a quick
midafternoon coffee. We'd intended to spend the whole day and night together, but Miranda had needed an emergency babysitter for Cassidy so she
could take Caroline to the doctor, and I had been recruited. I'd gotten home
too late to spend any real time with him, and he'd recently stopped camp-
ing out in my bed just to get a glimpse of me, which I understood. He'd
wanted to stay over the night before, but I was still in that stage of parent-
pretending: even though all parties involved knew that Alex and I were
sleeping together, nothing could be done, said, or implied to actually confirm it. And so I hadn't wanted him there when my parents arrived.

"Hey, babe. I thought you guys could use some help today." He held
up a Bagelry bag that I knew would contain salt bagels, my favorite, and
some large coffees. "Are your parents here yet? I brought them coffees,
too."

"I thought you had to tutor today," I said just as Shanti emerged
from her bedroom wearing a black pantsuit. She hung her head as she
walked past us, mumbled something about working all day, and left. We
so seldom talked, I wondered if she realized today was my last day in the
apartment.

"I did, but I called the two little girls' parents and both said that tomorrow morning was fine with them, so I'm all yours!"

"Andy! Alex!" My father stood in the doorway behind Alex, beaming
as though this were the best morning on earth. My mom looked so awake
I wondered if she was on drugs. I did a quick once-over of the situation
and figured that they would rightly assume that Alex had just arrived
since he was still wearing his shoes and was obviously holding recently
purchased food. Besides, the door was still open. Phew.

"Andy said you couldn't make it today," my dad said, setting down what looked like a bag of bagels—also salt, no doubt—and coffees on the table in the living room. He deliberately avoided eye contact. "Are you on your way in or out?"

I smiled and looked at Alex, hoping he wasn't already regretting what he'd gotten himself into so early in the morning.

"Oh, I just got here, Dr. Sachs," Alex said gamely. "I rearranged my tutoring because I thought you two could use another pair of hands."

"Great. That's great—I'm sure it'll be a big help. Here, help yourself to bagels. Alex, I'm sorry to say that we didn't get three coffees since we didn't know you'd be here." My dad looked genuinely upset, which was touching. I knew he still had trouble with his youngest daughter having a boyfriend, but he did his best not to show it.

"No worries, Dr. S. I brought some stuff, too, so it looks like there's plenty." And somehow, my dad and my boyfriend sat down on the futon together—without a trace of awkwardness—and shared an early-morning breakfast.

I sampled salt bagels from each of their bags and thought about how much fun it would be to live with Lily again. We'd been out of college for nearly a year now. We'd tried to talk at least once a day, but it still felt like we hardly ever saw each other. Now, we would come home to each other and bitch about our respective hellish days—just like old times. Alex and my dad prattled on about sports (basketball, I think) while my mom and I labeled the boxes in my room. Sadly, there wasn't much: just a few boxes of bed linens and pillows, another of photo albums and assorted desk supplies (even though I lacked a desk), some makeup and toiletries, and a whole bunch of garment bags filled with un-*Runway*-esque clothes. Hardly enough to warrant labels; I guess it was the assistant in me kicking in.

"Let's get moving," my dad called from the living room.

"Shhh! You'll wake Kendra," I loudly whispered back. "It is only nine in the morning on a Saturday, you know."

Alex was shaking his head. "Didn't you see her leave with Shanti before? At least, I think that was her. There were definitely two of them, and they were both wearing suits and looking unhappy. Check their bedroom."

The door to the room they managed to share by bunking their beds was ajar, and I pushed it open slightly. Both beds were made meticulously, pillows fluffed and matching stuffed Gund dogs propped up on each. I didn't realize until then that I'd never so much as stepped foot in their room—in the few months I'd lived with these girls, we hadn't had a conversation of longer than thirty seconds—I didn't know exactly what they did, where they went, or if they had any friends besides each other. I was glad to be leaving.

Alex and my dad had cleaned up the leftover food and were trying to map out a game plan. "You're right, they're both gone. I don't even think they know I'm leaving today."

"Maybe leave them a note?" my mom suggested. "Maybe on your Scrabble board." I'd inherited my father's addiction to Scrabble, and he had a theory that each new home required a new board so I was leaving the old one behind.

I took the last five minutes in the apartment to make the tiles read, "Thanks for everything and good luck XO Andy." Fifty-nine points. Not bad.

It took an hour to pack both of the cars up, with me not doing much more than propping open the door to the street and guarding the vehicles while they went back upstairs. The bed movers—who were charging more than the actual cost of the damn thing—were running late, so my dad and Alex each started downtown. Lily had found our new apartment through an ad in the *Village Voice*, and I hadn't even seen it yet. She'd called me at work from her cell phone in the middle of the day, screaming, "I found it! I found it! It's perfect! There's a bathroom with running water, a wooden floor that only has minimal warping, and I've been here four full minutes and haven't seen a single mouse or even a roach. Can you come see it immediately?"

"Are you high right now?" I whispered. "*She's* here, which means I'm not going anywhere."

"You have to come *now*. You know what it's like. I have my folder and everything."

"Lily, be reasonable. I couldn't leave the office right now for an emergency heart transplant if I needed one, without getting fired. How can I come look at an apartment?"

"Well, it's not going to be here in thirty more seconds. There are at least twenty-five other people at this open house, and they're all filling out applications. I need to do this *now*."

In the obscene world of Manhattan real estate, semilivable apartments were rarer—and more desirable—than seminormal straight guys. When you added semiaffordable into the mix, they became harder to rent than your private island somewhere off the southern coast of Africa. Or probably harder. No matter that most boasted fewer than three hundred square feet of dirt and rotted wood, pockmarked walls, and prehistoric appliances. No roaches? No mice? This one was a keeper!

"Lily, I trust you, just do it. Can you e-mail me a description?" I was trying to get off the phone as quickly as possible since Miranda was due back from the art department any second. If she saw me on a personal call, I was finished.

"Well, I have copies of your paychecks—which, by the way, really suck . . . and I've got both our bank statements and printouts of our credit histories and your employment letter. The only problem is our guarantor. It has to be a tristate resident who makes more than forty times our monthly rent, and my grandmother sure as hell doesn't make a hundred grand. Can your parents sign for us?"

"Jesus, Lil, I don't know. I haven't asked them, and I can't very well call them right now. You call."

"Fine. They do make enough, don't they?"

I wasn't really sure, but who else could we ask? "Just call them," I told her. "Explain about Miranda. Tell them I'm sorry for not calling myself."

"Will do," she said. "But let me make sure we can get the place. I'll call you back," she said and clicked off the phone. The phone rang again twenty seconds later, and I saw her cell phone number on the office phone caller ID. Emily raised her eyes in that special way she did when she heard me once again talking to a friend. I grabbed the phone but spoke to Emily.

"It's important," I hissed in her direction. "My best friend is trying to rent me an apartment over the phone because I can't leave here for a goddamn—"

Three voices attacked me at once. Emily's was measured and calm and carried with it a warning tone. "Andrea, please," she'd started, at the exact same time that Lily was shrieking, "They'll do it, Andy, they'll do it! Are you listening to me?" But even though both of them were clearly addressing me, I couldn't really hear either one of them. The only voice that came through loud and clear was Miranda's.

"Do we have a problem here, Ahn-dre-ah?" Shocker—she got my name right this time. She was hovering over me, appearing ready to strike.

I immediately hung up on Lily, hoping she'd understand, and braced myself for the onslaught. "No, Miranda, no problem at all."

"Good. Now, I'd like a sundae and I'd like to actually eat it before the entire thing melts. Vanilla ice cream—not yogurt, mind you, not ice milk, and nothing sugar-free or low-fat—with chocolate syrup and real whipped cream. Not canned, you understand? Genuine whipped cream. That's all." She walked purposefully back toward the art department, and I was left with the distinct impression that she'd come in just to check on me. Emily smirked. The phone rang. Lily again. Dammit— couldn't she just e-mail me? I picked it up and pressed it to my ear but said nothing.

"OK, I know you can't talk, so I will. Your parents will be our guar- antors, which is great. The apartment is a big one-bedroom, and once we put the wall up in the living room, there will still be room for a two- person couch *and* a chair. The bathroom doesn't have a bath, but the shower looks OK. No dishwasher, natch, and no AC, but we can get win- dow units. Laundry in the basement, part-time doorman, one block from the six train. And get this. A balcony!"

I must've breathed audibly, because she got even more excited at my excitement. "I know! Crazy, right? It looks like it might fall right off the side of the building, but it's there! And we could both fit on it and have a place to smoke, and oh, it's just perfect!"

"How much?" I croaked, determined that these would be the ab- solute last words I'd utter.

"All ours for the grand total of twenty-two eighty a month. Do you believe that we'll get a balcony for eleven hundred forty dollars apiece? This place is the find of the century. So, can I do it?"

I was silent. I wanted to talk, but Miranda was inching her way back to her office as she upbraided the public events coordinator in front of everyone. She was in a wicked mood, and I'd already had enough for one day. The girl she was currently abusing had her head hung in shame, cheeks bright red, and I prayed for her own sake that she wouldn't cry.

"Andy! This is fucking ridiculous. Just say yes or no! It's bad enough that I have to cut class today and you can't so much as leave work to come look at this place, but you can't even bother to say yes or no? What am I—" Lily had reached her breaking point and I totally understood, but there was nothing I could do except hang up on her. She was screaming so loud into the phone that it was reverberating in the quiet office, and Miranda was standing less than five feet away. I was so frustrated, I wanted to grab the PR coordinator and hit the ladies' room and cry with her. Or maybe if we worked together we could throw Miranda into a toilet stall and tighten that Hermès scarf that hung loosely around her skinny neck. Would I hold her down or pull? Or perhaps it'd be more effective to just shove the damn thing down her throat and watch her gasp for air and—

"Ahn-dre-ah!" Her voice was clipped, steely. "What did I ask you for a mere five minutes ago?" Shit! The sundae. I'd forgotten the sundae. "Is there a particular reason why you're still sitting there instead of doing your job? Is this your idea of a joke? Did I do or say something to indicate that I wasn't entirely serious? Did I? Did I?" Her blue eyes were bulging out of her face, and although she hadn't fully raised her voice yet, of course, she was coming awfully close. I opened my mouth to speak but heard Emily talking instead.

"Miranda, I'm so sorry. It's my fault. I asked Andrea to answer the phone because I thought it might be Caroline or Cassidy and I was on the other line ordering that shirt from Prada you wanted. Andrea was just on her way out. I'm sorry, and it won't happen again."

Miracle of miracles! The Perfect One had spoken, and in my defense, no less.

Miranda looked momentarily mollified. "Well, all right then. Get my sundae now, Andrea." And with that, she walked in her office and picked up the phone, where she promptly started cooing to B-DAD.

I looked at Emily, but she was pretending to work. I shot her a one-word e-mail. *Why?* I wrote.

Because I wasn't entirely sure she wasn't going to fire you, and I don't really feel like training someone new, she wrote back instantly. I left to go in search of this perfect sundae and called Lily from my cell phone as soon as the elevator hit the lobby.

"I'm sorry, I really am. It's just that—"

"Look, I don't really have time for this," Lily said flatly. "I think you're overreacting just a little bit, don't you? I mean, you can't so much as say yes or no on the phone?"

"It's hard to explain, Lil, it's just that—"

"Forget it. I've got to run. I'll call you if we get it. Not that you really care either way."

I tried to protest, but she'd hung up. Dammit! It wasn't fair to expect Lily to understand when I would've thought I was ridiculous a mere four months earlier. It really wasn't fair to send her all over Manhattan in search of an apartment we could both share when I wouldn't even take her phone calls, but what choice did I have?

When she answered one of my calls right after midnight, she told me we got the apartment.

"That's amazing, Lil. I can't thank you enough. I swear I'll make it up to you. I promise!" And then I had a thought. Be spontaneous! Call an Elias car and get up to Harlem and thank your best friend in person. Yes, that was it! "Lil, are you home? I'm coming up to celebrate, OK?"

I thought she'd be thrilled, but she was quiet. "Don't bother," she said quietly. "I've got a bottle of So-Co and Tongue Ring Boy is here. I've got everything I want."

It stung, but I understood. Lily rarely got mad, but when she did, no one could talk her out of it until she was good and ready. I heard liquid swishing into a glass and ice clinking, and I heard her take a deep, long swig.

"OK. But call me if you need anything, OK?"

"Why? So you can sit in silence on the other end? No thanks."

"Lil—"

"Don't worry about me. I'm just fine." Another gulp. "I'll talk to you later. And hey, congratulations to us."

"Yeah, congratulations to us," I repeated, but she'd already hung up once again.

I'd called Alex on his cell to ask if I could go over to his place, but he didn't sound as delighted to hear from me as I'd hoped.

"Andy, you know I'd love to see you, but, well, I'm out with Max and the guys. You're never really around during the week anymore, so I made plans to see them tonight."

"Oh, well, are you guys in Brooklyn or around here somewhere? I could come meet you?" I asked, knowing that of course they were some-where on the Upper East Side, probably very close to me, because that's where all the other guys lived as well.

"Listen, any other night that'd be great, but tonight is definitely just a guys' night."

"Oh, sure, OK. I was going to meet Lily to celebrate the new apart-ment, but we, uh, sort of got in a fight. She doesn't understand why I can't really talk from work."

"Well, Andy, I have to say, sometimes I don't totally understand, ei-ther. I mean, I know she's a tough lady—trust me, I do—it just seems that you take everything pretty seriously when it comes to her, you know?" He sounded like he was trying very hard to keep his tone ac-commodating and nonconfrontational.

"Maybe that's because I do!" I shot back at him, pissed off at him for not wanting to see me and not begging me to go out with his friends and for taking Lily's side even though she had a point and so did he. "It is my life, you know? My career. My *future*. What the hell am I supposed to do? Treat it like a joke?"

"Andy, you're twisting my words. You know that's not what I meant."

But I was already screaming back—I couldn't help myself. First Lily and now Alex? Both on top of Miranda, all day, every day? It was too much, and I wanted to cry but all I could do was yell.

"A big fucking joke, huh? That's what my job is to both of you! *Oh, Andy, you work in fashion, how hard can it be?*" I mimicked, hating my-self more with every passing second. "Well, excuse me if we can't all be do-gooders or Ph.D. candidates! Excuse me if—"

"Call me when you calm down," he stated. "I'm not going to listen to this anymore." And he hung up. Hung up! I waited for him to call back, but he never did, and by the time I'd finally fallen asleep, close to three, I hadn't heard from either Alex or Lily.

Now it was moving day—a full week later—and while neither was still visibly mad, neither seemed exactly the same either. There hadn't been time to make amends in person with either one since we were in the middle of closing an issue, but I figured things would fall into place when Lily and I moved into our new apartment. Our shared apartment, where everything would go back to the way it was when we were in college and life was much more palatable.

The movers finally came at eleven, and it took them all of nine minutes to disassemble my beloved bed and throw the pieces in back of their van. Mom and I hitched a ride with them over to my new building, where my dad and Alex were schmoozing with the doorman—who, bizarrely enough, was a dead ringer for John Galliano—with my boxes piled against a wall in the lobby.

"Andy, glad you're here. Mr. Fisher here won't open the apartment unless there's a tenant present," my dad said with a huge smile on his face. "Which is very smart of him," he added, winking at the doorman.

"Oh, is Lily not here yet? She said she'd get here by ten, ten-thirty."

"Nope, haven't seen her. Should I call her?" Alex asked.

"Yeah, I guess so. Why don't I go up with, er, Mr. Fisher so we can start bringing stuff up. Ask her if she needs any help."

Mr. Fisher smiled a way that could only be described as lecherous. "Please, we're like family now," he said, looking at my chest. "Call me John."

I almost choked on the now cold coffee I was holding and wondered if the man revered the world over for reviving the Dior brand had died without my knowing and been reincarnated as my doorman.

Alex nodded and wiped his glasses on his T-shirt. I loved it when he did that. "You go with your parents. I'll call."

I wondered if it was a good or bad thing that my father was now best friends with my (designer) doorman, the man who would inevitably know every detail of my life. The lobby looked nice, if a little retro. It was done in a light-colored stone of some sort, and there were a few uncomfortable-looking benches in front of the elevators and behind the mailroom. Our apartment was number 8C, and it faced southwest, which, from what I'd heard, was a good thing. John opened the door with his master key and stood back like a proud papa.

"Here she is," he announced grandly.

I walked in first, expecting to be hit with an overpowering smell of sulfur or perhaps see a few bats winging their way around our ceiling, but it was surprisingly clean and bright. The kitchen was on the right, a narrow, one-person-wide strip with white tile floors and reasonably white Formica cabinets. The countertops were some sort of flecked granite imitation, and there was a microwave built in above the stove.

"This is great," my mom said, pulling open the refrigerator. "It's already got ice trays." The movers pushed past us, grunting while they lugged my bed.

The kitchen opened to the living room, which had already been divided in two by a temporary wall to create a second bedroom. Of course, that meant that all the windows had been cut out of the living room entirely, but that was OK. The bedroom was a decent size—definitely bigger than the one I'd just left—and the sliding glass door leading to the balcony made up one whole wall. The bathroom was between the living room and the real bedroom and was done in Pepto pink tiling and pink paint. Oh well. Could be kitschy. I walked into the real bedroom, which was significantly bigger than the living room one and looked around. A tiny closet, a ceiling fan, and a small, dirty window that looked directly into an apartment in the building next door. Lily had wanted this one and I'd happily agreed. She preferred having the extra space since she spent so much time in her bedroom studying, but I'd rather have the light and the balcony entrance.

"Thanks, Lil," I whispered to myself, knowing that Lily couldn't possibly hear me.

"What'd you say, honey?" my mom asked, coming up behind me.

"Oh, nothing. Just that Lily did really, really well. I had no idea what to expect, but this is great, don't you think?"

She looked like she was trying to find the most tactful way of saying something. "Yes, for New York, it's a great apartment. It's just hard to imagine paying so much and getting so little. You know your sister and Kyle only pay fourteen hundred a month total for their condo, and they have central air, marble bathrooms, brand-new dishwasher and washer-dryer, and three bedrooms and two bathrooms?" she pointed out, as if she were the first to make this realization. For $2,280 you could get a beachfront townhouse in LA, a three-story condo on a tree-lined street in Chicago, a four-bedroom split-level in Miami, or a goddamn castle with a moat in Cleveland. Yes, we knew this.

"And two parking spots, access to the golf course, gym, and pool," I added helpfully. "Yeah, I know. But believe it or not, this is a great deal. I think we'll be very happy here."

She hugged me. "I think you will be, too. As long as you don't work too hard to enjoy it," she said lightly.

My dad walked in and opened the duffel bag that he'd been dragging around all day, one I'd assumed held racquetball clothes for his game later. But he pulled out a maroon box emblazoned with "Limited Edition!" across the front. Scrabble. The collector's edition, where the board came mounted on its own lazy Susan and the squares had little raised borders so the letters didn't slide around. We'd been admiring them together in specialty game stores for the past ten years, but no occasion had ever warranted purchasing one.

"Oh, Dad. You shouldn't have!" I knew the board cost well over two hundred dollars. "Oh! I just love it!"

"Use it in good health," he said, hugging me back. "Or better yet, to kick your old man's ass, as I know you will. I remember when I used to let you win. I had to, or you'd stomp around the house, sulking all night. And now! Well, now my old brain cells are fried and I couldn't beat you if I tried. Not that I won't," he added.

I was about to tell him that I'd learned from the best, but Alex had walked in. And he didn't look happy.

"What's wrong?" I immediately asked as he fidgeted with his sneakers.

"Oh, nothing at all," he lied while glancing in the direction of my parents. He shot me a "just hold on a sec" look and said, "Here, I brought a box."

"Let's go get a few more," my dad said to my mom, moving toward the door. "Maybe Mr. Fisher has some sort of cart. We could bring a bunch up at once. Be right back."

I looked at Alex, and we both waited until we'd heard the elevator open and close.

"So, I just talked to Lily," he said slowly.

"She's not still mad at me, is she? She's been so weird all week."

"No, I don't think it's that."

"So what is it?"

"Well, she wasn't at home . . ."

"So where is she? Some guy's apartment? I can't believe she's late for her own moving day." I yanked open one of the windows in the converted bedroom to let some of the cold air dissipate the smell of new paint.

"No, she was actually at a police precinct in midtown." He looked at his shoes.

"She was where? Is she OK? Ohmigod! Was she mugged or raped? I have to go to her right away."

"Andy, she's fine. She was arrested." He said it quietly, as if he were breaking the news to a parent that their child wasn't going to pass fourth grade.

"Arrested? She was arrested?" I tried to stay calm, but I realized too late that I was screaming. My dad walked in, pulling a giant cart that looked ready to topple under the weight of unevenly stacked boxes.

"Who was arrested?" he asked off-handedly. "Mr. Fisher brought all this stuff up for us."

I was racking my brain for a lie, but Alex stepped in before I could think of anything remotely plausible. "Oh, I was just telling Andy that I saw on VH-1 last night that one of the girls from TLC was arrested on drug charges. And she always seemed like one of the straighter ones . . ."

My dad shook his head and surveyed the room, only half listening and probably wondering when exactly Alex or myself had become so interested in female pop stars that we actually discussed it. "I'm thinking that the only real place your bed can go is with the head against the far wall," he said. "Speaking of which, I better go see how they're doing."

I literally flung my body in front of Alex the minute the apartment door closed.

"Quickly! Tell me what happened. What happened?"

"Andy, you're shrieking. It's not so bad. Actually, it's kind of funny." His eyes crinkled as he laughed, and for a brief second he looked just like Eduardo. Ew.

"Alex Fineman, you better fucking tell me right now what happened with my best friend—"

"OK, OK, relax." He was clearly enjoying this. "She was out with some guy last night that she referred to as Tongue Ring Boy—do we know who that is?"

I stared at him.

"Anyway, they went out for dinner and Tongue Ring Boy was walking her home, and she thought it'd be fun to flash him, right there on the street outside the restaurant. 'Sexy,' she said. To get him interested."

I envisioned Lily unwrapping a dinner mint and strolling outside after a romantic meal, only to pull away and yank up her shirt for a guy who'd paid to have someone ram a post through his tongue. Jesus.

"Oh no. She didn't . . ."

Alex nodded somberly, trying not to laugh.

"You're telling me my friend got arrested for showing her breasts? That's ridiculous. This is New York. I see women every day who are practically topless—and that's in the workplace!" I was shrieking again, but I couldn't help it.

"Her bottom." He was looking at his shoes again, and his face was so red, I couldn't tell if he was embarrassed or hysterical.

"Her what?"

"Not her breasts. Her bottom. Her lower half. Like, all of it. Front and back." An ear-to-ear grin had finally broken out, and he looked so delighted that I thought he might wet himself.

"Oh, say it isn't true," I moaned, wondering what my friend had gotten herself into now. "And a cop saw her and arrested her?"

"No, evidently two little kids saw her do it and pointed it out to their mother . . ."

"Oh, god."

"So, the mother asked her to pull her pants back up, and Lily loudly told her what she could do with her opinions, and the woman went and found a cop standing on the next street over."

"Oh, stop. Oh, please, just stop."

"It gets better. By the time the woman and the cop came back, Lily and Tongue Ring Boy were going at it on the street, pretty hot and heavy from what she said."

"Who is this? This is my friend Lily Goodwin? My sweet, adorable best friend from eighth grade now gets naked and hooks up on street corners? With guys who have tongue rings?"

"Andy, calm down. Really, she's fine. The only reason the cop actually arrested her was because she gave him the finger when he asked if she had, in fact, pulled her pants down . . ."

"Oh, my god. I can't take it anymore. This is what it must feel like to be a mother."

". . . but they let her go with just a warning, and she's going back to her apartment to recover—sounds like she was pretty drunk. I mean, why else would someone flip off a police officer? So don't worry. Let's get you moved in and then we can go see her if you want." He headed toward the cart my dad had left in the middle of the living room and started unloading boxes.

I couldn't wait until later; I had to see what had happened. She picked up on the fourth ring, right before it clicked into voice mail, as if she'd been debating whether or not to answer it.

"Are you OK?" I asked her the second I heard her voice.

"Hey, Andy. Hope I'm not screwing up the move at all. You don't need me, right? Sorry about all this."

"No, I don't care about that, I care about you. Are you OK?" It had just occurred to me that Lily may have spent the night at the police station, considering that it was early Saturday morning and she was just leaving. "Did you stay overnight? In *jail?*"

"Well, yeah, I guess you could say that. It wasn't so bad, nothing like TV or anything. I just slept in this room with one other totally harmless girl who was in for something just as stupid. The guards were totally cool—it really wasn't a big deal. No bars or anything." She laughed, but it sounded hollow.

I digested this for a moment, tried to reconcile the image of sweet little hippie Lily getting cornered in a urine-flooded cell by an extremely angry and possessive lesbian. "Where the hell was Tongue Ring Boy through all of this? Did he just leave you to rot in jail?" But before she could answer, it occurred to me: Where the hell was I through all of this? Why hadn't Lily called me?

"He was actually really great, he—"

"Lily, why—"

". . . offered to stay with me and even called his parents' lawyer—"

"Lily. Lily! Stop for a second. Why didn't you call me? You know I would've been there in a second and not left until they'd let you go. So why? Why didn't you call me?"

"Oh, Andy, it doesn't matter anymore. It really wasn't that bad, I swear. I can't believe how stupid I was, and trust me, I'm over getting that drunk. It's just not worth it."

"Why? Why didn't you call? I was home all night."

"It's not important, really. I didn't call because I figured you were either working or really, really tired, and I didn't want to bother you. Especially on a Friday night."

I thought back to what I'd been doing the night before and the only thing that stuck clearly in my mind was watching *Dirty Dancing* on TNT for exactly the sixty-eighth time in my life. And out of all those times, that had been the first that I'd fallen asleep before Johnny announced, "No one puts Baby in the corner," and proceeded to, quite literally, lift her off her feet, until Dr. Houseman admits that he knows Johnny wasn't the one who got Penny in trouble, and claps him on the back and kisses Baby, who has recently reclaimed the name Frances. I considered the whole scene a defining factor in my identity.

"Working? You thought I was working? And what does too tired have to do with it when you need help? Lil, I don't get it."

"Look, Andy, let's drop it, OK? You work constantly. Day and night, and lots of times on weekends. And when you're not working, you're complaining about work. Not that I don't understand, because I know how tough your job is, and I know you work for a lunatic. But I wasn't going to be the one to interrupt a Friday night when you might actually be relaxing or hanging out with Alex. I mean, he says he never sees you, and I didn't want to take that away from him. If I'd really needed you, I would've called, and I know you would've come running. But I swear, it wasn't so bad. Please, can we forget it? I'm exhausted and I really need a shower and my own bed."

I was so stunned I couldn't speak, but Lily took my silence for acquiescence.

"You there?" she asked after nearly thirty seconds, during which I was desperately trying to find the words to apologize or explain or something. "Listen, I just got home. I need sleep. Can I call you later?"

"Um, uh, sure," I managed. "Lil, I'm so sorry. If I've ever given you the impression that you can't—"

"Andy, don't. Nothing's wrong—I'm fine, we're fine. Let's just talk later."

"OK. Sleep well. Call me if I can do anything . . ."

"Will do. Oh, how's the new place, by the way?"

"It's great, Lil, it really is. You did a fantastic job with it. It's better than I'd ever imagined. We're going to love it here." My voice sounded empty to my own ears, and it was obvious I was talking just for the sake of it, keeping her on the phone to make sure our friendship hadn't changed in some inexplicable but permanent way.

"Great. I'm so glad you like it. Hopefully Tongue Ring Boy will like it, too," she joked, although that, too, sounded hollow.

We hung up and I stood in the living room, staring at the phone until my mom walked in to announce that they were going to take Alex and me out for lunch.

"What's wrong, Andy? And where's Lily? I figured she'd need some help with her stuff, too, but we're not going to stick around much after three. Is she on her way?"

"No, she's, uh, she got sick last night. It's been coming on for a few days, I guess, so she probably won't move in until tomorrow. That was just her on the phone."

"Well, you're sure she's all right? Do you think we should go over there? I always feel so badly for that girl—no real parents, just that cranky old bat of a grandmother." She put her hand on my shoulder, as if to drive home the pain. "She's lucky she's got you for a friend. Otherwise she'd be all alone in the world."

My voice caught in my throat, but after a few seconds I managed a few words. "Yeah, I guess so. But she's fine, she really is. Just going to sleep it off. Let's get sandwiches, OK? The doorman said there's a great deli four blocks down."

◄—►

"Miranda Priestly's office," I answered in my now usual bored tone that I hoped conveyed my misery to whoever was daring to interrupt my e-mailing time.

"Hi, is that Em-Em-Em-Emily?" asked a lisping, stuttering voice on the other end.

"No, it's Andrea. I'm Miranda's new assistant," I said, even though I'd already introduced myself to a thousand curious callers.

"Ah, Miranda's new assistant," the strange female voice roared. "Aren't you the luckiest girl in the w-w-w-world! How are you finding your tenure with supreme evil thus far?"

I perked up. This was new. In all the days I'd worked at *Runway*, I'd never met a single person who dared to badmouth Miranda so boldly. Was she serious? Could she be baiting me?

"Um, well, working at *Runway* has been a really great learning experience," I heard myself stutter. "It's a job a million girls would die for, of course." Did I just say that?

There was a moment of silence, followed by a hyena-like howl. "Oh, that's just f-f-f-fucking perfect!" she screeched, doing some sort of simultaneous laugh-choke. "Does she lock you in your West Village studio apartment and deprive you of all things G-g-g-gucci until you're brainwashed enough to actually say shit like that? F-f-f-fantastic! That woman is really a piece of work! Well, Miss Learning Experience, I'd heard through the grapevine that Miranda had actually hired herself a thinking l-l-l-l-lackey this time around, but I see that the grapevine, as usual, is wrong. You like Michael Kors t-t-twinsets and all the pretty fur coats at J. Mendel's? Yes, sweetie, you'll do just fine. Now put that skinny-ass boss of yours on the phone."

I was conflicted. My first impulse was to tell her to fuck off, tell her she didn't know me, that it's easy to see she tries to compensate for her stuttering with a major attitude problem. More than that, though, I wanted to press the phone close to my lips and urgently whisper, "I am a prisoner, more than you can imagine—please, oh, please, come and rescue me from this brainwash hell. You're right, it's just the way you describe, but I'm different!" But I didn't get the chance to do either, because it finally occurred to me that I had no idea who owned the raspy, stuttering voice on the other end of the phone.

I sucked in my breath and decided to hit her point for point—on every subject but Miranda. "Well, I do adore Michael Kors, of course, but I must tell you that it's certainly not because of his *twinsets*. Furs from J. Mendel's are wonderful, of course, but a real *Runway* girl—that is, someone with discriminating and impeccable taste—would probably prefer something custom made from Pologeorgis on Twenty-ninth Street. Oh, and for the future, I'd prefer if you used the more casual 'hired help' instead of something as stiff and unforgiving as 'lackey.' Now, of course, I'll be happy to correct any more incorrect assumptions you'd care to make, but maybe I could ask with whom am I speaking first?"

"Touché, Miranda's new assistant, touché. You and I m-m-may be friends after all. I d-d-d-don't much like the usual robots she hires, but it's fitting because I don't much like her. My name is Judith Mason, and in c-c-case you aren't aware, I author your travel articles each m-m-m-month. Now, tell me this, since you're still relatively new now: Is the h-h-honeymoon over?"

I was silent. What did she mean by this? It was like talking to a ticking bomb.

"Well? You're in that fascinating window of time w-w-w-where you've been there long enough for everyone to know your name, but not long enough that they uncover and exploit all your weaknesses. It's a really sweet feeling when th-th-th-that happens, trust me. You're working in a really special place."

But before I could respond, she said, "Enough f-f-f-flirting for now, my new friend. Don't b-b-b-bother telling her it's me, because she never takes my c-c-calls anyway. Stuttering pisses her off, I think. Just be sure to put my n-n-n-name down on the Bulletin so she can make someone else call me back. Thanks, l-l-love." Click.

I hung up the phone, dumbfounded, and started to laugh. Emily looked up from one of Miranda's expense reports and asked who it was. When I told her it was Judith, she rolled her eyes so deeply they almost didn't resurface and whined, "She's such a supreme bitch. I have, like, no idea how Miranda even speaks to her. She won't take her calls, though, so you don't even have to tell her she's on the phone. Just put her on the Bulletin and Miranda will have someone else call her back." It seems Judith understood the inner workings of our office better than I.

I double-clicked on the icon on my sleek turquoise iMac called "Bulletin" and glanced over its contents so far. The Bulletin was the *pièce de résistance* of Miranda Priestly's office and, as far as I could see, her sole reason for living. Developed many years before by some high-strung, compulsive assistant, the Bulletin was simply a Word document that lived in a shared folder both Emily and I could access. Only one of us could open it at a time and add a new message, thought, or question to the itemized list. Then we'd print out the updated version and place it on the clipboard that sat on the shelf over my desk, removing the old ones as we went. Miranda would examine it every few minutes throughout the day as Emily and I struggled to type, print, and clip as quickly as the calls came in. Often we'd hiss at each other to close the Bulletin so the other could access it and write a message. We'd print to our separate printers simultaneously and dive for the clipboard, not knowing whose was the most recent until we were face to face.

"Judith's the latest message on mine," I said, exhausted from the pressure of trying to finish it before Miranda entered the suite. Eduardo had called from the security desk downstairs to warn us that she was on her way upstairs. We hadn't gotten a call from Sophy yet, but we knew it'd be only seconds.

"I have the concierge from the Ritz Paris after Judith," Emily near-shouted, triumphantly, while clipping her sheet to the Lucite clipboard. I took my four-second outdated Bulletin back to the desk and glanced over it. Dashes in phone numbers were not permissible, only periods. There were to be no colons in the time, only periods. Times must be rounded up or down to the nearest quarter-hour. Call-back phone numbers always got their own lines to make them easier to distinguish. A time listed indicated that someone had called in. The word "note" was something that Emily or I had to tell her (since addressing her without being first addressed was out of the question, all relevant info went on the Bulletin). "Reminder" was something Miranda had most likely left on one of our voice mails sometime between one and five A.M. the previous night, knowing that once it was recorded for us, it was as good as done. We were to refer to ourselves in the third person—if it was absolutely crucial for us to refer to ourselves at all.

She often asked us to find out exactly when and at what number a particular person would be available to speak. In this case it was a tossup whether the fruits of our investigation would go under "note" or "reminder." I remember once thinking that the Bulletin read like a who's who in the Prada crowd, but the names of the superbigmoney, the superhigh-fashion, and the generally superimpressive had ceased to register as "special" on my desensitized brain. In my new *Runway* reality, the White House social secretary held little more interest than the vet who needed to speak to her about the puppy's vaccinations (fat chance of him getting a call back!).

Thursday, April 8

7.30: Simone called from the Paris office. She figured out dates with Mr. Testino for the Rio shoot and also confirmed with Giselle's agent, but she still needs to discuss the fashion with you. Please call her.
011.33.1.55.91.30.65

8.15: Mr. Tomlinson called. He is on cell. Please call him.

Note: Andrea spoke with Bruce. He said that the large mirror in your foyer has a piece of decorative plaster missing from the upper left-hand corner. He located an identical mirror at an antique shop in Bordeaux. Would you like him to order it?

8.30: Jonathan Cole called. He is leaving for Melbourne on Saturday and would like to clarify the assignment before he leaves. Please call him.
555.7700

Reminder: To call Karl Lagerfeld about the Model of the Year party. He will be reachable at his home in Biarritz this evening from 8.00–8.30 P.M. his time.
011.33.1.55.22.06.78: home
011.33.1.55.22.58.29: home studio
011.33.1.55.22.92.64: driver
011.33.1.55.66.76.33: assistant's number in Paris, in case you cannot find him

9.00: Natalie from Glorious Foods called to see whether you'd prefer that the Vacherin be filled with mixed berries praline or warm rhubarb compote. Please call her.
555.9887

9.00: Ingrid Sischy called to congratulate you on the April issue. Says the cover is "spectacular, as always" and wants to know who styled the front-of-book beauty shoot. Please call her.
555.6246: office
555.8833: home

Note: Miho Kosudo called to apologize for being unable to de-
       liver Damien Hirst's flower arrangement. They said to be
       sure to tell you that they waited outside his building for
       four hours, but since he doesn't have a doorman, they
       had to leave. They will try again tomorrow.

9.15: Mr. Samuels called. He will be unreachable until
       after lunch, but wants to remind you of parent-teacher
       conferences tonight at Horace Mann. He would like
       to discuss Caroline's history project with you before
       hand. Please call him after 2.00 P.M. but before 4.00 P.M.
       555.5932

9.15: Mr. Tomlinson called again. He asked Andrea to make
       reservations for dinner tonight after parent-teacher con-
       ferences. Please call him. He is on cell.

Note: Andrea made reservations for you and Mr. Tomlinson
       tonight at 8.00 P.M. at La Caravelle. Rita Jammet said
       she is looking forward to seeing you again, and she's de-
       lighted you chose her restaurant.

9.30: Donatella Versace called. She said everything's confirmed
       for your visit. Will you be needing any staff besides a
       driver, a chef, a trainer, a hair and makeup person, a per-
       sonal assistant, three maids, and a yacht captain? If so,
       please let her know before she leaves for Milan. She will
       also provide cell phones, but won't be able to join you as
       she'll be preparing for the shows.
       011.3901.55.27.55.61

9.45: Judith Mason called. Please call her back.
       555.6834

I crumpled the sheet and tossed it in the basket under my desk,
where it immediately soaked up the leftover grease from Miranda's third
morning breakfast that I'd already thrown out. So far, a relatively normal day as far as the Bulletin was concerned. I was just about to click
"inbox" on my Hotmail account to see if anyone had e-mailed yet when
she cruised into the office. Damn that Sophy! She'd forgotten the warning call again.

"I expect the Bulletin is updated," she said icily without making eye contact or otherwise acknowledging our presence.

"It is, Miranda," I replied, holding it up to her so she needn't so much as reach for it. *Three words and counting*, I thought to myself, predicting—and praying—it wouldn't be more than a seventy-five-word day on my part. She removed her waist-length mink, so plush I had to restrain myself from burying my face into it right there, and tossed it onto my desk. As I went to hang that magnificent dead animal in the closet, trying to rub it discreetly against my cheek, I felt a quick shock of cold and wet: there were tiny bits of still-frozen sleet stuck to the fur. How fabulously apropos.

Pulling the lid from a lukewarm latte, I carefully arranged today's greasy pile of bacon, sausage, and cheese-filled pastry on a filthy plate. I tiptoed into her office and carefully placed everything unobtrusively on a corner of her desk. She was concentrating on writing a note on her ecru Dempsey and Carroll stationery and spoke so softly I almost didn't hear.

"Ahn-dre-ah, I need to discuss the engagement party with you. Get a notebook."

I nodded, simultaneously realizing that nodding doesn't count as a word. This engagement party had already become the bane of my existence and it was still more than a month away, but since Miranda was leaving for the European shows soon and would be gone for two weeks, planning this party had occupied the vast majority of both our recent workdays. I returned to her office with a pad and pen, preparing myself to not understand a single word she'd say. I considered sitting for just a moment since it'd make taking dictation much more comfortable, but wisely resisted.

She sighed as though this were so taxing she wasn't sure if she'd make it and tugged on the white Hermès scarf that she'd woven into a braceletlike thing around her wrist. "Find Natalie at Glorious Foods and tell her that I prefer the rhubarb compote. Do not let her convince you that she needs to speak with me directly, because she does not. Also talk to Miho and make sure they understand my orders for the flowers. Get Robert Isabell on the phone for me sometime before lunch to go over tablecloths, place cards, and serving trays. Also that girl from the Met to see when I can go over to make sure everything is set up properly, and tell her to fax over the table configurations so I may do seating charts. That's all for now."

She had rattled off that list without a single pause in her note writing, and when she finished speaking she handed me her newly crafted note to mail. I finished scribbling on my pad, hoping I'd understood everything correctly, which, considering the accent and the rapid-fire cadence, wasn't always simple.

"OK," I muttered and turned to go, bringing up my Total Miranda Words to four. *Maybe I won't break fifty*, I thought. I could feel her eyes examining the size of my butt as I walked back to my desk and briefly considered whipping around to walk backward like a religious Jew would do when leaving the Wailing Wall. Instead, I tried to glide toward the hidden safety of my desk while picturing thousands and thousands of *Hasidim* in Prada black, walking backward circles around Miranda Priestly.

12 The blissful day I'd been waiting for, dreaming of, had finally, finally arrived. Miranda had not only departed the office, but she'd left the country as well. She'd jumped into her Concorde seat less than an hour before to meet with a few of the European designers, making me at present the indisputably happiest girl on the planet. Emily kept trying to convince me that Miranda was even more demanding when she was abroad, but I wasn't buying it. I was in the middle of mapping out exactly how I was going to spend every ecstatic moment of the next two weeks when I got an e-mail from Alex.

Hey babe, how are you? Hope your day is at least ok. You must be loving that
she left, right? Enjoy it. Anyway, just wanted to see if you think you'll be able
to call me around three-thirty today. I have a free hour then before the reading program starts and I need to talk to you. Nothing major, but I would like to
talk. Love, A

To which I immediately worried and replied to ask if everything was
OK, but he must have logged off right away because he never wrote back
again. I made a mental note to call him at exactly three-thirty, loving the
feeling of freedom that comes from knowing that She wouldn't be around
to screw it up. But just in case, I pulled a piece of *Runway* stationery
from the pile and wrote CALL A, 3:30 P.M. TODAY and taped it to the
side of my monitor. Just as I was going to call back a friend from school
who'd left a message on my home machine a week earlier, the phone
rang.

"Miranda Priestly's office," I all but sighed, figuring that there wasn't
a single person on earth I wanted to speak with at that moment.

"Emily? Is that you? Emily?" The unmistakable voice filled the
phone line and seemed to seep into the air in the office. Even though she
couldn't have possibly heard from across the suite, Emily looked up
at me.

"Hello, Miranda. This is Andrea. May I help you with something?"
How on earth was this woman calling? I quickly checked the itinerary
that Emily had typed for everyone while Miranda was in Europe and saw
that her flight had taken off a mere six minutes before and she was already calling from the seat phone.

"Well, I should hope so. I've looked at my itinerary and I just noticed
that hair and makeup for Thursday before dinner is not confirmed."

"Um, well, Miranda, that's because Monsieur Renaud wasn't able to
get an absolute confirmation from the Thursday people, but he said it
was ninety-nine percent that they'd be able to and—"

"Ahn-dre-ah, answer me this: Is ninety-nine percent the same as a
hundred? Is it the same as *confirmed*?" But before I could answer I heard
her tell someone, most likely a flight attendant, that she wasn't "particularly interested in the rules and regulations regarding the use of elec-
tronics" and to "please bore someone else with them."

"But ma'am, it's against the rules, and I'm going to have to ask that you disconnect your call until we've reached a cruising altitude. It's simply unsafe," she said beseechingly.

"Ahn-dre-ah, can you hear me? Are you listening . . ."

"Ma'am, I'm going to have to insist. Now please, hang up the phone." My mouth was starting to ache from smiling so widely—I could only imagine how much Miranda was hating being addressed as "ma'am," which, as everyone knows, connotes old lady all the way.

"Ahn-dre-ah, the *stewardess* is forcing me to end this call. I'll call you back when the *stewardess* allows me to do so. In the meantime, I want hair and makeup confirmed, and I'd like you to begin interviewing new girls for the nanny position. That's all." It clicked off, but not before I heard the flight attendant call her "ma'am" one last time.

"What did she want?" Emily asked, her forehead wrinkling in intense worry.

"She called me the right name three times in a row," I gloated, happy to prolong her anticipation. "Three times, do you believe it? I think that means we're best friends, doesn't it? Who would've thought? Andrea Sachs and Miranda Priestly, BFF."

"Andrea, what did she say?"

"Well, she wants the Thursday hair and makeup confirmed because clearly ninety-nine percent isn't reassuring enough. Oh, and she said something about interviewing for a new nanny? I must've misunderstood that one. Whatever—she'll call back in thirty seconds."

Emily took a deep breath and willed herself to endure my stupidity with grace and style. It clearly wasn't easy for her. "No, I don't think you misunderstood at all. Cara is no longer with Miranda, so obviously she'll be needing a new nanny."

"What? What do you mean no longer 'with Miranda'? If she's no longer 'with Miranda,' then where the hell is she?" I found it really hard to believe Cara wouldn't have told me about her abrupt departure.

"Miranda thought Cara might be happier working for someone else," Emily said in what I'm sure was much more diplomatic phrasing than Miranda herself had used. As if Miranda had ever been attuned to other people's happiness!

"Emily, please. Please tell me what really happened."

"I gathered from Caroline that Cara had grounded the girls in their rooms after they talked back to her the other day. Miranda didn't feel it was appropriate for Cara to be making these decisions. And I agree. I mean, Cara is not these girls' mother, you know?"

So Cara had gotten fired because she made two little girls sit in their bedrooms after they'd surely given her attitude? "Yeah, I see your point. It's definitely not a nanny's job to look out for the well-being of her charges," I said, nodding solemnly. "Cara was out of line there."

Emily not only didn't react to my dripping sarcasm, but didn't seem to detect so much as a hint of it. "Exactly. And besides, Miranda never liked that Cara didn't speak French. How are the girls supposed to learn to speak it without an American accent?"

Oh, I don't know. Maybe from their $18,000-a-year private school, where French was a required subject and all three of the French teachers were native speakers? Or perhaps from their own fluent mother who had herself lived in France, still visited a half-dozen times a year and could read, write, and speak the language with perfect, lilting pronunciation? But instead I said, "Hey, you're right. No French, no nanny. I hear you."

"Well, regardless, it's going to be your responsibility to find the girls a new nanny. Here's the number of the agency we work with," she said, sending it to me in an e-mail. "They know how discriminating Miranda is—and rightfully so, of course—so they usually give us good people."

I looked at her warily and wondered what her life had been before Miranda Priestly. I got to sleep with my eyes open for a little while longer before the phone rang again. Blessedly, Emily answered it.

"Hello, Miranda. Yes, yes, I can hear you. No, no problem at all. Yes, I have confirmed hair and makeup for that Thursday. And yes, Andrea has already begun looking for new nannies. We'll have three solid candidates ready for you to interview on your first day back." She cocked her head to the side and touched her pen to her lips. "Mmm, yes. Yes, it's definitely confirmed. No, it's not ninety-nine percent, it's one hundred percent. Definitely. Yes, Miranda. Yes, I confirmed it myself, and I'm quite positive. They're looking forward to it. OK. Have a nice flight. Yes, it's confirmed. I'll fax it right now. OK. Good-bye." She hung up the phone and appeared to be shaking.

"Why doesn't that woman understand? I told her the hair and

makeup were confirmed. And then I told her again. Why did I have to tell her fifty more times? And do you know what she said?"

I shook my head.

"Do you know what she said? She said that since this has all been such a headache for her, she'd like me to redo the itinerary so that it will reflect that hair and makeup is now confirmed and fax it to the Ritz so she'll have the correct one when she arrives. I do everything for that woman—I give her my *life*—and this is how she talks to me in return?" She looked ready to cry. I was thrilled for the rare opportunity to see Emily turn on Miranda, but I knew that a *Runway* Paranoid Turnaround was imminent, so I had to proceed with caution. Strike just the right note of sympathy and indifference.

"It's not you, Em, I promise. She knows how hard you work—you're an amazing assistant to her. If she didn't think you did a great job, she'd have gotten rid of you already. She's not exactly scared to do it—you know what I mean?"

Emily had stopped tearing and was approaching the defiant zone where, even though she agreed with me, she'd defend Miranda if I said anything too outrageous. I'd learned about the Stockholm Syndrome in psych, in which the victims identify with their captors, but I hadn't really understood how it all played out. Maybe I'd videotape one of the little sessions here between Emily and me and send it to the prof so next year's freshmen could actually see it happening firsthand. All efforts to proceed carefully began to feel superhuman, so I took a deep breath and dove right in.

"She's a lunatic, Emily," I said softly and slowly, willing her to agree with me. "It's not you, it's her. She's an empty, shallow, bitter woman who has tons and tons of gorgeous clothes and not much else."

Emily's face tightened noticeably, the skin on her neck and around her cheeks pulling taut, and her hands stopped shaking. I knew she was going to bulldoze me at any moment, but I couldn't stop.

"Have you ever noticed that she has no friends, Emily? Have you? Sure, her phone rings day and night with the world's coolest people, but they're not calling to talk about their kids or their jobs or their marriages, are they? They're calling because they need something from her. It sure seems awesome looking in, but can you imagine if the only reason anyone ever called you was because they—"

"Stop it!" she screamed, the tears streaming down her face again. "Just fucking shut up already! You march into this office and think you understand everything. Little Miss I'm So Sarcastic and So Above All This! Well, you don't understand anything. Anything!"

"Em—"

"Don't 'Em,' me, Andy. Let me finish. I know Miranda is difficult. I know she sometimes seems crazy. I know what it's like to never sleep and always be scared she's calling you and have none of your friends understand. I know all that! But if you hate it so much, if you can't do anything but complain about it and her and everyone else all the time, then why don't you just leave? Because your attitude is really a problem. And to say that Miranda is a lunatic, well, I think there are many, many more people out there who think she's gifted and gorgeous and talented and would think you're a lunatic for not doing your best to help out someone so amazing. Because she is amazing, Andy—she really is!"

I considered this for a moment and decided she had a point. Miranda was, as far as I could tell, a truly fantastic editor. Not a single word of copy made it into the magazine without her explicit, hard-to-obtain approval, and she wasn't afraid to scrap something and start over, regardless of how inconvenient or unhappy it made everyone else. Although the various fashion editors called in the clothes to shoot, Miranda alone selected the looks she wanted and which models she wanted wearing each one; the sittings editors might be the ones at the actual shoots, but they were simply executing Miranda's specific and incredibly detailed instructions. She had the final—and often even the preliminary—say over every single bracelet, bag, shoe, outfit, hair style, story, interview, writer, photo, model, location, and photograph in every issue, and that made her, in my mind, the main reason for the magazine's stunning success each month. *Runway* wouldn't be *Runway*—hell, it wouldn't be much of anything at all—without Miranda Priestly. I knew it and so did everyone else. What it hadn't yet done was convince me that any of this gave her a right to treat people the way she did. Why was the ability to put together a Balmain evening gown and a brooding, leggy Asian girl on a side street in San Sebastian worshiped so much that Miranda wasn't accountable for her behavior? I still wasn't building the bridge, but what the hell did I know? Emily obviously got it.

"Emily, all I'm saying is that you're a really great assistant to her, that she's lucky she has someone who works as hard as you do, who's so committed to the job. I just wish you'd realize that it's not your fault if she's unhappy with something. She's just an unhappy person. There's nothing more you could have done."

"I know that. I really do. But you don't give her enough credit, Andy. Think about it. I mean, really think about it. She is so incredibly accomplished, and she's had to sacrifice a lot to get there, but couldn't the same be said of supersuccessful people in every industry? Tell me, how many CEOs or managing partners or movie directors or whatever don't have to be tough sometimes? It's part of the job."

I could tell we weren't going to see eye to eye on this one. It was clear that Emily was deeply invested in Miranda, in *Runway*, in all of it, but I just couldn't understand why. She wasn't any different from the hundreds of other personal assistants and editorial assistants and assistant editors and associate editors and senior editors and editors in chief of fashion magazines. But I just didn't understand why. From everything I'd seen so far, each one was humiliated, degraded, and generally abused by their direct superior, only to turn around and do it to those under them the second they got promoted. And all of it so they could say, at the end of the long and exhausting climb, that they'd gotten to sit in the front row at Yves Saint-Laurent's couture show and had scored a few free Prada bags along the way?

Time to just agree. "I know," I sighed, surrendering to her insistence. "I just hope you know that you're doing her the favor by putting up with her shit, not the other way around."

I expected a quick counter-attack, but Emily grinned. "You know how I just told her like a hundred times that her Thursday hair and makeup were confirmed?"

I nodded. She looked positively giddy.

"I was totally lying. I didn't call a single person or confirm anything!" She practically sang the last part.

"Emily! Are you serious? What are you going to do now? You just swore up and down that you'd personally confirmed it." For the first time since starting work, I wanted to hug the girl.

"Andy, be serious. Do you honestly think that any sane person is going to say no to doing her hair and makeup? It could make his whole career—he'd be crazy to turn her down. I'm sure the guy was planning to do it all along. He was probably just rearranging his travel plans or something. I don't have to confirm with him, because I'm that sure he'll do it. How could he *not*? She's Miranda Priestly!"

Now I thought I would cry, but instead I just said, "So what do I need to know to hire this new nanny? I should probably get started right away."

"Yeah," she agreed, still looking delighted with her own cleverness. "That's probably a good idea."

←→

The first girl I interviewed for the nanny position looked positively shell-shocked.

"Oh my god!" she'd howled when I asked her over the phone if she'd mind coming to the office to meet with me. "Oh my god! Are you serious? Oh my god!"

"Um, is that a yes or a no?"

"God, yes. Yes, yes, yes! To *Runway*? Oh my god. Wait until I tell my friends. They'll die. They'll absolutely die. Just tell me where to be and when."

"You understand that Miranda's away right now, so you won't be meeting with her, right?"

"Yep. Totally."

"And you also know that the job is being a nanny to Miranda's two daughters, right? That it won't have anything to do with *Runway*?"

She sighed as if to resign herself to the sad, unfortunate fact. "Yes, of course. A nanny, I totally get it."

Well, she hadn't really gotten it, because even though she looked the part (tall, impeccably groomed, reasonably well dressed, and seriously underfed), she kept asking which parts of the job would require her to be at the office.

I shot her a specialty Withering, but she didn't seem to notice. "Um, none. Remember, we talked about this? I'm just doing some initial screening for Miranda, and we just happen to be doing it in the office. But that's it. Her twins don't live here, you know?"

"Right, right," she'd agreed, but I'd already nixed her.

The next three the agency had waiting in the reception area weren't much better. Physically, all fit the Miranda profile—the agency really did know exactly what she wanted—but not one had what I'd be looking for in a nanny who'd be taking care of my future niece or nephew, the standard I'd set for the process. One had a master's in child development from Cornell but glazed over when I tried to describe the subtle ways this job might be different from others she'd held. Another had dated a famous NBA player, which she felt gave her "insight into celebrity." But when I'd asked her if she'd ever worked with the children of celebrities, she'd instinctively wrinkled her nose and informed me that "famous people's kids always have, like, major issues." Nixed. The third and most promising had grown up in Manhattan and had just graduated from Middlebury and wanted to spend a year as a nanny to save some money for a trip to Paris. When I asked if that meant she spoke French, she nodded. The only problem was that she was a city girl through and through and therefore didn't have a driver's license. Was she willing to learn? I'd asked. No, she'd answered. She didn't believe that the streets needed another car clogging them. Nix number three. I spent the rest of the day trying to figure out a tactful way of telling Miranda that if a girl is attractive, athletic, comfortable with celebrity, lives in Manhattan, has a driver's license, can swim, has an advanced degree, speaks French, and is completely and entirely flexible with her time, then chances are she does not want to be a nanny.

She must have read my mind, because the phone rang immediately. I did a few calculations and realized that Miranda would have just landed at de Gaulle, and a quick glance at the second-by-second itinerary Emily had so painstakingly constructed showed she would now be in the car on her way to the Ritz.

"Miranda Pri—"

"Emily!" she practically shrieked. I wisely decided now wasn't the time to correct her. "Emily! The driver did not give me my usual phone, and as a result I don't have anyone's phone number. This is unacceptable. Entirely unacceptable. How am I supposed to conduct business with no phone numbers? Connect me immediately to Mr. Lagerfeld."

"Yes, Miranda, please hold just a moment." I jabbed the hold button and called out to Emily for help, although I would've had better luck simply eating the receiver whole than actually locating Karl Lagerfeld in less time than it took Miranda to get so annoyed that she'd smash down the phone and keep calling to ask, "Where the hell is he? Why can't you find him? Do you not know how to use a phone?"

"She wants Karl," I called over to Emily. The name immediately sent her flying, racing, tearing through papers all over her desk.

"OK, listen. We have twenty to thirty seconds. You take Biarritz and the driver, I'll get Paris and the assistant," she called, her fingers already flying across the keypad. I double-clicked on the thousand-plus name contact list that we shared on our hard drives and found exactly five numbers I'd have to call: Biarritz main, Biarritz second main, Biarritz studio, Biarritz pool, and Biarritz driver. A quick glance over the other listings for Karl Lagerfeld indicated that Emily had a grand total of seven, and there were still more numbers for New York and Milan. We were dead before we started.

I'd tried Biarritz main and was in the middle of dialing Biarritz second main when I saw that the flashing red light had stopped blinking. Emily announced that Miranda had hung up, in case I hadn't noticed. Only ten or fifteen seconds had passed—she was feeling particularly impatient today. Naturally, the phone rang again immediately, and Emily responded to my pleading puppy eyes and answered it. She didn't get halfway through her canned greeting before she was nodding gravely and trying to reassure Miranda. I was still dialing and had—miraculously—made it to Biarritz pool, where I was currently talking to a woman who didn't speak a single word, a single syllable, of English. Maybe this was the obsession with speaking French?

"Yes, yes, Miranda. Andrea and I are calling right now. It should only be a few more seconds. Yes, I understand. No, I know it's frustrating. If you'll allow me to just put you on hold for ten seconds or so, I'm sure we'll have him on the line. OK?" She punched "hold" and kept right on jabbing numbers. I heard her trying in what sounded like horrifically accented and broken French to talk to someone who appeared to not know the name Karl Lagerfeld. We were dead. Dead. I was getting ready to hang up on the crazy French woman who was shrieking into the receiver when I saw the flashing red light go out again. Emily was still frantically dialing.

"She's gone!" I called with the urgency of an EMT performing emergency CPR.

"Your turn to get it!" she screamed back, fingers flying, and sure enough, the phone rang again.

I picked it up and didn't even attempt to say anything, since I knew the voice on the other end would speak up immediately. It did.

"Ahn-dre-ah! Emily! Whoever the hell I'm talking to . . . why is it that I'm speaking with you and not with Mr. Lagerfeld? Why?"

My first instinct was to remain silent, since it didn't appear that the verbal barrage was over, but as usual, my instincts were wrong.

"Hell-*ooo*? Anyone there? Is the process of connecting one phone call to another really too difficult for *both* my assistants?"

"No, Miranda, of course not. I'm sorry about this—" My voice was shaking a little, but I couldn't get it under control. "—it's just that we can't seem to find Mr. Lagerfeld. We've already tried at least eight—"

"*Can't seem to find him?*" she mimicked in a high-pitched voice. "What do you mean, you 'can't seem to find' him?"

What part of that simple five-word sentence did she not comprehend, I wondered. Can't. Seem. To. Find. Him. Seemed rather clear and precise to me: We can't fucking find him. That is why you're not talking to him. If *you* can find him, then *you* can talk to him. A million barbed responses raced around my head, but I could only sputter like a first-grader who'd been singled out by the teacher for talking in class.

"Um, well, Miranda, we've called all of the numbers we have listed for him, and he doesn't appear to be at any of them," I managed.

"Well of course he's not!" She was almost screaming now, that precious, well-guarded cool was precariously close to collapsing. She took a deep, exaggerated breath and said calmly, "Ahn-dre-ah. Are you aware that Mr. Lagerfeld is in Paris this week?" I felt like we were doing English As a Second Language lessons.

"Of course, Miranda. Emily has been trying all the numbers in—"

"And are you aware that Mr. Lagerfeld said he'd be available on his mobile phone while he was in Paris?" Every muscle in her throat strained to keep her voice even and calm.

"Well, no, we don't have a cell number listed in the directory, so we didn't know that Mr. Lagerfeld even had a cell phone. But Emily is on the phone with his assistant right now, and I'm sure she'll have that number in just a minute." Emily gave me the thumbs-up right before she scribbled something and exclaimed, *"Merci,* oh yes, thank you, I mean, *merci"* over and over again.

"Miranda, I have the number right here. Would you like me to connect you now?" I could feel my chest puff out with confidence and pride. A job well done! A superior performance under the most pressure-filled conditions. Never mind that my really cute peasant blouse that had been complimented by two—not one, but two—fashion assistants was now sporting sweat stains under the arms. Who cared? I was about to get this stark raving mad lunatic of an international caller off my back, and I was thrilled.

"Ahn-dre-ah?" It sounded like a question, but I was only concentrating on trying to figure out a pattern for indiscriminate name mix-ups. At first I'd thought she did it deliberately in an attempt to belittle and humiliate us even more, but then I figured out that she was probably quite satisfied with the levels of belittlement and humiliation we endured and so she did it only because she couldn't be bothered to keep straight details so inane as her two assistants' names. Emily had confirmed this by saying that she called her Emily about half the time but called her a mixture of Andrea and Allison—the assistant before her—the other half. I felt better.

"Yes?" Squeaking again. Dammit! Wasn't it possible for me to have just a tiny bit of dignity with this woman?

"Ahn-dre-ah, I don't know what all the fuss is over finding Mr. Lagerfeld's mobile number when I have it right here. He gave it to me just five minutes ago, but we were disconnected and I can't seem to dial correctly." She said the last part as though the entire world was to blame for this irritation and inconvenience except for herself.

"Oh. You, um, you have the number? And you knew he was on that number the whole time?" I was saying it for Emily's benefit, and it only served to enrage Miranda even more.

"Am I not making myself perfectly clear here? I need you to connect me to 03.55.23.56.67.89. Immediately. Or is that too difficult?"

Emily was slowly shaking her head in disbelief as she crumpled up the number we'd both just fought so hard to get.

"No, no, Miranda, of course that's not too difficult. I'll connect you right away. Hold just a minute." I hit "conference," dialed the numbers, heard an older man shout "Allo!" into the phone, and hit conference again. "Mr. Lagerfeld, Miranda Priestly, you're connected," I stated like one of those manual operators from the *Little House on the Prairie* days. And instead of putting the whole call on mute and then hitting speaker so Emily and I could listen in on the call together, I just hung up. We sat in silence for a few minutes as I tried to refrain from badmouthing Miranda immediately. Instead, I mopped some dampness from my forehead and took long, deep breaths. She spoke first.

"So, let me just get this straight. She had his number the entire time but just didn't know how to dial it?"

"Or maybe she just didn't feel like dialing it," I added helpfully, always enthusiastic for the chance to team up against Miranda, especially considering how rare the opportunities were with Emily.

"I should've known," she said, shaking her head like she was horribly disappointed with herself. "I really should've known that. She always calls to have me connect her to people who are staying in the next room, or who are in a hotel two streets over. I remember I thought that was the weirdest thing, calling from Paris to New York to have someone connect you to someone in Paris. Now it just seems normal, of course, but I can't believe I didn't see that one coming."

I was about to run to the dining room for lunch, but the phone rang again. Operating under the lightning-doesn't-strike-twice theory, I decided to be a sport and answer the phone.

"Miranda Priestly's office."

"Emily! I am standing in the pouring rain on the rue de Rivoli and my driver has vanished. Vanished! Do you understand me? Vanished! Find him immediately!" She was hysterical, my very first time hearing her that way, and I wouldn't have been surprised to learn it was the only time.

"Miranda, just a moment. I have his number right here." I turned to scan my desk for the itinerary I'd set down a moment earlier, but all I saw were papers, old Bulletins, stacks of back issues. Only three or four seconds had passed, but I felt as if I were standing right next to her, watching as the rain poured down on her Fendi fur and caused the makeup to melt down the side of her face. Like she could just reach out and slap my face, tell me I'm a worthless piece of shit with zero talent, no skill set, a complete and total loser. There wasn't time to talk myself down, remind myself that this was merely a human being (theoretically) who wasn't happy to be standing in the rain and was taking it out on her assistant 3,600 miles away. It's not my fault. It's not my fault. It's not my fault.

"Ahn-dre-ah! My shoes are *ruined*. Do you hear me? Are you even listening? Find my driver *now!*"

I was at risk of some inappropriate emotion—I could feel the knot in the back of my throat, the tightening of the muscles in the back of my neck, but it was too early to tell if I would laugh or cry. Either one: not good. Emily must have sensed as much, because she leapt out of her seat and handed me her copy of the itinerary. She'd even highlighted the driver's contact numbers, three in all, one for the car phone, his mobile phone, and his home phone. Naturally.

"Miranda, I'm going to need to put you on hold while I call him. Can I put you on hold?" I didn't wait for a response, which I knew would drive her crazy, and threw the call on hold. I dialed Paris again. The good news was the driver picked up on the first ring of the first number I tried. The bad news was he didn't speak English. Although I'd never been self-destructive before, I couldn't help but smash my forehead firmly into the Formica. Three times of this, and Emily had picked up the line at her desk. She'd resorted to screaming, not so much in attempt to make the driver understand her own bad French, but simply because she was trying to impress upon him the urgency of the current situation. New drivers always took a little breaking in, mostly because they foolishly believed that if Miranda had to wait forty-five seconds to a minute extra, she'd be all right. This was precisely the notion of which Emily and I were to disabuse them.

We both put our heads down a few minutes later, after Emily had managed to insult the driver enough that he'd hightailed it back to where he'd left Miranda three or four minutes earlier. I wasn't particularly hungry for lunch anymore, a phenomenon that made me nervous. Was *Runway* rubbing off? Or was it just the adrenaline and nerves mixing together to guarantee no appetite? That was it! The starvation so endemic at *Runway* was not, in fact, self-induced; it was merely the physiological response of bodies that were so consistently terrified and all-around anxiety-ridden that they were never actually hungry. I vowed to look into this a little more and perhaps explore the possibility that Miranda was smarter than all of this and had deliberately created a persona so offensive on every level that she literally scared people skinny.

"Ladies, ladies, ladies! Pick those heads up off those desks! Can you imagine Miranda seeing you now? She wouldn't be very happy!" James sang from the doorway. He had slicked back his hair using some greasy, waxy stuff called Bed Head ("Hot name—how can you resist?") and was wearing some sort of skintight football jersey with the number 69 on both the front and the back. As always, a picture of subtlety and understatement.

Neither of us so much as glanced at him. The clock said it was only four, but it felt like midnight.

"OK then, let me guess. Mama's been calling off the hook because she lost an earring somewhere between the Ritz and Alain Ducasse and she wants you to find it, even though it's in Paris and you're in New York."

I snorted. "You think that would put us in this condition? That's our *job*. We do that every day. Give us something difficult."

Even Emily laughed. "Seriously, James, not good enough. I could find an earring in under ten minutes in any city in the world," she said, all of a sudden inspired to join in for reasons I didn't understand. "It'd only be a challenge if she didn't tell us what city she'd lost it in. But I bet even then we could do it."

James was backing himself away from the office, a look of feigned horror on his face. "All right, then, ladies, you have a great day, you hear? At least she hasn't fucked you both up for good. I mean, seriously, thank god for that, right? You're both *tooootally* sane. Yeah. Um, have a great day . . ."

"NOT SO FAST THERE, YOU PANSY!" shrieked someone very loud

and very high-pitched. "I WANT YOU TO MARCH YOUR WAY BACK IN THERE AND TELL THE GIRLS WHAT YOU WERE THINKING WHEN YOU PUT THAT SHMATA ON THIS MORNING!" Nigel grabbed James by the left ear and dragged him into the area between our desks.

"Oh, come on, Nigel," James whined, pretending to be annoyed but obviously delighted that Nigel was touching him. "You know you love this top!"

"LOVE THAT TOP? YOU THINK I LOVE THAT FRATTY, GAY-JOCK LOOK YOU'VE GOT GOING? JAMES, YOU NEED TO RE-THINK HERE, OK? OK?"

"What's wrong with a tight football jersey? I think it looks hot." Emily and I nodded in quiet alliance with James. It may not have been exactly tasteful, but he did look incredibly hip. And besides, it was kind of tough to be taking fashion advice from a man who was, at that precise moment, wearing zebra-print boot-cut jeans and a black V-neck sweater with a keyhole cut out in the back to reveal rippling back muscles. The whole ensemble was topped off with a floppy straw hat and a touch (subtle, I'll give him that!) of kohl eyeliner.

"BABY BOY, FASHION IS NOT FOR ADVERTISING YOUR FAVE SEX ACTS ON YOUR SHIRT. UNH-UNH, NO IT'S NOT! YOU WANNA SHOW A LITTLE SKIN? THAT'S HOT! YOU WANNA SHOW SOME OF THOSE TIGHT, YOUNG CURVES OF YOURS? *THAT'S* HOT. CLOTHING IS NOT FOR TELLING THE WORLD WHAT POSITION YOU PREFER, BOYFRIEND. NOW DO YOU UNDERSTAND?"

"But, Nigel!" A look of defeat was carefully constructed to disguise how pleased he was to be the center of Nigel's attention.

"DON'T 'NIGEL' ME, HONEY. GO TALK TO JEFFY AND TELL HIM I SENT YOU. TELL HIM TO GIVE YOU THE NEW CALVIN TANK WE CALLED IN FOR THE MIAMI SHOOT. IT'S THE ONE THAT GORGEOUS BLACK MODEL—OH MY, HE'S AS TASTY AS A THICK, CHOCOLATE MILKSHAKE—IS ASSIGNED TO WEAR. GO ON NOW, SHOO. BUT BE SURE TO COME BACK HERE AND SHOW ME WHAT YOU LOOK LIKE!"

James scampered off like a recently fed bunny rabbit, and Nigel turned to look at us. "HAVE YOU PUT IN HER CLOTHING ORDER YET?" he asked no one in particular.

"No, she won't choose until she has the look-books," Emily answered, looking bored. "She said she'll do it when she gets back."

"WELL, JUST BE SURE TO LET ME KNOW AHEAD OF TIME SO I CAN CLEAR MY SCHEDULE FOR THAT PARTY!" He took off in the direction of the Closet, probably to try to catch a glimpse of James changing.

I'd already lived through one round of Miranda wardrobe ordering, and it hadn't been pretty. When at the shows, she went from runway to runway, sketchbook in hand, preparing herself to come back to the States and tell New York society what they would be wearing—and middle America what they'd like to be wearing—via the only runway that actually mattered. Little did I know that Miranda was also paying particular attention to the outfits cruising down the runways because it was her first glance at what she herself would be wearing in the upcoming months.

A couple weeks after returning to the office, Miranda had handed Emily a list of designers whose look-books she'd like to see. As the usual suspects rushed to get their books put together for her—their runway photographs often weren't even developed, never mind airbrushed and bound, before she demanded to see them—everyone at *Runway* was put on alert that the books would be arriving. Nigel would need to be ready, of course, to help her flip through them all and select her personal outfits. An accessories editor should be on hand to choose bags and shoes, and perhaps an extra fashion editor to ensure that everyone was in agreement—especially if the order included something big, like a fur coat or an evening gown. When the various houses had finally pieced together the different items she'd requested, Miranda's personal tailor would come to *Runway* for a few days to fit everything. Jeffy would completely empty out the Closet, and no one would really be able to get any work done at all, since Miranda and her tailor would be holed up in there for hours on end. On the first go-round of fittings, I'd walked by the Closet just in time to hear Nigel shouting, "MIRANDA PRIESTLY! TAKE THAT RAG OFF THIS SECOND. THAT DRESS MAKES YOU LOOK LIKE A SLUT! A COMMON WHORE!" I'd stood outside with my ear pressed to the door—literally risking life and limb if it were to swing open—and waited for her to upbraid him in that special way of hers, but all I heard was a quiet murmur of agreement and the rustling of the fabric as she removed the dress.

Now that I had been there long enough, it seemed as though the honor of ordering Miranda's clothes would fall to me. Four times a year, like clockwork, she flipped through look-books like they were her own personal catalogs and selected Alexander McQueen suits and Balenciaga pants like they were T-shirts from L.L.Bean. A yellow sticky on this pair of Fendi pencil pants, another placed squarely over the Chanel skirt suit, a third with a big "NO" plastered across the matching silk top. Flip, stick, flip, stick, on and on it went, until she had selected a full season's wardrobe directly from the runway, clothes that had most likely not yet even been made.

I'd watched as Emily had faxed Miranda's choices to the different designers, omitting any size or color preference, since anyone worth their Manolos knew what would work for Miranda Priestly. Of course, merely being made to the correct size wasn't enough—when the clothes did arrive at the magazine, they'd need to be cut and tucked to make them appear custom-made. Only when the entire wardrobe was completely ordered, shipped, snipped, and delivered expressly to her bedroom closet by chauffeured limousine would Miranda relinquish last season's clothes and heaps of Yves and Celine and Helmut Lang would find their way— in garbage bags—back to the office. Most were only four or six months old, stuff that had been worn once or twice or, most often, not at all. Everything was still so incredibly stylish, so ludicrously hip, that it wasn't yet available in most stores, but once it was last season, it was about as likely to show up on Miranda as a pair of pleather pants from Target's new Massimo line.

Occasionally I'd find a tank top or an oversize jacket I could keep, but the fact that everything was in a size zero was a bit of a problem. Mostly we distributed the clothes to anyone with preteen daughters, the only ones who had a shot in hell of actually fitting into the stuff. I pictured little girls with bodies like little boys strutting around in Prada lipstick skirts and slinky Dolce and Gabbana dresses with spaghetti straps. If there was something really dynamite, really expensive, I'd pull it from the garbage bag and stash it under my desk until I could smuggle it

home safely. A few quick clicks on eBay or perhaps a little visit to one of
the upscale consignment shops on Madison Avenue, and my salary all of
a sudden wasn't so depressing. Not stealing, I rationalized, simply utiliz-
ing what was available to me.

Miranda called six more times between the hours of six and nine in
the evening—midnight to three A.M. her time—to have us connect her to
various people who were already in Paris. I fielded them listlessly, un-
eventfully, until I went to gather my things and try to sneak out for the
night before the phone rang again. It wasn't until I was climbing ex-
haustedly into my coat that I caught a glimpse of the note that I'd stuck
to my monitor just so this very thing wouldn't happen: CALL A,
3:30 P.M. TODAY. My head felt like it was swimming, my contacts had
long before dried to tiny, hard shards covering my eyes, and at this point
my head started to throb. No sharp pains, just that nebulous, dull kind
of ache where you can't pinpoint the center but you know it will build
and build in a slow, burning intensity until you either manage to pass out
or your head just explodes. In the frenzy of all the calls that had produced such anxiety, such panic, from across an ocean, I had forgotten to
take the thirty seconds out of my day and call Alex when he'd asked me
to. Simply up and forgotten to do something so simple for someone who
never seemed to need anything from me.

I sat down in the now darkened and silent office and picked up the
phone that was still a little wet from my sweaty hands during Miranda's
last call a few minutes earlier. His home line rang and rang until the machine picked up, but he answered on the first ring when I tried his cell
phone.

"Hi," he said, knowing it was me from the caller ID. "How was your
day?"

"Whatever, usual. Alex, I'm so sorry I didn't call you at three-thirty.
I can't even get into it—it's just that things were so crazy here, she just
kept calling and—"

"Hey, forget it. Not a big deal. Listen, now's not really a great time
for me. Can I call you tomorrow?" He sounded distracted, his voice taking on that faraway quality of someone talking from an international
payphone on the beach of a tiny village across the world.

"Um, sure. But is everything OK? Will you just quickly tell me what you wanted to talk about before? I've been really worried that everything's not OK."

He was quiet for a moment and then said, "Yeah, well it doesn't seem like you were all that worried. I ask you one time to call me at a time that's convenient for me—not to mention that your boss isn't even in the country right now—and you can't manage to do that until six hours after the fact. Not really a sign of someone who's genuinely concerned, you know?" He stated all of this with no sarcasm, no disapproval, just a simple summary of the facts.

I was twisting the phone cord around my finger until it cut off the circulation entirely, making the knuckle bulge out and the tip turn white; there was also a brief, metallic taste of blood in my mouth, the first realization that I had been gnawing on the inside of my bottom lip.

"Alex, it's not that I forgot to call," I lied openly, trying to extricate myself from his nonaccusatory accusation. "I simply didn't have a single second free, and since it sounded like something serious, I didn't want to call just to have to hang up again. I mean, she must have called me two dozen times just this afternoon, and each one is an absolute emergency. Emily took off at five and left me all alone with that phone, and Miranda just didn't stop. She just kept calling and calling and calling, and every time I went to call you, it'd be her again on the other line. I, uh, you know?"

My rapid-fire list of excuses sounded pathetic even to me, but I couldn't stop. He knew I had just forgotten, and so did I. Not because I didn't care or wasn't concerned, but because all things non-Miranda somehow ceased to be relevant the moment I arrived at work. In some ways I still didn't understand and certainly couldn't explain—never mind ask anyone else to understand—how the outside world just melted into nonexistence, that the only thing remaining when everything else vanished was *Runway*. It was especially difficult to explain this phenomenon when it was the single thing in my life I despised. And yet, it was the only one that mattered.

"Listen, I have to get back to Joey. He has two friends over and they've probably torn apart the entire house by this point."

"Joey? Does that mean you're in Larchmont? You don't usually watch him on Wednesdays. Is everything OK?" I was hoping to steer him away from the blatantly obvious fact that I had gotten too wrapped up at work for six straight hours, and this seemed like the best path. He'd tell me how his mom had gotten held up at work accidentally or perhaps had to go see Joey's teacher for conferences that night when the regular babysitter canceled. He'd never complain of course—that just wasn't his style—but he'd at least tell me what was going on.

"Yeah, yeah, everything's fine. My mom just had an emergency client meeting tonight. Andy, I can't really talk about it now. I was just calling before with some good news. But you didn't call me back," he said flatly.

I wrapped the phone cord, which had begun to slowly unravel, so tight around my pointer and middle fingers that they began to pulsate. "I'm sorry" was all I could manage, because even though I knew he was right, that I was insensitive not to have called, I was too worn out to present a huge defense. "Alex, please. Please don't punish me by not telling me something good. Do you know how long it's been since anyone has called with good news? Please. Give me that at least." I knew he'd respond to my rational approach, and he did.

"Look, it's not that exciting. I just went ahead and made all the arrangements for us to go back for our first homecoming together."

"You did? Really? We're going?" I'd brought it up a couple times before in what I'd liked to believe had been an offhand and casual way, but in a decidedly non-Alex fashion he'd been hedging on committing to our going together. It was really early to be planning any of it, but the hotels and restaurants in Providence were always full months ahead of time. I'd dropped it a few weeks earlier, figuring that we would figure something out, find a place to stay somewhere. But somehow, of course, he'd picked up on just how badly I wanted to go with him, and he'd figured out everything.

"Yeah, it's done. We have a rental car—a Jeep, actually—and I reserved a room at the Biltmore."

"At the Biltmore? You're kidding? You got a room there? That's amazing."

"Yeah, well, you've always talked about wanting to stay there, so I figured we should try it. I even made a reservation for brunch on Sunday at Al Forno for ten people, so we can each gather up the troops and have everyone in one place at one time."

"No way. You did all of this already?"

"Sure. I thought you'd be really psyched. That's why I was really looking forward to telling you about it. But apparently you were too busy to call back."

"Alex, I'm thrilled. I can't even tell you how excited I am, and I can't believe you figured everything out already. I'm really sorry about before, but I can't wait for October. We're going to have the best time, thanks to you."

We talked for another couple minutes. By the time I hung up, he didn't sound mad anymore, but I could barely move. The effort to win him back, to find the right words not only to convince him that I hadn't overlooked him but also to reassure him that I was appropriately grateful and enthusiastic had drained the last reserves of my energy. I don't remember getting into the car or the ride home or whether or not I said hello to John Fisher-Galliano in the lobby of my building. Besides a bone-deep exhaustion that hurt so much it almost felt good, the only thing I remember feeling at all was relief that Lily's door was shut and no light peeked out from under it. I thought about ordering in some food, but the mere thought of locating a menu and a phone was too overwhelming—another meal that simply wasn't happening.

Instead, I sat on the crumbling concrete of my furnitureless balcony and leisurely inhaled a cigarette. Lacking the energy to actually blow the smoke out, I let it seep from my mouth and hang in the still air around me. At some point I heard Lily's door open, her footsteps shuffling along the hallway, but I quickly turned out my lights and sat in the darkened silence. There had just been fifteen straight hours of talking, and I could talk no more.

13

"Hire her," Miranda had decreed when she met Annabelle, the twelfth girl I'd interviewed and one of only two that I'd decided were fit to even meet Miranda. Annabelle was a native French speaker (she actually spoke so little English I had to have the twins translate for me), a graduate of the Sorbonne, and the possessor of a long, hard body, with gorgeous brown hair. She had style. She wasn't afraid to wear stilettos on the job and didn't seem to mind Miranda's brusque manner. In fact, she was rather aloof and brusque herself and never really seemed to make any sort of eye contact. Always kind of bored, a touch disinterested, and supremely confident. I was thrilled when Miranda wanted her, both because it saved

me weeks more of meeting nanny wannabes and because it indicated—
in some teeny, tiny way—that I was starting to get it.

Get what, exactly, I wasn't sure, but things were going as smoothly as
I could have hoped at this point. I'd pulled off the clothing order with
only a few noticeable screwups. She hadn't exactly been psyched when
I'd shown her everything she'd ordered from Givenchy and accidentally
pronounced it precisely as it appears—give-EN-chee. After much glaring
and a few snide comments, I was informed of the correct pronunciation,
and everything went reasonably well until she had to be told that the
Roberto Cavalli dresses she'd requested hadn't been made yet and
wouldn't be ready for another three weeks. But I'd handled that and had
managed to coordinate fittings in the Closet with her tailor and had assembled nearly everything in the closet in her home dressing room, a
space roughly the size of a studio apartment.

The party planning had continued in Miranda's absence and picked
up again full-force with her return, but there was surprisingly little
panic—it appeared that everything was in order, and that the upcoming
Friday was set to go off without a hitch. Chanel had delivered a one-of-
a-kind, floor-length red beaded sheath while Miranda was in Europe,
and I'd immediately sent it to the cleaners for a once-over. I'd seen a similar Chanel dress in black in the pages of *W* the month before, and when
I pointed it out to Emily, she'd nodded somberly.

"Forty thousand dollars," she'd said, moving her head up and down,
up and down. She double-clicked on a pair of black pants on style.com,
where she'd spent months scouring for ideas for her upcoming trip to
Europe with Miranda.

"Forty thousand WHAT?"

"Her dress. The red one from Chanel. It costs forty thousand dollars
if you were to buy it retail. Of course, Miranda isn't paying full price, but
she didn't get this one for free, either. Isn't it wild?"

"Forty thousand DOLLARS?" I'd asked again, still unable to believe
that I'd held a single item worth so much money in my hands just hours
earlier. I couldn't help a quick conceptualization of forty grand: two full
years' college tuition, a down payment on a new home, an average *yearly*
salary for a typical American family of four. Or, at the very least, one hell
of a lot of Prada bags. But one dress? I thought I'd seen it all at that

point, but I was due another zinger when the dress came back from the couture dry cleaner with a calligraphic envelope that read *Ms. Miranda Priestly*. Inside was a hand-printed invoice on cream-colored cardstock that read:

Garment type: *Evening gown*. Designer: *Chanel*. Length: *Ankle*. Colour: *Red*. Size: *Zero*. Description: *Hand-beaded, sleeveless with slight scoop neckline, invisible side zipper, heavy silk lining*. Service: *Basic, first-time cleaning*. Fee: *$670*.

There was an additional note underneath the actual bill part from the shop's owner, a woman I was sure paid both the rent for her store and her home with the money she received from Elias on behalf of Miranda's extensive dry-cleaning addiction.

We were delighted to work on such a gorgeous gown and we hope you enjoy wearing it to your party at the Metropolitan Museum of Art. As directed, we will pick up the gown on Monday, May 24, for its post-party cleaning. Please let us know if we may be of any additional service. All the best, Colette.

Either way, it was only Thursday and Miranda had a brand-new and newly cleaned gown resting gently in her closet, and Emily had located the exact silver Jimmy Choo sandals she'd requested. The hair stylist was due at her house at five-thirty P.M. on Friday, the makeup artist at five forty-five, and Uri was on call for exactly six-fifteen to take Miranda and Mr. Tomlinson to the museum.

Miranda had already left for the day to watch Cassidy's gymnastics meet, and I was hoping to duck out early to surprise Lily. She'd just finished her last exam of the year and I wanted to take her out for a celebration.

"Hey, Em, do you think I could leave by six-thirty or seven today? Miranda said she didn't need the Book because there really wasn't anything new," I added quickly, irritated that I had to beg my equal, my peer for permission to leave work after only twelve hours instead of the usual fourteen.

"Um, sure. Yeah, whatever. I'm leaving now." She checked her computer screen and saw that it was a little after five. "Stay for another couple hours and then head out. She's with the twins tonight, so I don't think she should be calling much." She had a date that night with the guy she'd met in LA over New Year's. He'd finally made it to New York and, surprise of all surprises, he'd actually called. They were headed to Craftbar for drinks, at which point she would treat him to Nobu if he was behaving himself. She'd made the reservations five weeks earlier when he'd e-mailed that he might be in New York, but Emily still had to use Miranda's name to score the time slot.

"Well, what are you going to do when you show up there and you're clearly not Miranda Priestly?" I asked stupidly.

As usual, I received an expert eye-roll-deep-sigh combo. "I'll simply tell them that Miranda had to be out of town unexpectedly, show them a business card, and tell them she wanted me to have her reservation. Hardly a big deal."

Miranda called only once after Emily left to tell me that she wouldn't be in the office until noon tomorrow, but she'd like a copy of the restaurant review she'd read today "in the paper." I had the presence of mind to ask if she recalled the name of the restaurant or the paper in which she read about it, but this annoyed her greatly.

"Ahn-dre-ah, I'm already late for the meet. Don't grill me. It was an Asian fusion restaurant and it was in today's paper. That's all." And with that, she snapped her Motorola V60 shut. I hoped, as I usually did when she cut me off midsentence, that one day the cell phone would simply clamp down on her perfectly manicured fingers and swallow them whole, taking special time to shred those flawless red nails. No luck yet.

I wrote a quick note to myself to find the restaurant first thing in the morning in the notebook I kept with Miranda's myriad and ever-changing requests and bolted for the car. I called Lily from my cell and she picked up just as I was about to get out and go up to the apartment, and so I waved to John Fisher-Galliano (who had grown his hair a little longer and adorned his uniform with a few chains and looked more like the designer each and every day) but didn't move.

"Hey, what's up? It's me."

"*Hiiiiiiiiii,*" she sang, happier than I'd heard her in weeks, maybe months. "I am so done. Done! No early summer session, nothing but a little, insignificant proposal due for a master's thesis that I can change ten times after the fact if I want. So that leaves nothing until mid-July. Do you believe it?" She sounded positively gleeful.

"I know, I'm so excited for you! You up for a celebratory dinner? Anywhere you want, it's on *Runway*."

"Really? Anywhere?"

"Anywhere. I'm downstairs and I have a car. Come down; we'll go somewhere great."

She squealed. "Fun! I've been meaning to tell you all about Freudian Boy. He's beautiful! Hold on one second. I'm putting on jeans and I'll be right down."

She bounded out five minutes later looking trendier and happier than I'd seen her in a very long time. She wore a pair of tight, faded boot-cut jeans that hugged her hips, paired with a long-sleeve flowy white peasant blouse. A pair of flip-flops I'd never seen before—brown leather straps with turquoise beads—completed the look. She was even wearing makeup, and her curls looked as though they had seen a blow-dryer at some point in the last twenty-four hours.

"You look great," I said as she bounded into the backseat. "What's your secret?"

"Freudian Boy, of course. He's amazing. I think I'm in love. So far, he's going strong at nine-tenths. Do you believe it?"

"First, let's decide where we're going. I didn't make a reservation anywhere, but I can call ahead and use Miranda's name. Anywhere you want."

She was rubbing on some Kiehl's lip gloss and staring at herself in the driver's rearview mirror. "Anywhere?" she said absentmindedly.

"Anywhere. Maybe Chicama for those mojitos?" I suggested, knowing that the way to sell Lily on a restaurant was by advertising its drinks, not its food. "Or there are those amazing Cosmos at Meet. Or the Hudson Hotel—maybe we can even sit outside? If you want wine, though, I'd love to try—"

"Andy, can we go to Benihana? I've been craving it forever." She looked sheepish.

"Benihana? You want to go to *Benihana*? Like, the chain restaurant where they seat you with tourists who have lots of whining children and unemployed Asian actors cook the food right on your table? *That* Benihana?"

She was nodding so enthusiastically, I had no choice but to call for the address.

"No, no, I have it right here. Fifty-sixth between Fifth and Sixth, north side of the street," she called to the driver.

My weirdly excited friend didn't seem to notice that I was staring. Instead, she chatted happily about Freudian Boy, aptly named because he was in his last year of a Ph.D. program in psychology. They'd met in the graduate student lounge in the basement of Low Library. I got the full rundown on all of his qualifications: twenty-nine years old ("So much more mature, but not at all too old"), originally from Montreal ("Such a cute French accent, but like, totally Americanized"), longish hair ("But not freaky ponytail long"), and just the right amount of stubble ("He looks just like Antonio Banderas when he doesn't shave for three days").

The samurai chef-actors did their thing, slicing and dicing and flipping cubes of meat all over the place while Lily laughed and clapped her hands like a little girl at her first circus. Although it seemed impossible to believe that Lily actually liked a guy, it appeared to be the only logical explanation for her obvious elation. Even more impossible to believe was her claim that she hadn't slept with him yet ("Two and a half full weeks of hanging out constantly at school and nothing! Aren't you proud of me?"). When I asked why I hadn't seen him around the apartment at all, she'd smiled proudly and said, "He hasn't been invited over to the apartment yet. We're taking things slow." We were standing directly outside the restaurant as she regaled me with all the funny stories he'd told her when Christian Collinsworth appeared in front of me.

"Andrea. The lovely Andrea. I have to say, I'm rather surprised to discover that you're a fan of Benihana . . . What would Miranda think?" he asked teasingly, sliding his arm around my shoulder.

"I, uh, well . . ." The stammering was immediately all-consuming. There was no room for words when the thoughts were bouncing off each side of my head, pinging between my ears. *Eating at Benihana. Christian knows it! Miranda at Benihana! Looks so adorable in leather bomber jacket! Must be able to smell the Benihana on me! Don't kiss him on the cheek! Kiss him on the cheek!* "Well, it's not that, uh, that . . ."

"We were actually just discussing where we would be going next," Lily stated crisply, extending her hand to Christian, who, it finally occurred to me, was alone. "We must've gotten so caught up that we didn't even realize we'd stopped in the middle of the street! Hah, hah! How do like that, Andy? My name's Lily," she said to Christian, who shook her hand and then pushed a curl away from his eye, just like he'd done so many times at the party. Once again I had an odd feeling that I could be entranced for hours, maybe days, just watching him push that single, adorable curl away from his perfect face.

I stared at her and at him and became vaguely aware that I had to say something, but the two of them seemed to be holding up just fine on their own.

"Lily," Christian rolled the name around on his tongue. "*Lily.* Great name. Almost as great as *Andrea.*" I had the presence of mind to at least look at them, and I noticed that Lily was beaming. She was thinking to herself that this guy was not only older and hot, but he was also charming. I could see the wheels turning, weighing whether I was interested in him, if I'd actually do anything because of Alex, and, if so, if there was anything she could do to expedite it. She adored Alex because, really, how could you not, but she refused to understand how two people so young could spend so much time together—or, at least, that's what she claimed, although I knew that it was only the monogamy part that really blew her away. If there was a speck of a chance of some drama between Christian and me, then Lily would die fanning the fire.

"Lily, it's a pleasure to meet you. I'm Christian, a friend of Andrea's. Do you always stop in front of Benihana to talk?" His smile actually prompted a shooting-sinking feeling in my stomach.

Lily threw back her own brown curls with the back of her hand and said, "Well of course not, Christian! We just had dinner at Town and were trying to figure out a good place to get a drink. Any suggestions?"

Town! It was one of the hottest and most expensive restaurants in the city. Miranda went there. Jessica and her fiancé went there. Emily talked obsessively about wanting to go there. But Lily?

"Well, that's weird," Christian said, obviously buying the whole thing. "I just came from a dinner with my agent there. Strange that I didn't see you two . . ."

"We were all the way in the back, kind of tucked behind the bar," I said quickly, regaining a modicum of composure. Thankfully I'd paid attention when Emily had made me look at the tiny picture of the restaurant's bar listed on citysearch.com when she was trying to decide if it was a good date place.

"Mmm." He nodded, looking a little distracted and cuter than ever. "So, you girls are on your way to get a drink?"

I felt an overwhelming need to shower the Benihana stink from my clothes and hair, but Lily wasn't giving me a chance. I briefly wondered if it was as obvious to Christian as it was to me that I was being whored out, but he was hot and she was determined, so I kept my mouth shut.

"Yep, we were just discussing where to go. Any suggestions? We'd both just love for you to join us," Lily declared, tugging on his arm playfully. "What's around here that you like?"

"Well, midtown isn't exactly known for its bar scene, but I'm meeting my agent at Au Bar if you girls would like to come along. He just ran back to the office to pick up a few papers, but he should be there in a little. Andy, maybe you'd like to meet him—you never know when you're going to need an agent. So, Au Bar, how about it?"

Lily was peering at me with an encouraging look, one that screamed, *He's beautiful, Andy! Beautiful! I may not know who the hell he is, but he wants you so pull yourself together and tell him how much you love Au Bar!*

"I love Au Bar," I said somewhat convincingly, even though I'd never been. "I think it's perfect."

Lily smiled and Christian smiled and together we set off for Au Bar. Christian Collinsworth and I were going to get a drink together. Did this qualify as a date? *Of course not, don't be ridiculous,* I berated myself. *Alex, Alex, Alex,* I silently chanted, both determined to remember that I had a very loving boyfriend and disappointed with myself for having to force myself to remember that I had a very loving boyfriend.

Even though it was a random Thursday night, the velvet rope police were out in full force, and, while they had no problem letting the three of us in, no one was offering reduced admission of any sort: twenty bucks just to get in the door.

But before I could hand over my cash, Christian deftly peeled three twenties from a huge wad he pulled from his pocket and handed them over without a word.

I tried to protest, but Christian put two fingers to my lips. "Darling Andy, don't worry your pretty little head about it." And before I could move my mouth out from underneath his touch, he reached his other hand behind my head and took my face in both hands. Somewhere deep in the recesses of my completely addled brain, the firing synapses were warning me that he was going to kiss me. I knew it, sensed it, but couldn't move. He took my split-second hesitation to move away as permission, leaned over, and touched his lips to my neck. Just quickly, a brush, really, with perhaps a little tongue, right underneath my jaw and near my ear but still firmly on the neck, and then he reached for my hand and pulled me inside.

"Christian, wait! I, uh, I need to tell you something," I started, not quite sure whether one uninvited, nonlip, minimal-tongue kiss really demanded a whole long explanation of having a boyfriend and not meaning to send the wrong signals. Apparently Christian didn't think it was necessary, because he had walked me to a couch in a dark corner and ordered me to sit. Which I did.

"I'm getting us drinks, OK? Don't worry so much. I don't bite." He laughed, and I felt myself turn red. "Or, if I do, I promise you'll enjoy it." And he turned and walked toward the bar.

To keep from passing out or having to actually consider what had just transpired, I scanned the dark, cavernous room for Lily. We'd been there less than three minutes, but she was already deep in conversation with a tall black guy, hanging on his every word and throwing her head back with delight. I weaved through the throngs of international drinkers. How did they all know that this was the place to come if you didn't have an American passport? I passed a group of men in their thirties shouting in what I think was Japanese, two women flapping their hands and talking passionately in Arabic, and a young, unhappy-looking couple glaring at each other and whispering angrily in something that sounded like Spanish but could have been Portuguese. Lily's guy had his hand on the small of her back already and was looking utterly charmed. No time for niceties, I decided. Christian Collinsworth had just massaged my neck with his mouth. Ignoring the guy, I clamped my hand down on her right arm and turned to drag her back to the couch.

"Andy! Stop it," she hissed, pulling her arm free but remembering to smile for her guy. "You're being rude. I'd like to introduce you to my friend. William, this is my best friend, Andrea, who doesn't usually act like this. Andy, this is William." She smiled benevolently as we shook hands.

"So, may I ask why you're stealing your friend from me, Ahn-dre-ah?" William asked in a deep voice that almost echoed in the subterranean space. Perhaps in another place or at another time or with another person I would've noticed his warm smile or the chivalrous way he'd immediately stood and offered his seat when I approached, but the only thing I could focus on was that British accent. Didn't matter that this was a man, a large black man, who didn't exactly resemble Miranda Priestly in any way, shape, or form. Just hearing that accent, the way he pronounced my name *just like she did*, was enough to literally make my heart beat a little faster.

"William, I'm sorry, it's nothing personal. It's just that I have a little problem and I'd like to talk to Lily in private. I'll bring her right back." And with that, I grabbed her arm more firmly this time and yanked. Enough of this shit: I needed my friend.

Once we'd settled into the couch where Christian had placed me and I checked to ensure he was still trying to get the bartender's attention (straight guy at the bar—he may be there all night), I took a deep breath.

"Christian kissed me."

"So what's the problem? Was he a bad kisser? Oh, that's it, isn't it? No quicker way to ruin a good fraction than—"

"Lily! Good, bad, what's the difference?"

Her eyebrows reached up her forehead and she opened her mouth to talk, but I kept going.

"And not that it's at all relevant, but he kissed my neck. The problem is not *how* he did, it's that it happened at all in the first place. What about Alex? I don't exactly go around kissing other guys, you know."

"Don't I ever," she mumbled under her breath before speaking up. "Andy, you're being ridiculous. You love Alex and he loves you, but it's perfectly okay if you feel like kissing another guy once in a while. You're twenty-three years old, for chrissake. Cut yourself a little slack!"

"But I didn't kiss him . . . He kissed me!"

"First of all, let's get something very clear. Remember when Monica went down on Bill and the whole country and all our parents and Ken Starr rushed to call that sex? That was not sex. In much the same way, some guy who probably means to kiss your cheek but gets your neck instead does not qualify as 'kissing someone.' "

"But—"

"Shut up and let me finish. More important than what actually happened is that you wanted it to happen. Just admit it, Andy. You wanted to kiss Christian regardless of whether that's 'wrong' or 'bad' or 'against the rules.' And if you don't admit it, you're lying."

"Lily, seriously, I don't think it's fair that—"

"I've known you for nine years, Andy. You don't think I can see it written all over your face that you worship him? You know you shouldn't—he doesn't quite play by your rules, does he? But that's probably exactly why you like him. Just go with it, enjoy it. If Alex is right for you, he'll always be right for you. And now, you'll have to excuse me, because I have found someone who's right for me . . . for right now." She literally jumped off the couch and skipped back to William, who looked undeniably happy to see her.

I felt self-conscious sitting on the oversize velvet couch alone and looked around to find Christian, but he wasn't at the bar anymore. It would just take a little more time, I decided. Everything would just sort itself out if I just stopped worrying so much. Maybe Lily was right and I did like Christian—what was so wrong with that? He's smart and undeniably gorgeous, and the whole take-charge confidence thing was incredibly sexy. Hanging out with someone who just happened to be sexy didn't exactly translate as cheating. I'm sure there had been situations over the years in which Alex had worked with or studied with or gotten to know a cool, attractive girl, and he may have had thoughts. Did that make him disloyal? Of course not. With renewed confidence (and a now-desperate attempt to see, watch, hear, just be near Christian again), I began cruising the lounge.

I found him leaning on his right hand, talking intently to an older man, probably in his late forties, who was wearing a very dapper three-piece suit. Christian was gesturing wildly, hands flailing, with a look on his face that registered somewhere between amused and supremely annoyed, while the man with salt-and-pepper hair looked at him earnestly. I was still too far away to hear what they were discussing, but I must have been staring rather intently, because the man's eyes locked on mine and he smiled. Christian pulled back a little, followed his gaze, and saw me watching them both.

"Andy, darling," he said, his tone entirely different from what it had been just a few minutes earlier. I noticed he made the transition from seducer to friend of your parent quite smoothly. "Come here, I'd like you to meet a friend of mine. This is Gabriel Brooks, my agent, business manager, and all-around hero. Gabriel, this is Andrea Sachs, currently of *Runway* magazine."

"Andrea, a pleasure to meet you," Gabriel said, extending a hand and taking mine in one of those annoyingly delicate I'm-not-shaking-your-hand-as-I-would-a-man's-because-I'm-sure-I'd-just-snap-your-girly-little-bones-in-half clutches. "Christian has told me a lot about you."

"Really?" I said, pressing a bit more firmly, which only caused him to loosen his already slack grip. "All good, I hope?"

"Of course. He said you're an aspiring writer, like our mutual friend here." He smiled.

I was surprised to hear that he actually had heard about me from Christian, since our conversation about writing had sounded like just small talk. "Yes, well, I love to write, so hopefully someday . . ."

"Well, if you're half as good as some of the other people he's sent my way, then I look forward to reading your work." He dug around in an inside pocket and produced a leather case, from which he drew out a business card. "I know you're not ready yet, but when it does come time to show your stuff to someone, I hope you'll keep me in mind."

It took every ounce of willpower and strength to remain standing upright, to make sure that my mouth had not flopped open or my knees had not just given out. *Hope you'll keep me in mind?* The man who represented Christian Collinsworth, literary boy genius extraordinaire, had just asked if I would keep him in mind. This was craziness.

"Why thank you," I croaked, tucking the card into my bag, from where I knew I would pull it out and examine every inch of it the first chance I got. They both smiled at me, and it took a minute for me to recognize this as my cue to leave. "Well, Mr. Brooks, um, Gabriel, it was really great meeting you. I've got to be getting home now, but hopefully we'll cross paths soon."

"My pleasure, Andrea. Congratulations again on scoring such a fantastic job. Right out of college and working at *Runway*. Very impressive."

"I'll walk you out," Christian said, placing a hand on my elbow and motioning to Gabriel that he'd be right back.

We stopped at the bar so I could tell Lily that I was heading home, and she unnecessarily told me—in between William's nuzzlings—that she wouldn't be joining me. At the foot of the stairs that would take me back to street level, Christian kissed me on the cheek.

"Great running into you tonight. And I have a feeling I'm going to have to hear Gabriel talk about how great you are now, too." He grinned.

"We barely exchanged two words," I pointed out, wondering why everyone was being so complimentary.

"Yes, Andy, but what you don't seem to realize is that the writing world is a small one. Whether you write mysteries or feature stories or newspaper articles, everyone knows everyone. Gabriel doesn't have to know much about you to know that you have potential: you were good enough to get a job at *Runway*; you sound bright and articulate when you talk, and hell, you're a friend of mine. He's got nothing to lose by giving you his card. What does he know? He could have just discovered the next best-selling author. And trust me—Gabriel Brooks is a good man for you to know."

"Hmm, I guess you're right. Well, anyway, I've got to get home since I've got to be at work again in a few hours anyway. Thanks for everything. I really appreciate it." I leaned up to kiss him on the cheek, half expecting him to turn his face forward and half wanting him to, but he just smiled.

"More than my pleasure, Andrea Sachs. Have a good night." And before I could come up with anything remotely clever to say, he was headed back to Gabriel.

I rolled my eyes at myself and headed to the street to hail a cab. It had started to rain—nothing torrential, just a light, steady stream—so of course there wasn't a single cab free anywhere in Manhattan. I called the Elias-Clark car service, gave them my VIP number, and had a car screeching to the curb exactly six minutes later. Alex had left a voice mail asking me how my day was and saying that he'd be home all night writing lesson plans. It had been too long since I surprised him. It was time to make a little effort and be spontaneous. The driver agreed to wait as long as I needed, so I ran upstairs, jumped in the shower, took a little extra time making my hair look good, and threw together a bag with stuff for work the next day. Since it was already after eleven, traffic was tame and we made it to Alex's apartment in Brooklyn in under fifteen minutes. He looked genuinely happy to see me when he opened the door, saying over and over and over again how he couldn't believe that I'd come all the way to Brooklyn so late on a work night and it was the best surprise he could've hoped for. And as I lay with my head on my favorite spot on his chest, watching Conan and listening to the rhythmic sound of his breathing as he played with my hair, I barely thought about Christian at all.

"Um, hi. May I speak with your food editor please? No? OK, maybe an editorial assistant, or someone who can tell me when a restaurant review ran?" I asked an openly hostile receptionist at the *New York Times*. She had answered the phone by barking, "What!" and was currently pretending—or perhaps not—that we didn't speak a common language. Persistence paid off, though, and after asking her name three times ("We can't tell our names, lady"), threatening to report her to her manager ("What? You think he cares? I'll put him on right now"), and finally swearing rather emphatically that I would personally show up at their Times Square offices and do everything in my power to have her fired on the spot ("Oh, really? I'm not so worried"), she tired of me and connected me to someone else.

"Editorial," snapped another hassled-sounding woman. I wondered if this is what I sounded like answering Miranda's phone, and if not, then I aspired to it. It was such an enormous turnoff hearing a voice that was so incredibly, undeniably unhappy to hear from you that it almost made you just want to hang up.

"Hi, I just had a quick question." The words tumbled out in a desperate attempt to be heard before she inevitably slammed down the phone. "I'm wondering if you ran any reviews of Asian fusion restaurants yesterday?"

She sighed as though I'd just asked her to donate one of her limbs to science and then sighed again. "Have you looked online?" Another sigh.

"Yes, yes, of course, but I can't—"

"Because that's where they would be if we'd done one. I can't keep track of every word that goes in the paper, you know."

I took a deep breath myself and tried to stay calm. "Your charming receptionist connected me to you since you work in the archives department. So it does in fact appear that it's your job to keep track of every word."

"Listen, if I had to try to track down every vague description that everyone called me with every day, I wouldn't be able to do anything else. You really need to check online." She sighed twice more, and I began to worry that she might hyperventilate.

"No, no, *you* just listen for a minute," I started, feeling primed and ready to lay into this lazy girl who had a far better job than my own. "I'm calling from Miranda Priestly's office, and it just so happens that—"

"I'm sorry, did you say you were calling from Miranda Priestly's office?" she asked, and I could feel her ears perk up across the phone line. "Miranda Priestly . . . from *Runway* magazine?"

"The one and only. Why? Heard of her?"

It was here that she transformed from highly put-upon editorial assistant to gushing fashion slave. "Heard of her? Of course! Is anybody not familiar with Miranda Priestly? She is, like, the ultimate woman in fashion. What was it you said she was looking for?"

"A review. Yesterday's paper. Asian fusion restaurant. I didn't see it online, but I'm not sure I checked properly." That was a bit of a lie. I had checked online and was quite sure there hadn't been any reviews of

Asian fusion restaurants in the *New York Times* any day in the past week, but I wasn't telling her that. Maybe Schizophrenic Editorial Girl here would work a miracle.

So far I'd called the *Times*, the *Post*, and the *Daily News*, but nothing had turned up. I'd plugged in her corporate card number to access the *Wall Street Journal*'s paid archives and had actually found a blurb on a new Thai restaurant in the Village, but I had to immediately discount it when I noticed that the average entrée price was only seven dollars and citysearch.com listed only a single dollar sign next to it.

"Well, sure, hold on just a second here. I'm going to check that right out for you." And all of a sudden, Little Miss "I Can't Be Expected to Remember Every Word That Goes in the Paper" was tapping away on a keyboard and humming excitedly to both of us.

My head ached from the debacle the night before. It had been fun to surprise Alex and amazingly relaxing to just laze around his apartment, but for the first time in many, many months, I couldn't fall asleep. Over and over and over again, I had pangs of guilt, flashbacks of Christian kissing my neck and my then jumping in a car to see Alex but tell him nothing. Even though I tried to push it all out of my mind, they kept returning, each one more intense than the last one. When I finally did manage to fall asleep, I dreamed that Alex was hired to be Miranda's nanny and—even though in reality hers didn't live in—he was to move in with the family. Whenever I wanted to see Alex in my dream, I would have to share a car home with Miranda and visit him in her apartment. She would insist on calling me Emily and send me out on inane errands even though I told her repeatedly that I was just there to visit my boyfriend. By the time morning had finally rolled around, Alex had fallen under Miranda's spell and couldn't understand why I thought she was so evil and, even worse, Miranda had started dating Christian. Blessedly, my hell ended when I woke in a start after dreaming that Miranda, Christian, and Alex all sat around in Frette robes together each Sunday morning and read the *Times* and laughed while I prepared breakfast, served everyone, and cleaned up afterward. Sleep last night was about as relaxing as a solo stroll down Avenue D at four in the morning, and now this restaurant review was wrecking whatever hope I had of having an easy Friday.

"Hmm, no, we really haven't run anything lately on Asian fusion. I'm trying to think, just personally, you know, if there are any new hot Asian fusion places. You know, places that Miranda would actually consider going?" she said, sounding like she'd do anything to prolong the conversation.

I ignored her transition into first-name familiarity with Miranda and worked on getting her off the phone. "OK, well, that's what I thought. Thanks anyway, though. I appreciate it. 'Bye."

"Wait!" she cried out, and even though the phone was already halfway to the base, her urgency made me listen again. "Yes?"

"Oh, well, I, uh, I just wanted to let you know that if there's, like, anything else I can do—or any of us here—feel free to call, you know? We love Miranda here, and we'd, like, uh, want to help with anything we could?"

You would've thought that the First Lady of the United States of America had just asked Schizophrenic Editorial Girl if she might be able to locate an article for the president, an article that included information crucial to an imminent war, and not an unnamed review on an unnamed restaurant in an unnamed newspaper. The saddest part of all was that I wasn't surprised: I knew she'd come around.

"OK, I'll be sure to pass that along. Thanks so much."

Emily looked up from preparing yet another expense account and said, "No luck there either?"

"Nope. I have no idea what she's talking about, and apparently, neither does anyone else in this city. I've spoken to someone at every Manhattan paper she reads, checked online, talked to archivists, food writers, chefs. Not a single person can think of a suitable Asian fusion place that has so much as been open in the past week, never even mind one that's been reviewed in the past twenty-four hours. She's clearly lost her mind. So what now?" I flopped back into my chair and pulled my hair into a ponytail. It still wasn't yet nine in the morning, and already the headache had spread to my neck and shoulders.

"I guess," she said slowly, regrettably, "you have no choice but to ask her to clarify."

"Oh, no, not that! However will she react?"

Emily, as usual, didn't appreciate my sarcasm. "She'll be in at noon. If

I were you, I'd figure out what you are going to say ahead of time, because she is not going to be happy if you don't have that review. Especially since she asked for it last night," she pointed out with a barely suppressed smile. She was clearly delighted that I was about to get abused.

There was little left to do but wait. It was my luck that Miranda was at her monthly marathon shrink session ("She just doesn't have time to go all the way over there once a week," Emily had explained when I asked why she went for three straight hours), the only chunk of time during the entire day or night when she wouldn't call us and, of course, the only time I needed her to. A mountain of mail that I'd neglected to open for the past two days threatened to topple off the desk, and another two full days' worth of dirty dry cleaning was heaped under it, around my feet. Huge sigh to let the world know just how unhappy I was, and I dialed the cleaners.

"Hi, Mario. It's me. Yeah, I know—two whole days, no talk. Can I get a pickup, please? Great. Thanks." I hung up the phone and forced myself to pull some of the clothes onto my lap, where I would sort through them and record them on the computerized list I kept of her outgoing clothes. When Miranda called the office at 9:45 P.M. and demanded to know where her new Chanel suit was, all I had to do was open up the document and tell her that they'd gone out the day before and were due to be delivered the following day. I logged today's clothes in (one Missoni blouse, two identical pairs of Alberta Ferretti pants, two Jil Sander sweaters, two white Hermès scarves, and one Burberry trench coat), threw them in a shopping bag emblazoned with *Runway*, and called for a messenger to take them downstairs to the area where the cleaners would pick them up.

I was on a roll! Cleaning was one of the more dreaded tasks, because no matter how many times I had to do it, I was still repulsed to be sorting through someone else's dirty clothes. After I finished sorting and bagging every day, I had to wash my hands: the lingering smell of Miranda was all-pervasive, and even though it consisted of a mixture of Bulgari perfume and moisturizer and occasionally a whiff of B-DAD's cigarette smoke and was not at all unpleasant, it made me feel physically ill. British accents, Bulgari perfume, white silk scarves—just a few of life's simpler pleasures that were forever ruined for me.

The mail was the usual, ninety-nine percent garbage that Miranda would never see. Everything that was just labeled "Editor in Chief" went

directly to the people who edited the Letters pages, but many of the readers had gotten more savvy and now addressed their correspondence directly to Miranda. It took me about four seconds to skim one and see that
it was a letter to the editor and not a charity ball invitation or a quick note
from a long-lost friend, and those I just threw aside. Today there were tons.
Breathless notes from teenage girls and housewives and even a few gay
men (or, in all fairness, maybe straight and just very fashion-conscious):
"Miranda Priestly, you're not only the darling of the fashion world, you're
the Queen of my world!" one gushed. "I couldn't agree more with your
choice to run the article about red being the new black in the April issue—
it was ballsy, but genius!" another exclaimed. A few letters ranted about a
Gucci ad being too sexual since it depicted two women in stilettos and
garters who lay together on a rumpled bed and pressed their bodies together, and a few more decried the sunken-eyed, starvation-wracked,
heroine-chic models that *Runway* had used in its "Health First: How to
Feel Better" article. One was a standard-issue post office postcard that was
addressed in flowery script to Miranda Priestly on one side and read, quite
simply, on the other: "Why? Why do you print such a boring, stupid magazine?" I laughed out loud and tucked that one in my bag for later—my
collection of critical letters and postcards was growing, and soon there
wasn't going to be any fridge space left. Lily thought it was bad karma to
bring home other people's negative thoughts and hostility, and she shook
her head when I insisted that any bad karma originally intended toward
Miranda could only make me happy.

The last letter of the massive pile before I'd begin tackling the two
dozen invitations Miranda received each day was addressed in the loopy,
girly writing of a teenager, complete with *i*'s dotted with hearts and
smiley faces next to happy thoughts. I planned to only skim it, but it
wouldn't allow itself to be skimmed: it was too immediately sad and honest—it was bleeding and pleading and begging all over the page. The initial four-second period came and went and I was still reading.

Dear Miranda,
My name is Anita and I am seventeen years old and I am a senior at
Barringer H.S. in Newark, NJ. I am so ashamed of my body even
though everyone tells me I'm not fat. I want to look like the models

you have in your magazine. Every month I wait for Runway to come in the mail even though my mama says it's stupid to pay all my allowance for a fashion magazine. But she doesn't understand that I have a dream, but you do, dontcha? It has been my dream since I was a little girl, but I don't think it's gonna happen. Why, you ask? My boobs are very flat and my behind is bigger than the ones your models have and this makes me very embarased. I ask myself if this is the way I wanna live my life and I answer NO!!! because I wanna change and I wanna look and feel better and so I'm asking for your help. I wanna make a positive change and look in the mirror and love my breasts and my behind because they look just like the ones in the best magazine on earth!!!

Miranda, I know you're a wonderful person and fashion editor and you could transform me into a new person, and trust me, I would be forever grateful. But if you can't make me a new person, maybe you can get me a really, really, really nice dress for special occasions? I don't ever have dates, but my mama says it's OK for girls to go out alone so I will. I have one old dress but its not a designer dress or anything you would show in Runway. My favorite designers are Prada (#1), Versace (#2), John Paul Gotier (#3). I have many faves, but those are my first three I love. I do not own any of their clothes and I haven't even seen them in a store (I'm not sure if anywhere in Newark sells these designers, but if you know of one, please tell me so I can go look at them and see what they look like up close), but I've seen there clothes in Runway and I have to say that I really, really love them.

I'm gonna stop bothering you now, but I want you to know that even if you throw this letter in the garbage, I will still be a big fan of your magazine because I love the models and the clothes and everything, and of course I love you too.

> *Sincerely,*
> *Anita Alvarez*

P.S. My phone number is 973-555-3948. You can write or call but please do so before the week of July 4 because I really need a nice dress before then. I LOVE YOU!! Thank you!!!!!

The letter smelled like Jean Naté, that acrid-smelling toilet water–spray preferred by preteen girls the country over. But that wasn't what was causing the tightness in my chest, the constriction in my throat. How many Anitas were there out there? Young girls with so little else in their lives that they measured their worth, their confidence, their entire existence around the clothes and the models they saw in *Runway*? How many more had decided to unconditionally love the woman who put it all together each month—the orchestrator of such a seductive fantasy—even though she wasn't worth one single second of their adoration? How many girls had no idea that the object of their worship was a lonely, deeply unhappy, and oftentimes cruel woman who didn't deserve the briefest moment of their innocent affection and attention?

I wanted to cry, for Anita and all her friends who expended so much energy trying to mold themselves into Shalom or Stella or Carmen, trying to impress and please and flatter the woman who would only take their letters and roll her eyes or shrug her shoulders or toss them without a second thought to the girl who'd written down a piece of herself. Instead, I tucked the letter into my top desk drawer and vowed to find a way to help Anita. She sounded even more desperate than the others who wrote, and there was no reason that with all the excess stuff around I couldn't find her a decent dress for a date she would hopefully have soon.

"Hey, Em, I'm just going to run down to the newsstand and see if they have *Women's Wear* yet. I can't believe it's so late today. Do you want anything?"

"Will you bring me a Diet Coke?" she asked.

"Sure. Just a minute," I said, and weaved quickly through the racks and past the doorway to the service elevator, where I could hear Jessica and James sharing a cigarette and wondering who would be at Miranda's Met party that night. Ahmed was finally able to produce a copy of *Women's Wear Daily*, which was a relief, and I grabbed a Diet Coke for Emily and a can of Pepsi for me, but on second thought, I took a Diet for myself as well. The difference in taste and enjoyment wasn't worth the disapproving looks and/or comments I was sure to receive during the walk from reception to my desk.

I was so busy examining the front page's color photo of Tommy Hilfiger, I didn't even notice that one of the elevators had opened and was available. Out of the corner of my eye, I caught a quick glimpse of green, a very distinct green. Particularly noteworthy because Miranda had a Chanel suit in just that shade of greeny tweed, a color I'd never really seen before but liked a whole lot. And although my mind knew better, it couldn't stop my eyes from looking up and into the elevator, where they were sort of not really surprised to find Miranda peering back. She stood ramrod straight, her hair pulled severely off her face as usual, her eyes staring intently at what must have been my shocked face. There was absolutely no alternative but to step inside the elevator with her.

"Um, good morning, Miranda," I said, but it came out sounding like a whisper. The doors closed behind us: we would be the only two riding for the entire seventeen floors. She said nothing to me, but she pulled out her leather organizer and began flipping through the pages. We stood side by side, the depth of the silence increasing tenfold with every second that she didn't respond. *Does she even recognize me?* I wondered. Was it possible that she was entirely unaware that I had been her assistant for the past seven months—or perhaps I really had whispered so softly that she hadn't heard? I wondered why she didn't immediately ask me about the restaurant review or whether I'd received her message about ordering new china, or if everything was in place for the evening's party. But she acted as though she were all alone in that elevator, that there was not another human being—or, to be precise, not one worth acknowledging—inside that small vestibule with her.

It wasn't until nearly a full minute later that I noticed we weren't progressing through the floors. Ohmigod! She *had* seen me because she'd assumed that I would press the button, but I'd been too stunned to move. I reached forward slowly, fearfully, pressed the number seventeen, and instinctively waited for something to explode. But we immediately whisked upward, and I wasn't even sure if she had noticed we hadn't been moving all along.

Five, six, seven . . . it felt as though it took ten minutes for the elevator to pass each floor, and the silence had begun humming in my ears. When I worked up enough nerve to steal a glance in Miranda's direction, I discovered that she was looking me up and down. Her eyes moved unabashedly as they checked out first my shoes and then my pants and then my shirt, and continued upward to my face and hair, all the while avoiding my eyes. The expression on her face was one of passive disgust, the way the desensitized *Law & Order* detectives appear when they're faced with yet another beaten and bloodied corpse. I did a quick review of myself and wondered what exactly had triggered the reaction. Short-sleeve, military-style shirt, a brand-new pair of Seven jeans I'd been sent free from their PR department simply for working at *Runway*; and a pair of relatively flat (two-inch heels) black slingbacks that were to date the only nonboots/nonsneakers/nonloafers that allowed me to make four-plus trips to Starbucks a day without shredding my feet to bits. I usually tried to wear the Jimmy Choos that Jeffy had given me, but I needed a day off every week or so to allow the arches in my feet to stop aching. My hair was clean and assembled in the kind of deliberately messy top-knot that Emily always wore without comment, and my nails—though unpainted—were long and reasonably well shaped. I had shaved under my arms within the last forty-eight hours. At least as far as the last time I'd checked, there were no massive facial eruptions. My Fossil watch was turned around so the face was sitting on the inside of my wrist just in case anyone tried to catch a glimpse of the brand; and a quick check with my right hand indicated that no bra straps were visible. So what was it? What exactly had made her look at me that way?

Twelve, thirteen, fourteen . . . the elevator stopped and swept open to yet another stark white reception area. A woman of around thirty-five stepped forward to board, but stopped two feet from the door when she saw Miranda standing inside.

"Oh, I, uh . . ." she stammered loudly, looking frantically around her for an excuse not to enter our private hell. And although it would've been nicer for me to have her come aboard, I privately rooted for her to escape. "I, um, oh! I forgot the photos I need for the meeting," she finally managed, whipping around on a particularly unsteady Manolo and high-tailing it back toward the office area. Miranda hadn't appeared to notice, and once again, the doors swept shut.

Fifteen, sixteen, and finally—finally!—seventeen, where the doors opened to reveal a group of *Runway* fashion assistants on their way to pick up the cigarettes, Diet Coke, and mixed greens that would consti-tute their lunch. Each young, beautiful face looked more panicked than the next, and they almost trampled one another trying to move out of Miranda's way. They parted directly down the middle, three to one side and two to the other, and she deigned to walk past them. They were all staring after her, silent, as she made her way across the reception area, and I was left with no choice but to follow her. Wouldn't notice a thing, I figured. We'd just spent what felt like an entire insufferable week locked together in a five-by-three-foot box, and she hadn't so much as acknowledged my presence. But as soon as I stepped onto the floor, she turned around.

"Ahn-dre-ah?" she asked, her voice cutting through the tense silence that filled the entire room. I didn't respond since I figured it was rhetorical, but she waited.

"Ahn-dre-ah?"

"Yes, Miranda?"

"Whose shoes are you wearing?" She placed one hand lightly on a tweed-swathed hip and peered over at me. By now the elevator had left without the fashion assistants, since they were too engrossed in actually getting to see—and hear!—Miranda Priestly in the flesh. I could feel six pairs of eyes on my feet, which, although they had been quite comfortable mere moments before, were now beginning to burn and itch under the intense scrutiny of five fashion assistants and one fashion guru.

The anxiety from the unexpected shared elevator ride (a first) and the unwavering stares of all these people addled my brain, so when Miranda asked whose shoes I was wearing, I thought that perhaps *she* thought I was not wearing my own.

"Um, mine?" I said, without realizing until the words had been spoken that it sounded not only disrespectful, but downright obnoxious. The gaggle of Clackers began to twitter, until Miranda turned her wrath on them.

"I'm wondering why the vahst majority of my fashion assistants appear as though they have nothing better to do than gossip like little girls." She began singling them out by pointing at each one, since she wouldn't have been able to produce a single one's name if you put a gun to her head.

"You!" she said crisply to the coltish new girl who was probably seeing Miranda for the first time. "Did we hire you for this or did we hire you to call in clothes for the suits shoot?" The girl hung her head and opened her mouth to apologize, but Miranda barreled on.

"And you!" she said, walking over and standing directly in front of

Jocelyn, the highest-ranking among them and a favorite of all the editors. "You think there aren't a million girls who want your job and who understand couture just as well as you?" She took a step back, slowly moved her eyes up and down each of their bodies, lingering just long enough to make each feel fat, ugly, and inappropriately clad, and commanded them all to return to their desks. They nodded their heads furiously while keeping their heads bowed. A few murmured heartfelt apologies while they moved quickly back to the fashion area. It wasn't until they'd all left that I realized we were alone. Again.

"Ahn-dre-ah? I won't tolerate being spoken to that way by my assistant," she declared, walking toward the door that would lead us to the hallway. I was unsure whether I should follow her or not, and I briefly hoped that either Eduardo or Sophy or one of the fashion girls had warned Emily that Miranda was on her way back.

"Miranda, I—"

"Enough." She paused at the door and looked at me. "Whose shoes are you wearing?" she asked again in a none-too-pleased voice.

I checked out my black slingbacks again and wondered how to tell the most stylish woman in the western hemisphere that I was wearing a pair of shoes I'd purchased at Ann Taylor Loft. Another glance at her face and I knew I couldn't.

"I bought them in Spain," I said quickly, averting my eyes. "It was at some adorable boutique in Barcelona right off Las Ramblas that carried this new Spanish designer's line." Where the hell had I pulled that one from?

She folded her hand into a fist, put it over her mouth, and cocked her head. I saw James approaching the glass door from the other side, but as soon as he saw Miranda he turned and fled. "Ahn-dre-ah, they're unacceptable. My girls need to represent *Runway* magazine, and those shoes are not the message I'm looking to convey. Find some decent footwear in the Closet. And get me a coffee." She looked at me and looked at the door, and I understood I was to reach forward and open it for her, which I did. She walked through without saying thank you and headed back to the office. I needed to get money and my cigarettes for the coffee run, but neither was worth having to walk behind her like an abused but loyal duckling, and so I turned to walk back toward the elevator. Eduardo could spot me the five bucks for the latte, and Ahmed would just charge a new pack to *Runway*'s house account, as he'd been doing for months now. I hadn't counted on her even noticing, but her voice hit the back of my head like a shovel.

"Ahn-dre-ah!"

"Yes, Miranda?" I stopped in my tracks and turned to face her.

"I expect the restaurant review I asked you for is on my desk?"

"Um, well, actually, I've had a little trouble locating it. You see, I've spoken to all the papers and it seems none of them have run a review of an Asian fusion restaurant in the past few days. Do you, uh, happen to remember the name of the restaurant?" Without realizing it, I was holding my breath and bracing for the onslaught.

It appeared my explanation held little interest for her, because she had resumed walking toward her office. "Ahn-dre-ah, I already told you that it was in the *Post*—is it really that difficult to find?" And with that, she was gone. The *Post*? I'd spoken to their restaurant reviewer just that morning and he had sworn there were no reviews that fit my description—nothing noteworthy had opened that week whatsoever. She was cracking up, for sure, and I was the one who was going to get blamed.

The coffee run took only a few minutes since it was midday, so I felt free to tack on an extra ten minutes to call Alex, who would be having lunch at exactly twelve-thirty. Thankfully, he answered his cell phone, so I didn't have to deal with any of the teachers again.

"Hey babe, how's your day going?" He sounded cheerful to the point of excess, and I had to remind myself not to be irritated.

"Awesome so far, as always. I really do love it here. I've spent the past five hours researching an imaginary article that was dreamed up by a delusional woman who would probably rather take her own life than admit she's wrong. What about you?"

"Well, I've had a great day. Remember I told you about Shauna?" I nodded into the phone even though he couldn't see me. Shauna was one of his little girls who had yet to utter a single word in class, and whether he threatened her or bribed her or worked with her one on one, Alex couldn't get her to talk. He'd been near-hysterical the first time she'd shown up in his class, placed there by a social worker who'd discovered that even though she was nine years old she'd never been in the inside of a school, and he'd been obsessed with helping her ever since.

"Well, it seems she won't shut up! All it took was a little singing. I had a folk singer come in today to play the guitar for the kids, and Shauna was singing away. And once she broke the ice, she's been jabbering away with everyone since. She knows English. She has an age-appropriate vocabulary. She's completely and totally normal!" His obvious elation made me smile, and all of a sudden I started to miss him. Miss him in the way that you do when you've seen someone frequently and regularly but haven't really connected with him in any significant way. It had been great to surprise him the night before, but, as usual, I'd been too frazzled to be much company. We both inherently understood that we were just waiting out my sentence, waiting for me to complete my year of servitude, waiting until everything went back to the way it was. But I still missed him. And I still felt not a little guilty for the whole Christian situation.

"Hey, congratulations! Not that you needed a testament to the fact that you're a great teacher, but you got one anyway! You should be thrilled."

"Yeah, it's exciting." I could hear the bell ring in the background.

"Listen, is that offer still open for a date tonight—just you and me?" I asked, hoping he hadn't made plans yet but expecting that he had. As I'd pulled myself out of bed this morning and dragged my exhausted and sore body into the shower, he'd called out that he wanted to just rent a movie, order some food, and hang out. I'd mumbled something unnecessarily sarcastic about it not being worth his time because I wouldn't get home until late and would just fall asleep, and at least one of us should have a life and enjoy their Friday night. I wanted to tell him now that I was angry at Miranda, at *Runway*, at myself, but not at him, and that there was nothing I'd rather do than curl up on the couch and cuddle for fifteen straight hours.

"Sure." He sounded surprised, but pleased. "Why don't I just wait at your place and then we can figure out what we want to do? I'll just hang out with Lily until you get home."

"Sounds absolutely perfect. You can hear all about Freudian Boy."

"Who?"

"Never mind. Listen, I've got to run. The Queen will wait for coffee no longer. See you tonight—can't wait."

Eduardo allowed me upstairs after chanting only two refrains—my choice—of "We Didn't Start the Fire," and Miranda was talking animatedly when I set down her coffee spread on the left-hand corner of her desk. I spent the rest of the afternoon arguing with every assistant and editor I could reach at the *New York Post*, trying to insist that I knew their paper better than they did, and could I please just have one little copy of the Asian fusion restaurant review they'd run the day before?

"Ma'am, I've told you a dozen times and I'll tell you again: *we did not review any such restaurant*. I know Ms. Priestly is a crazy woman and I don't doubt that she's making your life a living hell, but I just can't produce an article that doesn't exist. Do you understand?" This had come finally from an associate who, even though he worked on *Page Six*, had been assigned the task of finding my article to shut me up. He'd been patient and willing, but he'd reached the end of his charity work. Emily was on the other line with one of their freelance food writers, and I'd forced James to call one of his ex-boyfriends who worked in the advertising department there to see if there was anything—anything—he could do. It was already three o'clock the day *after* she'd requested something, and this was the very first time I hadn't gotten it immediately.

"Emily!" Miranda called from inside her deceptively bright office.

"Yes, Miranda?" we both answered, jumping up to see which one of us she would motion to.

"Emily, I can hear that you just spoke to the people at the *Post*?" she said, directing her attention in my direction. The real Emily looked relieved and sat down.

"Yes, Miranda, I just hung up with them. I've actually spoken to three different people there and all of them insist that they haven't reviewed a single new Asian fusion restaurant in Manhattan at any point in the last week. Maybe it was before then?" I was now tottering in front of her desk with my head bowed just enough so I could stare at the black Jimmy Choo slingbacks with four-inch heels that Jeffy had provided so smugly.

"Manhattan?" She looked confused and pissed off all at once. "Who said anything about Manhattan?"

It was my time to be confused.

"Ahn-dre-ah, I've told you at least five times now that the review was written about a new restaurant in *Washington*. Since I'll be there next week, I need you to make a reservation." She cocked her head and moved her lips into what can only be described as a wicked smile. "What exactly about this project do you find so challenging?"

Washington? Five times she'd told me the restaurant was in *Washington*? I don't think so. She was clearly losing her mind or just taking sadistic pleasure in watching me lose mine. But being the idiot she took me for, I again spoke without thinking.

"Oh, Miranda, I'm fairly certain that the *New York Post* doesn't do reviews of restaurants in Washington. It appears they only actually visit and review places new to New York."

"Is that supposed to be funny, Ahn-dre-ah? Is that your idea of having a sense of humor?" Her smile had disappeared and she was leaning forward in her seat, looking like a hungry vulture that was impatiently circling its prey.

"Um no, Miranda, I just thought that—"

"Ahn-dre-ah, as I've made clear a *dozen times already*, the review I'm looking for is in the *Washington Post*. You've heard of that little newspaper, right? Just like New York has the *New York Times*, Washington, D.C., has its own paper, too. See how that works?" Her voice was now beyond mocking: she was so incredibly patronizing that she was only one step away from actually addressing me in baby talk.

"I'll get it for you right away," I stated as calmly as I could and quietly walked out.

"Oh, and Ahn-dre-ah?" My heart lurched and my stomach wondered if it could take another "surprise." "I expect you to attend the party tonight to greet the guests. That's all."

I looked to Emily, who looked absolutely baffled, her crinkled forehead making her appear as dumbfounded as I felt. "Did I hear her correctly?" I whispered to Emily, who could do nothing but nod and motion for me to come to her side of the suite.

"I was afraid of this," she whispered gravely, like a surgeon telling a patient's family member that they'd found something horrible upon opening the chest cavity.

"She can't be serious. It's four o'clock on Friday. The party starts at seven. It's black tie, for chrissake—there is no way on earth she expects me to go." I looked again at my watch in disbelief and tried to remember her exact words.

"Oh, she's quite serious," she said, picking up the phone. "I'll help you, OK? You go find the review in the *Washington Post* and get her a copy before she leaves—Uri is coming for her soon to take her home for her hair and makeup. I'll get you a dress and everything else you need for tonight. Don't worry. We'll figure it out." She began rapid-fire dialing and whispering urgent-sounding instructions into the phone. I stood and stared, but she waved her hand without looking up and I snapped back to reality.

"Go," she whispered, looking at me with a rare hint of sympathy. And I went.

"You can't show up in a cab," Lily said to me as I jabbed helplessly at my eyes with my brand-new Maybelline Great Lash mascara. "This is black-tie. Call a car, for chrissake." She watched for a minute more and then grabbed the clumpy wand from my hand and tapped my eyelids closed.

"I guess you're right," I sighed, still refusing to accept that my Friday night was to be spent in a formal gown at the Met, greeting wealthy-but-still-rednecks from Georgia and North and South Carolina and plastering fake smile after fake smile on my poorly made-up face. The announcement had left me all of three hours to find a dress, buy makeup, get ready, and revamp all my weekend plans, and in the craziness of the situation, I'd forgotten to arrange transportation.

Luckily, working at one of the biggest fashion magazines in the country (the job a million girls would die for!) has its advantages, and by 4:40 P.M. I was the proud borrower of a knockout floor-length black Oscar de la Renta number, provided kindly by Jeffy, Closet maven and lover of all things feminine ("Girl, you go black-tie, you go Oscar, and that's that. Now don't be shy, take those pants off and try this on for Jeffy." I began to unbutton and he shuddered. I asked him if he really found my half-naked body that repulsive, and he said of course not; it was merely my panty lines that he found so disgusting). The fashion assistants had already called in a pair of silver Manolos in my size, and someone in accessories had selected a flashy silver Judith Leiber evening bag with a long, clanking chain. I'd expressed interest in an understated Calvin Klein clutch, but she snorted at the suggestion and handed me the Judith. Stef was debating whether I should wear a choker or a pendant, and Allison, the newly promoted beauty editor, was on the phone with her manicurist, who made office calls.

"She'll meet you in the conference room at four forty-five," Allison said when I picked up my extension. "You're wearing black, right? Insist on Chanel Ruby Red. Just tell her to bill us."

The entire office had worked itself up to a nearly hysterical frenzy trying to make me look appropriate for the night's gala affair. It certainly wasn't because they all adored me so much and killed themselves trying to help me out; rather, they knew Miranda had mandated the makeover and were eager to prove to her the high level of their taste and class.

Lily finished her charity makeup lesson and I briefly wondered if I looked ridiculous wearing a floor-length Oscar de la Renta gown and Bonne Belle Lipsmackers in Fudgsicle. Probably, but I had turned down all offers of having a makeup artist come to the apartment. Everyone on staff tried to insist—and none too subtly—but I adamantly refused. Even I had limits.

I hobbled into the bedroom on my four-inch Manolo stilettos and kissed Alex on the forehead. He barely looked up from the magazine he was reading.

"I'll definitely be home by eleven, so we can go get some dinner or drinks then, OK? I'm sorry I have to do this, I really am. If you do decide to go out with the guys, call so I can come meet you, OK?" He had, as promised, come directly from school to spend the night together, and hadn't been all that thrilled when I'd arrived home with the news that he could definitely have a relaxing night at home but that I wouldn't be a part of the plans. He was sitting on the balcony off my bedroom, reading an old copy of *Vanity Fair* we had lying around and drinking one of the beers Lily kept in the fridge for guests. It wasn't until after I'd explained that I had to work tonight that I even noticed he and Lily weren't hanging out.

"Where is she?" I asked. "She has no classes, and I know she's not working Fridays all summer."

Alex took a swig of his Pale Ale and shrugged. "I'm guessing she's here. Her door's closed, but I saw some guy walking around before."

"Some guy? Could you be a little more descriptive? What guy?" I wondered if someone had broken in, or perhaps Freudian Boy had finally been invited over.

"I don't know, but he's scary-looking. Tattoos, piercings, wife-beater—the whole nine. Can't imagine where she met this one." He took another nonchalant swig.

I couldn't imagine where she'd found him, either, considering I'd left her at eleven the night before in the company of a very polite guy named William who, as far as I could see, was not a wife-beater-wearing, tattoo-donning kind of guy.

"Alex, seriously! You're telling me there's some thug cruising around my apartment—a thug who may or may not have been invited over—and you don't care? This is ridiculous! We need to do something," I said, getting up from the chair and wondering, as always, if the weight shift was going to cause the balcony to fall off the side of the building.

"Andy, relax. He's definitely *not* a thug." He flipped a page. "He might be a punk-grunge-freak, but he's not a thug."

"Great, that's just fucking great. Now are you going to come see what's going on, or are you just going to sit there all night?"

He still refused to look at me, and I finally understood how annoyed he was about tonight. Understandable, entirely, but I was just as irritated to have to work, and there wasn't a damn thing I could do about it. "Why don't you call if you need me?"

"Fine," I huffed and made a big production of storming inside. "Don't feel guilty when you find my dismembered body on the bathroom floor. Really, no big deal . . ."

I stomped inside and around the apartment for a little while, looking for evidence of this guy's presence. The only thing that seemed at all out of place was an empty bottle of Ketel One in the sink. Had she really managed to buy, open, and drink an entire bottle of vodka sometime after midnight last night? I knocked on her door. No response. I knocked a little more insistently, and I heard a guy's voice state the very obvious fact that someone was knocking on the door. When still no one responded, I turned the doorknob.

"Hello? Anyone home here?" I called out, trying not to look inside the room but only being able to hold out for about five seconds. My eyes skipped over the two pairs of jeans that were tangled up on the floor and the bra that was hanging from the desk chair and the overflowing ashtray that made the room stink like a frat house and went directly to the bed, where my best friend was stretched out on her side, back to me, completely naked. A sickly looking guy with a line of sweat above his lip and a head full of greasy hair blended into her sheets: his dozens of snaking, winding, scary tattoos acted as the perfect camouflage against her green and blue plaid comforter. There was a gold hoop through his eyebrow, much glittering metal from each ear, and two small, rounded spikes coming out of his chin. Thankfully he was wearing a pair of boxers, but they looked so dirty and dingy and old that I almost—almost—wished he weren't. He pulled on his cigarette, exhaled slowly and meaningfully, and nodded in my general direction.

"Yo," he said, waving his cigarette toward me. "You mind shuttin' the door there, m'friend?"

What? "M'friend"? Was this sleazy-looking Aussie actually giving *me* attitude?

"Are you smoking *crack*?" I asked, no longer interested in manners of any sort, and not at all scared. He was shorter than me and couldn't have weighed more than a hundred thirty—as far as I could tell, the worst thing he could do to me at that point would be to touch me. I shuddered when I thought about the myriad ways he'd probably touched Lily, who was still sleeping soundly underneath his protective hover. "Who the hell do you think you are? This is *my* apartment, and I'd like you to leave. Now!" I added, my courage fueled by the time demands: I had exactly one hour to get gorgeous for the single most stressful night of my career, and dealing with this strung-out freak had not been part of the game plan.

"*Duuuuuuuude*. Chill out," he breathed and inhaled again. "It doesn't look like your friend here wants me to leave . . ."

"She would want you to leave if she HAPPENED TO BE CONSCIOUS, YOU ASSHOLE!" I screamed, horrified that Lily had—in all likelihood—had sex with this guy. "I assure you, I speak for both of us when I say GET THE FUCK OUT OF OUR APARTMENT!"

I felt a hand on my shoulder and whipped around to see Alex, looking concerned, checking out the situation. "Andy, why don't you get in the shower and let me take care of this, OK?" Although no one could call him a big guy, he looked like a pro wrestler compared to the emaciated mess that was currently nuzzling his facial metal against my best friend's bare back.

"I. WANT. HIM."—I pointed here, just to be clear.—"OUT. OF. MY. APARTMENT."

"I know you do, and I think he's about ready to leave, too, aren't you, buddy?" Alex asked in the kind of soothing voice you'd use with a rabid-looking dog you were frightened of upsetting.

"*Duuuuuuuude*, no issues here. Just havin' a little fun with Lily is all. She was all over me last night at Au Bar—ask anyone, they'll tell you. Fuckin' begged me to come back with her."

"I don't doubt that," Alex said soothingly. "She's a really friendly girl when she wants to be, but sometimes she gets too drunk to know what she's doing. So as her friend, I'm going to have to ask you to leave now."

The freak mashed his cigarette out and made a big show of throwing up his hands in mock surrender. "Dude, no problem whatsoever. I'll just take a quick shower and give m'little Lily here a proper good-bye, and then I'll be on m'way." He swung his legs over the side of the bed and reached for the towel that hung next to her desk.

Alex moved forward, swiftly removed the towel from his hands, and looked him directly in the eye. "No. I think you should leave now. Right now." And in a way that I'd never seen him do in the almost three years

I'd known him, he placed himself squarely in front of Freak Boy and allowed his height to insinuate the threat that was clearly intended.

"Dude, no worries. I'm outta here," he crooned after taking one look at Alex and realizing he had to crane his neck to look at his face. "Just get m'self dressed and out the door." He picked up his jeans from the floor and located his ripped-up T-shirt from underneath Lily's still exposed body. She moved when he pulled it out from under her, and a few seconds later her eyes managed to open.

"Cover her!" Alex commanded gruffly, now clearly enjoying his new role as threatening-man-in-charge. And without comment, Freak Boy pulled the cover over her shoulders so that only a tangle of her black curls was visible.

"What's going on?" Lily croaked while willing her eyes to stay open. She turned to see me trembling in anger in her doorway, Alex hulking about doing manly poses, and Freak Boy scrambling to tie his blue and canary yellow Diadoras and get the hell out before things got really ugly. Too late. Her gaze stopped on Freak Boy.

"Who the hell are you?" she asked him, bolting upright without even realizing that she was now completely naked. Alex and I instinctively turned away while she pulled the covers up, looking shocked, but Freak Boy grinned lecherously and ogled her breasts.

"Baby, you tellin' me you don't remember who I am?" he asked, his thick Australian accent becoming less adorable with every passing second. "You sure knew who I was last night." He walked over to her and looked like he was about to sit down on the bed, but Alex had already grabbed his arm and pulled him upright.

"Out. Now. Or I'm going to have to carry you myself," he commanded, looking tough and very cute and not a little proud of himself.

Freak Boy threw up his hands and made clucking noises. "I'm outta here. Call me sometime, Lily. You were great last night." He moved quickly through the bedroom door toward the living room with Alex in pursuit. "Man, she sure as hell is a feisty one," I heard him say to Alex right before the front door slammed shut, but it didn't appear that Lily had heard. She had pulled on a T-shirt and managed to pull herself out of bed.

"Lily, who the hell was that? He was the biggest jerk I've ever met, not to mention absolutely *disgusting*."

She shook her head slowly and appeared to be concentrating very hard, trying to remember where he'd entered her life. "Disgusting. You're right, he is absolutely disgusting, and I have no idea what happened. I remember you leaving last night and talking to some really nice guy in a suit—we were doing shots of Jaeger, for some reason—and that's it."

"Lily, just imagine how drunk you had to be to agree to not only have sex with someone who looks like that, but to bring him back to our apartment!" I thought I was pointing out the obvious, but her eyes widened into surprised realization.

"You think I had sex with him?" she asked softly, refusing to acknowledge what seemed certain.

Alex's words from a few months before came back to me: Lily did drink more than was normal—all the signs were there. She was missing classes regularly, had gotten arrested, and now had dragged home the scariest-looking mutant of a guy I'd ever laid eyes on. I also remembered the message one of her professors had left on our machine right after finals, something to the effect that while Lily's final paper had been stellar, she'd missed too many classes and handed things in too late to give her the "A" she deserved. I decided to tread carefully. "Lil, sweetie, I don't think the problem is the guy. I think it's the drinking that's causing it."

She had begun brushing her hair, and it wasn't until now that I realized it was already six o'clock on a Friday night and she was just getting out of bed. She wasn't protesting, so I continued.

"It's not that I have any issue with drinking," I said, trying to keep the conversation relatively peaceful. "Clearly, I'm not antidrinking. I just wonder if it's gotten a little bit out of control lately, you know? Has everything been OK at school?"

She opened her mouth to say something, but Alex popped his head in the door and handed me my shrieking cell phone. "It's her," he said and left again. *Argghhh!* The woman had a very special gift for wrecking my life.

"Sorry," I said to Lily, looking at the phone warily as the display screamed MP CELL over and over again. "It usually only takes a second for her to humiliate or reprimand me, so hold that thought." Lily set down her brush and watched me answer.

"Miran—" Again, I'd almost answered the line as though it were her own. "This is Andrea," I corrected, bracing for the barrage.

"Andrea, you know I expect you there at six-thirty tonight, do you not?" she barked into the phone without a greeting or identification of any sort.

"Oh, um, you had said seven o'clock earlier. I still need to—"

"I said six-thirty before and I'm saying it again now. *Siiiiix-thiiiiirty.* Get it?" Click. She'd hung up. I looked at my watch. 6:05 P.M. This was a problem.

"She wants me there in twenty-five minutes," I stated out loud to no one in particular.

Lily looked relieved for the distraction. "Let's get you moving then, OK?"

"We're midconversation here, and this is important. What were you going to say before?" The words were right, but it was clear to both of us that my mind was already a million miles away. I'd already decided there was no time to shower, as I now had fifteen minutes to zip myself into black-tie and get into a car.

"Seriously, Andy, you've got to move. Go get ready—we'll do this later."

And once again I was left with no choice but to move quickly, heart racing, climbing into my gown and running a brush through my hair and trying to match some of the names with the pictures of the evening's guests that Emily had helpfully printed out earlier. Lily watched the whole thing unwind with mild amusement, but I knew she was worrying about the incident with Freak Boy, and I felt terrible I couldn't deal with it right then. Alex was on his phone with his little brother, trying to convince him that he really was too young to go to a movie at nine o'clock and that their mother wasn't cruel in forbidding him to do so.

I kissed him on the cheek as he whistled and told me that he'd probably meet some people for dinner but to call him later if I wanted to meet up, and ran as best one can in stilts back to the living room, where Lily was holding a gorgeous piece of black silk fabric. I looked at her questioningly.

"A wrap, for your big night," she sang, shaking it out like a bedsheet. "I want my Andy to look just as sophisticated as all the big-money Carolina rednecks she'll be serving tonight like a common waitress. My grandmother bought it for me years ago to wear to Eric's wedding. I can't decide if it's gorgeous or hideous, but it's black-tie enough and it's Chanel, so it should do."

I hugged her. "Just promise if Miranda kills me for saying the wrong thing that you'll burn this dress and make sure I'm buried in my Brown sweatpants. Promise me!" She grabbed the mascara wand I was waving about and started working on me.

"You look great, Andy, really you do. Never thought I'd see you in an Oscar gown going to one of Miranda Priestly's parties, but, hey, you look the part. Now go."

She handed me the dangling, obnoxiously bright Judith Leiber bag and held the door as I walked into the hallway. "Have fun!"

The car was waiting outside my building and John—who was shaping up to be a first-class pervert—whistled as the driver held the door open for me.

"Knock 'em dead, hottie," he called after me with an exaggerated wink. "See ya late-night." He had no idea where I was going, of course, but it was comforting that he thought I'd at least be coming home. *Maybe it won't be that bad*, I thought as I settled into the cushy back-seat of the Town Car. But then my dress slid up over my knees and the back of my legs touched the ice-cold leather seats, and I lurched forward. *Or, maybe, it will suck just as much as I think it will?*

The driver jumped out and ran around to open the door for me, but I was standing on the curb by the time he'd made it around. I'd been to the Met once before, on a day trip to New York with my mom and Jill to see some of the tourist sights. I didn't remember any of the actual exhibits we saw that day—only how much my new shoes had hurt by the time we got there—but I recalled the never-ending white staircase out front and the feeling that I could climb those stairs forever.

The stairs stood where I remembered them but looked different in the haze of dusk. Still accustomed to the short, miserable days of winter, I thought it seemed strange that the sky was just darkening and it was already six-thirty. That night the stairs looked positively regal. They were prettier than the Spanish Steps or the ones outside the library at Columbia, or even the awe-inspiring spread at the Capitol building in D.C. It wasn't until I'd made it to about the tenth one of those white beauties that I began to loathe them. What cruel, cruel sadist would make a woman in a skintight, floor-length gown and spiked heels climb such a hill of hell? Since I couldn't very well hate the architect or even the museum official who'd commissioned him, I was forced to hate Miranda, who could usually be blamed for directly or indirectly causing all the misery and bad will in my life.

The top felt like a mile away, and I flashed back to the spinning classes I used to take when I still had time to go to the gym. Some Nazi instructor would sit atop her little bike and bark out orders in perfect military staccato: "Pump, pump, and breathe, breathe! Climb, people, climb that hill. You're almost at the top! Don't lose it now! Climb for your life!" I closed my eyes and tried to envision pedaling instead, the wind in my hair, running over the instructor, but climbing, still climbing. Oh, anything to forget the fiery pain that shot from little toe to heel to back again. Ten more steps, that was all that was left, just ten more, oh, god, was that wetness in my shoes blood? Would I have to walk before Miranda in a sweaty Oscar gown and bloody feet? Please, oh please, say that I was almost there and . . . there! The top. The feeling of victory was no less than that of a world-class sprinter who'd just won her first gold medal. I inhaled mightily, clenched my fingers to fight off the urge for a victory cigarette, and reapplied my Fudgsicle Lipsmackers. It was time to be a lady.

The guard opened the door for me, bowed slightly, and smiled. He probably thought I was a guest.

"Hi, miss, you must be Andrea. Ilana said to have a seat right over there, and she'll be out in a minute." He turned away and spoke discreetly into a microphone on his sleeve and nodded when he heard a response through his earpiece. "Yes, right over there, miss. She'll be here as soon as she can."

I looked around the enormous entryway but didn't feel like going through the dress-adjustment hassle of actually sitting. Besides, when would I ever again have the chance to be in the Metropolitan Museum of Art, after hours, with apparently no one else there? The ticket booths were empty and the ground-level galleries dark, but the sense of history, of culture, was awesome. The silence itself was deafening.

After nearly fifteen minutes of peering around, being careful not to wander too far from the aspiring Secret Service agent, a rather ordinary-looking girl in a long navy dress crossed the massive foyer and walked toward me. I was surprised that someone with a job as glamorous as hers (working in the special events office of the museum) could be so plain, and I felt instantly ridiculous, like a girl from a small town trying to dress for a big-city black-tie affair—which, ironically enough, was exactly who I was. Ilana, on the other hand, looked like she hadn't even bothered to change out of work clothes, and I learned later that she hadn't.

"Why bother?" She'd laughed. "It's not like these people are here to look at me." Her brown hair was clean and straight but lacking in style, and her brown flats were horrifically unfashionable. But her blue eyes were bright and kind, and I knew instantly that I would like her.

"You must be Ilana," I said, sensing that I somehow had seniority in the situation and was expected to take charge. "I'm Andrea. I'm Miranda's assistant, and I'm here to help in any way I can."

She looked so relieved, I instantly wondered what Miranda had said to her. The possibilities were endless, but I imagined it had something to do with Ilana's *Ladies' Home Journal* getup. I shuddered to think what wicked thing she'd uttered to such a sweet girl and prayed she wouldn't start to cry. Instead, she turned to me with those big innocent eyes, leaned forward, and declared none-too-quietly, "Your boss is a first-rate bitch."

I stared, shocked, for just a moment before recovering. "She is, isn't she?" I said, and we both laughed. "What do you need me to do? Miranda's going to be able to sense that I'm here in about ten seconds, so I should look like I'm doing something."

"Here, I'll show you the table," she said, walking down a darkened hallway toward the Egyptian exhibits. "It's dynamite."

We arrived in a smaller gallery, perhaps the size of a tennis court with a rectangular, twenty-four-seat table stretched down the middle. Robert

Isabell was worth it, I could see. He was the New York party planner, the only one who could be trusted to strike just the right note with astonishing attention to detail: fashionable without being trendy, luxe but not ostentatious, unique without being over the top. Miranda insisted that Robert do everything, but the only time I'd ever seen his work before was at Cassidy and Caroline's birthday party. I knew he could manage to turn Miranda's colonial-style living room into a chic downtown lounge (complete with soda bar—in martini glasses, of course—ultra-suede, built-in banquettes, and a fully heated, tented balcony dance floor with a Moroccan theme) for ten-year-olds, but this was truly spectacular.

Everything glowed white. Light white, smooth white, bright white, textured white, and rich white. Bundles of milky white peonies looked as if they grew from the table itself, deliciously lush but low enough to allow people to talk over them. Bone white china (with a white checked pattern) rested on a crisp white linen tablecloth, and high-backed white oak chairs were covered in luscious white suede (the danger!), all atop a plush white carpet, specially laid for the evening. White votive candles in simple white porcelain holders gave off a soft white light, highlighting (but somehow not burning) the peonies from underneath and providing subtle, unobtrusive illumination around the table. The only color in the entire room came from the elaborate multihued canvases that hung on the walls surrounding the table, shocking blues and greens and golds from the depictions of early Egyptian life. The white table as a deliberate contrast to the priceless, detailed paintings was exquisite.

As I turned my head around to take in the wonderful contrast of the color and the white ("That Robert really is a genius!"), a vibrant red figure caught my eye. In the corner, standing ramrod straight under a looming painting was Miranda, wearing the beaded red Chanel that had been commissioned, cut, fitted, and precleaned just for tonight. And although it'd be a stretch to say that it had been worth every penny (since those pennies added up to tens of thousands of dollars), she did look breathtaking. She herself was an *objet d'art*, chin jutted upward and muscles perfectly taut, a neoclassical relief in beaded Chanel silk. She wasn't beautiful—her eyes were a bit too beady and her hair too severe and her face much too hard—but she was stunning in a way I couldn't make sense of, and no matter how hard I tried to play it cool, to pretend to be admiring the room, I couldn't take my eyes off her.

As usual, the sound of her voice broke my reverie. "Ahn-dre-ah, you do know the names and faces of our guests this evening, do you not? I assume you have properly studied their portraits. I expect you won't humiliate me tonight by failing to greet someone by name," she announced, looking nowhere, with only my name indicating that her words might somehow be directed toward me.

"Um, yes, I've got it covered," I answered, suppressing the urge to salute and still acutely aware that I was staring. "I'll take a few minutes now and make sure I'm positive." She looked at me as if to say *You sure will, you idiot,* and I forced myself to look away and walk out of the gallery. Ilana was right behind me.

"What's she talking about?" she whispered, leaning toward me. "Portraits? Is she crazy?"

We sat down on an uncomfortable wooden bench in a darkened hallway, both of us overwhelmed with the need to hide. "Oh, that. Yeah, normally I would've spent the last week trying to find pictures of the guests tonight and memorizing them so I could greet them by name," I explained to a horrified Ilana. She stared at me incredulously. "But since she just told me I had to come today, I only had a few minutes in the car to look them over.

"What?" I asked. "You think *this* is strange? Whatever. It's standard stuff for a Miranda party."

"Well, I thought there wouldn't be anyone famous here tonight," she said, referring to Miranda's past parties at the Met. Since she was a huge contributor, Miranda was often granted the very special privilege of renting out, oh, THE METROPOLITAN MUSEUM OF ART for private parties and cocktail hours. Mr. Tomlinson had had to ask only once, and Miranda was scrambling to make her brother-in-law's party the best the Met had ever seen. She figured it would impress the rich Southerners and their trophy wives to dine for a night at the Met. She was right.

"Yeah, there won't be anyone we'd recognize right away, just a lot of billionaires with homes below the Mason-Dixon line. Usually when I have to memorize the guests' faces, they're easier to find online or in

WWD or something. I mean, you can generally locate a picture of Queen Noor or Michael Bloomberg or Yohji Yamamoto if you have to. But just try to find Mr. and Mrs. Packard from some rich suburb of Charleston or wherever the hell they live and it's not so easy. Miranda's other assistant was looking for these people while everyone else was getting me ready, and she eventually found almost everyone in the society pages of their hometown newspapers or on various companies' web sites, but it was really annoying."

Ilana continued to stare. I think somehow I knew that I was sounding like a robot, but I couldn't stop. Her shock only made me feel worse.

"There's only one couple I haven't identified yet, so I guess I'll know them by default," I said.

"Oh, my. I don't know how you do it. I'm annoyed I have to be here on a Friday night, but I can't imagine doing your job. How do you take it? How do you stand being spoken to and treated like that?"

It took me a moment to realize that this question caught me off-guard: no one had really ever volunteered anything negative about my job. I'd always thought I was the only one—among the millions of imaginary girls that would "die" for my job—who saw anything remotely disturbing about my situation. It was more horrifying to see the shock in her eyes than it was to witness the hundreds of ridiculous things I saw each and every day at work; the way she looked at me with that pure, unadulterated pity triggered something inside me. I did what I hadn't done in months of working under subhuman conditions for a nonhuman boss, what I always managed to keep suppressed for a more appropriate time. I started to cry.

Ilana looked more shocked than ever. "Oh, sweetie, come here! I'm so sorry! I didn't mean anything by it. You're a saint for putting up with that witch, you hear me? Come with me." She pulled me by the hand and led me down another darkened hallway toward an office in the back. "Here, now sit for a minute and forget all about what these stupid people look like."

I sniffled and started to feel stupid.

"And don't feel strange, you hear? I have a feeling you kept that inside for a long, long time and you have to have a good cry every now and then."

She was fumbling around in her desk for something while I tried to wipe the mascara from my cheeks. "Here," she proclaimed proudly. "I'm destroying this right after you see it, and if you even think of telling anyone about it, I'll wreck your life. But just look, it's amazing." She handed me a manila envelope sealed with a "Confidential" sticker and smiled.

I tore off the sticker and pulled a green folder out. Inside was a photo—a color photocopy, actually—of Miranda stretched out on a restaurant banquette. I recognized it immediately as a picture taken by a famous society photographer during a recent birthday party for Donna Karan at Pastis. It had already appeared on the pages of *New York* magazine and was bound to keep showing up. In it she was wearing her signature brown and white snakeskin trench coat, the one I always thought made her look like a snake.

Well, it seems I wasn't alone, because in this version, someone had subtly—expertly—attached a scaled-to-size cutout of a rattlesnake's rattle directly where her legs should have been. The effect was a fabulous rendition of Miranda as Snake: she rested her elbow on the banquette, cradled her chiseled chin in her palm, and stretched out across the leather, with her rattle curled in a semicircle and hanging off the edge of the bench. It was perfect.

"Isn't it great?" Ilana asked, leaning over my shoulder. "Linda came into my office one afternoon. She'd just spent the entire day on the phone with Miranda, selecting which gallery they'd dine in. Linda naturally insisted on one gallery because it's by far the best size and most beautiful, but Miranda mandated that it be held in the other one near the gift shop. They went back and forth for a while before Linda finally—after days of negotiations—got permission from the board to hold it in Miranda's gallery, and she was so excited to call Miranda and tell her the great news. Guess what happened when . . ."

"She changed her mind, obviously," I said quietly, feeling her irritation. "She decided to do exactly as Linda suggested in the first place, but only once she was sure everyone would jump through all her hoops."

"Precisely. Well, this irritated the hell out of me. I've never seen the entire museum turn itself upside down for anyone—I mean, christ, the president of the United States could ask to have a State Department dinner here and they wouldn't let him! And then your boss thinks she can march in and order everyone around, make our lives a living hell for days on end. Anyway, I made this pretty little picture as a pick-me-up for Linda. You know what she did with it? Shrunk it on the copier so she could have a little one for her wallet! I just thought you'd get a kick out of this. Even if it's just to remind you that you're not alone. You're definitely the worst off, but you're not alone."

I stuck the picture back in its confidential envelope and handed it back to Ilana. "You're the best," I said, touching her shoulder. "I really, really appreciate it. I promise to never, ever tell anyone where I got this, but will you please send this to me? I don't think it'll fit in the Leiber bag, but I'd give anything if you'd send it to me at home. Please?"

She smiled and motioned for me to write my address, and we both stood up and walked (I hobbled) back to the museum's foyer. It was just about seven, and the guests were due to arrive any minute. Miranda and B-DAD were talking to his brother, the honored guest and groom, who looked like he had played soccer, football, lacrosse, and rugby at a Southern school—one where he was always surrounded by cooing blondes. The cooing blonde of twenty-six who was to become his bride was standing quietly by his side, gazing up at him adoringly. She was holding a snifter of something and chortling at his jokes.

Miranda was hanging on to B-DAD's forearm with the fakest of smiles plastered across her face. I didn't have to hear what they were saying to know that she was barely responding at the appropriate time. Social graces were not her strength, as she had little tolerance for small talk—but I knew she'd be on her best kiss-ass behavior tonight. I'd come to realize that her "friends" all fell into one of two categories. There were those she perceived as "above" her and who must be impressed. This list was short, but it generally included people like Irv Ravitz, Oscar de la Renta, Hillary Clinton, and any first-rate, A-list movie star. Then there were those "below" her, who must be patronized and belittled so they don't forget their place, which included basically everyone else: all *Runway* employees, all family members, all parents of her children's friends—unless they coincidentally fell into category number one—almost all designers and other magazine editors, and every single solitary person in the service industry, both here and abroad. Tonight was sure to be amusing because these were category two people who would have to be treated like category ones, merely because of their association with Mr. Tomlinson and his brother. I always enjoyed the rare occasions when I got to watch Miranda try to impress those around her, mostly because she wasn't naturally charming.

I felt the first guests arrive before I saw them. The tension in the room was palpable. Remembering my color printouts, I rushed over to the couple and offered to take the woman's fur wrap. "Mr. and Mrs. Wilkinson, thank you so much for joining us this evening. Please, I'll take that. And Ilana here will show you to the atrium, where cocktails are being served." I hoped I wasn't staring during my monologue, but the spectacle was truly outrageous. I'd seen women dressed like hookers and men dressed like women and models not dressed at all at Miranda's parties, but never before had I seen people dressed like this. I knew it wasn't going to be a trendy New York crowd, but I was expecting them to look like something out of *Dallas*; instead, they looked like a dressier version of the cast from *Deliverance*.

Mr. Tomlinson's brother, himself distinguished looking with silver hair, made the horrible mistake of wearing white tails—in May, no less—with a plaid handkerchief and a cane. His fiancée had on an emerald green taffeta nightmare. It swirled and puffed and gathered and forced her enormous bust up and over the top of the dress so that it appeared her own silicon breasts might actually suffocate her. Diamonds the size of Dixie cups hung from her ears, and an even larger one sparkled from her left hand. Her hair was bleached white with peroxide, as were her teeth, and her heels were so high and so skinny, she walked as if she'd been a running back in the NFL for the past twelve years.

"Dah-lings, I am *so* delighted you could join us for a little pah-ty! Everyone loves pahties, now don't they?" Miranda sang in a falsetto voice. The soon-to-be Mrs. Tomlinson looked as if she'd pass out. Right there before her was the one and only Miranda Priestly! Her glee embarrassed us all, and the whole wretched crowd moved into the atrium with Miranda leading the way.

The rest of the night went on much like the beginning. I recognized all the guests' names and managed not to utter anything too humiliating. The parade of white tuxes, chiffon, big hair, bigger jewels, and barely postadolescent women ceased to amuse me as the hours wore on, but I never grew tired of watching Miranda. She was the true lady and the envy of every woman in that museum that night. And even though they understood that all the money in the world could never buy them her class and elegance, they never stopped wanting it.

I smiled genuinely when she dismissed me halfway through dinner, as usual without a thank-you or a good-night. ("Ahn-dre-ah, we won't be needing you anymore this evening. See yourself out.") I looked for Ilana, but she had already sneaked out. The car took only about ten minutes to arrive after I called for it—I had briefly considered taking the subway, but wasn't sure how well the Oscar or my feet would've held up—and I sunk, exhausted but calm, into the backseat.

When I walked past John on my way to the elevator, he reached under his little table and pulled out a manila envelope. "Just got this a few minutes ago. It says 'Urgent.' " I thanked him and sat down in a corner of the lobby, wondering who would be messengering me something at ten o'clock on a Friday night. I tore it open and pulled out a note:

> *Dearest Andrea,*
> *It was so great to meet you tonight! Can we please get together next week for sushi or something? I dropped this off on my way home— figured you could use the pick-me-up after a night like the one we just had. Enjoy.*
>
> > *Xoxo,*
> > *Ilana*

Inside was the picture of Miranda as Snake, only Ilana had enlarged this one to a ten by thirteen size. I looked at it carefully for a few minutes, massaging the feet I'd finally pulled from the Manolos, and looked into Miranda's eyes. She looked intimidating and mean and just like the bitch I stared at every day. But tonight she'd also looked sad, and not a little lonely. Adding this picture to my fridge and making fun of it with Lily and Alex wasn't going to make my feet hurt any less, or give me back my Friday night. I tore it up and hobbled upstairs.

"Andrea, it's Emily," I heard a voice croak from the phone. "Can you hear me?" It had been months since Emily had called me at home late at night, so I knew it had to be serious.

"Hi, sure. You sound like hell," I said, bolting upright in bed, immediately wondering if Miranda had done something to make her sound that way. The last time Emily had called this late was when Miranda had called her at eleven on a Saturday night to demand that Emily charter her and Mr. Tomlinson a private jet to get home from Miami since bad weather had canceled their regularly scheduled flight. Emily was just getting ready to leave her apartment to attend her own birthday party when the call came in, and she'd immediately called me and begged me to deal with it. I hadn't gotten the message until the next day, though, and when I called her back, she was still in tears.

"I missed my own birthday party, Andrea," she'd wailed the second she picked up the phone. "I missed my own birthday party because I had to charter them a flight!"

"They couldn't get a hotel room for one night and come back the next day like normal people?" I'd asked, pointing out the obvious.

"Don't you think I thought of that? I had penthouse suites reserved for them at the Shore Club, the Albion, and the Delano within seven minutes of her first phone call, figuring she couldn't possibly be serious—I mean, my god, it was a Saturday night. How the hell do you charter a flight on a Saturday night?"

"I'm guessing she wasn't so into that idea?" I'd asked soothingly, feeling genuinely guilty that I hadn't been around to help her out and simultaneously ecstatic that I'd dodged that particular bullet.

"Yeah. Not so into it at all. She called every ten minutes, demanding to know why I hadn't found her anything yet, and I had to keep putting these people on hold to answer her call, and when I went back to them, they'd hang up." She gulped air. "It was a nightmare."

"So what finally happened? I'm almost scared to ask."

"What finally happened? What *didn't* finally happen? I called every single private charter company in the state of Florida and, as you might imagine, they weren't answering their phones at midnight on a Saturday. I paged individual pilots, I called domestic airlines to see if they had any recommendations, I even managed to talk to some sort of supervisor at the Miami International Airport. Told him I needed a plane in the next half hour to fly two people to New York. Know what he did?"

"What?"

"He laughed. Hysterically. Accused me of being a front for terrorists, for drug smugglers, everything. Told me I had a better chance of getting hit by lightning exactly twenty times than I did of securing a plane and a pilot at that hour—regardless of how much I was willing to pay. And that if I called back again, he'd be forced to direct my inquiry to the FBI. Do you believe it?" She was screaming at this point. "Do you fucking believe it? The FBI!"

"And I assume Miranda didn't like that, either?"

"Yeah, she *loooooved* that one. She spent twenty minutes refusing to believe that there wasn't a single plane available. I assured her that it wasn't that they were all taken, just that it was a difficult time of night to be attempting to charter a flight."

"So what happened?" I didn't see this one ending happily.

"At about one-thirty in the morning she finally accepted that she wasn't going to get home that night—not that it mattered whatsoever, since the girls were with their father and the nanny was around all day Sunday if they needed her—and she had me buy her a ticket for the first flight out in the morning."

This was puzzling. If her flight had been canceled, I'd assumed the airlines would've rescheduled her for the first flight out in the morning, especially considering her premier-advantage-plus-gold-platinum-diamond-executive-VIP mileage status and the original cost of her first-class tickets. I said as much.

"Yeah, well, Continental scheduled them for their first flight out, which was at six-fifty A.M. But when Miranda heard that someone else had managed to get on a Delta flight at six-thirty-five A.M., she went ballistic. She called me an incompetent idiot, asked me over and over what good an assistant was if I couldn't do something as simple as arrange for a private plane." She'd sniffed and took a sip of something, probably coffee.

"Ohmigod, I know what you're going to say. Tell me you didn't!"

"I did."

"You didn't. You've got to be kidding. For fifteen minutes?"

"I did! What choice did I have? She was really unhappy with me—at least this way, it seemed like I was actually doing something. It came to another couple thousand bucks—not exactly a big deal. She was bordering on *happy* when we hung up. What else can you ask for?"

By this point we'd both started laughing. I knew without Emily's telling me—and she knew I knew—that she'd gone ahead and purchased two additional business-class tickets on the Delta flight for Miranda just to shut her up, to make the incessant demands and insults finally, blissfully, cease.

I was nearly choking at this point. "So, wait. By the time you arranged for a car to take her to the Delano—"

"—it was just before three in the morning, and she'd called my cell phone exactly twenty-two times since eleven. The driver waited while they showered and changed in their penthouse suite and then took them right back to the airport in time for their *earlier* flight."

"Stop! You've got to stop," I howled, doubled over at this charming series of events. "This did not really happen."

Emily stopped laughing and tried to feign seriousness. "Oh, really? You think all of this is good? I haven't even told you the best part."

"Oh, tell me, tell me!" I was positively gleeful that Emily and I had, for once, managed to find something funny at the exact same time. It felt good to be part of a team, one half in the battle against the oppressor. I realized then for the first time what a different year it would have been if Emily and I could've truly been friends, if we could have covered and protected and trusted each other enough to face Miranda as a united front. Things probably wouldn't have been quite so unbearable, but, except for rare times like these, we didn't agree on just about everything.

"The best part of all of it?" She was silent, dragging out the joy we shared a few moments longer. "She didn't realize this, of course, but even though the Delta flight took off earlier, it was actually scheduled to land eight minutes after her original Continental!"

"Shut up!" I'd howled, delighted with this delicious new nugget of information. "You've *got* to be kidding me!"

When we finally hung up, I was surprised to see that we'd been talking for more than an hour, just like a couple of real friends would. Of course, we immediately reverted back to just-contained hostility on Monday, but my feelings for Emily were always a bit more affectionate after that weekend. Until now, of course. I sure didn't like her enough to hear whatever surely irritating or inconvenient thing she was preparing to dump on me.

"Really, you sound horrible. Are you sick?" I tried valiantly to interject a touch of sympathy in my voice, but the question came out sounding aggressive and accusatory.

"Oh yeah," she rasped before breaking into hacking coughs. "Really sick."

I never really believed it when anyone said they were really sick: without a diagnosis of something very official and potentially life-threatening, you were well enough to work at *Runway*. So when Emily finished hacking and reiterated that she was really ill, I didn't even consider the possibility that she wouldn't be at work on Monday. After all, she was scheduled to fly to Paris to meet Miranda on October 18 and that was only slightly more than a week away. And besides, I'd managed to ignore a couple strep throats, a few bouts of bronchitis, a horrific round of food poisoning, and a perpetual smoker's cough and cold and hadn't taken a single sick day in nearly a year of work.

I'd sneaked in a single doctor's appointment when I was desperate for antibiotics with one of the cases of strep throat (I ducked into his office and ordered them to see me right away when Miranda and Emily thought that I was out scouting for new cars for Mr. Tomlinson), but there was never time for preventative work. Although I'd had a dozen sets of highlights from Marshall, quite a few free massages from spas that felt honored to have Miranda's assistant as a guest, and countless manicures, pedicures, and makeovers, I hadn't seen a dentist or a gynecologist in a year.

"Anything I can do?" I asked, trying to sound casual while I racked my brain thinking of why she'd called to tell me that she didn't feel well. As far as we were both concerned, it was completely and entirely irrelevant. She'd be at work on Monday whether she felt well or not.

She coughed deeply and I heard phlegm rattling in her lungs. "Um, yeah, actually. God, I can't believe this is happening to me!"

"What? What's happening?"

"I can't go to Europe with Miranda. I have mono."

"What?"

"You heard me, I can't go. The doctor called today with the blood results, and as of right now, I'm not allowed to leave my apartment for the next three weeks."

Three weeks! She had to be kidding. There wasn't time to feel badly for her—she'd just told me she wasn't going to Europe, and it was that thought alone—the idea that both Miranda and Emily would be out of my life—that had sustained me through the past couple months.

"Em, she's going to kill you—you have to go! Does she know yet?"

There was a foreboding silence on the other end. "Um, yeah, she knows."

"You called her?"

"Yes. I had my doctor call her, actually, because she didn't think that having mono really qualified me as sick, so he had to tell her that I could infect her and everyone else, and anyway . . ." Her sentence trailed off, and her tone was suggestive of something far, far worse.

"Anyway what?" My self-preservation instincts had kicked into overdrive.

"Anyway . . . she wants you to go with her."

"She wants me to go with her, huh? That's cute. What'd she really say? She didn't threaten to fire you for getting sick, did she?"

"Andrea, I'm—" a deep, mucousy cough shook her voice and I thought for a moment that she might very well die right there on the phone with me "—serious. Completely and totally serious. She said something about the assistants they give her abroad being idiots and that even you'd be better to have around than them."

"Oh, well, when you put it like that, sign me up! Nothing quite like some over-the-top flattery to convince me to do something. Seriously, she shouldn't have said such nice things. I'm blushing!" I didn't know whether to focus on the fact that Miranda wanted me to go to Paris with her, or that she only wanted me to go because she considered me slightly less brain-dead than the anorexic French clones of, well . . . me.

"Oh, just shut up already," she croaked in between fits of now annoying coughing. "You're the luckiest fucking person in the world. I've been waiting two years—over two years—for this trip, and now I can't go. The irony of this is painful—you realize that, don't you?"

"Of course I do! It's one giant cliché: this trip is your sole reason for living and it's the bane of my existence, yet I'm going and you're not. Life is funny, huh? I'm laughing so hard I can barely stop," I deadpanned, sounding not the least bit amused.

"Yeah, well, I think it sucks, too, but what can you do? I already called Jeffy to tell him to start calling in clothes for you. You'll have to bring a ton since you'll need different outfits for each of the shows you attend, any dinners, and, of course, for Miranda's party at the Hotel Costes. Allison will help you out with makeup. Talk to Stef in accessories for bags and shoes and jewelry. You only have a week, so get on it first thing tomorrow, OK?"

"I still don't really believe she expects me to do this."

"Well, believe it, because she sure wasn't kidding. Since I'm not going to be able to come to the office at all this week, you're also going to—"

"What? You're not even going to come into the *office*?" I might not have taken a sick day or spent a single hour outside the office while Miranda was there, but Emily hadn't, either. The one time it had been close—when her great-grandfather had died—she'd managed to get home to Philadelphia, attend the funeral, and be back at her desk without missing a minute of work. This was how things worked. Period. Short of death (immediate family only), dismemberment (your own), or nuclear war (only if confirmed by the U.S. government to be directly affecting Manhattan), one was to be present. This would be a watershed moment in the Priestly regime.

"Andrea, I have mononucleosis. I'm highly infectious. It's really serious. I'm not supposed to leave my apartment for a cup of coffee, never mind go to work for the day. Miranda understands that, and so you'll need to pick up the slack. There will be a lot to do to get both of you ready for Paris. Miranda leaves on Wednesday for Milan, and then you'll be leaving to meet her in Paris the following Tuesday."

"She understands that? C'mon! Tell me what she really said." I refused to believe that she'd accepted something as mundane as mono for an excuse to not be available. "Just give me that small pleasure. After all, my life will be hell for the next few weeks."

Emily sighed, and I could feel her eyes roll over the phone. "Well, she wasn't thrilled. I didn't actually talk to her, you see, but my doctor said she kept asking if mono is a 'real' disease. But when he assured her that it was, she was very understanding."

I laughed out loud. "I'm sure she was, Em, I'm sure she was. Don't worry about a thing, OK? You just concentrate on feeling better, and I'll take care of everything else."

"I'll e-mail you a checklist, just so you don't forget anything."

"I won't forget anything. She's been to Europe four times in the past year. I've got it down. I'll get the cash from the basement bank, change a few grand into euros, buy a few more grand's worth of traveler's checks, and triple confirm all of her hair and makeup appointments while she's there. What else? Oh, I'll make sure the Ritz gives her the right cell phone this time, and I'll speak to the drivers ahead of time to make sure they know they can't ever leave her waiting. I'm already thinking of all the people who'll need copies of her itinerary—which I'll type up, no problem—and I'll see to it that it gets passed around. And of course she'll have a detailed itinerary as to the twins' classes, lessons, practices, and play dates, and full listings of the entire household staff's work schedules. See! You don't have to worry—I've got it all under control."

"Don't forget about the velvet," she chided, singing the last couple words as if on autopilot. "Or the scarves!"

"Of course not! They're already on my list." Before Miranda packed for anything—or rather, had her housekeeper pack her—either Emily or I would purchase massive rolls of velvet at a fabric store and bring them to Miranda's apartment. There, we'd work with the housekeeper to cut them in the exact shape and size of every article of clothing she was planning to bring, and individually wrap each item in the plush material. The velvet packages were then neatly stacked in dozens of Louis Vuitton suitcases, with plenty of extra pieces included for when she inevitably threw the first batch out upon unpacking in Paris. In addition, usually one half of a suitcase was occupied by a couple dozen orange Hermès boxes, each containing a single white scarf just waiting to be lost, forgotten, misplaced, or simply discarded.

I hung up with Emily after making a good effort to sound sincerely sympathetic and found Lily stretched out on the couch, smoking a cigarette and sipping a clear liquid that was definitely not water from a cocktail glass.

"I thought we weren't allowed to smoke in here," I said, flopping down next to her and immediately putting my feet on the scuffed wooden coffee table my parents had handed down to us. "Not that I care, but that was *your* rule." Lily wasn't a full-time, committed smoker like yours truly; she usually smoked only when she drank and wasn't one to even buy packs. A brand-new box of Camel Special Lights peeked out of the chest pocket of her oversize button-down. I nudged her thigh with my slippered foot and nodded toward the cigarettes. She handed them over with a lighter.

"I knew you wouldn't care," she said, taking a leisurely drag off her cigarette. "I'm procrastinating and it helps me concentrate."

"What do you have due?" I asked, lighting my own cigarette and tossing back the lighter. She was taking seventeen credits this semester in an effort to pull up her GPA after last spring's mediocre showing. I watched as she took another drag and washed it down with a healthy gulp of her nonwater beverage. It didn't appear that she was on the right track.

She sighed heavily, meaningfully, and let the cigarette hang suspended from the corner of her mouth as she spoke. It flapped up and down, threatening to fall at any moment and, combined with her wild, unwashed hair and smeared eye makeup, made her look—just for a moment—like a defendant on *Judge Judy* (or maybe a plaintiff, since they always looked the same—lack of teeth, greasy hair, dull eyes, and propensity for using the double negative). "An article for some totally random, esoteric academic journal that no one will ever read but I still have to write, just so I can say I'm published."

"That's annoying. When's it due?"

"Tomorrow." Total nonchalance. She looked completely unfazed.

"Tomorrow? For real?"

She shot me a warning look, a quick reminder that I was supposed to be on her team. "Yes. Tomorrow. It really blows, considering that Freudian Boy is the one who's assigned to edit it. No one seems to care that he's a candidate in psych, not Russian lit—they're just short copy editors, so he's mine. There's no *way* I'm getting that to him on time. Screw him." Once again, she poured some of the liquid down her throat, making an obvious effort not to taste it, and grimaced.

"Lil, what happened? Granted, it's been a few months, but last I heard, you were taking things slow and he was perfect. Of course, that was before that, that *thing* you dragged home, but . . ."

Another warning look, this time followed by a glare. I'd tried to talk to her about the whole Freak Boy incident a few dozen times, but it seemed like we were never really alone and neither of us had much time

lately for heart-to-hearts. She immediately changed the subject whenever I brought it up. I could tell that more than anything she was embarrassed; she had acknowledged that he was vile, but she wouldn't
participate in any discussion whatsoever about the excessive drinking
that was responsible for the whole episode.

"Yes, well, apparently at some point that night I called him from Au
Bar and begged him to come meet me," she said, avoiding eye contact,
instead concentrating intently on using the remote control to switch
tracks on the mournful Jeff Buckley CD that seemed to be on permanent
replay in the apartment.

"So? Did he come and see you talking to, uh, to someone else?" I was
trying not to push her away even more by being critical of her. There was
obviously a lot going on inside her head, what with the problems at
school and the drinking and the seemingly limitless supply of guys, and
I wanted her to open up to someone. She'd never kept anything from me
before, if for no other reason than I was all she had, but she hadn't been
telling me much of anything lately. It occurred to me how strange it was
that we hadn't bothered to discuss this until four months after the fact.

"No, not quite," she said bitterly. "He came all the way there from
Morningside Heights only to find me not there. Apparently he called my
cell phone and Kenny answered and wasn't all that nice."

"Kenny?"

"That *thing* I dragged home at the beginning of the summer, remember?" She said it sarcastically, but this time she smiled.

"Ah-hah. I'm guessing Freudian Boy didn't take that well?"

"Not so much. Whatever. Easy come, easy go, right?" She scampered
off to the kitchen with her empty glass and I saw her pour from a half-
full bottle of Ketel One. A very small splash of soda, and she was back
on the couch.

I was just about to inquire as gently as possible why she was inhal-
ing vodka when she had an article due the next day, but the buzzer rang
from downstairs.

"Who's there?" I called to John by holding down the button.

"Mr. Fineman is here to see Ms. Sachs," he announced formally, all
business now that other people were around.

"Really? Um, great. Send him up."

Lily looked at me and raised her eyebrows, and I realized that once again we weren't going to have this conversation. "You look psyched," she said with obvious sarcasm. "Not exactly thrilled that your boyfriend is surprising you, are you?"

"Of course I am," I said defensively, and we both knew I was lying. Things with Alex had been strained the past few weeks. Really strained. We went through all the motions of being together and we did it well: after almost four years, we certainly knew what the other wanted to hear or needed to do. But he'd compensated for all the time I spent at work by being even more angelic at school—volunteering to coach, tutor, mentor, and chair just about every activity someone could think up—and the time we did actually see each other was about as exciting as if we'd been married for thirty years. We had an unspoken understanding that we'd just wait things out until my year of servitude was over, but I wouldn't let myself think about where the relationship might be headed then.

But still. That made two close people in my life—first Jill (who'd called me out on the miserable state of affairs on the phone the other night), and now Lily—who'd pointed out that Alex and I were less than adorable together lately, and I had to admit that Lily had, in her buzzed but nonetheless perceptive way, noticed that I was not happy to hear that Alex had arrived. I was dreading telling him that I had to go to Europe, dreading the inevitable fight that would ensue, a fight I very much would have liked to put off for a few more days. Ideally, not until I was in Europe. But no such luck, as he was currently knocking on my door.

"Hi!" I said a bit too enthusiastically as I pulled open the door and threw my arms around his neck. "What a great surprise!"

"You don't mind that I just stopped by, do you? I met Max for a drink right around the corner and I thought I'd say hi."

"Of course I don't mind, silly! I'm thrilled. Come in, come in." I knew I sounded positively manic, but any armchair shrink could easily point out that my outward enthusiasm was meant to overcompensate for all that was lacking inwardly.

He grabbed a beer and kissed Lily on the cheek and settled into the bright orange armchair my parents had saved from the seventies, just knowing that one day they could bestow it proudly on one of their off-spring. "So, what's going on here?" he asked, nodding toward the stereo, where a positively heart-wrenching version of "Hallelujah" was blaring.

Lily shrugged. "Procrastinating. What else?"

"Well, I have some news," I said, trying to sound enthusiastic to convince both myself and Alex that this was, in fact, a positive development. He'd been so excited about arranging all the plans for our homecoming weekend—and I'd been so pushy in getting him to do it—that it seemed downright cruel to be canceling on him less than a week and a half before we were going. We'd spent an entire night figuring out whom we wanted to invite to our big Sunday brunch, and even knew exactly where and with whom we'd be tailgating before the Brown–Dartmouth game on Saturday.

They both looked at me, not a little warily, until Alex finally managed, "Yeah? What's up?"

"Well! I just got the call—I'm going to Paris for a week!" I said this with the exuberance of telling an infertile couple that they were having twins.

"You're going where?" Lily asked, looking puzzled and distracted, not entirely interested.

"You're going *why*?" Alex asked at the exact same moment, looking about as pleased as if I'd just announced that I had tested positive for syphilis.

"Emily just found out she has mono, and Miranda wants me to accompany her to the shows. Isn't that awesome?" I said, a chipper smile on my face. This was exhausting. I was dreading having to go myself, but it made it ten times worse to have to convince him that it was actually a really great opportunity.

"I don't understand. Doesn't she go to the shows like a thousand times a year?" he asked. I nodded. "So why does she all of a sudden need you to go with her now?"

Lily had tuned out at this point and seemed to be engrossed in flipping through an old issue of *The New Yorker*. I'd saved every copy from the past five years.

"She throws this massive party at the spring shows in Paris and just likes to have one of her American assistants be there. She'll go to Milan first and then we'll meet in Paris. To, you know, oversee everything."

"And that American assistant has to be you, and it has to mean you'll be missing homecoming," he said flatly.

"Well, it's not normally the way it works. Since it's considered a huge privilege, usually the senior assistant is the only one who gets to go, but since Emily is sick, then, yes, now I will be going. I have to leave next Tuesday, so I can't go to Providence that weekend. I'm really, really sorry." I moved off my chair and went to sit closer to him on the couch, but he immediately stiffened.

"So it's just that simple, right? You know, I already paid for the entire room to guarantee the rate. Never mind the fact that *I* rearranged *my* whole schedule to go with you that weekend. I told my mom she had to find a sitter because *you* wanted to go. Not a big deal, though, right? Just another *Runway* obligation." In all the years we'd spent together, I'd never seen him so angry. Even Lily looked up from her magazine long enough to excuse herself and get the hell out of the room before this turned into an all-out war.

I tried to curl up on his lap, but he crossed his legs and waved his hand. "Seriously, Andrea—" He called me that only when he was really annoyed. "Is all of this really worth it? Be honest with me for a second. Is it worth it to you?"

"All of what? Is missing a homecoming weekend when there will be dozens more worth it to do something I'm required to do for my job? A job that is going to open doors for me I never thought possible, and sooner than I ever expected? Yes! It's worth it."

His chin dropped to his chest and for a moment I thought he was crying, but when he lifted it again, his face revealed nothing but rage.

"Don't you think I'd rather go with you than go be someone's slave twenty-four-seven for a straight week?" I shouted, forgetting entirely that Lily was somewhere in the apartment. "Can't you stop for one second to think about the fact that I may not want to go either, but I have no choice?"

"No choice? You have nothing *but* choices! Andy, this job isn't just a job anymore, in case you've failed to notice—it's taken over your entire life!" he yelled back, the redness in his face expanding to his neck and ears. Normally I thought this was very cute, even sexy, but tonight I just wanted to go to sleep.

"Alex, listen, I know—"

"No, *you* listen! Forget about me for a second, not like that's such a stretch, but forget that we never, ever see each other anymore because of the hours you keep at work, because of your never-ending work emergencies. What about your parents? When was the last time you actually saw them? And your sister? You do realize that she just had her first baby and you haven't even seen your own nephew yet, don't you? Doesn't that mean anything?" He lowered his voice and leaned in closer. I thought he might be getting ready to apologize, but he said, "What about Lily? Have you not noticed that your best friend has turned into a raging alcoholic?" I must have looked absolutely shocked, because he barreled on. "You can't even think of saying you didn't realize that, Andy. It's the most obvious thing in the world."

"Yes, of course she drinks. So do you and so do I and so does everyone we know. Lily's a student, and that's what students do, Alex. What's so weird about that?" It sounded even more pathetic when I said it out loud, and he only shook his head. We were both quiet for a few minutes until he spoke.

"You just don't get it, Andy. I'm not exactly sure how it happened, but I feel like I don't even know you anymore. I think we need a break."

"What? What are you saying? You want to break up?" I asked, realizing much too late that he was very, very serious. Alex was so understanding, so sweet, so available, that I'd begun to take for granted that he'd always be around to listen or talk me down after a long day or cheer me up when everyone else had felt free to take a swing. The only problem with all of this was that I wasn't exactly holding up my end of the deal.

"No, not at all. Not break up, just take a break. I think it would help both of us if we reevaluate what we've got going here. You sure don't seem happy with me lately, and I can't say I'm thrilled with you. Maybe a little time away would be good for both of us."

"Good for both of us? You think it'll 'help us'?" I wanted to scream at the triteness of his words, at the idea that "taking some time" would actually help draw us closer. It seemed selfish that he was doing this now, just as I was going into what I hoped was the last of my one-year *Runway* sentence and mere days before I had to pull off the biggest challenge of my career. Any quick jabs of sadness or concern from a few minutes ago had been swiftly replaced with irritation. "Fine, then. Let's 'take a break,' " I said sarcastically, meanly. "A breather. Sounds like a great plan."

He stared at me with those big brown eyes with a look of overwhelming surprise and hurt, and then pressed them tightly shut in an apparent effort to push away the image of my face. "OK, Andy. I'll put you out of your obvious misery and leave now. I hope you have a great time in Paris, I really do. I'll talk to you soon." And before I even realized that it was actually happening, he'd kissed me on the cheek like he would Lily or my mother and walked toward the door.

"Alex, don't you think we should talk about this?" I said, trying to keep my voice calm, wondering if he would actually walk out right now.

He turned and smiled sadly and said, "Let's not talk any more tonight, Andy. We should've been talking the past few months, the past *year*, not trying to cram it all in right now. Think about everything, OK? I'll call you in a couple weeks, when you're back and settled. And good luck in Paris—I know you'll be great." He opened the door, stepped through it, and quietly closed it behind him.

I ran to Lily's room so she could tell me that he was overreacting, that I had to go to Paris because it was the best thing for my future, that she didn't have a drinking problem, that I wasn't a bad sister for leaving the country when Jill had just had her first baby. But she was passed out on top of her covers, fully dressed, the empty cocktail glass on her bedside table. Her Toshiba laptop was open beside her on the bed, and I wondered if she'd managed to write a single word. I looked. Bravo! She'd written the heading, complete with her name, the class number, the professor's name, and her presumably temporary version of the article's title: "The Psychological Ramifications of Falling in Love with Your Reader." I laughed out loud, but she didn't stir, so I moved the computer back to her desk and set her alarm for seven and turned out the lights.

My cell phone rang as soon as I walked in my bedroom. After the initial five-second usual heart-pounding session I endured each time it rang for fear that it was Her, I flipped it open immediately, knowing it was

Alex. I knew he couldn't leave things so unfinished. This was the same guy who couldn't fall asleep without a good-night kiss and a verbal wish for sweet dreams; there was no way he was just prancing out of here, totally fine with the suggestion that we not talk for a few weeks.

"Hi, baby," I breathed, missing him already but still happy to be on the phone with him and not necessarily having to deal with everything in person right now. My head ached and my shoulders felt like they were glued to my ears, and I just wanted to hear him say that the whole thing had been a big mistake and he'd call me tomorrow. "I'm glad you called."

" 'Baby'? Wow! We're making progress, aren't we, Andy? Better be careful or I might have to consider the possibility that you want me," Christian said smoothly with a grin I could hear over the phone line. "I'm glad I called, too."

"Oh. It's you."

"Well, that's not the warmest welcome I've ever received! What's the matter, Andy? You've been screening me lately, haven't you?"

"Of course not," I lied. "I've just had a bad day. As usual. What's up?"

He laughed. "Andy, Andy, Andy. Come on now. You have no reason to be so unhappy. You're on the fast-track to great things. Speaking of which, I'm calling to see if you wanted to come to a PEN award ceremony and reading tomorrow night. Should be lots of interesting people, and I haven't seen you in a while. Purely professional, of course."

For a girl who had read way too many "How to Know if He's Ready to Commit" articles in *Cosmo*, one might think the warning flags would've gone up on this one. And they did—I just chose to ignore them. It had been a very long day, and so I allowed myself to think—just for a few minutes—that he might, might, MIGHT actually be sincere. Screw it. It felt good to talk to a noncritical male for a few minutes, even if he did refuse to accept that I was taken. I knew I wouldn't actually accept his invitation, but a few minutes of innocent phone flirting wouldn't hurt anyone.

"Oh really?" I asked coyly. "Tell me all about it."

"I'm going to list all the reasons that you should come with me, Andy,

and the first one is the simplest: I know what's good for you. Period."
God, he was arrogant. Why did I find it so endearing?

Game on. We were off and running, and it took only a few more minutes until the trip to Paris and Lily's nasty little vodka habit and Alex's sad
eyes faded to the background of my acknowledged-unhealthy-and-
emotionally-dangerous-but-really-sexy-and-fun-nonetheless conversation
with Christian.

16

It was planned that Miranda would be in Europe for a week before I was due to arrive. She settled for using some local assistants for the Milan shows—and would be arriving in Paris the same morning I was so we could work out the details of her party together, like old friends. Hah. Delta had refused to simply change the name on the ticket from Emily's to mine, so rather than get even more frustrated and hassled than I already was, I just charged a new one. Twenty-two hundred dollars because it was fashion week and I was buying at the last minute. I paused for one ridiculous minute before forking over the corporate card number. *Whatever*, I thought. *Miranda can spend that in a week on hair and makeup alone.*

As Miranda's junior assistant, I was the lowest-ranking human being at *Runway*. However, if access is power, then Emily and I were the two most powerful people in fashion: we determined who got meetings, when they were scheduled (early morning was always preferred because people's makeup would be fresh and their clothes unwrinkled), and whose messages got through (if your name wasn't on the Bulletin, you didn't exist).

So when either of us needed help, the rest of the staff were obliged to pull through. Yes, of course there was something disconcerting about the realization that if we didn't work for Miranda Priestly these same people would have no compunction in running over us with their chauffeured Town Cars. As it was, when called upon, they ran and fetched and retrieved for us like well-trained puppies.

Work on the current issue ground to a halt as everyone rallied to send me off to Paris adequately prepared. Three Clackers from the fashion department hastily pulled together a wardrobe that included every single item that I could conceivably require for any event Miranda could conceivably call on me to attend. By the time I left, Lucia, the fashion director, promised I would have in my possession not only an assemblage of clothing appropriate for any contingency, but also a full sketchbook complete with professionally rendered charcoal sketches depicting every imaginable way of pairing the aforementioned clothing in order to maximize style and minimize embarrassment. In other words: leave nothing to my own selection or pairing, and I'd quite possibly have a shot in hell—albeit slim—of looking presentable.

Might I need to accompany Miranda to a bistro and stand, mummy-like, in the corner while she sipped a glass of Bordeaux? A pair of cuffed, charcoal gray Theory pants with a black silk turtleneck sweater by Celine. Attend the tennis club where she'd receive her private lessons so that I could fetch water and, if required, white scarves in case she *schvitzed*? A head-to-toe athletic outfit complete with bootleg workout pants, zip-up hooded jacket (cropped to show off my tummy, natch), a $185 wife-beater to wear under it, and suede sneakers—all by Prada. And what if maybe—just maybe—I actually did make it to the front row of one of those shows like everyone swore I would? The options were limitless. My favorite so far (and it was still only late afternoon on Monday) was a pleated school-girl skirt by Anna Sui, with a very sheer and very frilly white Miu Miu blouse, paired with a particularly naughty-looking pair of midcalf Christian Laboutin boots and topped with a Katayone Adeli leather blazer so fitted it bordered on obscene. My Express jeans and Franco Sarto loafers had been buried under a film of dust in my closet for months now, and I had to admit I didn't miss them.

I also discovered that Allison, the beauty editor, did, in fact, deserve her title by literally *being* the beauty industry. Within twenty-four hours of being "put on notice" that I would be needing some makeup and more than a few tips, she had created the Be-All, End-All Cosmetic Catchall. Included in the decidedly oversize Burberry "toiletry case" (it actually more closely resembled a wheeled suitcase slightly larger than those approved by the airlines for carry-on) was every imaginable type of shadow, lotion, gloss, cream, liner, and type of makeup. Lipsticks came in matte, high-shine, long-lasting, and clear. Six shades of mascara—ranging in color from a light blue to a "pouty black"—were accompanied by an eyelash curler and two eyelash combs in case of (gasp!) clumps.

Powders, which appeared to account for half of all the products and fixed/accentuated/accented/hid the eyelids, the skin tone, and the cheeks, had a color scheme more complex and subtler than a painter's palette: some were meant to bronze, others to highlight, and still others to pout, plump, or pale. I had the choice whether to add that healthy blush to my face in the form of a liquid, solid, powder, or a combination thereof. The foundation was the most impressive of all: it was as if someone had managed to remove an actual sample of skin directly from my face and custom-mix a pint or two of the stuff. Whether it "added sheen" or "covered blemishes," every single solitary little bottle matched my skin tone better than, well, my own skin. Packed in a slightly smaller matching plaid case were the supplies: cotton balls, cotton squares, Q-tips, sponges, somewhere in the vicinity of two dozen different-size application brushes, washcloths, two different types of eye makeup remover (moisturizing and oil-free), and no less than twelve—TWELVE—kinds of moisturizer (facial, body, deep-conditioning, with SPF 15, glimmering, tinted, scented, nonscented, hypoallergenic, with alpha-hydroxy, antibacterial, and—just in case that nasty October Parisian sun got the best of me—with aloe vera).

Tucked in a side pocket of the smaller case were legal-size pieces of paper with preprinted faces rendered on each one, enlarged to fit the page. Each face bragged an impressive makeover: Allison had applied the actual makeup she'd included in the kit to the paper faces. One face was eerily labeled "Relaxed Evening Glamour" but had a caveat under it in big, bold marker that read: NOT FOR BLACK-TIE!! TOO CASUAL!! The nonformal face had a light covering of the matte foundation under a slight brush of bronzing powder, a light dab of liquid or "crème" blush, some very sexy, dark-lined and heavily shadowed eyelids accented by jet black mascara'd lashes, and what appeared to be a quick, casual swipe of high-gloss lip color. When I'd mumbled under my breath to Allison that this would be utterly impossible for me to recreate, she looked exasperated.

"Well, hopefully you won't have to," she said in a voice that sounded so taxed, I thought she might collapse under the weight of my ignorance.

"No? Then why do I have nearly two dozen 'faces' suggesting different ways to use all this stuff?"

Her withering glance was worthy of Miranda.

"Andrea. Be serious. This is for emergencies only, in case Miranda asks you to go somewhere with her at the last minute, or if your hair and makeup person can't make it. Oh, that reminds me, let me show you the hair stuff I packed."

As Allison demonstrated how to use four different types of round brushes to blow my hair straight, I tried to make sense of what she'd just said. I would have a hair and makeup person, too? I hadn't arranged for anyone to do me when I'd booked all of Miranda's people, so who had? I had to ask.

"The Paris office," Allison replied with a sigh. "You're representing *Runway*, you know, and Miranda is very sensitive to that. You'll be attending some of the most glamorous events in the world alongside Miranda Priestly. You don't think you could achieve the right look on your own, do you?"

"No, of course not. It's definitely better that I have professional help for this. Thank you."

Then Allison kept me cornered an additional two hours until she was satisfied that if any of the fourteen hair and makeup appointments

I had scheduled over the course of the week fell through, I wouldn't humiliate our boss by smearing the mascara across my lips or shaving the sides of my head and spiking the center into a mohawk. When we were through, I thought I'd finally get a moment to race down to the dining room and grab some calorie-enriched soup, but Allison picked up Emily's extension—her old phone line—and dialed Stef in the accessories department.

"Hi, I'm done with her and she's here right now. You want to come over?"

"Wait! I need to go get lunch before Miranda comes back!"

Allison rolled her eyes just like Emily. I wondered if it was something about that particular position that inspired such expert demonstrations of irritation. "Fine. No, no, I was talking to Andrea," she said into the phone, raising her eyebrows at me—surprise, surprise—just like Emily. "It seems that she's *hungry*. I know. Yes, I know. I told her that, but she seems intent on . . . *eating*."

I walked out of the office and picked up a large cup of cream of broccoli with cheddar cheese and returned within three minutes to find Miranda sitting at her desk, holding the phone receiver away from her face like it was covered in leeches. She was due to fly to Milan that very evening but I wasn't sure I'd survive to see it happen.

"The phone rings, Andrea, but when I pick it up—because you're apparently not interested in doing so—no one's there. Can you explain this phenomenon?" she asked.

Of course I could explain it, just not to her. On the rare occasion that Miranda was in her office alone, she sometimes picked up the phone when it rang. Naturally callers were so shocked to hear her voice on the other end that they promptly hung up. No one was actually prepared to *speak* with her when they called, since the likelihood of being put through was next to nil. I'd gotten dozens of e-mails from editors or assistants informing me—as if I didn't know—that Miranda was answering the phone again. "Where are you guys???" The panicked missives would read, one after another. "She's answering her own phone!!!!"

I mumbled something about how I, too, received hang-ups every now and then, but Miranda had already lost interest. She was peering not at me but at my cup of soup. Some of the creamy green fluid was dripping

slowly down the side. Her gaze turned to one of disgust when she realized I was not only holding something edible, but that I had clearly
planned to consume it as well.

"Dispose of that immediately!" she barked from fifteen feet away.
"The smell of it alone is enough to make me ill."

I dropped the offending soup in the garbage can and gazed wistfully
after the lost nourishment before her voice jerked me back to reality.

"I'm ready for the run-throughs!" she screeched, settling back into
her chair more easily now that the food she'd spotted at *Runway* had
been discarded. "And the moment we're through here, call the features
meeting."

Each word caused another adrenaline surge; since I was never sure
what exactly she'd be requesting, I was never sure if I'd be able to handle it or not. Since it was Emily's job to schedule the run-throughs and
the weekly meetings, I had to race over to her desk and check her appointment book. In the three o'clock slot she had scribbled: *Sedona
Shoot run-through, Lucia/Helen.* I jabbed Lucia's extension and spoke as
soon as she picked up the phone.

"She's ready," I stated, like a military commander. Helen, Lucia's assistant, hung up without saying a word, and I knew she and Lucia were
already halfway to the office. If they didn't arrive within twenty to
twenty-five seconds, I would be sent out to hunt them down and remind
them in person—just in case they might have forgotten—that when I'd
called thirty seconds before and said that Miranda was ready right then,
I meant right *then*. Generally this was a mere annoyance, yet another
reason why the enforced footwear of spiky stilettos made life even more
miserable. Running through the office, frantically searching for someone
who was most likely hiding from Miranda was never fun, but it was only
really miserable when that person happened to be in the bathroom.
Whatever one does in a men's or ladies' room, however, is no excuse for
not being available at the exact moment your presence is expected, and
so I had to charge right in—sometimes checking underneath the stalls for
recognizable footwear—and politely ask in whatever humiliated way I
could manage that they finish up and head to Miranda's office. Immediately.

Luckily for everyone involved, Helen arrived within seconds, pushing an overflowing, off-kilter wheeled rack in front of her and pulling another behind her. She hesitated briefly outside Miranda's French door before she received one of Miranda's imperceptible nods and then dragged the racks through the thick carpeting.

"This is all of it? Two racks?" Miranda asked, barely looking up from the copy she was reading.

Helen was clearly surprised at being addressed, since, as a rule, Miranda didn't speak to other people's assistants. But Lucia hadn't shown up with her own racks yet, so there was little choice.

"Um, uh, no. Lucia will be here in just a moment. She has the other two. Would you like me to, uh, begin showing you what we've called in?" Helen asked nervously as she pulled her ribbed tank top down over her prairie skirt.

"No."

And then: "Ahn-dre-ah! Find Lucia. By my watch it's three o'clock. If she's not prepared, then I have better things to do than sit here and wait for her." Which wasn't exactly true, since it appeared she hadn't yet stopped reading copy and it was now only approximately thirty-five seconds since I'd made the initial phone call. But I wasn't about to point this out.

"No need, Miranda, I'm right here," sang a breathless Lucia, herself pushing and pulling racks past me just as I stood to begin the search. "So sorry. We were waiting for one last coat from the YSL people."

She arranged the racks, which were organized by clothing type (shirts, outerwear, pants/skirts, and dresses) in a half-circle in front of Miranda's desk and gave the signal for Helen to leave. Miranda and Lucia then went through each item, one by one, and bickered over its place or lack thereof in the upcoming fashion shoot that was to take place in Sedona, Arizona. Lucia was pushing for an "urban cowgirl chic" look, which she thought would play out perfectly against a backdrop of the red-rock mountains, but Miranda kept announcing snidely that she'd prefer "just chic," since "cowgirl chic" was clearly an oxymoron. Maybe she'd had her fill of "cowgirl chic" at B-DAD's brother's party. I managed to tune them out until Miranda called my name, this time ordering me to call in the accessories people for their run-through.

Immediately I checked Emily's book again, but it was just as I thought: there was no accessories run-through scheduled. Praying that

Emily had simply forgotten to put it in the book, I called Stef and told her Miranda was ready for the Sedona run-through.

No such luck. They weren't scheduled for their run-through until late afternoon the following day, and at least a quarter of the things they needed hadn't been delivered yet from their PR companies.

"Impossible. Can't do it," announced Stef, sounding much less confident than her words implied.

"Well, what the hell do you expect me to tell her?" I whispered back.

"Tell her the truth: the run-through wasn't supposed to take place until tomorrow and a lot of the stuff isn't here. I mean, seriously! Right now we're still waiting for one evening bag, one clutch, three different fringed purses, four pairs of shoes, two necklaces, three—"

"OK, OK, I'll tell her. But wait by the phone and pick up if I call you back. And if I were you, I'd get ready. I'm betting she doesn't really care when it was scheduled for."

Stef hung up on me without another word and I approached Miranda's doors and waited patiently for her to acknowledge me. When she looked in my general direction and waited, I said, "Miranda, I just spoke with Stef and she said that since the run-through wasn't scheduled until tomorrow, they're still waiting for quite a few items. But they should all be here by—"

"Ahn-dre-ah, I simply cannot visualize how these models will look in these clothes without shoes or bags or jewelry and by tomorrow I'll be in Italy. Tell Stef I want her to give me a run-through of whatever she's got and be prepared to show me photos of whatever isn't here yet!" She turned back to Lucia and together they returned to the racks.

Conveying this to Stef gave new meaning to "don't shoot the messenger." She freaked.

"I cannot fucking pull a run-through together in thirty seconds, do you understand me? It's fucking impossible! Four of my five assistants aren't here, and the only one who is here is a complete fucking idiot. Andrea, what the fuck am I going to do?" She was hysterical, but there wasn't much room for negotiation.

"OK, great then," I said sweetly, eyeing Miranda, who had a knack of hearing everything. "I'll tell Miranda you'll be right here." I hung up before she dissolved into tears.

I wasn't surprised to see Stef arrive two and a half minutes later with her one fucking idiot accessories assistant, a fashion assistant she'd borrowed, and James, also borrowed from beauty, all looking terrified as they carried oversize wicker baskets. They stood cowering by my desk until Miranda gave another imperceptible nod, at which point they all shuffled forward for the genuflection exercises. Since Miranda obviously refused to leave her office—ever—she required that all the overflowing racks of clothes and carts full of shoes and baskets brimming over with accessories must be schlepped to her.

When the accessories people finally managed to lay out their wares in neat rows on the carpet for her to inspect, Miranda's office morphed into a Bedouin bazaar—one that just so happens to look more Madison Avenue than Sharm-el-Sheik. One editor was presenting her with $2,000 snakeskin belts while another tried to sell her a large Kelly bag. A third hawked a short Fendi cocktail dress, while someone else tried to sell her on the merits of chiffon. Stef had managed to assemble a near-perfect run-through with only thirty seconds' notice and a whole lot of pieces missing; I saw she had filled the gaps with things from past photo shoots, explaining to Miranda that the accessories they were still waiting for were similar but even better. They were all masters at what they do, but Miranda was the ultimate. She was the ever-aloof consumer, coolly moving from one gorgeous stall to the next, never feigning any show of interest. When she finally, blessedly, did decide, she pointed and commanded (much like a judge at a dog show, "Bob, she's chosen the Border Collie . . ."), and the editors nodded obsequiously ("Yes, excellent choice," "Oh, definitely, the perfect choice") and they wrapped up their wares and scuttled back to their respective departments before she inevitably changed her mind.

The whole hellish ordeal only took a few minutes, but by the time it was over, we were all exhausted from anxiety. She'd already announced earlier in the day that she'd be leaving early, around four, to spend a couple hours with the girls before the big trip, so I canceled the features meeting, to the relief of the entire department. At precisely 3:58 P.M. she began packing her bag to leave, a not-so-strenuous activity, since I'd be bringing anything of any heft or significance to her apartment later on that evening in time for her flight. Basically, it involved tossing her Gucci wallet and her Motorola cell phone into that Fendi bag that she kept abusing. The past few weeks, the $10,000 beauty had been serving as Cassidy's school bag and many of the beads—in addition to one of the handles—had snapped off. Miranda had dropped it on my desk one day and ordered me to have it fixed or, if it was impossible to fix, to just throw out. I'd proudly resisted all temptation to tell her the bag was unfixable so I could keep it and instead had a leatherworker repair it for her for a mere twenty-five dollars.

When she finally walked out, I instinctively reached for the phone to call Alex and whine about my day. It wasn't until I'd dialed half of his number that I remembered we were taking a break. It hit me that this would be the first day in more than three years that we wouldn't talk. I sat with the phone in my hand, staring at an e-mail he'd sent the day before, one that he'd signed "love," and wondered if I'd made a horrible mistake in agreeing to this break. I dialed again, this time ready to tell him that we should talk about everything, figure out where we'd gone wrong, that I take responsibility for the part I'd played in the slow and steady fading of our relationship. But before it even had a chance to ring, Stef was standing over my desk with the Accessories War Plan for my Paris trip, pumped up from her run-through with Miranda. There were shoes and bags and belts and jewelry and hosiery and sunglasses to discuss, so I replaced the receiver and tried to focus on her instructions.

Logically, it would seem that a seven-hour flight in steerage decked out in a pair of skintight leather pants, open-toe strappy sandals, and a blazer over a tank top would be the utmost in hellish travel experiences. Not so. The seven hours in flight were the most relaxing I could remember. Since Miranda and I were both flying to Paris at the same time on different flights—she from Milan and me from New York—it appeared I'd stumbled on the single situation where she could not call me for seven straight hours. For one blessed day, my inaccessibility wasn't my fault.

For reasons I still didn't understand, my parents hadn't been nearly as thrilled as I thought they'd be when I'd called to tell them about the trip.

"Oh, really?" my mother asked in that special way of hers that implied so much more than those two little words really meant. "You're going to Paris now?"

"What do you mean, 'now'?"

"Well, it just doesn't seem like the best time to be jetting off to Europe, is all," she said vaguely, although I could tell that an avalanche of Jewish-mother guilt was ready to begin its slide in my direction.

"And why is that? When *would* be a good time?"

"Don't get upset, Andy. It's just that we haven't seen you in months—not that we're complaining, Dad and I both understand how demanding your job is—but don't you want to see your new nephew? He's a few months old already and you haven't even met him yet!"

"Mom! Don't make me feel guilty. I'm dying to see Isaac, but you know I can't just—"

"You know Dad and I will pay for your ticket to Houston, right?"

"Yes! You've told me four hundred times. I know it and I appreciate it, but it's not the money. I can't get any time off work and now with Emily out, I can't just up and leave—even on weekends. Does it make sense to you to fly across the country only to have to come back if Miranda calls me on Saturday morning to pick up her dry cleaning? Does it?"

"Of course not, Andy, I just thought—we just thought—that you might be able to visit them in the next couple weeks, because Miranda was going to be away and all, and if you were going to fly out there, then Dad and I would go also. But now you're going to Paris."

She said it in the way that implied what she was really thinking. "But now you're going to Paris" translated to "But now you're jetting off to Europe to escape all of your family obligations."

"Mother, let me make something very, very clear here. I am not going on vacation. I have not chosen to go to Paris rather than meet my baby nephew. It's not my decision at all, as you probably know but are refusing to accept. It's really very simple: I go to Paris with Miranda in three days for one week, or I get fired. Do you see a choice here? Because if so, I'd love to hear it."

She was quiet for a moment before she said, "No, of course not, honey. You know we understand. I just hope—well, I just hope that you're happy with the way things are going."

"What's that supposed to mean?" I asked nastily.

"Nothing, nothing," she rushed to say. "It doesn't mean anything other than just what I said: your dad and I only care that you're happy, and it seems that you've really been, um, well, uh, pushing yourself lately. Is everything OK?"

I softened a bit since she was clearly trying so hard. "Yeah, Mom, everything's fine. I'm not happy to be going to Paris, just so you know. It's going to be a week of sheer hell, twenty-four-seven. But my year will be up soon, and I can put this kind of living behind me."

"I know, sweetie, I know it's been a tough year for you. I just hope this all ends up being worth it for you. That's all."

"I know. So do I."

We hung up on good terms, but I couldn't shake the feeling that my own parents were disappointed in me.

The baggage claim at de Gaulle was a nightmare, but I found the elegantly dressed driver who was waving a sign with my name on it when I exited customs, and the moment he closed his own door, he handed me a cell phone.

"Ms. Priestly asked that you call her upon arrival. I took the liberty of programming the hotel's number into the automatic dialing. She's in the Coco Chanel suite."

"Um, oh, OK. Thanks. I guess I'll call right now," I announced rather unnecessarily.

But before I could press the star key and the number one, the phone bleated and flashed a frightening red color. If the driver hadn't been watching me expectantly I would have muted the ring and pretended I hadn't yet seen it, but I was left with the distinct feeling that he had been ordered to keep a close eye on me. Something about his expression suggested that it was not in my best interest to ignore that call.

"Hello? This is Andrea Sachs," I said as professionally as possible, already making over/under bets with myself as to the chance it was anyone besides Miranda.

"Ahn-dre-ah! What time does your watch read at this moment?"

Was this a trick question? A preface to accusing me of being late?

"Um, let me see. Actually, it says that it's five-fifteen in the morning, but obviously I haven't switched it yet to Paris time. Therefore, my watch should read that it's eleven-fifteen A.M." I said cheerily, hoping to start off the first conversation of our interminable trip on as high a note as I dared.

"Thank you for that never-ending narrative, Ahn-dre-ah. And may I ask what, exactly, you've been doing for the past thirty-five minutes?"

"Well, Miranda, the flight landed a few minutes late and then I still had—"

"Because according to the itinerary *you* created for me, I'm reading that your flight arrived at ten-thirty-five this morning."

"Yes, that's when it was scheduled to arrive, but you see—"

"I'll not have you tell me what I see, Ahn-dre-ah. That is most certainly not acceptable behavior for the next week, do you understand me?"

"Yes, of course. I'm sorry." My heart began pounding what felt like a million beats a minute, and I could feel my face grow hot with humiliation. Humiliation at being spoken to that way, but more than anything, my own shame in pandering to it. I had just apologized—most sincerely—to someone for not being able to make my international flight land at the correct time and then for not being savvy enough to figure out how to avoid French customs entirely.

I pressed my face rather uncouthly against the window and watched as the limo weaved its way through Paris's bustling streets. The women seemed so much taller here, the men so much more genteel, and just about everyone was beautifully dressed, thin, and regal in their stance. I'd only been to Paris once before, but living out of a backpack in a hostel on the wrong side of town didn't quite have the same feel as watching the chic little clothing boutiques and adorable sidewalk cafés from the backseat of a limousine. *I could get used to this*, I thought, as the driver turned around to show me where I might find a few bottles of water if I was so inclined.

When the car pulled up to the hotel entrance, a distinguished-looking gentleman wearing what I guessed was a custom-made suit opened the back door for me.

"Mademoiselle Sachs, what a pleasure to finally meet you. I am Gerard Renaud." His voice was smooth and confident, and his silver hair and deeply lined face indicated he was much older than I'd pictured when I spoke to the concierge over the phone.

"Monsieur Renaud, it's great to finally meet you!" Suddenly all I wanted to do was crawl into a nice, soft bed and sleep off my jet lag, but Renaud quickly quashed my hopes.

"Mademoiselle Andrea, Madame Priestly would like to see you in her room immediately. Before you've settled into yours, I'm afraid." He had an apologetic expression on his face, and for a brief moment I felt sorrier for him than I did for myself. Clearly he didn't enjoy conveying this news.

"That's fucking great," I muttered, before noticing how distressed this made Monsieur Renaud. I plastered on a winning smile and began again. "Please excuse me, it was a terribly long flight. Will someone please tell me where I may find Miranda?"

"Of course, mademoiselle. She is in her suite and from what I can gather, very eager to see you." When I looked over at Monsieur Renaud I thought I detected a slight eye-roll and even though I'd always found him oppressively proper over the phone, I reconsidered. Although he was much too professional to show it, never mind actually say anything, I considered that he might loathe Miranda as much as I did. Not because of any real proof I had, but simply because it was impossible to imagine anyone *not* hating her.

The elevator opened and Monsieur Renaud smiled and ushered me inside. He said something in French to the bellman who was escorting me upstairs. Renaud bid me adieu and the bellman led me to Miranda's suite. He knocked on the door and then fled, leaving me to face Miranda alone.

I briefly wondered if Miranda herself would answer the door, but it was impossible to imagine. In the eleven months I'd been letting myself in and out of her apartment, I'd yet to catch her doing anything that even resembled work, including such pedestrian tasks as answering the phone, removing a jacket from a closet, or pouring a glass of water. It was as if her every day was *Shabbat* and she was once again the observant Jew, and I was, of course, her *Shabbes goy*.

A pretty, uniformed maid opened the door and ushered me inside, her sad eyes moist and staring directly at the floor.

"Ahn-dre-ah!" I heard from somewhere in the deep recesses of the most magnificent living room I'd ever seen. "Ahn-dre-ah, I'll need my Chanel suit pressed for tonight, since it was practically ruined with wrinkles on the flight over. You'd think the Concorde would know how to handle luggage, but my things look dreadful. Also, call Horace Mann and confirm that the girls made it to school. You'll be doing that every day—I just don't trust that Annabelle. Make sure you speak to both Caroline and Cassidy each night and write out a list of their homework assignments and upcoming exams. I'll expect a written report in the morning, right before breakfast. Oh, and get Senator Schumer on the phone immediately. It's urgent. Lastly, I need you to contact that idiot Renuad and tell him I expect him to supply me with competent staff during my stay, and if that's too difficult I'm sure the general manager would be able to assist me. That dumb girl he sent me is mentally challenged."

My eyes swiveled to the sorrowful girl who was currently cowering in the foyer, looking as fearful as a cornered hamster as she trembled and tried not to cry. I had to assume she understood English, so I shot her my best sympathetic look, but she just continued to shake. I looked around the room and tried desperately to remember everything Miranda had just rattled off.

"Will do," I called in the general direction of her voice, past the baby grand piano and the seventeen separate flower arrangements that had been lovingly placed around the house-size suite. "I'll be back in just a moment with everything you've asked for." I quietly berated myself for ending a sentence with a preposition and took one last look around the magnificent room. It was, undoubtedly, the plushest, most luxurious place I'd ever seen, with its brocade curtains, thick, cream-colored carpeting, richly woven damask bedspread on the king-size bed, and gold painted figurines tucked discreetly on mahogany shelves and tables. Only a flat-screen TV and a sleek, silver stereo system gave any indication that the entire place hadn't been created and designed in the previous century by highly skilled craftsmen plying their trade.

I ducked past the quaking maid and into the hallway. The terrified bellman had reappeared.

"Could you show me to my room, please?" I asked as kindly as I could, but he clearly thought that I would be abusing him as well, and so once again he scurried ahead of me.

"Here, mademoiselle, I hope this is acceptable."

About twenty yards down the hall was a door without a separate number on it. It opened to a minisuite, nearly an exact replica of Miranda's but with a smaller living room and a queen-size bed instead of a king. A large mahogany desk outfitted with a multiline corporate-style phone, sleek desktop computer, laser printer, scanner, and fax machine had taken the place of the baby grand piano, but otherwise the rooms were remarkably similar in their rich, soothing décor.

"Miss, this door leads to the private hallway connecting your room and Ms. Priestly's," he explained as he moved to open the door.

"No! It's fine, I don't need to see it. Just knowing it's there is good enough." I glanced at the engraved nametag placed discreetly on the pocket of his well-pressed uniform shirt. "Thank you, uh, Stephan." I rooted around in my bag for cash to tip him but realized that I'd never thought to change my American dollars to euros and hadn't yet stopped at an ATM. "Oh, I'm sorry, I, uh, only have American dollars. Is that OK?"

His face flushed crimson and he began apologizing profusely. "Oh, no, miss, please do not worry about such things. Ms. Priestly takes care of these details when she departs. However, since you will be needing local currency when you leave the hotel, allow me to show you this." He walked over to the behemoth of a desk, slid open the top drawer, and handed me an envelope with French *Runway*'s logo on it. Inside was a pile of euro bills, about 4,000 American dollars' worth in all. The note, scribbled by Briget Jardin, the editor in chief who'd borne the brunt of planning and scheduling for both this trip and Miranda's upcoming party, read:

Andrea, darling, delighted to have you join us! Please find enclosed euros for your use while in Paris. I've spoken with Monsieur Renaud and he will be on call for Miranda twenty-four hours a day. See below for a listing of his work and personal numbers, as well as the numbers for the hotel's chef, physical fitness trainer, director of transportation, and, of course, the general manager. They are all familiar with Miranda's stays during the shows and so there should be no

problems. Of course, I may always be reached at work or, if neces-
sary, by cell, home phone, fax, or pager if either of you requires any-
thing at all. If I don't see you before Saturday's big soiree, I'll look
forward to meeting you there. Lots of Love, Briget

Folded on a sheet of *Runway* stationery and tucked underneath the
cash was a list of nearly a hundred phone numbers, encompassing everything one could need in Paris, from a chic florist to an emergency surgeon. These same numbers were repeated on the last page of the detailed
itinerary I'd created for Miranda using information Briget had updated
daily and faxed over, so as of this moment there didn't appear to be a
single contingency—short of an all-out world war—that would prevent
Miranda Priestly from viewing the spring line with the least possible
amount of stress, anxiety, and concern.

"Thank you so much, Stephan. This is most helpful." I peeled off a
few bills for him anyway, but he courteously pretended not to see it and
ducked back into the hallway. I was pleased to see that he appeared significantly less terrorized than he had just a few moments earlier.

I somehow managed to find the people she had asked for and figured
I had a few minutes to rest my head on the four-hundred-thread-count
pillowcase, but the phone rang the moment I closed my eyes.

"Ahn-dre-ah, come to my room immediately," she barked before
slamming down the phone.

"Yes, of course, Miranda, thank you for asking so nicely. It'd be my
pleasure," I said to absolutely nobody. I heaved my jet-lagged body off
the bed and concentrated on not getting a heel stuck in the carpeted hallway that connected my room to hers. Once again, a maid answered the
door when I knocked.

"Ahn-dre-ah! One of Briget's assistants just rang me to see how long
my speech is for today's brunch," she announced. She was paging
through a copy of *Women's Wear Daily* that someone from the office—
probably Allison, who knew the drill from her tenure in Miranda's office—had faxed earlier, and two beautiful men were working on her hair
and makeup. A cheese plate sat on the antique table beside her.

Speech? What speech? The only thing besides shows that was on the
itinerary today was some sort of awards luncheon that Miranda planned

to spend her usual fifteen minutes at before bolting out of sheer boredom.

"I'm sorry. Did you say a speech?"

"I did." She carefully closed the paper, calmly folded it in half, and then tossed it angrily to the floor, narrowly missing one of the men who knelt in front of her. "Why the hell was I not informed that I'd be receiving some nonsense award at today's luncheon?" she hissed, her face contorting with a hatred I'd never seen before. Displeasure? Sure. Dissatisfaction? All the time. Annoyance, frustration, generalized unhappiness? Of course, every minute of every day. But I'd never seen her look so downright *pissed off*.

"Um, Miranda, I'm so sorry, but it was actually Briget's office that RSVP'd you to the event today, and they never—"

"Stop speaking. Stop speaking this instant! All you ever offer me are excuses. *You* are my assistant, *you* are the person I designated to work things out in Paris, *you* are the one who should be keeping me abreast of these things." She was nearly shouting now. One of the makeup guys asked softly in English if we would like a moment alone, but Miranda ignored him entirely. "It's noon right now and I'll be needing to leave here in forty-five minutes. I expect a short, succinct, and articulate speech legibly typed and waiting in my room. If you cannot accomplish this, see yourself home. *Permanently*. That's all."

I fled down the hallway faster than I'd ever run in heels and whipped open my international cell phone before I'd made it into my room. It was nearly impossible to dial Briget's work number since my hands were shaking so badly, but somehow the call went through. One of her assistants answered.

"I need Briget!" I shrieked, my voice breaking when I pronounced her name. "Where is she? *Where is she?* I need to talk to her. *Now!*"

The girl was momentarily shocked into silence. "Andrea? Is that you?"

"Yes, it's me and I need Briget. It's an emergency—where the hell is she?"

"She's at a show, but don't worry, she always has her cell phone on. Are you at the hotel? I'll have her call you right back."

The phone on the desk rang a mere few seconds later, but it felt like a week. "Andrea," she lilted in her lovely French accent. "What is it, dear? Monique said you were hysterical."

"Hysterical? Damn right I'm hysterical! Briget, how could you do this to me? Your office made the arrangements for this fucking luncheon and no one bothered to tell me that she is not only receiving an award but also expected to give a speech?"

"Andrea, calm down. I'm sure we told—"

"And I have to write it! Are you listening to me? I have forty-five fucking minutes to write an acceptance speech for an award I know nothing about in a language I don't speak. Or I'm finished. What am I going to do?"

"All right, relax, I'm going to walk you through this. First of all, the ceremony is right there, at the Ritz, in one of the salons."

"The what? Which salon?" I hadn't had a chance to look around the hotel yet, but I was reasonably sure there weren't any pubs in the place.

"It is French for, oh, what do you call them? Meeting rooms. So, she will only need to go downstairs. It is for the French Council on Fashion, an organization here in Paris that always has its awards during the shows because everyone is in town. *Runway* will be receiving an award for fashion coverage. It is not such a, how do you say, big deal, almost like a formality."

"Great, well at least I know what it's for. What exactly am I supposed to write? Why don't you just dictate in English and I can get Monsieur Renaud to translate it, OK? You start. I'm ready." My voice had regained some confidence, but I could still barely grip the pen. The combination of exhaustion, stress, and hunger was making it hard to focus my eyes on the Ritz stationery that was laid out on my desk.

"Andrea, you are in luck again."

"Oh, really? Because I'm not feeling so lucky right now, Briget."

"These things are always conducted in English. There is no need for translation. So you can write it, yes?"

"Yes, yes I'll write it," I mumbled and dropped the phone. There wasn't even time to consider that this was my very first chance to show Miranda that I was capable of doing something more sophisticated than fetching lattes.

After I hung up and began typing away at sixty words a minute—typing was the only useful class I'd taken in all of high school—I realized the whole thing would only take two, maybe three minutes for Miranda to read. There was just enough time to gulp some of the Pellegrino and devour a few of the strawberries someone had thoughtfully left on my small bar. *If only they could've left a cheeseburger*, I thought. I remembered that I had tucked a Twix bar in my luggage that had been neatly piled in the corner, but there wasn't time to look for it. Exactly forty minutes had passed since I'd received my marching orders. It was time to see if I'd passed.

A different—but equally as terrified—maid answered Miranda's door and ushered me into the living room. Obviously, I should've remained standing, but the leather pants I'd been wearing since the day before felt like they were permanently stuck to my legs, and the strappy sandals that hadn't bothered me so much on the plane were beginning to feel like long, flexible razor blades affixed to my heels and toes. I chose to perch on the overstuffed couch, but the moment my knees bent and my butt made contact with the cushion, her bedroom door flew open and I instinctively launched to my feet.

"Where's my speech?" she asked automatically, while yet another maid followed after her holding a single earring that Miranda had forgotten to put in. "You did write something, did you not?" She was wearing one of her classic Chanel suits—round collars with fur trim—and a looping strand of extraordinarily large pearls.

"Of course, Miranda," I said proudly. "I think this will be appropriate." I walked toward her since she was making no effort to retrieve it herself, but before I could offer her the paper she snatched it from my hand. I didn't realize until her eyes had finished moving back and forth that I'd been holding my breath.

"Fine. This is fine. Certainly nothing groundbreaking, but fine. Let's go." She picked up a matching quilted Chanel purse and placed the chain handle over her shoulder.

"Pardon?"

"I said, let's go. This silly little ceremony starts in fifteen minutes, and with any luck we'll be out of there in twenty. I truly loathe these things."

There was no way to deny that I'd heard her say both "let's" and "we": I was definitely expected to go with her. I glanced down at my leather pants and fitted blazer and figured that if she had no problem with it—and I certainly would've heard if she had—then what did it really matter? There would probably be fleets of assistants roaming around, tending to their bosses, and surely no one would care what we were wearing.

The "salon" was exactly what Briget had said it would be—a typical hotel meeting room, complete with a couple dozen round luncheon tables and a slightly raised presentation stage with a podium. I stood along the back wall with a few other employees of various kinds and watched as the president of the council showed an incredibly unfunny, uninteresting, wholly uninspired movie clip on how fashion affects all of our lives. A few more people hogged the mike for the next half hour, and then, before a single award had been presented, an army of waiters began bringing out salads and filling wine glasses. I looked warily at Miranda, who appeared acutely bored and irritated, and tried to shrink smaller behind the potted tree I was currently leaning against to keep from falling asleep. I can't be sure how long my eyes were closed, but just as I lost all control of my neck muscles and my head started to nod forward uncontrollably, I heard her voice.

"Ahn-dre-ah! I don't have time for this nonsense," she whispered loudly enough that a few Clackers from a nearby table glanced up. "I wasn't told that I would be receiving an award, and I wasn't prepared to do so. I'm leaving." And she turned around and began striding toward the door.

I hobbled after her but thought better of grabbing her shoulder. "Miranda? Miranda?" She was clearly ignoring me. "Miranda? Whom would you like to accept the award on behalf of *Runway*?" I whispered as quietly as I could and still have her hear me.

She whipped around and stared me straight in the eyes. "Do you think I care? Go up there and accept it yourself." And before I could say another word, she was gone.

Oh my god. This wasn't happening. I would surely wake up in my own, unglamorous, negative-thread-count-sheeted bed in just a minute and discover that the entire day—hell, the entire year—had just been a particularly horrid dream. That woman didn't really expect me—the *junior* assistant—to go up there and accept an award for *Runway*'s fashion coverage, did she? I looked around the room frantically to see if anyone else from *Runway* was attending the lunch. No such luck. I slumped down in a seat and tried to figure out whether I should call Emily or Briget for advice, or whether I should just leave myself since Miranda apparently cared nothing about receiving this honor. My cell phone had just connected to Briget's office (who I was hoping could make it over there in time to take the goddamn award herself) when I heard the words ". . . extend our deepest appreciation to American *Runway* for its accurate, amusing, and always informative fashion coverage. Please welcome its world-famous editor in chief, a living fashion icon herself, Ms. Miranda Priestly!"

The room erupted into applause at precisely the same moment I felt my heart stop beating.

There was no time to think, to curse Briget for letting this all happen, to curse Miranda for leaving and taking the speech with her, to curse myself for ever accepting this hateful job in the first place. My legs moved forward on their own, *left-right, left-right*, and climbed the three steps to the podium with no incident whatsoever. Had I not been utterly shell-shocked, I might have noticed that the enthusiastic clapping had given way to an eerie silence as everyone tried to figure out who I was. But I didn't. Instead, some greater force prompted me to smile, reach out to take the plaque from the severe-looking president's hands, and place it shakingly on the podium in front of me. It wasn't until I lifted my head and saw hundreds of eyes staring back—curious, probing, confused eyes, all of them—that I knew for sure I would cease breathing and die right there.

I imagine I stood like that for no longer than ten or fifteen seconds, but the silence was so overwhelming, so all-consuming, that I wondered if I had, in fact, died already. No one uttered a word. No silver scraped plates, no glasses clinked, no one even whispered to a neighbor about who was standing in for Miranda Priestly. They just watched me, moment after moment, until I was left with no choice but to speak. I didn't remember a word of the speech that I had written an hour earlier, so I was on my own.

"Hello," I began and heard my voice reverberate in my ears. I couldn't tell if it was the microphone or the sound of blood pounding inside my head, but it didn't matter. The only thing I could hear for sure was that it was shaking—uncontrollably. "My name is Andrea Sachs and I'm Mir—uh, I'm on staff at *Runway*. Unfortunately, Miranda, um, Ms. Priestly had to step out for a moment, but I would like to accept this award on her behalf. And, of course, on behalf of everyone at *Runway*. Thank you, um"—I couldn't remember the name of the council or the president here—"all so much for this, uh, this wonderful honor. I know I speak for everyone when I say that we are all so honored." Idiot! I was stuttering and um-ing and shaking, and I was even conscious enough at this point to notice that the crowd had begun to twitter. Without another word, I walked in as dignified a manner as I could manage from the podium and didn't realize until I'd reached the back doors that I'd forgotten the plaque. A staffer followed me to the lobby, where I'd just collapsed in a fit of exhaustion and humiliation, and handed it to me. I waited until she left and asked one of the janitors to throw it out. He shrugged and tossed it in his bag.

That bitch! I thought, too angry and tired to conjure up any really creative names or methods of ending her life. My phone rang and, knowing it was her, I turned off the ringer and ordered a gin and tonic from one of the front desk people. "Please. Please just have someone send one out. Please." The woman took one look at me and nodded. I sucked the entire thing down in just two long gulps and headed back upstairs to see what she wanted. It was only two in the afternoon of my first day in Paris, and I wanted to die. Only death was not an option.

17

"Miranda Priestly's room," I answered from my new Parisian office. My four glorious hours that were supposed to constitute a full night's sleep had been rudely interrupted by a frantic call from one of Karl Lagerfeld's assistants at six A.M., which is precisely when I'd discovered that all of Miranda's phone calls were being routed directly to *my* room for answering. It appeared the entire city and surrounding area knew Miranda stayed here during the shows, and so my phone had been ringing incessantly since the moment I stepped inside. Never mind the two dozen messages that had already been left on the voice mail.

"Hi, it's me. How's Miranda doing? Is everything OK? Did anything go wrong yet? Where is she and why aren't you with her?"

"Hey, Em! Thanks for caring. How are you feeling, by the way?"

"What? Oh, I'm fine. A little weak, but getting better. Whatever. How is *she*?"

"Yes, well, I'm fine, too, thanks for asking. Yes, it was a long flight to get here and I haven't slept for more than twenty minutes at a time since the phone keeps ringing and I'm pretty sure it's never going to stop, and, oh! I gave a completely impromptu speech—after writing an impromptu speech—to a group of people who wanted Miranda's company but apparently weren't interesting enough to warrant it. Looked like a giant fucking idiot, actually, and nearly gave myself a heart attack in the process, but hey, other than that, things are just great."

"Andrea! Be serious! I've been really worried about everything. There wasn't a lot of time to prepare for this, and you know that if anything goes wrong over there she's going to blame me anyway."

"Emily. Please don't take this personally, but I can't talk to you right now. I just can't do it."

"Why? Is something wrong? How did her meeting go yesterday? Did she get there on time? Do you have everything you need? Are you making sure to wear appropriate clothes? Remember, you're representing *Runway* over there, so you always have to look the part."

"Emily. I need to hang up now."

"Andrea! I'm concerned. Tell me what you've been doing."

"Well, let's see. In all the free time I've had, I've gotten a half-dozen or so massages, two facials, and a few manicures. Miranda and I have really bonded over doing the whole spa thing together. It's great fun. She's really trying hard not to be too demanding, says she really wants me to enjoy Paris since it's such a wonderful city and I'm lucky to be here. So basically we just hang out and have fun. Drink great wine. Shop. You know, the usual."

"Andrea! This is really not funny, OK? Now tell me what the hell is going on." With every degree more annoyed she sounded, my mood improved a notch.

"Emily, I'm not sure what to tell you. What do you want to hear? How it's been so far? Let's see, I've spent most of my time trying to figure out how best to sleep through a phone that won't stop ringing while simultaneously shoving enough food down my throat between the hours of two and six A.M. to sustain me for the remaining twenty hours. It's like fucking Ramadan here, Em—no eating during daylight hours. Yeah, you should be really sorry you're missing this one."

The other line began blinking and I put Emily on hold. Every time it rang my mind went quickly, uncontrollably, to Alex, wondering if he just might call and say that everything was going to be just fine. I'd called twice on my international cell since I'd arrived and he'd answered both times, but like the expert prank caller I'd been in junior high, I'd hung up the moment I'd heard his voice. It'd been the longest we'd ever gone without talking and I wanted to hear what was going on, but I also couldn't help feeling like life had gotten significantly simpler since we'd taken a break from the bickering and the guilt-mongering. Still, I held my breath until I heard Miranda's voice screeching from across the wires.

"Ahn-dre-ah, when is Lucia due to arrive?"

"Oh, hello, Miranda. Let me just check the itinerary I have for her. Here it is. Let's see, it says here that she was flying in directly from the shoot in Stockholm today. She should be at the hotel."

"Connect me."

"Yes, Miranda, just a moment, please."

I put her on hold and switched her back to Emily. "That's her, hold on."

"Miranda? I just found Lucia's number. I'll connect you now."

"Wait, Ahn-dre-ah. I'll be leaving the hotel in twenty minutes for the rest of the day. I'll need some scarves before I return, and a new chef. He should have a minimum of ten years' experience in mostly French restaurants and be available for family dinners four nights a week and dinner parties twice a month. *Now* connect me to Lucia."

I knew I should've gotten hung up on the fact that Miranda wanted me to hire her a New York chef from Paris, but all I could focus on was that she was leaving the hotel—without me, and for the entire day. I clicked back to Emily and told her that Miranda needed a new chef.

"I'll work on it, Andy," she announced while coughing. "I'll do some preliminary screening and then you can talk to a few of the finalists. Just find out if Miranda would like to wait until she gets home to meet them or if she'd prefer if you arranged for a couple to fly there and meet with her now, OK?"

"You can't be serious."

"Well, of course I'm serious. Miranda hired Cara when she was in Marbella last year. Their last nanny had just quit and she had me fly three finalists to her so she could find someone right away. Just find out, OK?"

"Sure," I muttered. "And thanks."

Just talking about those massages had sounded so good, I decided to book one for myself. There wasn't an appointment available until early evening, so I called room service in the meantime and ordered a full breakfast. When the butler delivered it to me, I'd already crawled back into one of the plush robes, donned a pair of the matching slippers, and prepared myself to feast on the omelet, croissants, Danishes, muffins, potatoes, cereal, and crepes that arrived smelling so good. After devouring all the food and two cups of tea, I waddled back to the bed I hadn't really slept in the night before and fell asleep so quickly that I wondered if someone had slipped something in my orange juice.

The massage was the perfect way to top off what had been a blessedly relaxed day. Everyone else was doing my work for me, and Miranda had only called and woken me once—once!—to request that I make her a lunch reservation the following day. *This isn't so bad*, I thought, as the woman's strong hands kneaded my twisted neck muscles. Not a bad perk at all. But just as I started to drift off once again, the cell phone that I'd grudgingly brought along began its persistent ring.

"Hello?" I said brightly, as if I weren't lying naked on a table covered in oil, half-asleep.

"Ahn-dre-ah. Move my hair and makeup earlier and tell the Ungaro people I can't make it tonight. I'll be attending a small cocktail party instead, and I expect you to come with me. Be ready to leave in an hour."

"Um, sure, uh, sure," I stammered, trying to process the fact that I was actually going somewhere with her. A flashback from yesterday—the last time I was told at the very last minute that I was to go somewhere with her—flooded my brain, and I felt as though I would hyperventilate. I thanked the woman and charged the massage to the room even though I'd made it through only the first ten minutes, and I ran upstairs to figure out how to best maneuver around this newest obstacle. This was getting old. Quickly.

It took just a few minutes to page Miranda's hair and makeup people (who, incidentally, were different from my own—I was pieced together by an angry-looking woman whose look of despair on seeing me for the first time haunted me still, while Miranda had a pair of gay guys who looked like they stepped directly out of the pages of *Maxim*) and change her appointment.

"No problem," Julien squealed in a thick French accent. "We will be there, how you say? Wearing bells! We clear our schedules this week just in the case that Madame Priestly need us at different times!"

I paged Briget yet again and asked her to deal with the Ungaro people. Time to hit the wardrobe. The sketchbook with all my different "looks" was displayed prominently on the bedside table, just waiting for a lost fashion victim like myself to turn to it for spiritual guidance. I flipped through the headings and subheadings and tried to make sense of it all.

Shows:
1. Daytime
2. Evening
Meals:
   1. Breakfast meeting
   2. Lunch
      A. Casual (hotel or bistro)
      B. Formal (The Espadon in the Ritz)
   3. Dinner
      A. Casual (bistro, room service)
      B. Midrange (decent restaurant, casual dinner party)
      C. Formal (Le Grand Vefour restaurant, formal dinner party)
Parties:
   1. Casual (champagne breakfasts, afternoon teas)
   2. Stylish (cocktail parties by nonmajor people, book parties, "meet for drinks")
   3. Dressy (cocktail parties by major people, anything at a museum or gallery, postshow parties hosted by design team)

Miscellaneous:
1. To and from the airport
2. Athletic events (lessons, tournaments, etc.)
3. Shopping excursions
4. Running errands
    A. To couture salons
    B. To upscale shops and boutiques
    C. To the local food store and/or health and beauty aid

There didn't appear to be any suggestions for what to wear when one was unable to establish the major-ness or non-major-ness of the hosts. Clearly, there was the opportunity to make a big mistake here: I could narrow the event down to "Parties," which was a good first step, but at that point things got gray. Was this party going to be a simple number 2, where I'd just pull out something chic, or was it really a 3, in which case I'd better pay attention to choose something from the more elegant choices? There were no instructions for "gray area" or "uncertainty," but someone had helpfully included a last-minute handwritten note toward the bottom of the table of contents: *When in doubt (and you never should be), better to be underdressed in something fabulous than overdressed in something fabulous.* Well, OK then, it looked like I now squarely fit into category, party; subcategory, stylish. I turned to the six looks that Lucia had sketched for that specific description and tried to figure out what might look less ridiculous once it was actually on.

After a particularly embarrassing run-in with a feather-covered tank top and patent-leather thigh-high (as in yes, over the knee) boots, I finally selected the outfit on page thirty-three, a flowy patchwork skirt by Roberto Cavalli with a baby-T and a pair of biker-chick black boots by D&G. Hot, sexy, stylish—but not too dressy—without actually making me look like an ostrich, an eighties throwback, or a hooker. What more could you ask for? Just as I was attempting to choose a workable bag, the hair and makeup woman showed up to begin her frowning and disapproving attempts at making me not look half as horrific as she clearly thought I did.

"Um, could you maybe lighten the stuff under my eyes just a little?" I asked carefully, desperately trying not disparage her handiwork. It

probably would've been better to have a go at the makeup myself—
especially since I had more supplies and instructions than the NASA sci-
entists commissioned to build the space shuttle—but the Makeup
Gestapo showed up like clockwork whether I liked it or not.

"No!" she barked, clearly not striving for the same sensitivity as myself. "It looks better this way."

She finished painting on the thick black paint along my bottom
lashes and vanished as quickly as she'd arrived; I grabbed my bag (alli-
gator Gucci bowling bag) and headed to the lobby fifteen minutes before
our estimated time of departure so I could double-check that the driver
was ready. Just as I was debating with Renaud whether Miranda would
prefer for us to each take separate cars so she wouldn't have to speak to
me or actually use the same one and risk catching something from sharing a backseat with her assistant, she appeared. She looked me up and
down very slowly, her expression remaining completely passive and indifferent. I'd passed! This was the first time since I'd started working
there that I hadn't received a look of all-out disgust or, at the very least,
a snarky comment, and all it had taken was a SWAT team of New York
fashion editors, a collection of Parisian hair and makeup stylists, and a
hefty selection of the world's finest and most expensive clothing.

"Is the car here, Ahn-dre-ah?" She looked stunning in a short,
shirred velvet cocktail dress.

"Yes, Ms. Priestly, right this way," Monsieur Renaud interrupted
smoothly, leading us past a group of what could only be other American
fashion editors also there for the shows. A deferential hush fell over the
super-hip-looking crowd of über-Clackers when we walked past, Miranda
two steps in front me, looking thin and striking and very, very unhappy. I
nearly had to run to keep up, even though she was six inches shorter than
me, and I waited until she gave me a "Well? What the hell are you waiting
for?" look before I ducked into the backseat of the limo after her.

Thankfully the driver appeared to know where he was going, because
I'd been paranoid for the past hour that she would turn to me and ask
me where the unknown cocktail party was being held. She did turn to
me, but she said nothing, choosing instead to chat with B-DAD on her
cell phone, repeating over and over that she expected him to arrive with
plenty of time to change and have a drink before the big party on Sat-

urday night. He was flying over in his company's private jet, and they were currently debating whether or not to bring Caroline and Cassidy; since he wouldn't be returning until Monday, she didn't want the girls to have to miss a day of school. It wasn't until we'd actually pulled up in front of a duplex apartment on Boulevard Saint Germain that I wondered what it was exactly that I was supposed to do all night. She'd always been rather good about not abusing Emily or me or any of her staff in public, which indicated—at least on some level—that she knew she was doing it in the first place. So if she couldn't really order me to fetch her drinks or find her someone on the phone or have something dry-cleaned while we were standing there, what was I to do?

"Ahn-dre-ah, this party is being hosted by a couple with whom I was friendly when we lived in Paris. They requested that I bring along an assistant to entertain their son, who generally finds these events rather dull. I'm sure the two of you will get along well." She waited until the driver opened her door, then she daintily stepped out in her perfect Jimmy Choo pumps. Before I could open my own door, she had climbed the three steps and was already handing her coat to the butler, who was clearly awaiting her arrival. I slumped back into the soft leather seat for just a minute, trying to process this new gem of information she'd so coolly relayed. The hair, the makeup, the rescheduling, the panicked consultation with the style book, the biker-chick boots, were all so I could spend the night babysitting some rich couple's snot-nosed kid? And a *French* snot-nosed kid, no less.

I spent three full minutes reminding myself that *The New Yorker* was now only a couple months away, that my year of servitude was about to pay off, that I could surely make it through one more night of tedium to get my dream job. It didn't help. All of a sudden, I desperately wanted to curl up on my parents' couch and have my mom microwave me some tea while my dad set up the Scrabble board. Jill and even Kyle would be visiting, too, with baby Isaac, who would coo and smile when he saw me and Alex would call and tell me he loved me. No one would care that my sweatpants were stained or my toes were frightfully unpedicured or that I was eating a big, fat chocolate éclair. Not a single person would even know that there were fashion shows going on somewhere across the Atlantic, and they sure as hell wouldn't be interested in hearing about them. But all of that seemed incredibly far away, a lifetime actually, and right now I had to contend with a coterie of people who lived and died on the runway. That, and what was sure to be a screaming, spoiled little boy speaking some French gibberish.

When I finally pulled my scantily-but-stylishly clad self from the limo, the butler was no longer expecting anyone. There was music coming from a live band and the smell of scented candles wafted outside from a window above the small garden. I took a deep breath and reached up to knock, but the door swung open. It's safe to say that never, ever, in my young life had I been more surprised than I was that night: Christian was smiling back at me.

"Andy, darling, so glad you could make it," he said, leaning in and kissing me full on the mouth—a bit intimate considering my mouth had been hanging wide open in disbelief.

"What are you doing here?"

He grinned and pushed that ever-present curl off his forehead. "Shouldn't I be asking you the same thing? Because you seem to follow me everywhere I go, I'm going to have to assume you want to sleep with me."

I blushed and, always the lady, snorted loudly. "Yeah, something like that. Actually, I'm not here as a guest, I'm just a very well dressed babysitter. Miranda asked me to come along and didn't tell me until the last second that I'm supposed to be watching the hosts' bratty son tonight. So, if you'll excuse me, I better go make sure he has all the milk and crayons he'll need."

"Oh, he's just fine, and I'm pretty sure the only thing he'll be needing tonight is another kiss from his babysitter." And he cupped my face in his hands and kissed me again. I opened my mouth to protest, to ask him what the hell was going on, but he took that as enthusiasm and slid his tongue into my mouth.

"Christian!" I was hissing quietly, wondering just how quickly Miranda would fire me if she caught me making out with some random guy at one of her own parties. "What the hell are you doing? Let go of me!" I squirmed away, but he just continued to grin that annoyingly adorable smile.

"Andy, since you seem to be a little slow on the uptake here, this is *my* house. *My* parents are hosting this party, and I was clever enough to have them ask your boss to bring you along. Did she tell you I was ten years old, or did you just decide that for yourself?"

"You're joking. Tell me you're joking. Please?"

"Nope. Fun, right? Since I can't seem to pin you down any other way, I thought this might work. My stepmother and Miranda used to be friendly when Miranda worked at French *Runway*—she's a photographer and does shoots for them all the time—so I just had her tell Miranda that her lonely son wouldn't mind a little company in the form of one attractive assistant. Worked like a charm. Come on, let's get you a drink." He put his hand on the small of my back and led me toward a massive oak bar in the living room, which currently had three uniformed bartenders administering martinis and glasses of Scotch and elegant flutes of champagne.

"So, let me just get this straight: I don't have to babysit for anyone tonight? You don't have a baby brother or anything like that, do you?" It was incomprehensible that I had driven to a party with Miranda Priestly and had no responsibilities for the entire night except to hang out with a Hot Smart Writer. Maybe they'd invited me because they were planning to make me dance or sing to entertain the guests, or perhaps they were really short one cocktail waitress and figured I was the easiest last-minute fill-in? Or maybe we were headed to the coat check, where I would relieve the girl who sat there now, looking bored and tired? My mind refused to wrap itself around Christian's story.

"Well, I'm not saying you don't have to babysit at all tonight, because I plan on needing lots and lots of attention. But I think it'll be a better night than you'd anticipated. Wait right here." He kissed me on the cheek and disappeared into the crowd of partygoers, mostly distinguished-looking men and sort of artsy, fashionable women in their forties and fifties, what appeared to be a mix of bankers and magazine people, with a few designers, photographers, and models thrown in for good measure. There was a small, elegant stone patio in the back of the townhouse, all lit by white candles, where a violinist played softly, and I peeked outside. Immediately I recognized Anna Wintour, looking absolutely ravishing in a cream-colored silk slip dress and beaded Manolo sandals. She was talking animatedly to a man I presumed to be her boyfriend, although her giant Chanel sunglasses prevented me from being able to tell if she was amused, indifferent, or sobbing. The press loved to compare the antics and attitudes of Anna and Miranda, but I found it impossible to believe that anyone could be quite as unbearable as my boss.

Behind her stood what I presumed to be a few *Vogue* editors, eyeing Anna warily and wearily like our own Clackers eye Miranda, and next to them was a screeching Donatella Versace. Her face was so caked with makeup, her clothes were so phenomenally tight, that she actually looked like a caricature of herself. Like the first time I visited Switzerland and couldn't help thinking how much it resembled the mock-up town in EPCOT, Donatella actually looked more like the character on *Saturday Night Live* than herself.

I sipped my glass of champagne (and I thought I wouldn't be having any!) and made small talk with an Italian guy—one of the first ugly ones I'd ever met—who spoke in florid prose about his innate appreciation for the female body, until Christian reappeared again.

"Hey, come with me for a minute," he said, once again navigating me smoothly through the crowd. He was wearing his uniform: perfectly faded Diesels, a white T-shirt, a dark sport coat, and Gucci loafers, and he blended into the fashion crowd seamlessly.

"Where are we going?" I asked, keeping my eyes peeled for Miranda, who, no matter what Christian said, was still probably expecting me to be banished to the corner, faxing or updating the itinerary.

"First, we're getting you another drink, and maybe another for me as well. Then, I'm going to teach you how to dance."

"What makes you think I don't know how to dance? It just so happens that I'm a gifted dancer."

He handed me another glass of champagne that seemed to appear out of thin air and led me into his parents' formal living room, which was done in gorgeous shades of deep maroon. A six-piece band was playing hip music, of course, and the couple dozen people under thirty-five had congregated here. As if on cue, the band started playing Marvin Gaye's "Let's Get It On" and Christian pulled me against him. He smelled of masculine, preppy cologne, something old-school like Polo Sport. His hips moved naturally to the music, no thinking involved, we just moved together all over the makeshift dance floor, and he sang quietly in my ear. The rest of the room became fuzzy—I was vaguely aware there were others dancing, too, and somewhere someone was making a toast to something, but at that moment the only thing with any definition was Christian. Somewhere in the deep recesses of my mind, there was a tiny but insistent reminder that this body against mine was not Alex's, but it didn't matter at all. Not now, not tonight.

It was after one when I actually remembered that I was there with Miranda; it had been hours since I'd last seen her, and I was certain she'd forgotten all about me and headed back to the hotel. But when I finally pulled myself away from the couch in his father's study, I saw her happily chatting with Karl Lagerfeld and Gwyneth Paltrow, all of them apparently oblivious to the fact that they would all be waking up for the Christian Dior show in just a few hours. I was debating whether or not I should approach her when she spotted me.

"Ahn-dre-ah! Come over here," she called, her voice sounding almost merry over the din of the party that had become noticeably more festive in the last few hours. Someone had dimmed the lights, and it was abundantly clear that the partyers who remained had been well taken care of by the smiling bartenders. The annoying way she pronounced my name didn't even bother me in my warm and fuzzy champagne buzz. And even though I thought the evening couldn't get any better, she was clearly calling me over to introduce me to her celebrity friends.

"Yes, Miranda?" I cooed in my most ingratiating, thank-you-for-bringing-me-to-this-fabulous-place tone. She didn't even look in my general direction.

"Get me a Pellegrino and then make sure the driver's out front. I'm ready to leave now." The two women and one man standing next to her snickered, and I felt my face turn bright red.

"Of course. I'll be right back." I fetched the water, which she accepted without a thank-you, and made my way through the thinning crowd to the car. I considered finding Christian's parents to thank them but thought better of it and headed straight toward the door, where he was leaning up against the frame with a smugly satisfied expression.

"So, little Andy, did I show you a good time tonight?" he slurred just a little bit, and it seemed nothing short of adorable at that moment.

"It was all right, I suppose."

"Just all right? Sounds to me like you wish I would've taken you upstairs tonight, huh, Andy? All in good time, my friend, all in good time."

I smacked him playfully on the forearm. "Don't flatter yourself,

Christian. Thank your parents for me." And, for once, I leaned over first and kissed him on the cheek before he could do anything else. "G'night."

"A tease!" he called, slurring just a little bit more. "You're quite the little tease. Bet your boyfriend loves that about you, doesn't he?" He was smiling now, and not cruelly. It was all part of the flirty game for him, but the reference to Alex sobered me for a minute. Just long enough to realize that I'd had a better time tonight than I could remember having had in many years. The drinking and the close dancing and his hands on my back as he pulled me against him had made me feel more alive than in all the months since I'd been working at *Runway*, months that had been filled with nothing but frustration and humiliation and a body-numbing exhaustion. Maybe this was why Lily did it, I thought. The guys, the partying, the sheer joy of realizing you're young and breathing. I couldn't wait to call and tell her all about it.

Miranda joined me in the backseat of the limo after another five minutes, and she even appeared to be somewhat happy. I wondered if she'd gotten drunk but ruled that out immediately: the most I'd ever seen her drink was a sip of this or that, and then only because a social situation demanded it. She preferred Perrier or Pellegrino to champagne and certainly a milkshake or a latte to a cosmo, so the chances she was actually drunk right now were slim.

After grilling me about the following day's itinerary for the first five minutes (luckily I'd thought to tuck a copy in my bag), she turned and looked at me for the first time all evening.

"Emily—er, Ahn-dre-ah, how long have you been working for me?"

It came out of left field, and my mind couldn't work fast enough to figure out the ulterior motive for this sudden question. It felt strange to be the object of any question of hers that wasn't explicitly asking why I was such a fucking idiot for not finding, fetching, or faxing something fast enough. She'd never actually asked about my life before. Unless she remembered the details of our hiring interview—and it seemed unlikely, considering she'd stared at me with utterly blank eyes my very first day of work—then she had no idea where, if anywhere, I'd attended college, where, if anywhere, I lived in Manhattan, or what, if anything, I did in the city in the few precious hours a day I wasn't racing around for her. And although this question most certainly did have a Miranda element to it, my intuition said that this might, just maybe, be a conversation about me.

"Next month it will be a year, Miranda."

"And do you feel you've learned a few things that may help you in your future?" She peered at me, and I instantly suppressed the urge to start rattling off the myriad things I'd "learned": how to find a single store or restaurant review in a whole city or out of a dozen newspapers with few to no clues about its genuine origin; how to pander to preteenage girls who'd already had more life experiences than both my parents combined; how to plead with, scream at, persuade, cry to, pressure, cajole, or charm anyone, from the immigrant food delivery guy to the editor in chief of a major publishing house to get exactly what I needed, when I needed it; and, of course, how to complete just about any challenge in under an hour because the phrase "I'm not sure how" or "that's not possible" was simply not an option. It had been nothing if not a learning-rich year.

"Oh, of course," I gushed. "I've learned more in one year working for you than I could've hoped to have learned in any other job. It's been fascinating, really, seeing how a major—*the* major—magazine runs, the production cycle, what all the different jobs are. And, of course, being able to observe the way you manage everything, all the decisions you make—it's been an amazing year. I'm so thankful, Miranda!" So thankful that two of my molars had been aching for weeks, too, but I wasn't ever able to get in to see a dentist during working hours, but whatever. My newfound, intimate knowledge of Jimmy Choo's handicraft had been well worth the pain.

Could this possibly sound believable? I stole a glance, and she seemed to be buying it, nodding her head gravely. "Well, you know, Ahn-dre-ah, that if ah-fter a year my girls have performed well, I consider them ready for a promotion."

My heart surged. Was it finally happening? Was this where she told me that she'd already gone ahead and secured a job for me at *The New Yorker*? Never mind that she had no idea I would kill to work there. Maybe she had just figured it out because she cares.

"I have my doubts about you, of course. Don't think I haven't noticed your lack of enthusiasm, or those sighs or faces you make when I ask you to do something that you quite obviously don't feel like doing. I'm hoping that's just a sign of your immaturity, since you do seem reasonably competent in other areas. What exactly are you interested in doing?"

Reasonably competent! She may as well have announced I was the most intelligent, sophisticated, gorgeous, and capable young woman she'd ever had the pleasure of meeting. Miranda Priestly had just told me I was reasonably competent!

"Well, actually, it's not that I don't love fashion, because of course I do. Who wouldn't?" I rushed on to say, keeping a careful appraisal of her expression, which, as usual, remained mostly unchanged. "It's just that I've always dreamt of becoming a writer, so I was hoping that might, uh, be an area I could explore."

She folded her hands in her lap and glanced out the window. It was clear that this forty-five-second conversation was already beginning to bore her, so I had to move quickly. "Well, I certainly have no idea if you can write a word or not, but I'm not opposed to having you write a few short pieces for the magazine to find out. Perhaps a theater review or a small writeup for the Happenings section. As long as it doesn't interfere with any of your responsibilities for me, and is done only during your own time, of course."

"Of course, of course. That would be wonderful!" We were talking, really communicating, and we hadn't so much as mentioned the words "breakfast" or "dry cleaning" yet. Things were going too well not to just go for it, and so I said, "It's my dream to work at *The New Yorker* one day."

This seemed to catch her now drifting attention, and once again she peered at me. "Why ever would you want to do that? No glamour there, just nuts and bolts." I couldn't decide if the question was rhetorical, so I played it safe and kept my mouth shut.

My time was about twenty seconds from expiring, both because we were nearing the hotel and her fleeting interest in me was fading fast. She was scrolling through the incoming calls on her cell phone, but still managed to say in the most offhanded, casual way, "Hmm, *The New Yorker*. Condé Nast." I was nodding wildly, encouragingly, but she wasn't looking at me. "Of course I know a great many people there. We'll see how the rest of the trip goes, and perhaps I'll make a call over there when we return."

The car pulled up to the entrance, and an exhausted-looking Monsieur Renaud eclipsed the bellman who was leaning forward to open Miranda's door and opened it himself.

"Ladies! I hope you had a lovely evening," he crooned, doing his best to smile through the exhaustion.

"We'll be needing the car at nine tomorrow morning to go to the Christian Dior show. I have a breakfast meeting in the lobby at eight-thirty. See that I'm not disturbed before then," she barked, all traces of her previous humanness evaporating like spilled water on a hot sidewalk. And before I could think how to end our conversation or, at the very least, kiss up a little more for having had it at all, she walked toward the elevators and vanished inside one. I shot a weary, understanding look to Monsieur Renaud and boarded an elevator myself.

The small, tastefully arranged chocolates on a silver tray on my bed-side table only highlighted the perfection of the evening. In one random, unexpected night, I'd felt like a model, hung out with one of the hottest guys I'd seen in the flesh, and had been told by Miranda Priestly that I was reasonably competent. It felt like everything was finally coming to-gether, that the past year of sacrifice was showing the first early signs of potentially paying off. I collapsed on top of the covers, still fully dressed, and gazed at the ceiling, still unable to believe that I'd told Miranda straight up that I wanted to work at *The New Yorker*, and she hadn't laughed. Or screamed. Or in any way, shape, or form freaked out. She hadn't even scoffed and told me that I was ridiculous for not wanting to get promoted somewhere within *Runway*. It was almost as though—and I might be projecting here, but I don't think so—she had listened to me and *understood*. Understood and *agreed*. It was almost too much to com-prehend.

I undressed slowly, making sure to savor every minute of tonight, going over and over in my mind the way Christian had led me from room to room and then all over the dance floor, the way he looked at me through those hooded lids with the persistent curl, the way Miranda had almost, imperceptibly, nodded when I'd said what I really wanted was to write. A truly glorious night, I had to say, one of the best in re-cent history. It was already three-thirty in the morning Paris time, mak-ing it nine-thirty New York time—a perfect time to catch Lily before she went out for the night. Although I should've just dialed with no re-gard for the insistent, blinking light that announced—surprise, sur-prise—that I had messages, I cheerfully pulled out a pad of the Ritz stationery and got ready to transcribe. There were bound to be long lists of irritating requests from irritating people, but nothing could take away my Cinderella-esque evening.

The first three were from Monsieur Renaud and his assistants, confirming various drivers and appointment for the next day, always remembering to wish me a good night as though I were actually a person instead of just a slave, which I appreciated. Between the third and the fourth message I found myself both wishing and not wishing that one of the messages to come was from Alex, and as a result, was both delighted and anxious when the fourth was from him.

"Hi, Andy, it's me. Alex. Listen, I'm sorry to bother you over there, I'm sure you're incredibly busy, but I need to talk to you, so please call me on my cell phone as soon as you get this. Doesn't matter how late it is, just be sure to call, OK? Uh, OK. 'Bye."

It was so strange that he hadn't said he loved me or missed me or was waiting for me to get back, but I guess all those things fall squarely into the "inappropriate" category when people decide to "take a break." I hit delete and decided, rather arbitrarily, that the lack of urgency in his voice meant I could wait until tomorrow—I just couldn't handle a long "state of our relationship" conversation at three o'clock in the morning after as wonderful a night as I'd just had.

The last and final message was from my mom, and it, too, sounded strange and ambiguous.

"Hi, honey, it's Mom. It's about eight our time, not sure what that makes it for you. Listen, no emergency—everything's fine—but it'd be great if you could call me back when you hear this. We'll be up for a while, so anytime is fine, but tonight is definitely better than tomorrow. We both hope you're having a wonderful time, and we'll talk to you later. Love you!"

This was definitely strange. Both Alex and my mother had called me in Paris before I'd gotten a chance to call either of them, and both had requested that I call them back regardless of what time I got the message. Considering my parents defined a late night by whether or not they managed to stay awake for Letterman's opening monologue, I knew something had to be up. But at the same time, no one sounded particularly panicked or even a little frantic. Perhaps I'd take a long bubble bath with some of the Ritz products provided and slowly work up the energy to call everyone back; the night had just been too good to wreck by talking to my mother about some petty concern or to Alex about "where we stand."

The bath was just as hot and luxurious as you'd expect it to be in a junior suite adjacent to the Coco Chanel suite at the Ritz Paris, and I took a few extra minutes to apply some of the lightly scented moisturizer from the vanity to my entire body. Then, finally wrapped in the plushest terry-cloth robe I'd ever pulled around me, I sat down to dial. Without thinking, I dialed my mother first, which was probably a mistake: even her "hello" sounded seriously stressed out.

"Hey, it's me. Is everything OK? I was going to call you guys tomorrow, it's just that things have been so hectic. But, wait until I tell you about the night I just had!" I knew already that I'd be omitting any romantic references to Christian, since I hadn't felt like explaining the entire Alex scenario to my parents, but I knew they'd both be thrilled to hear that Miranda seemed to respond well when I'd brought up the idea of *The New Yorker*.

"Honey, I don't mean to interrupt you, but something's happened. We got a call today from Lenox Hill Hospital, which is on Seventy-seventh Street, I think, and it seems that Lily's been in an accident."

And although it's quite conceivably the most clichéd expression in the English language, my heart stopped for just a moment. "What? What are you talking about? What kind of an accident?"

She had already switched into worried-mom mode and was clearly trying to keep her voice steady and her words rational, following what was sure to have been my dad's suggestion of passing along to me a feeling of calm and control. "A car accident, honey. A rather serious one, I'm afraid. Lily was driving—there was also a guy in the car, someone from school, I think they said—and she turned the wrong way down a one-way street. It seems she hit a taxicab head-on, going nearly forty miles an hour on a city street. The police officer I spoke with said it was a miracle she's alive."

"I don't understand. When did it happen? Is she going to be OK?" I had started choke-crying at some point, because as calm as my mother was trying to remain, I could hear the severity of the situation in her carefully chosen words. "Mom, where is Lily now, and is she going to be OK?"

It wasn't until this point that I noticed my mom was crying also, just quietly. "Andy, I'm putting Dad on. He spoke to the doctors most recently. I love you, honey." The last part came out like a squeak.

"Hi, honey. How are you? Sorry we have to call with news like this." My dad's voice sounded deep and reassuring, and I had a fleeting feeling that everything was going to work out. He was going to tell me that she'd broken her leg, maybe a rib or two, and someone had called in a good plastic surgeon to stitch up a few scrapes on her face. But she was going to be just fine.

"Dad, will you please tell me what happened? Mom said Lily was driving and hit a cab going really fast? I don't understand. None of this makes any sense. Lily doesn't have a car, and she hates to drive. She'd never be cruising around Manhattan. How did you hear about this? Who called you? And what's wrong with her?" Again, I'd worked myself up to nearly hysterical, but again his voice was commanding and soothing all in one.

"Take a deep breath—I'll tell you everything I know. The accident happened yesterday, but we just found out about it today."

"Yesterday! How could this have happened yesterday and no one called me? Yesterday?"

"Sweetie, they did call you. The doctor said that Lily had filled out the front information page in her daily planner and had listed you as her emergency contact, since her grandmother's really not doing all that well. Anyway, I guess the hospital called you at home and on your cell, but of course you weren't checking either one. When no one called them back or showed up in twenty-four hours, they went through her planner and noticed that we have the same last name as you, and so the hospital called here to see if we knew how to reach you. Mom and I couldn't remember where you were staying, so we called Alex for the name of the hotel."

"Oh my god, it was a day ago. Has she been alone this whole time? Is she still in the hospital?" I couldn't ask the questions fast enough, but I still felt like I wasn't getting any answers. All I knew for sure was that Lily had decided on me as the primary person in her life, the emergency

contact you always had to list but never, ever took seriously. And here
she'd really needed me—didn't have anyone else, in fact—and I'd been
nowhere to be found. My choking had subsided, but the tears continued
to pour down my cheeks in hot, angry streaks, and my throat felt as
though it had been scraped raw with a pumice stone.

"Yes, she's still in the hospital. I'm going to be very honest with you,
Andy. We're not sure if she's going to be all right."

"What? What are you saying? Will someone just tell me something
concrete already?"

"Honey, I've spoken to her doctor a half-dozen times already, and I
have complete confidence that she's getting the best attention. But Lily's
in a coma, sweetie. Now, the doctor did reassure me that—"

"A coma? Lily is in a coma?" Nothing was making sense anymore;
the words were refusing to take on meaning.

"Honey, try to calm down. I know this is shocking for you and I hate
to do this over the phone. We considered not telling you until you got
back, but since that's still half a week away, we figured you had a right
to know. But also know that Mom and I are doing everything we can to
make sure that Lily gets the best help. She's always been like a daughter to us, you know that, so she's not going to be alone."

"Oh my god, I have to come home. Dad, I have to come home! She
doesn't have anybody but me, and I'm across the Atlantic. Oh, but that
fucking party is the night after tomorrow and it's the sole reason she
brought me and she'll definitely fire me if I'm not there. Think! I need
to think!"

"Andy, it's late there. I think the best thing you could do is get some
sleep, take a little time to think things over. Of course I knew you'd want
to come home right away, because that's the kind of person you are, but
keep in mind that for right now Lily is not conscious. Her doctor assured
me that the chances are excellent that she'll come out of this in the next
forty-eight to seventy-two hours, that her body is just using this as an extended and deeper sleep to help itself heal. But nothing is certain," he
added, softly.

"And if she does come out of it? I'm assuming she could have all sorts
of brain damage and horrible paralysis and things like that? Oh my god,
I can't stand it."

"They just don't know yet. They said that she is responsive to stimuli in her feet and legs, which is a good indication that there's no paralysis. But there's a lot of swelling around her head, and it won't be possible to know anything for sure until she comes out of this. We just need to wait."

We spoke for a few minutes longer before I hung up abruptly and called Alex's cell phone.

"Hi, it's me. Have you seen her?" I asked without so much as a hello. I was now a mini-Miranda.

"Andy. Hi. So you know?"

"Yeah, I just got off the phone with my parents. Have you seen her?"

"Yes, I'm at the hospital now. They won't let me in her room right now since it's not visiting hours and I'm not family, but I wanted to be here just in case she wakes up." He sounded very, very far away, completely lost in his own thoughts.

"What happened? My mom said something about how she was driving and hit a cab or something? None of it makes any sense to me."

"Uch, it's a nightmare," he sighed, clearly unhappy that no one else had told me the story yet. "I'm not sure I know exactly, but I did talk to the guy she was with when it happened. You remember Benjamin, that guy she was seeing in college who she walked in on having a threesome with those girls?"

"Of course, he works in my building now. I see him sometimes. What the hell was she doing with him? Lily hates him—she's never gotten over that."

"I know, that's what I thought, too, but it seems they've been hanging out lately and they were together last night. He says they had gotten tickets to see Phish at Nassau Coliseum and drove out there together. I guess Benjamin smoked too much and decided he shouldn't drive his car home, so Lily volunteered. They made it back to the city with no problems until Lily ran a red light and then turned the wrong way down Madison, straight into oncoming traffic. They hit a cab head-on, on the driver's side, and, well, uh, you know." He choked up at this point, and I knew things must be worse than anyone had let on.

I'd done nothing but ask questions the last half hour—to my mom, my dad, and now Alex—but I couldn't bring myself to ask the most obvious one: Why had Lily run a red light and then tried to drive south on an avenue that only ran north? But I didn't need to, because Alex, as always, knew exactly what I was thinking.

"Andy, her blood alcohol level was nearly twice the legal limit." He stated this matter-of-factly, trying not to swallow the words so I wouldn't ask him to repeat them.

"Oh my god."

"If—when—she wakes up, she's going to have even more to deal with than her health: she's in a lot of trouble. Luckily, the cabbie was OK, just a few bumps and bruises, and Benjamin's left leg is completely smashed up, but he'll be fine, too. We just need to wait for Lily. When are you coming home?"

"What?" I was still trying to process the fact that Lily had been "seeing" a guy I'd always thought she hated, that she'd ended up in a coma because she was so drunk when she was with him.

"I said, when are you coming home?" When I was silent for a moment, he continued. "You are coming home, aren't you? You're not seriously considering staying there while your best friend on earth lies in a hospital bed, are you?"

"What are you suggesting, Alex? Are you suggesting that this is my fault because I didn't see it coming? That she's lying in that hospital bed because I'm in Paris right now? That if I had known she was hanging out with Benjamin again none of this would have happened? What? What exactly are you saying?" I shrieked, all of the confusing emotions of the night boiling over into a simple, urgent need to scream at someone else.

"No, I didn't say any of that. You did. I just assumed that of course you'd be coming home to be with her as soon as possible. I'm not passing judgment on you, Andy—you know that. I also know that it's really late for you already and there's nothing you can do in the next couple hours, so why don't you call me when you know what flight you're on. I'll pick you up at the airport and we can come straight to the hospital."

"Fine. Thanks for being there for her. I really appreciate it and I know Lily does, too. I'll call you when I know what I'm doing."

"OK, Andy. I miss you. And I know you'll do the right thing." The line went dead before I could pounce all over that one.

Do the right thing? The *right* thing? What the hell did that mean? I hated that he had just assumed I would jump on a plane and race home because he told me to. Hated his condescending, preachy tone of voice that immediately made me feel like one of his students who'd just been caught talking during class. Hated that he was the one who was with Lily now even though she was my friend, that he was the one acting as a liaison between my own parents and me, that he was once again sitting on his moral high horse and calling the shots. Gone were the old days, when I might have hung up comforted by his presence, knowing that we were in this together and would get through it together, instead of as warring factions. When had things become like this?

There was no energy left to point out the obvious to him, namely, that if I left early to come home, I'd be fired immediately and my entire year of servitude would have been for nothing. I had managed to suppress that awful thought before it took full form in my mind: that my being there or not being there would mean absolutely nothing to Lily right now, since she was unconscious and unaware in a hospital bed. The options swirled around in my mind. Perhaps I would stay just long enough to help with the party and then try to explain to Miranda what happened and make a plea for my job. Or, if it appeared that Lily was awake and alert, someone could explain that I would be on my way as soon as possible, at that point probably just a couple more days. And while both of these explanations sounded somewhat reasonable in the dark hours of early morning after a long night of dancing and many glasses of bubbly and a phone call telling me my best friend was in a coma because of her own drunk driving, somewhere down deep I knew—I knew—that neither of them was.

←→

"Ahn-dre-ah, leave a message at Horace Mann that the girls will be missing school on Monday because they'll be in Paris with me, and make sure you get a list of all the work they'll need to make up. Also, push back my dinner tonight until eight-thirty, and if they're not happy about that, then just cancel it. Have you located a copy of that book I asked you for yesterday? I need four copies—two in French, two in English—before I meet them at the restaurant. Oh, and I want a final copy of the edited menu for tomorrow's party to reflect the changes I made. Make certain that there will be no sushi of any kind, do you hear me?"

"Yes, Miranda," I said, scribbling as quickly as possible in the Smythson notebook the accessories department had thoughtfully included with my array of bags, shoes, belts, and jewelry. We were in the car on our way to the Dior show—my first—with Miranda spitting out rapid-fire instructions with no regard for the fact that I'd gotten less than two hours of sleep. The knock on my door came at 7:45 A.M. from one of Monsieur Renaud's junior concierges who was there personally to wake me up and see that I was dressed in time to attend the show with Miranda, who had herself decided she'd like my assistance just six minutes earlier. He had politely ignored my being quite obviously passed out on the still made bed and had even dimmed the lights, which had blazed all night. I had twenty-five minutes to shower, consult the fashion book, dress myself, and do my own makeup, since my woman was not scheduled to come this early.

I awoke with a minor champagne headache, but the real jolt of pain came when the previous night's phone calls came flashing back. Lily! I needed to call Alex or my parents and see if anything had happened in the last couple hours—god, it seemed like a week ago—but now there was no time.

By the time the elevator had hit the first floor, I'd decided that I had to stay for one more day, just one lousy day to tend to this party, and then I'd be home with Lily. Maybe I'd even take a short leave of absence once Emily returned, to spend some time with Lil, help her recuperate and deal with some of the inevitable fallout from the accident. My parents and Alex would hold down the fort until I got there—*it's not as though she's all alone,* I told myself. And this was my life. My career, my entire future, was on the line here, and I didn't see how two days either way made all that much difference to someone who wasn't yet conscious. But to me—and certainly to Miranda—it made all the difference in the world.

Somehow I'd made it to the backseat of the limo before Miranda did, and even though her eyes were currently fixating on my chiffon skirt, she hadn't yet commented on any one part of the outfit. I had just tucked the

Smythson book into my Bottega Venetta bag when my new, international cell phone rang. It had never rung in Miranda's presence before, I realized, so I scrambled quickly to turn off the ringer, but she ordered me to answer it.

"Hello?" I kept one eye on Miranda, who was paging through the day's itinerary and pretending not to listen.

"Andy, hi honey." Dad. "Just wanted to give you a quick update."

"OK." I was trying to say the bare minimum, since it seemed incredibly strange to be talking on the phone in front of Miranda.

"The doctor just called and said that Lily is showing signs that indicate she may come out of it soon. Isn't that great? I thought you'd want to know."

"That's great. Definitely great."

"Have you decided if you're coming home or not?"

"Um, no, I haven't decided. Miranda's having a party tomorrow night and she definitely needs my help, so . . . Listen, Dad, I'm sorry, but now's not a great time. Can I call you back?"

"Sure, call anytime." He tried to sound neutral, but I could hear the disappointment in his voice.

"Great. Thanks for calling. 'Bye."

"Who was that?" Miranda asked, still peering at her itinerary. It had just begun raining and her voice was nearly drowned out by the sound of water hitting the limo.

"Hmm? Oh, that was my father. From America." Where the hell did I come up with this stuff? From *America*?

"And what did he want you to do that conflicted with your working at the party tomorrow night?"

I considered a million potential lies in the course of two seconds, but there wasn't enough time to work out the details of any of them. Especially when she had turned her full attention to me now. I was left with no choice but to tell the truth.

"Oh, it was nothing. A friend of mine was in an accident. She's in the hospital. In a coma, actually. And he was just calling to tell me how she was doing and to see if I was coming home."

She considered this, nodding slowly, and then picked up the copy of the *International Herald Tribune* paper the driver had thoughtfully provided. "I see." No "I'm sorry," or "Is your friend OK?," just an icy, vague statement and a look of extreme displeasure.

"But I'm not, I'm definitely not going home. I understand how important it is that I'm at the party tomorrow, and I'll be there. I've thought a lot about it, and I want you to know that I plan to honor the commitment I've made to you and to my job, so I'll be staying."

At first Miranda said nothing. But then she smiled slightly and said, "Ahn-dre-ah, I'm very pleased with your decision. It is absolutely the right thing to do, and I appreciate that you recognize that. Ahn-dre-ah, I have to say, I had my doubts about you from the start. Clearly, you know nothing about fashion and more than that, you don't seem to care. And don't think I've failed to notice all the rich and varied ways you convey to me your displeasure when I ask you to do something that you'd rather not. Your competency in the job has been adequate, but your attitude has been substandard at best."

"Oh, Miranda, please let me—"

"I'm speaking! And I was going to say that I'll be much more willing to help you get where you'd like to go now that you've demonstrated that you're committed. You should be proud of yourself, Ahn-dre-ah." Just when I thought I'd faint from the length and depth and content of the soliloquy—whether from joy or from pain, I wasn't sure—she took it one step further. In a move that was so fundamentally out of character for this woman on every level, she placed her hand on top of the one I had resting on the seat between us and said, "You remind me of myself when I was your age." And before I could conjure up a single appropriate syllable to utter, the driver screeched to a halt in front of the Carrousel du Louvre and leapt out to open the doors. I grabbed my bag and hers as well and wondered if this was the proudest or the most humiliating moment of my life.

My first Parisian fashion show was a blur. It was dark, that much I remember, and the music seemed much too loud for such understated elegance, but the only thing that stands out from that two-hour window into bizarreness was my own intense discomfort. The Chanel boots that Jocelyn had so lovingly selected to go with the outfit—a stretchy and therefore skintight cashmere sweater by Malo over a chiffon skirt—made my feet feel like confidential documents being fed through a shredder. My head ached from a combination of hangover and anxiety, causing my empty stomach to protest with threatening waves of nausea. I was standing in the very back of the room with assorted C-list reporters and others who didn't rank high enough to warrant a seat, keeping one eye on Miranda and the other scoping out the least humiliating places to be sick if the need arose. *You remind me of myself when I was your age. You remind me of myself when I was your age. You remind me of myself when I was your age.* The words kept reverberating over and over, keeping tune to the steady and persistent pounding of my forehead.

Miranda managed not to address me for nearly an hour, but after that she was off and running. Even though I was standing in the same room she was, she called my cell phone to request a Pellegrino. From that moment on, the phone rang in ten- to twelve-minute increments, each request sending another shock of pain directly to my head. *Brrring.* "Get Mr. Tomlinson on his air phone on the jet." (B-DAD didn't answer on his air phone when I tried calling it sixteen times.) *Brrring.* "Remind all the *Runway* editors in Paris that just because they're here does not mean they can neglect their responsibilities at home—I want everything in by original deadline!" (The couple of *Runway* editors I had gotten in touch with at their various hotels in Paris had simply laughed at me and hung up.) *Brrring.* "Get me a regular American turkey sandwich immediately—I'm tiring of all this ham." (I walked more than two miles in painful boots and with an upset stomach, but there was no turkey to be found anywhere. I'm convinced she knew, since she'd never once before asked for a turkey sandwich while in America—even though, of course, they're available on every street corner.) *Brrring.* "I expect dossiers prepared on the three best chefs you've found thus far to be waiting in my suite by the time we return from this show." (Emily hacked and whined and bitched but promised that she'd fax over whatever information she had on the candidates so far and I could make them into "dossiers.") *Brrring! Brrring! Brrring! You remind me of myself when I was your age.*

Too nauseated and crippled to watch the parade of anorexic models, I ducked outside for a quick cigarette. Naturally, the moment I flicked on my lighter, my cell phone shrilled again. "Ahn-dre-ah! Ahn-dre-ah! Where are you? Where the hell are you right now?"

I tossed out my still unlit cigarette and raced back inside, my stomach churning so violently that I knew I would be sick—it was just a matter of when and where.

"I'm right in the back of the room, Miranda," I said, sliding through the door and pressing my back against the wall. "Right to the left of the door. Do you see me?"

I watched as she swiveled her head back and forth until her eyes finally rested on mine. I was about to hang up the phone, but she was still stage whispering into it. "Don't move, do you hear me? Do not move! One would think that my assistant would understand she's here to assist me, not to gallivant around outside when I need her. This is unacceptable, Ahn-dre-ah!" By the time she'd made it to the back of the room and positioned herself in front of me, a woman in a glimmering floor-length silver gown with an empire waist and slight flare was sashaying through the reverent crowds, and the music switched from some sort of bizarre Gregorian chants to all-out heavy metal. My head began pounding almost in tune to the change in music. Miranda didn't stop hissing when she reached me, but she did, finally, flip her cell phone closed. I did the same.

"Ahn-dre-ah, we have a very serious problem here. *You* have a very serious problem. I just received a call from Mr. Tomlinson. It seems Annabelle brought it to his attention that the twins' passports expired last week." She stared at me, but all I could do was concentrate on not throwing up.

"Oh, really?" was all I could manage, but that clearly wasn't the right response. Her hand tightened around her bag and her eyes began to bulge with anger.

"*Oh, really?*" she mimicked in a hyena-like howl. People were beginning to stare at us. "Oh, really? That's all you have to say? 'Oh, really?' "

"No, uh, of course not, Miranda. I didn't mean it like that. Is there something I can do to help?"

"*Is there something I can do to help?*" she mimicked again, this time in a whiny child's voice. If she had been any other person on earth, I would have reached out and slapped her face. "You damn well better believe it, Ahn-dre-ah. Since you're clearly unable to stay on top of these things in advance, you'll need to figure out how to renew them in time for their flight tonight. I will not have my own daughters miss this party tomorrow night, do you understand me?"

Did I understand her? Hmm. A very good question indeed. I was thoroughly unable to understand how it was my fault that her ten-year-olds had expired passports when they, theoretically, had two parents, a stepfather, and a full-time nanny to oversee such things, but I also understood it didn't matter. If she thought it was my fault, it was. I understood that she would never understand when I told her that those girls were not getting on that plane tonight. There was virtually nothing I couldn't find, fix, or arrange, but securing federal documents while in a foreign country in less than three hours was not happening. Period. She had finally made her very first request of me in a full year that I could not accommodate—regardless of how much she barked or demanded or intimidated, it was not happening. *You remind me of myself when I was your age.*

Fuck her. Fuck Paris and fashion shows and marathon games of "I'm so fat." Fuck all the people who believed that Miranda's behavior was justified because she could pair a talented photographer with some expensive clothes and walk away with some pretty magazine pages. Fuck her for even thinking that I was anything like her. And most of all, fuck her for being right. What the hell was I standing here for, getting abused and belittled and humiliated by this joyless she-devil? So maybe, just maybe, I, too, could be sitting at this very same event thirty years from now, accompanied only by an assistant who loathes me, surrounded by armies of people who pretend they like me because they have to.

I yanked out my cell phone and punched in a number and watched as Miranda became increasingly more livid.

"Ahn-dre-ah!" she hissed, much too ladylike to ever make a scene. "What do you think you're doing? I'm telling you that my daughters need passports immediately, and you decide it's a good time to chat on your phone? Are you under the very mistaken impression that's why I brought you to Paris?"

My mother picked up on the third ring, but I didn't even say hello.

"Mom, I'm getting on the next flight I can. I'll call you when I get to JFK. I'm coming home." I clicked the phone shut before she could respond and looked up to see Miranda, who appeared genuinely surprised. I felt a smile break through the headache and nausea when I realized that I'd rendered her momentarily speechless. Unfortunately, she recovered quickly. There's a small chance I wouldn't have gotten fired if I'd immediately pleaded and explained and lost the defiant attitude, but I couldn't seem to muster one single, tiny shred of self-control.

"Ahn-dre-ah, you realize what you're doing, do you not? You do know that if you simply leave here like this, I'm going to be forced—"

"Fuck you, Miranda. *Fuck you.*"

She gasped audibly while her hand flew to her mouth in shock, and I felt not a few Clackers turn to see what the commotion was. They'd begun pointing and whispering, themselves as shocked as Miranda that some nobody assistant had just said that—and none too quietly—to one of the great living fashion legends.

"Ahn-dre-ah!" She grabbed my upper arm with her clawlike hand, but I wrenched it out of her grip and plastered on an enormous smile. I also figured it'd be an appropriate time to stop whispering and let everyone in on our little secret.

"So sorry, Miranda," I announced in a normal voice that for the first time since I'd landed in Paris wasn't shaking uncontrollably, "but I don't think I'll be able to make it to the party tomorrow. You understand don't you? I'm sure it'll be lovely, so please do enjoy it. That's all." And before she could respond, I hitched my bag higher up on my shoulder, ignored the pain that was searing from heel to toe, and strutted outside to hail a cab. I couldn't remember feeling better than that particular moment. I was going home.

18

"Jill, stop shout-
ing for your sister!" my mother screamed unhelpfully. "I think she's still
sleeping." And then, a voice came even louder from the bottom of the
stairs.

"Andy, are you still sleeping?" she screamed in the general direction
of my room.

I pried open an eye and checked the clock. Quarter after eight in the
morning. Dear god, what were these people *thinking*?

It took a few times of rocking from side to side before I could muster
enough strength to pull myself to sit, and when I finally did, my whole
body pleaded for more sleep, just a little more sleep.

"Morning," Lily smiled, her face coming within inches of my own when she turned to face me. "They sure do get up early around here." Since Jill and Kyle and the baby were home for Thanksgiving, Lily had been forced to vacate Jill's old room and move onto the lower half of my childhood trundle bed, which was currently pulled out and nearly level with my own twin-size bed.

"What are you complaining about? You look psyched to be awake right now, and I'm not sure why." She was propped up on one elbow, reading a newspaper and sipping a cup of coffee she kept picking up and placing down on the floor next to the bed.

"I've been up forever listening to Isaac cry."

"He's been crying? Really?"

"I can't believe you didn't hear him. It's been incessant since about six-thirty. Cute kid, Andy, but that whole early-morning thing has got to go."

"Girls!" my mother screamed again. "Is anyone awake up there? Anyone? I don't care if you're still sleeping, just please tell me one way or the other so I know how many waffles to defrost!"

"Please tell her one way or the other? I'm going to kill her, Lil." And then toward my still closed door: "We're still sleeping, can't you tell? Fast asleep, probably for hours more. We don't hear the baby or you screaming, or anything else!" I shouted back, collapsing backward on the bed. Lily laughed.

"Relax," she said in a very un-Lily-like way. "They're just happy you're home, and I, for one, am happy to be here. Besides, it's only a couple more months, and we've got each other. It's really not so bad."

"A couple more months? It's only been one so far, and I'm ready to put a bullet in my head." I yanked my nightshirt over my head—one of Alex's old workout ones—and put on a sweatshirt. The same jeans I'd been wearing every day for the past few weeks lay rumpled in a ball near my closet; when I pulled them over my hips, I noticed that were feeling snugger. Now that I no longer had to resort to gulping down a bowl of soup or subsisting on cigarettes and Starbucks alone, my body had adjusted itself accordingly and gained back the ten pounds I'd lost while working at *Runway*. And it didn't even make me cringe; I *believed* it when Lily and my parents told me I looked healthy, not fat.

Lily slipped on a pair of sweatpants over the boxers she'd slept in and tied a bandana over her frizzed-out curls. With her hair pulled off her face, the angry red marks where her forehead had met shards of the windshield were more noticeable, but the stitches had already come out and the doctor promised that there'd be minimal, if any, scarring. "Come on," she said, grabbing the crutches that were propped against the wall everywhere she went. "They're all leaving today, so maybe we'll get a decent night's sleep tonight."

"She's not going to stop screaming until we go down there, is she?" I mumbled, holding her elbow to help her to her feet. The cast around her right ankle had been signed by my entire family, and Kyle had even drawn annoying little messages from Isaac all over it.

"Not a chance."

My sister appeared in the doorway, cradling the baby, who currently had drool halfway down his chubby chin but was now giggling contentedly. "Look who I have," she cooed in baby talk, bouncing the happy boy up and down in her arms. "Isaac, tell your auntie Andy not to be such a tremendous bitch, since we're all leaving real, real soon. Can you do that for mommy, honey? Can you?"

Isaac sneezed a very cute baby sneeze in response, and Jill looked as though he'd just risen up from her arms a full-grown man and recited a few Shakespearean sonnets. "Did you see that, Andy? Did you *hear* that? Oh, my little guy is just the cutest thing ever!"

"Good morning," I said, kissing her on the cheek. "You know I don't want you to leave, right? And Isaac's welcome to stay as long as he can figure out how to sleep between the hours of midnight and ten A.M. Hell, even Kyle can stick around if he promises not to talk. See? We're easy here."

Lily had managed to hobble down the stairs and greet my parents, who were both dressed for work and saying their good-byes to Kyle.

I made my bed and tucked Lily's back underneath, making sure to fluff her pillow before sticking it in my closet for the day. She'd come out of the coma before I even got off the plane from Paris, and after Alex I was the first one to see her awake. They ran a million tests on every conceivable body part, but with the exception of some stitches on her face, neck, and chest, and the broken ankle, she was perfectly healthy. Looked like hell, of course—exactly what you'd expect for someone who'd danced with an oncoming vehicle—but she was moving around just fine and even seemed almost annoyingly upbeat for someone who'd just lived through what she did.

It was my dad's idea that we sublet our apartment for November and December and move in with them. Although the idea had been less than appealing to me, my zero-sum salary left me with few arguments. And besides, Lily seemed to welcome the chance to get out of the city for a little while and leave behind all the questions and gossip that she'd have to face as soon as she saw anyone she knew again. We'd listed the place on craigslist.org as a perfect "holiday rental" to enjoy all the sights of New York, and to both our shock and amazement, an older Swedish couple whose children were all living in the city paid our full asking price—six hundred dollars more per month than we ourselves paid. The three hundred bucks a month was more than enough for each of us to live on, especially considering my parents comped us food, laundry, and the use of a beat-up Camry. The Swedes were leaving the week after New Year's, just in time for Lily to start her semester over again and for me to, well, do something.

Emily had been the one who officially fired me. Not that I'd had any lingering doubts as to my employment status after my little foul-mouthed temper tantrum, but I suppose Miranda had been livid enough to drive home one last dig. The whole thing had taken only three or four minutes and had unfolded with the ruthless *Runway* efficiency that I loved so much.

I'd just managed to hail a cab and pry the left boot from my pulsating foot when the phone rang. Of course my heart instinctively lurched forward, but when I remembered that I'd just told Miranda what she could do with her *You remind me of myself when I was your age*, I realized it couldn't be her. I did a quick tabulation of the minutes that had passed: one for Miranda to shut her gaping mouth and recover her cool for all the Clackers who were watching, another for her to locate her cell phone and call Emily at home, a third to convey the sordid details of my unprecedented outburst, and a final one for Emily to reassure Miranda that she herself would "see to it that everything was taken care of." Yes, although the caller ID simply said "unavailable" on international phone calls, there wasn't a doubt in the world who was ringing.

"Hi, Em, how are you?" I practically sang while rubbing my bare foot and trying not to let it touch the filthy taxi floor.

She seemed to be caught off-guard by my downright chipper tone. "Andrea?"

"Hey, it's me, I'm right here. What's up? I'm kind of in a hurry, so . . ." I thought about asking her directly if she'd called to fire me but decided to give her a break for once. I braced myself for the verbal tirade she was sure to let loose on me—how could you let her down, me down, *Runway* down, the wide world of fashion, blah, blah, blah—but it never came.

"Oh yeah, of course. So, I just spoke to Miranda . . ." Her voice trailed off as though she was hoping I'd continue and explain that the whole thing had been a big mistake and not to worry because I'd managed to fix it in the last four minutes.

"And you heard what happened, I'm assuming?"

"Um, yeah! Andy, what's going on?"

"I should probably be asking you that, right?"

There was silence.

"Listen, Em, I have a feeling that you called to fire me. It's OK if you did; I know it's not your decision. So, did she tell you to call and get rid of me?" Even though I felt lighter than I had in many months, I still found myself holding my breath, wondering if maybe, through some dumb stroke of luck or misfortune, Miranda had respected my telling her to fuck off instead of been appalled by it.

"Yes. She asked me to let you know that you have been terminated, effective immediately, and she would like you to be checked out of the Ritz before she returns from the show." She said this softly and with a trace of regret. Perhaps it was for the many hours and days and weeks she was now facing of finding and training someone all over again, but there sounded like there might be something even more behind it.

"You're going to miss me, aren't you, Em? Go on, say it. It's OK, I won't tell anyone. As far as I'm concerned, this conversation never happened. You don't want me to go, do you?"

Miracle of miracles, she laughed. "What did you say to her? She just kept repeating that you were crass and unlady-like. I couldn't get anything more specific out of her than that."

"Oh, that's probably because I told her to fuck herself."

"You did not!"

"You're calling to fire me. I assure you, I did."

"Oh my god."

"Yeah, well, I'd be lying if I said it wasn't the single most satisfying moment of my pathetic life. Of course, I have now been fired by the most powerful woman in publishing. Not only do I not have a way to pay off my nearly maxed-out MasterCard, but future jobs in magazines are looking rather dismal. Maybe I should try to work for one of her enemies? They'd be happy to hire me, right?"

"Sure. Send your résumé over to Anna Wintour—they've never liked each other very much."

"Hmm. Something to think about. Listen, Em, no hard feelings, OK?" We both knew that we had absolutely, positively not a single thing in common but Miranda Priestly, but as long as we were getting on so famously, I figured I'd play along.

"Sure, of course," she lied awkwardly, knowing full well that I was about to enter into the upper stratosphere of social pariah-dom. The chances of Emily admitting she had so much as known me from this day forward were nonexistent, but that was OK. Maybe in ten years when she was sitting front and center at the Michael Kors show and I was still shopping at Filene's and dining at Benihana, we'd laugh about the whole thing. But probably not.

"Well, I'd love to chat, but I'm kind of screwed up right now, not sure what to do next. I've got to figure out a way to get home as soon as possible. Do you think I can still use my return ticket? She can't fire me and leave me stranded in a foreign country, can she?"

"Well of course she would be justified in doing so, Andrea," she said. Ah-hah! One last zinger. It was comforting to know that things never really changed. "After all, it's really you who are deserting your job—you forced her to fire you. But no, I don't think she's a vengeful kind of person. Just charge the change fee and I'll figure out a way to put it through."

"Thanks, Em. I appreciate it. And good luck to you, too. You're going to make a fantastic fashion editor someday."

"Really? You think so?" she asked eagerly, happily. Why my opinion as the biggest fashion loser ever to hit the scene was at all relevant, I didn't know, but she sounded very, very pleased.

"Definitely. Not a doubt in my mind."

Christian called the moment I hung up with Emily. He had, unsurprisingly, already heard what happened. Unbelievable. But the pleasure he took from hearing the sordid details, combined with all sorts of promises and invitations he offered up, made me feel sick again. I told him as calmly as possible that I had a lot to deal with right now, to please stop calling in the meantime, that I'd get in touch if and when I felt like it.

Since they miraculously didn't yet know that I'd flunked out of my job, Monsieur Renaud and entourage fell all over themselves on hearing that an emergency at home demanded I return immediately. It took only a half hour for a small army of hotel staff to book me on the next flight to New York, pack my bags, and tuck me into the backseat of a limo stocked with a full bar bound for Charles de Gaulle. The driver was chatty, but I didn't really respond: I wanted to enjoy my last moments as the lowest-paid but most highly perked assistant in the free world. I poured myself one final flute of perfectly dry champagne and took a long, slow, luxurious sip. It had taken eleven months, forty-four weeks, and some 3,080 hours of work to figure out—once and for all—that morphing into Miranda Priestly's mirror image was probably not such a good thing.

Instead of a uniformed driver with a sign waiting for me when I exited customs, I found my parents, looking immensely pleased to see me. We hugged, and after they got over the initial shock of what I was wearing (skintight, very faded D&G jeans with spike-heeled pumps and a completely sheer shirt—hey, it was listed in category, miscellaneous; subcategory, to and from airport, and it was by far the most plane-appropriate thing they'd packed for me), they gave me very good news: Lily was awake and alert. We went straight to the hospital, where Lily herself even managed to give me attitude about my outfit as soon as I walked in.

Of course, there was the legal problem for her to contend with; she had, after all, been speeding the wrong way down a one-way street in a drunken stupor. But since no one else was seriously hurt, the judge had shown tremendous leniency and, although she'd always have a DWI on her record, she'd been sentenced to only mandatory alcohol counseling and what seemed like three decades' worth of community service. We hadn't talked a lot about it—she still wasn't cool with admitting out loud that she had a problem—but I'd driven her to her first group session in the East Village and she'd admitted that it wasn't "too touchy-feely" when she came out. "Freakin' annoying" was how she put it, but when I raised my eyebrows and gave her a specialty withering look—à la Emily—she conceded that there were some cute guys there, and it wouldn't kill her to date someone sober for once. Fair enough. My parents had convinced her to come clean to the dean at Columbia, which sounded like a nightmare at the time but ended up being a good move. He not only agreed to let Lily withdraw without failing in the middle of the semester, but signed the approval for the bursar's office saying that she could just reapply for her tuition next spring.

Lily's life and our friendship seemed to be back on track. Not so with Alex. He'd been sitting by her side at the hospital when we arrived, and the minute I saw him I found myself wishing my parents hadn't diplomatically decided to wait in the cafeteria. There was an awkward hello and a lot of fussing over Lily, but when he'd shrugged on his jacket a half hour later and waved good-bye, we hadn't said a real word to each other. I called him when I got home, but he let it go to voice mail. I called a few times more and hung up, stalker-style, and tried one last time before I went to bed. He answered but sounded wary.

"Hi!" I said, trying to sound adorable and well adjusted.

"Hey." He clearly wasn't into my adorableness.

"Listen, I know she's your friend, too, and that you would've done that for anyone, but I can't thank you enough for everything you did for Lily. Tracking me down, helping my parents, sitting with her for hours on end. Really."

"No problem. It's what anyone would do when someone they know is hurt. No big deal." Implied in this, of course, was that anyone would do it except someone who happens to be phenomenally self-centered with whacked-out priorities, like yours truly.

"Alex, please, can we just talk like—"

"No. We really can't talk about anything right now. I've been around for the last year waiting to talk to you—begging, sometimes—and you haven't been all that interested. Somewhere in that year, I lost the Andy I fell in love with. I'm not sure how, I'm not exactly sure when it happened, but you are definitely not the same person you were before this job. My Andy would have never even entertained the idea of choosing a fashion show or a party or whatever over being there for a friend who really, really needed her. Like, *really* needed her. Now, I'm glad you decided to come home—that you know it was the right thing to do—but now I need some time to figure out what's going on with me, and with you, and with us. This isn't new, Andy, not to me. It's been happening for a long, long time—you've just been too busy to notice."

"Alex, you haven't given me a single second to sit down, face to face, and try to explain to you what's been going on. Maybe you're right, maybe I am a completely different person. But I don't think so—and even if I've changed, I don't think it's *all* been for the worse. Have we really grown apart that much?"

Even more than Lily, he was my best friend, of that I was certain, but he hadn't been my boyfriend for many, many months. I realized that he was right: it was time I told him so.

I took a deep breath and said what I knew was the right thing, even though it didn't feel so great then. "You're right."

"I am? You agree?"

"Yes. I've been really selfish and unfair to you."

"So what now?" he asked, sounding resigned but not heartbroken.

"I don't know. What now? Do we just stop talking? Stop seeing each other? I have no idea how this is supposed to work. But I want you to be a part of my life, and I can't imagine not being a part of yours."

"Me neither. But I'm not sure we're going to be able to do that for a long, long time. We weren't friends before we started dating, and it seems impossible to imagine just being friends now. But who knows? Maybe once we've both had a lot of time to figure things out . . ."

I hung up the phone that first night back and cried, not just for Alex but for everything that had changed and shifted during the past year. I'd strolled into Elias-Clark a clueless, poorly dressed little girl, and I'd staggered out a slightly weathered, poorly dressed semigrown-up (albeit one who now realized just how poorly dressed she was). But in the interim, I'd experienced enough to fill a hundred just-out-of-college jobs. And even though my résumé now sported a scarlet "F," even though my boyfriend had called it quits, even though I'd left with nothing more concrete than a suitcase (well, OK, four Louis Vuitton suitcases) full of fabulous designer clothes—maybe it had been worth it?

I turned off the ringer and pulled an old notebook from my bottom desk drawer and began to write.

My father had already escaped to his office and my mother was on her way to the garage when I made it downstairs.

"Morning, honey. Didn't know you were awake! I'm running out. I have a student at nine. Jill's flight is at noon, so you should probably leave sooner than later since there will be rush-hour traffic. I'll have my cell on if anything goes wrong. Oh, will you and Lily be home for dinner tonight?"

"I'm really not sure. I just woke up and haven't yet had a cup of coffee. Do you think I could decide on dinner in a little while?"

But she hadn't even stuck around to listen to my snotty response—she was halfway out the door by the time I opened my mouth. Lily, Jill, Kyle, and the baby were sitting around the kitchen table in silence, reading different sections of the *Times*. There was a plate of wet-looking, wholly unappetizing waffles in the middle, with a bottle of Aunt Jemima and a tub of butter straight from the fridge. The only thing anyone appeared to be touching was the coffee, which my father had picked up on his morning run to Dunkin Donuts—a tradition stemming from his understandable unwillingness to ingest anything my mother had made herself. I forked a waffle onto a paper plate and went to cut it, but it immediately collapsed into a soggy pile of dough.

"This is inedible. Did Dad pick up any donuts today?"

"Yeah, he hid them in the closet outside his office," Kyle drawled. "Didn't want your mother to see. Bring back the box if you're going?"

The phone rang on my way to seek out the hidden booty.

"Hello?" I answered in my best irritated voice. I'd finally stopped answering any ringing phone with "Miranda Priestly's office."

"Hello there. Is Andrea Sachs there, please?"

"Speaking. May I ask who's calling?"

"Andrea, hi, this is Loretta Andriano from *Seventeen* magazine."

My heart lurched. I'd pitched a 2,000-word "fiction" piece about a teenage girl who gets so caught up on getting into college that she ignores her friends and family. It had taken me all of two hours to write the silly thing, but I thought I'd managed to strike just the right chords of funny and touching.

"Hi! How are you?"

"I'm fine, thank you. Listen, your story got passed along to me, and I have to tell you—I love it. Needs some revisions, of course, and the language needs some tweaking—our readers are mostly pre- and early teens—but I'd like to run it in the February issue."

"You would?" I could hardly believe it. I'd sent the story to a dozen teen magazines and then wrote a slightly more mature version and sent that to nearly two dozen women's magazines, but I hadn't heard a word back from anyone.

"Absolutely. We pay one-fifty per word, and I'll just need to have you fill out a few tax forms. You've freelanced stories before, right?"

"Actually, no, but I used to work at *Runway*." I don't know how I thought this would help—especially since the only thing I ever wrote there were forged memos meant to intimidate other people—but Loretta didn't appear to notice the gaping hole in my logic.

"Oh, really? My first job out of college was as a fashion assistant at *Runway*. I learned more there that year than I did in the next five."

"It was a real experience. I was lucky to have it."

"What did you do there?"

"I was actually Miranda Priestly's assistant."

"Were you really? You poor girl, I had no idea. Wait a minute—were you the one who was just fired in Paris?"

I realized too late that I had made a big mistake. There'd been a sizable blurb in *Page Six* about the whole messy thing a few days after I got home, probably from one of the Clackers who'd witnessed my terrible manners. Considering they quoted me exactly, I couldn't figure out who else it could've been. How could I have forgotten that other people might have read that? I had a feeling that Loretta was going to be distinctly less pleased with my story than she was three minutes ago, but there was no escaping now.

"Um, yeah. It wasn't as bad as it seemed, really it wasn't. Things got totally blown out of proportion in that *Page Six* article. Really."

"Well, I hope not! Someone needed to tell that woman to go fuck herself, and if it was you, well, then, hats off! That woman made my life a living hell for the year I worked there, and I never even had to exchange a single word with her.

"Look, I've got to run to a press lunch right now, but why don't we set up a meeting? You need to come in and fill out some of these papers, and I'd like to meet you anyway. Bring anything else you think might work for the magazine."

"Great. Oh, that sounds great." We agreed to meet next Friday at three, and I hung up still not believing what had happened. Kyle and Jill had left the baby with Lily while they went to dress and pack, and he had commenced a sort of crying-whimpering thing that sounded as though he was two seconds away from all-out hysteria. I scooped him out of his seat and held him over my shoulder, rubbing his back through his terry-cloth footie pajamas, and, remarkably, he shut up.

"You'll never believe who that was," I sang, dancing around the room with Isaac. "It was an editor at *Seventeen* magazine—I'm going to be published!"

"Shut up! They're printing your life story?"

"It's not my life story—it's 'Jennifer's' life story. And it's only two thousand words, so it's not the biggest thing ever, but it's a start."

"Sure, whatever you say. Young girl gets super caught up in achieving something and ends up screwing over all the people who matter in her life. Jennifer's story. Uh-huh, whatever." Lily was grinning and rolling her eyes at the same time.

"Whatever, details, details. The point is, they're publishing it in the February issue and they're paying me three thousand dollars for it. How crazy is that?"

"Congrats, Andy. Seriously, that's amazing. And now you'll have this as a clip, right?"

"Yep. Hey, it's not *The New Yorker*, but it's an OK first step. If I can round up a few more of these, maybe in some different magazines, too, I might be getting somewhere. I have a meeting with the woman on Friday, and she told me to bring anything else I've been working on. And she didn't even ask if I speak French. And she hates Miranda. I can work with this woman."

I drove the Texas crew to the airport, picked up a good and greasy Burger King lunch for Lily and me to wash down our breakfast donuts with, and spent the rest of the day—and the next, and the next after that—working on some stuff to show the Miranda-loathing Loretta.

19

"Tall vanilla cappuccino, please," I ordered from a barista I didn't recognize at the Starbucks on 57th Street. It had been nearly five months since I'd been here last, trying to balance a whole tray of coffees and snacks and get back to Miranda before she fired me for breathing. When I thought about it like that, I figured it was far better to have gotten fired for screaming "fuck you" than it was to get fired because I'd brought back two packets of Equal instead of two raw sugars. Same outcome, but a totally different ballgame.

Who knew Starbucks had such huge turnover? There wasn't a single person behind the counter who looked remotely familiar, making all the time I'd spent there seem that much farther away. I smoothed my well-cut but nondesigner black pants and checked to make sure that the cuffed bottoms hadn't collected any of the city's muddy slush. I knew there was an entire magazine staff of fashionistas who would emphatically disagree with me, but I thought I looked pretty damn good for only my second interview. Not only did I now know that no one wears suits at magazines, but somewhere, somehow, a year's worth of high fashion had—by simple osmosis, I think—crammed itself into my head.

The cappuccino was almost too hot, but it felt fantastic on that chilly, wet day. The darkened, late-afternoon sky seemed to be misting the city with a giant Snow-Cone. Normally, a day like this would've depressed me. It was, after all, one of the more depressing days in the year's most depressing month (February), the kind when even the optimists would rather crawl under the covers and the pessimists didn't stand a chance of getting through without a fistful of Zoloft. But the Starbucks was warmly lit and just the right state of crowded, and I curled up in one of their oversize green armchairs and tried not to think of who had rubbed his dirty hair there last.

In the past three months, Loretta had become my mentor, my champion, my savior. We'd hit it off in that first meeting and she'd been nothing but wonderful to me ever since. As soon as I'd walked into her spacious but cluttered office and saw that she was—gasp!—fat, I had a weird feeling that I'd love her. She sat me down and read every word of the stuff I'd been working on all week: tongue-in-cheek pieces on fashion shows, some snarky stuff on being a celebrity assistant, a hopefully sensitive story about what it takes—and doesn't take—to bring down a three-year-long relationship with someone you love but can't be with. It was storybook-like, nauseating, really, how well we'd instantly hit it off, how effortlessly we shared our nightmares about *Runway* (I was still having them: a recent one had included a particularly horrid segment in which my own parents were shot dead by Parisian fashion police for wearing shorts on the street and Miranda had somehow managed to legally adopt me), how quickly we realized that we were the same person, just seven years apart.

Since I'd just had the brilliant idea of dragging all my *Runway* clothes to one of those snooty resale shops on Madison Avenue, I was a wealthy woman—I could afford to write for peanuts; anything for a by-line. I had waited and waited for Emily or Jocelyn to call to tell me they were sending a messenger to pick it all up, but they never did. So it was all mine. I packed up most of the clothes but set aside the Diane Von Furstenburg wrap-dress. While going through the contents of my desk drawers that Emily had emptied into boxes and mailed to me, I came across the letter from Anita Alvarez, the one in which she expressed her worship of all things *Runway*. I'd always meant to send her a fabulous dress, but I'd never found the time. I wrapped the bold-printed dress in tissue paper, tossed in a pair of Manolos, and forged a note from Miranda—a talent I was unhappy to discover I still possessed. This girl should know—just once—how it feels to own one beautiful thing. And, more importantly, to think there's someone out there who actually cares.

Except for the dress, the tight and very sexy D&G jeans, and the utterly classic, quilted, chain-handle purse I'd given to my mom as a gift ("Oh, honey, this is beautiful. What's this brand again?"), I sold every last filmy top, leather pant, spiked boot, and strappy sandal. The woman who worked the register called the woman who owned the store, and the two of them had decided it would be best if they just closed the shop down for a few hours to evaluate my merchandise. The Louis Vuitton luggage—two large suitcases, one medium-size accessories bag, and an oversize trunk—alone had netted me six grand, and when they were finally finished whispering and examining and giggling, I cruised out of there with a check for just over $38,000. Which, by my calculations, meant that I could pay rent and even feed myself for a year while I tried to get this writing gig together. And then Loretta strolled into my life and made it instantly better.

Loretta had already agreed to buy four pieces—one blurb, only slightly larger than a pull quote, two 500-word pieces, and the original 2,000-word story. But even more exciting was her bizarre obsession with helping me make contacts, her eagerness to get in touch with people at other magazines who might just be interested in some freelance stuff. Which is exactly what put me at that Starbucks on that overcast winter day—I was headed back to Elias-Clark. It had taken a lot of insisting on her part to convince me that Miranda wouldn't hunt me down the minute I walked in the building and knock me out with a blow dart, but I was still nervous. Not paralyzed with fear like the old days when a mere cell phone ring was enough to cause my heart to flip-flop, but jittery enough at the thought—however remote the possibility—of catching a glimpse of her. Or Emily. Or anyone else, for that matter, except for James, who had kept in touch.

Somehow, someway, for some *reason*, Loretta had called her old college roommate who just so happened to edit the city section of *The Buzz* and told her that she'd discovered the next new "it" writer. That was supposed to be me. She'd arranged an interview for me today, and even forewarned the woman that I'd been summarily dismissed from Miranda's employ, but the woman had just laughed and said something to the effect that if they refused to use anyone whom Miranda had fired at one point or another, they'd barely have any writers at all.

I finished my cappuccino and, newly energized, gathered my portfolio of different articles and headed—this time calmly, without either an incessantly ringing phone or an armload of coffees—toward the Elias-Clark building. A moment or two of reconnaissance from the sidewalk indicated that no *Runway* Clackers were amid the crowds in the lobby, and I proceeded to heave my weight against the revolving door. Nothing had changed in the five months since I'd last been there: I could see Ahmed behind the register in the newsstand, and a huge, glossy poster advertised that *Chic* would be hosting a party at Lotus that weekend. Although I technically should've signed in, I instinctively walked directly toward the turnstiles. Immediately, I heard a familiar voice call out, *"I can't remember if I cried when I read about his widowed bride, but something touched me deep inside, the day, the music died. And we were singing . . ."* "American Pie"! *What a sweetie,* I thought. This was the good-bye song that I'd never gotten to sing. I turned to see Eduardo, as large and sweaty as usual, grinning. But not at me. In front of the turnstile closest to him stood a toweringly skinny girl with jet black hair and green eyes, wearing a dynamite pair of tight, pinstripe pants and a navel-revealing tank top. She also happened to be balancing a small tray with three Starbucks coffees, an overflowing bag of newspapers and magazines, three hangers with complete outfits dangling from each one, and a duffel monogrammed with the initials "MP." Her cell phone began to ring just as I realized what was happening, and she looked so panicked

I thought she might cry on the spot. But when her repeated banging against the turnstile failed to elicit entry, she sighed deeply and sang, " 'Bye, 'bye, Miss American Pie, drove my Chevy to the levee, but the levee was dry, and good old boys were drinking whiskey and rye, singing this will be the day that I die, this will be the day that I die . . ." When I looked back to Eduardo, he smiled quickly in my direction and winked. And then, while the pretty brunette girl finished singing her verse, he buzzed me through like I was someone who mattered.